Readers love
The Kai Gracen Series

Kai is my fa[...] rappy,
outcast, snar[...]

—Gail Ca[...] torate
Series

Heart-pounding action, dramatic betrayals, and creepy backstories are all in a day's work for Kai.

—AudioFile Magazine

Black Dog Blues

—Library Journal Best Books of 2013
—AudioFile Earphones Award winner

"Awesome book that I'll absolutely recommend to fantasy lovers."

—It's About The Book

"This story is everything a fantasy should be."

—Love Bytes

Mad Lizard Mambo

—Paranormal Romance Guild
Reviewers Choice Award: Best Novel

"*Mad Lizard Mambo* is an outstanding sequel. Once again we are drawn into this crazy world author Rhys Ford has so lovingly created and carried away on an adventure beyond our imagination."

—Joyfully Jay

By Rhys Ford

Published by DSP PUBLICATIONS
www.dsppublications.com

RHYS FORD

JACKED CAT JIVE

DSP PUBLICATIONS

Published by
DSP PUBLICATIONS

5032 Capital Circle SW, Suite 2, PMB# 279,
Tallahassee, FL 32305-7886 USA
www.dsppublications.com

Jacked Cat Jive
© 2019 Rhys Ford.

Cover Art
© 2019 Chris McGrath.
www.christianmcgrath.com
Cover content is for illustrative purposes only and any person depicted
on the cover is a model.

Mass Market Paperback ISBN: 978-1-64108-136-8
Trade Paperback ISBN: 978-1-64080-969-7
Digital ISBN: 978-1-64080-968-0
Library of Congress Control Number: 2018961348
Mass Market Paperback published March 2019
v. 1.0

Printed in the United States of America
∞
This paper meets the requirements of
ANSI/NISO Z39.48-1992 (Permanence of Paper).

This one is going out to Michelle Mary Taylor, who really just wants to steal Kai away. And also to Harley, who came into our house, covered it with gray fur, and promptly steals my seat when I get up. If only she could type.

Acknowledgments

To MY beautiful Five—Penn, Tamm, Lea, and Jenn. Through thick and thin and through dangers untold, you are my true constant stars—kind of like a constellation… but with more bickering about tea and someone losing their knickers.

And much love to my other sisters—Ren, Ree, Mary, and Lisa.

Thanks will always go to Dreamspinner—Elizabeth, Lynn, Liz and her team, Naomi (who I drive insane), and everyone else who takes what I turn in and makes it marvelous.

Glossary

THE WORDS contained in *Jacked Cat Jive* have a base in current language and serve as representative words in Singlish, a polyglot common tongue spoken in the book. While many have retained their original meaning, some have experienced a lingual drift and have developed alternative definitions.

a'a—rough, crumbly lava
ainle—multiuse word, can be hero, champion, angel or if used in certain context, wild cat (Gaelic)
ainmhi dubh—black dog (Gaelic)
ampulla—orig: vial, blister; slang: piece of shit, waste of a person (Spanish)
arracht—monster (Gaelic)
bao—an Asian-centric bread, usually a soft white yeasty bread (Chinese origin word)
bebé—baby (Gaelic)

beathach sgeunach—skittish beast (Gaelic)

bonito—handsome, masculine pretty (Spanish)

chi wo de shi—slang: eat my shit, damn it (Mandarin)

chikusho—slang: damn it, fuck (Japanese)

deartháir—brother (Gaelic)

diu nei ah seng—fuck your family (Singapore slang)

fifl—idiot, fool (Old Norse)

gusano—worm (sometimes found in tequila) (Spanish)

hanai—adopted, calabash relative. Someone you would share a bowl of food with while eating with your fingers (Hawaiian)

hibiki—resonance, echo (Japanese)

hondashi—dried bonito (fish) flakes, mainly used for soup stock (Japanese)

Iesu—Jesus (Hawaiian)

Indios—indigenous Austronesian peoples living in Southern California / Mexico regions

jan-ken-po—rock, paper, and scissors (Hawaiian slang of Japanese phrase)

kimchee—pickled, spicy cabbage pickles, national dish of Korea. Also spelled kim chi or kim chee. (Korean)

kuso—crap (Japanese)

luranach—lover, intended (Gaelic)

malasadas—deep-fried yeast donuts rolled in granulated sugar (Portuguese)

meata—gone bad, turned rotten (Gaelic)

miso—soybean paste, commonly used in soup (Japanese)

muirnín—beloved, sweetheart, darling (Gaelic)

musang—wild cat, civet, feral cat (Filipino-Tagalog)

nori—seaweed, usually pressed into sheets (Japanese)

paho'eho'e—smooth, ropy lava (Hawaiian)

peata—pet (Gaelic)

Pele—Goddess of lava, volcanoes, passion and general bad-assery. Not someone to be fucked with. (Hawaiian)

saimin—local Hawaiian word for noodle soup dish based on Japanese ramen, Filipino pancit, and other Asian noodles. Possibly based on Japanese word ramen/sōmen or Chinese words xì and miàn.

shoyu—soy sauce (Japanese)

siao liao—crazy, out of your mind, insane. (Singapore slang)

Sidhe—fairy folk, also Seelie. Considered the "Dawn" court of the Underhill faerie / elves. Pronounced she. (Gaelic)

sláinte—health, salute (Gaelic)

sona ba bi tsi—son of a bitch (Chamorro)

sucio—filth, dirty things (Spanish)

tik-tik—bulbous triangular taxi cab, single driver car with wide back to accommodate passengers, suspended above roadways by upper rails and trolley lines, resembles a rounder version of a 1976 Ford Pinto (Indian origin word)

Unsidhe—fairy folk, also Unseelie. Considered the "Dusk" court of the Underhill faerie / elves. Pronounced un-she. (Gaelic)

One

"WHATEVER YOU do, boy, don't get eaten!" Jonas yelled at me from across the devastated schoolyard. "If you're going to die, you don't want to go as a giant squid's snack! Think about what that'll do to your reputation as a Stalker!"

Right. Because what people think of me and how I died should be my last thought as I drew my final breath. My reputation as a Stalker was already a sketchy one, mostly because I wasn't human and I'd been raised and trained by Dempsey, the most foul-mouthed, hot-tempered, itchy-trigger-fingered Stalker ever to be given a license.

And those were his best qualities.

It's a well-known fact being a Stalker for the SoCalGov meant long hours, lean pay, and an extremely short lifespan. It was a brutal existence with little thanks, and if you were like me, a chimera of

Sidhe and Unsidhe blood, it meant a lifetime of being viewed with skepticism and met with a loaded gun if you trespassed on a rancher's land in pursuit of a particularly nasty monster.

That's what Stalkers did—not the trespassing part so much, but the monsters. We were paid to take down, relocate, and sometimes eradicate anything that preyed on human settlements. I couldn't imagine there was much need for my job before the Merge, but when the elfin world folded into Earth, it brought more than the Sidhe and Unsidhe courts.

There were wars following the Merge. The introduction of two separate races already at odds with each other to a human world used to being on top of the food chain naturally led to conflict. On the human side, thousands died. On the elfin, at least a couple of hundred. Where Earth had technology, the Sidhe and the Unsidhe had magic and an unimaginable resistance to death. But they also couldn't reproduce like humans, so even the few casualties they suffered were catastrophic.

A peace was eventually struck, and the three races were reluctantly learning to live with one another over the subsequent decades—mostly because none of us had any choice. Everyone was struggling to survive in a world turned upside down by an event that nobody predicted or could control. The elfin courts had fought among themselves and against each other for centuries, and adding humans to the mix only made things worse. All sides were partners in an uneasy alliance, sharing resources and knowledge in little bits and pieces and opening up opportunities that no one ever imagined could exist.

Being a Stalker was an opportunity because the Merge didn't just bring elfin to Earth. It also brought their monsters—which was why I was deep in the bowels of San Diego's understreets, in the middle of an abandoned schoolyard, fighting a blue-spotted megacuttlefish the size of an elephant.

And by fighting, I meant letting myself get entangled in its tentacles to gain a clear shot at its underbelly when it drew me close enough to its snapping four-foot-wide beak. That hadn't been the original plan, but as I was about to go on a one-way ticket down a not-ready-for-dinnertime calamari appetizer, it was all I had.

"Stop getting in the way of its eyes," Jonas shouted at me from his very safe position a few yards away. "I'm trying to shoot its head, and you keep moving in front of it."

My *hanai* uncle was difficult to see in the perpetual gloom of the understreets. That seemed odd—how did anyone miss a brawny, nearly seven-foot-tall black man wielding two sawed-off shotguns?—but the black ink the cuttlefish sprayed on me might have clouded my vision, and the monster's hold on my foot as it swung me around like I was a piece of toilet paper it was trying to get off its shoe might have had something to do with my concentration difficulties.

"I can't even see its fucking eye!" I tried shouting back, but there was little hope Jonas heard me. The cuttlefish flailed me about and slammed me into a part of its body that felt like its head, but I couldn't be certain. Since I had a death grip on my knife, I stabbed at whatever I could reach, but the angle was all wrong and its skin was too slick, so all I did was irritate it. "Swear to Pele, I'm going to turn you into tacos."

It was a terrible pun, a play on the word *tako*, but since no one but me heard it, I wouldn't catch shit for it. The cuttlefish didn't have an opinion or a sense of humor. But then, we were trying to kill it, and since I've often bitten on the other side of that knife, I can attest that laughter is not normally my first go-to when I'm trying not to die.

Or maybe it is, because I just made a pun about cuttlefish and tacos.

Another circuit of the air above its body and the monster lost its hold and sent me careening into a decrepit chain-link fence. The slam of my body against the woven metal was like the cymbal finale of a symphony—a rattle of chimes and clashes loud enough to send a piercing shock wave through my eardrums. I rolled off of the fence and into the dirt and scraped my face on the scrabble of dead weeds clustered about a post.

I quickly considered staying put. Sure, the thing would probably graduate to munching on children in the next week or so, but they weren't my kids. I couldn't even have kids. I was a genetic cocktail of warring elfin DNA, incubated in a magical stew and hatched out of a crucible. The closest thing I would ever have to a child was my cat, who I found when it was eating one of my kills.

No, I couldn't think of one good reason to get back up on my feet and do battle with the rotten-tuna-smelling monster that was slithering free of the wading pool it now called home, but the bounty it would bring Jonas would be enough to feed his family for the next couple of months.

"Get off your ass, Kai," I scolded myself as I shook my nerves back into place. I'd lost my Glock as soon as the thing grabbed me, but I was still in possession of all of my knives, if not half of my wits. But damn, I ached. "It's a fucking appetizer. A couple of passes with your knife and you'll have *ika* for days."

This was supposed to be a simple bounty. A brief contract put out by the Post to eliminate a displaced foreign entity in the southern quadrant of San Diego's understreets. The job seemed pretty cut-and-dried.

The report sent over with the bounty stated that a small cephalopod of sea origins had somehow made its way through the sewage system and ended up at a brackish pond near New Barrio Logan. The SoCalGov inspector reported the mollusk was simply too large to go back through the grate it had come in through and was now trapped in the city proper. There had been some unverified instances of it preying on rodents, which we soon discovered from the locals was a big fat lie. The thing had been picking off dogs and cats for the past three weeks and had since moved on to slashing at any human who came too close.

I had just gotten too close.

Because twenty feet was too damned close when standing next to a wading pool with an angry, overgrown cuttlefish.

The understreets of San Diego were where the poor and disenfranchised gathered up what little they could scrape together and lived their lives in the belly of a vast metropolis. Efforts had been made to bring light and fresh water to the bowels of the sprawling city, but there was little return on investment for most politicians to do more than the bare minimum. Massive tracks of lights meant to replicate natural sunlight were affixed to the cement canopy separating lower San Diego from its upper regions, but they never seemed to be replaced when they broke. We were in a part of the understreets where copper piping was stripped from buildings for a few bucks and people sold wood scavenged from grocery store pallets a few blocks away.

Even the blue tik-tiks didn't make it in as far as we were, their overhead cables cut and tied off as though they were nothing more than a gigantic macramé plant hanger waiting for the world's most enormous fern.

Still, the neighborhood had its pride and its own fury. Someone had made enough noise for SoCalGov to send someone down to investigate their ravenous intruder, and when it was all done, I was definitely going to get some *elote* and carnitas fries from the kiosk on the corner to take home for dinner.

The fantastic smell coming from that grill had been driving me insane ever since we pulled up to the place, and oddly enough, even with the rotten-kelp-and-spoiled-seafoam odor caught in my nostrils, the kiosk's aromatic smoke stayed with me.

"You okay, boy?" Jonas shouted as I wiped the ink out of my eyes, hoping to shake off the ringing in my head and get back into the action. He let loose a volley of shot into the monster, but all it seemed to do was anger it. The flat head on one of its long tentacles lashed out, narrowly missing Jonas's face, and I was up on my feet before he could finish swearing.

By all rights the cuttlefish shouldn't have been there. The explanation of its arrival through a sewer pipe connected to the ocean was plausible only if we weren't nearly twenty-five miles inland. When we first got there, the wading pool appeared to be empty, half filled with algae-covered, garbage-choked water. But when we got closer, the monster erupted out in a flurry of tentacles and a snapping black beak.

The size of it made me lose speech. It was larger than a rhino, with pale angry eyes dominating its frilled triangular head, and its pale flesh rippled pink and purple beneath its startlingly bright cobalt spots. The bloated remains of a dog floated in the pool next to it, and the rank smell of the water made Jonas gag. I'd smelled worse. Hell, I'd *literally* smelled worse than that pool myself more than a few times in my life. It was the malevolence in its gaze that brought me up short.

Then it began to crawl out of the pool and the game changed drastically.

Most sea creatures needed water to breathe. As far as I knew, that was a truth that extended even to cuttlefish, no matter how big they were. But this one didn't seem to be bothered by the fact that it had lifted mostly out of the foul pool as it lurched its way toward Jonas and me.

I didn't move back fast enough, or maybe I just didn't believe the thing was as quick as it turned out to be. One moment I had my gun aimed at its bulbous head and then the next I was being used as a cat toy to draw out its next snack.

"I'm fine." It took me a bit to get up on my feet, but I forced my body to respond. "Let's kill this thing and go home."

"Planning on doing just that," Jonas replied with a shit-eating grin. The streetlamps were bright enough to catch the silver in his closely cropped hair—more silver than had been there a few months before—but his growl was still fierce, even though there was a hitch to his step when he moved out of the monster's reach. "If we do this right, we can have cuttlefish steaks for dinner. Meat's good once you get it skinned."

I didn't like how slowly Jonas was moving. Hell, I didn't like the fact that he was there at all, but he'd taken the bounty and asked me for help to bring the thing in. It took a lot for a man like Jonas to ask for help, but he was still recovering from a brutal attack months before, and he'd done right by me more times than I had hair on my head, so saying no wasn't on the table.

Honestly, I just *really* didn't like how slow he was responding or his wincing when he turned to take another shot at the monster.

"Bullets aren't working on it," I yelled at Jonas as I searched for at least one of my guns. I found my Glock on the pavement a few feet away and stumbled toward it. My hand closed down on the hilt, and my fingers felt like they were on fire from the mollusk's spew. The creature had left a viscous film on my body, and a sharp tingle began to spread over my skin. I wasn't up to date on my mollusk toxins, but something told me the cuttlefish had more surprises in it than just moving tentacles and a foul temper. "Jonas! *Pele take you*, don't let that thing grab you. It's—"

He got too near to the creature, and I saw his life flash before my eyes. I broke into a run—a hard, fast sprint toward an impossible target—as it aimed the flat sucker-filled end of its tentacle straight for Jonas's head. My elfin blood and body gave me a distinct advantage among humans, but where our monsters were concerned, it was pretty neck and neck.

Even with the ones missing a neck.

I went right by Jonas and launched myself at the creature. It saw me coming and tried to correct the angle of its tentacle, but it couldn't shift in time. I heard the slap of its meat hitting something, and I could only hope it wasn't my adopted human uncle, but Jonas's scream followed too closely on the heels of that horrific booming sound.

All I had left was my hope that he'd survived the strike.

My Glock was useless. I don't know what normal cuttlefish were made out of, but this one seemed to be constructed out of Kevlar and meanness. Bullets ricocheted off of its skin, and after I emptied a clip into its head, I tossed my gun aside and went after it with my knife. Sometimes killing had to happen up close, and this was going to get very messy.

I'd already gotten personal with the thing, but that hadn't prepared me for the stench. There was something wrong with it, or maybe there was more beneath its skin than flesh. Its eyes went wild and whirred about in their deep sockets as it spread its legs out, and it became a profane angel of suckers and featherless wings. Its beak lay at the juncture of its limbs and was broad enough to snap a man in half. For all I knew, I wouldn't be its first victim. Who knew what else lay beneath the water churning at the back of its body?

A tentacle whipped out, slapping my legs from under me, and I rolled with the motion and landed on my knees. The broken cement was hard on my joints, and I would have bruises down my legs, but they would be a small price to pay for not dying. It slapped down at the ground where I would have been had I not tucked my body in and let my shoulders take the brunt of my momentum. Bits of rock and dirt flew up from the impact of the cuttlefish's tentacle, and the surrounding concrete cracked and spit up small sprays of fine grit. I sucked in a mouthful of white sand and accidentally trapped it against the roof of my mouth with my tongue, caught between spitting it out or swallowing it.

I swallowed and got back on my feet before the thing could strike at me again.

"I've got your back, boy," Jonas shouted behind me. I didn't dare glance back. I took it as a good sign he was alive enough to yell, and then I held in an alarmed scream when he began to fire off shotgun volleys into the cuttlefish's gaping maw. "I'll keep it distracted!"

"You're going to get me killed," I muttered, knowing he couldn't hear me. When I was younger, that kind of mouthing off probably would've gotten me backhanded by my surrogate-father-of-sorts, Dempsey, but Jonas was a different breed of man. He was gentler and kinder by far than Dempsey, but then so was a dragon with an abscessed tooth. Still, just in case, I yelled back, "Just don't shoot me!"

A torrent of ink shot out from somewhere on the cuttlefish's body and nearly hit me. The sting of its fluid dissipated once it was dry, but the ink was milky and easily slid behind eyelids and into nostrils, making it difficult to see and breathe. It also turned the ground into a slippery mess. My boot heels caught something jagged beneath the slick, which gave me some traction. Then I hit the rim of the wading pool, its rough gravelly edge angled slightly up, and that provided enough of a hard lip to steady my leap.

To my right, a scatter of buckshot blackened its frills, and for a brief moment, I thought Jonas would hit me as well, but his next volley smacked directly into the creature's beak. I was in flight for less than a second and landed hard against the cuttlefish's flanged body. Its skin was slippery, and I couldn't find purchase, but when its eye rolled over to look at me as I slid across its length, I knew I had to strike quickly. Its tentacles threw shadows against the water and the ground as they folded back to grab me.

If it got hold of me again, there was a good chance it would slither back down to the wading pool and probably drown me in the muck. I would've liked to say I didn't know how elfin tasted, but my father was a sick, sadistic bastard who'd gone out of his way to ensure that I experienced that particularly horrific delicacy. I didn't imagine the cuttlefish was starving, as I'd been back then, but judging by the bits and pieces of animals floating in the murky water, it either had an eclectic palate or it just didn't give a shit about what it ate.

I was going to go with the latter.

Its skin was too slick, and there was nothing I could grab. Working my hand beneath the lip of its head and body slowed my descent down its side but left me open to its tentacles. Desperate, I sunk my knife into its eye and dug down deep in an effort to anchor myself, but my arm was nearly jerked out of its socket when I came to a screeching halt.

"Don't shoot!" I screamed back at Jonas, but the cuttlefish's writhing turned me around, and its body dipped back down into the filthy water. My boots skimmed a bit of debris, and my toe came back up wet and covered in a sticky green film. "Iesu. Why ask me to help you on a job if you're just going to kill me? Why not just shoot me back where my cat could eat my corpse?"

The tentacles slapped at my back and legs, nearly dislodging me, but I hung on tight and dug my boot heels into the edge of its frills. The slice in its eye gave me something to hold on to, so I plunged my hand past the cut, looking for anything to grab. I found it—a cluster of connective tissue that squished a bit through my fingers when I grabbed it. Where the cut didn't get a reaction, my grabbing at its innards did. The cuttle-fish spasmed beneath me. Its limbs began a furious dance to dislodge me, and one tip caught me across the ribs and found every single bruise forming along my torso from where I'd hit the fence.

I raised my knife to slice at it again, and that's when I noticed that Jonas had a bazooka.

Or it could have been a rocket launcher. I was never clear on the difference, and at that point, it didn't really matter. Jonas became a blur running toward me, and then all I saw was a flash of the neighborhood, because the monster was writhing beneath me, and I was forced to ride its body as though it were a bucking mechanical bull in a cowboy bar. Tightening my legs seemed like a good idea until I heard Jonas shout my name.

"Jump loose!" he shouted.

Jumping loose was not an option. I had my arm tangled up through the cuttlefish's tiny brain and its eyeball, beginning my own version of *yum pla muk* minus the lime juice, the fish sauce, and all the vegetables. A second later I discovered I really had no choice, because there was a large *kaboom* with enough concussive force to rattle the few remaining windows of the school building next to the pool and I was once again flying through the air.

Luckily for me there was a rusted wrought iron fence to catch me when I landed.

My pants were on fire, and I'd lost my knife. I also appeared to have lost a shoe, but what was most concerning me at that moment was the length of wrought-iron piercing through my ribs. The fence was at a slant, and I'd caught it at an incredibly wrong angle. My legs dangled a few inches off of the ground, and every effort I made to get loose only moved me down the iron spike.

The pain was both incredible and familiar—a gut-wrenching, spine-curling agony that stretched through every single nerve of my body as my elfin blood reacted to the iron cutting through my flesh. Flakes of rust were being caught up in my blood, or maybe it just felt that way. Within a few breaths of being hung up on the fence, my heart burned as though plunged into a vat of molten rock.

I knew the iron wouldn't kill me, but it would certainly make me wish I'd died back there on the twitching cuttlefish, waltzing alongside its death throes. Throwing up hurt even more, but I did it anyway, unable to hold back the instinctive reaction to the iron in me.

The chunks of cooked cuttlefish smacking the ground like sacks of wet cement only made matters worse.

I was suddenly no longer hungry for either the Mexican corn or the savory goodness of spiced shredded pork over crispy sliced potatoes. If I'd landed a few inches to the left, the wrought iron would've pierced my stomach. As it was I was fairly certain my liver was going to have to find one of its lobes in the area of my abdomen. For an elfin, the puncture itself wasn't a fatal wound, but the iron—the *fucking iron*—would be the death of any other in my race if it stayed in too long.

Lucky for me—if anyone could even stretch the truth and call it luck—I'd built up a pretty good immunity to Earth's most poisonous metal.

"Hold on, kid," Jonas said when he appeared at my side. His massive hands were under my back in an instant, taking the pressure off of my legs. "Grit your teeth. I'm going to pull you free."

I had carried iron under the skin of my back for countless decades—swirls of filigree and bars thick enough to leave a pair of black pearl dragon wings etched across my shoulder blades and on either side of my spine. It'd been a while since those pieces had been removed, but their memory remained. The fencing wasn't stuck to my flesh like the dragon wings, but it still hurt like fucking hell.

I clenched my jaw, but my stomach still tried to empty itself for a second time all over Jonas's back. It is a pity I had nothing in me but the cup of coffee we'd had before doing the job, because if anybody deserved to be thrown up on, it was Jonas for bringing out a bazooka and firing on me and the cuttlefish.

"What were you thinking?" I gasped and ground my teeth when he yanked me off of the shaft's flared end. "I was *on* the damned thing. And where the fuck did you get a bazooka?"

"I had it in the back of the truck. I use it some-times when I go after nightmares. I figured it couldn't hurt this time around." He made a face—a halfway apology through grimaces and sucking at his teeth. "Guess I forgot how powerful the thing is. One last pull and you'll be free."

"Good," I spat out. "Because as much as I love you, I'm going to kick your damned ass."

Jonas stopped his tugging and stared down at me, his soulful brown eyes welling with emotion. "Trust you to tell me you love me for the first time while I'm yanking you off of a wrought-iron fence."

"You gave me my first chocolate," I reminded him. "But I'm still going to kick you in the balls, espe-cially if you don't hurry up."

The last few inches were a horrific test of my will-power and the strength of my jaw. I felt the moment my body was free of the iron shaft—a wave of jangled relief passed underneath my skin, and my spine unclenched, willing to let go of the memories of screws and bolts through my shoulder blades and the slide of twisted barbs through my flesh. Laying me down on the cement as gently as he could, Jonas crouched by my side and of-fered me a mouthful of water from a bottle he'd brought with him. A long shadow fell across both of us, cast down from the flickering streetlamp I'd narrowly avoid-ed in my flight. I reached for my remaining knife and half yanked it out from the sheath tied to my thigh.

"Hey, mister." A little kid of indeterminate sex and dubious cleanliness held out a smoking chunk of our practically thoroughly cooked cuttlefish. "Are you going to eat all of this? Or can me and my friends take some of it home?"

Two

I WAS able to get a quick shower at Jonas's house before I headed home. After we packed the monster's remains in ice, I left it to him and his son Razor to get the cuttlefish's eyes and beak to the Post in order to collect the bounty. The money would've been nice—money is *always* nice—but I told him to leave my cut in the pot, a half-assed thank-you for introducing me to chocolate and saving my life more times than I could count.

Its eyes and its beak, along with some footage we took, were enough evidence of the kill for the Post, and we left about three hundred pounds of usable cuttlefish behind, even with a good amount of meat going into the back of Jonas's truck once we laid down some tarps. We salvaged a lot of its body—or maybe it was its head, I wasn't up on cuttlefish anatomy—but mostly everything behind its eyes had been blown back and remained raw.

My heart ached as I watched him battle his pride with practical necessity, but in the end, he knew I was only doing what was best for his family. The bounty on the cuttlefish was high, based on the size of the monster, and despite what the SoCalGov inspector put down in his report, the thing weighed in at a hefty chunk of change. The meat we scavenged would go into the freezer or the smokehouse to make jerky, and his spouses could sell it in their booth at the farmers' market on Saturday.

"We squeeze everything we can out of what we can get. You guys can do more with that than I can," I'd told him as I gingerly climbed into my own beat-up Chevy truck. "I'm good for now. Maybe one day when I'm not, I'll come knocking on your door for some soup."

"That day ever comes, boy," Jonas rumbled at me through the open window and grabbed at the back of my neck to give me a quick, intense squeeze, "I'll be the first one to fill your bowl and pass you the bread. After you pick all the good bits out of it."

We shared a grin, recalling days on a hunt where the bread was mostly weevils and we'd made jokes about being thankful for the extra protein. My younger self existed in a state of constant hunger and craved meat. The bugs were a welcome addition to my meal, and I'd been confused the others hadn't thought the same.

"They're nutty. Like cashews." I chuckled when Jonas's face curdled into a sour expression. "You better step away from the truck before one of your wives comes and drags me back inside to have dinner with you. Right now, while I'm thankful for the shower, I just want a long soak in a tub full of hot water and a glass of whiskey on ice."

"I'll get you some of that jerky once we're done with it. And you might want to check that backpack of yours when you get home. I had one of the kids put some cuttlefish scraps in an old butter container. That's not something you want to find two weeks from now." He ruffled my hair, and I snarled playfully out of habit. "I figured you would probably crawl home, throw some noodles into a bit of miso soup, so that cuttlefish would cook fast in the heat. Providing of course that damned cat of yours doesn't eat all of it."

"I'll make sure he doesn't." I wrinkled my nose. "Last time I give him some octopus, it was like I was under siege from a chemical weapons factory. I love the tiny asshole, but that cat farts napalm. Take care. And whatever you do, don't take another contract until you know exactly how big the monster is. I'm going to be feeling this one for days."

"You know that's a lie, boy." Jonas chuckled and slapped at my battered truck's roof. "You'll be healed of all your bruises by the time you get home."

"Doesn't mean I don't want that whiskey," I shot back and put my truck into gear.

The ride back into the city was shorter than the one I made every week to Dempsey's. Jonas and his sprawling, ever-growing family didn't live that far off of District 3, a homesteading initiative meant to populate the upper mesas near Mission Valley. All in all it had been a good plan—carve out pieces of land and hand farmers incentive to grow crops to support the hospitality industries San Diego was known for. The biggest problem with the homesteading idea was that they hadn't quite gotten rid of all the lions in Kearny Mesa, so anyone east of the 163 River often found themselves fighting to maintain their flocks.

Most gave up and sold off what they were never going to use. Jonas benefited from that immensely, scooping up low-priced properties already plumbed with irrigation lines and with outlying buildings. Farming was a hard life, but it was easier than being a Stalker, mostly because a rutabaga wasn't going to chew your face off. His wives and husband dealt with the day-to-day stuff, doing everything from supplying produce for farm-to-table restaurants to making herb-scented soaps. I usually left their house smelling like lemon and lavender, although one of the kids begged me to try out the loquat bars and promised me they were bubblegum scented.

Little bastard wasn't wrong.

A dip through the mesas and then over the rise and San Diego spread out in front of me. It was a glittering bristle of skyscrapers and neon, with a Buddha's-hand scramble of Medical dominating the shoreline where the upper and lower levels met. The crystal, glass, and steel spires were merely rich armor for the teeming gritty streets below. While the city's façade was beautiful to look at, I preferred the honest dirt the lower level provided. And sitting at the far east of the city, right up against the raging river that once was a freeway, sat the Southern Rise Court, home to the Sidhe lord who'd become the bane of my existence.

Ryder, Clan Sebac, Third in the House of Devon, got it into his head one day that San Diego needed an elfin presence, so he'd added another title to his long pedigree and become the High Lord of the Southern Rise Court, assumed ownership of Balboa Park and all surrounding properties, and set them aside for the elfin race.

He'd also tried to assume ownership of me.

We had a few words about *that*.

He was tricky—like most elfin—and as arrogant as all hell. When he rolled into San Diego, he convinced SoCalGov and the Post to make me the court's liaison between the elfin and the humans. On paper it made sense. I was elfin by blood but human by culture, and Ryder knew jack shit about how humans thought or lived.

Problem was, he made my blood sing, and I wanted him so badly I was willing to chew off my tongue after kissing him so he would be the last thing I ever tasted.

After what the Unsidhe did to me—*what my own father did to me*—the last person I would ever want to be involved with was one of my own kind. I'd felt the touch of their treachery, wore the sting of their torture in my bones, and carried their viciousness on my skin. The Sidhe weren't much better. The first thing Ryder's grandmother tried to do was kill me, and our relationship went downhill after that.

We'd come to an understanding, Ryder and I. It was an uneasy friendship at times—he would pull and I would push away—but he was getting under my skin, much like the iron my father, Tanic, the Wild Hunt Master of the Unsidhe, slid into my back. And I knew that if I let him in, he would leave me with much more horrific scars than what I had already.

I avoided him, but theoretically he was kind of still my boss if the court needed me, and we also shared a couple of nieces who were products of his twisted sister's depravity and my hopefully dead half brother. I didn't have high hopes regarding Valin's demise. He was like a cockroach—no matter how hard someone stomped on him, he always resurfaced.

"Yeah, a long bath sounds really good," I muttered as I checked my link to see if I had any messages. The band on my wrist glowed in the upper left, but nothing was flashing red to alert me to an emergency or, worse, Ryder contacting me to see how I was doing. The truck rattled and moaned its way along the freeway, but it held steady and strong when I coasted it into the cul-de-sac of warehouses where I lived.

I wanted a place of my own where I could sleep unmolested by Dempsey's earth-shattering snores, so I purchased the warehouse when he retired. It was furnished mostly from castoffs, but there were a few good pieces I'd gone out of my way to buy—a soft bed large enough to sleep ten if I needed it and an alarm system tight enough to electrocute anyone who tried to breach my defenses.

So I was surprised to find a woman leaning over the short wall that ran along the roof of my two-story warehouse. It was still early enough in the afternoon for the sun to cast her into silhouette, and after I threw the truck into Park, I reached for the Glock I'd recovered from the battle with our cuttlefish.

She knew me, or at least knew me well enough to throw her hands up so I could see she was unarmed. Then her lilting voice mocked me from where I stood on my roof.

"You can put the gun away, Kai," Duffy called out to me as she put her hands on the wide cement runner I'd laid down over the brick perimeter. "Why don't you go feed that damned cat of yours and come up here and have some of this preserved lemon with me. Because I can't get these fucking mayonnaise jars open to save my life."

DUFFY ALWAYS seemed ageless to me. I don't know if I saw her through the romanticized eyes of my younger self—the gangly, awkward elfin Pinocchio she took in and made a man of—or if she simply was a breathtaking woman, confident and strong and with more than a little bit of attitude and an air of mystery about her.

She'd been the first woman I'd fallen in love with and the first one to tell me she would never be mine.

We'd met in the Red Lantern district, during a foolhardy excursion where Dempsey, in the time-honored tradition of all Stalkers and their apprentices, took me to get laid and to get my first tattoo. At some point he decided I was domesticated enough for polite company or at least hired company, told me to take a good scrub at my grimy body and put on my best clothes, and drove us down to get drunk at an exclusive understreet brothel.

The drunk part was easy, and so was the tattoo, an exquisite Japanese rendition of the dragon I'd taken down earlier that day.

It was the getting laid part that proved to be hard.

The wars between the elfin and the humans left a bad taste in everyone's mouth, and no matter how much money Dempsey had, no one would come near me. I didn't know that at the time. I figured it out later. There were other Stalkers with us—not Jonas, because he probably would've pulled me out of there—and their conversation was hot, bright, and loud every time Dempsey returned to the table after he tried to chat up one of the workers.

"Don't think there's anybody here good enough for you, boy," he growled, but there was something off in his tone. He also usually thought I wasn't good for anything, so I couldn't imagine me being too good for the glittering, pretty people working the floor. "We might want to try the other place down the street. They have prettier there."

That's exactly when Duffy walked into the room. And she was definitely too good for the likes of me.

She was gentle and seductive, and though she sensed I wanted to escape, she made me feel so comfortable I didn't want to be anywhere else. We saw each other occasionally over the years and drifted from casual lovers to pretty decent friends. She'd left the brothel business and built up a steady clientele who clamored for her attention, but every once in a while, she took a walk down the streets, mostly to remind herself of where she came from.

But Duffy never came to my place without me being there, and she sure as hell hadn't ever broken in and gotten up to the roof.

"You'll have to tell me how you got up there," I said to her as I walked through the front door with a container of raw cuttlefish and fought off my cat, Newt. "Either that or tell me how you bypassed the alarms."

She sauntered down the staircase that led down from the loft, where I'd made my bedroom out of the built-in space I used for a garage. Her smile was as wicked as her walk, a swaying grin that kept her hips from being an erotic overload. On any other woman, a pair of jeans and a cinched red T-shirt would have been commonplace, but Duffy wore her garments as though she were stepping out onto starlight. Her long brown hair was loose and brushed the base of her spine, and a twinkle flashed in her dusky blue eyes when she leaned in to kiss my cheek.

I was very glad for the bath I'd taken at Jonas's.

"I see your decorating tastes haven't changed," she purred as she walked past me to run her hand over the big-block engine that sat on a rack between the front door and the entrance to the garage. "Still haven't found the car to put this in?"

"Not yet. I have hope." I jerked my thumb toward the garage. "I'm still working on getting the Mustang back on the road. That run I did with Ryder beat the shit out of it."

Sure, I was curious about why she was there, but no one rushed Duffy. She did things on her own time at her own pace. When she sat down on one of the three couches I'd placed in a U around a wooden chest, I almost warned her to not touch the disheveled cat when he stalked past her, but Newt simply leaped into her lap and began to purr, knead his little paws, and slit his eyes in sheer delight. The damned cat practically chewed my nose off to get fed every morning, and there the little bastard was, acting like a sweetheart.

"I love how he's such a tiny thing," Duffy murmured. She picked Newt up to hold him in front of her face. "Like he never made it past a half-grown kitten."

"Yeah, if I did that, I wouldn't have a face left." I headed into the kitchen area beneath the second-floor half-level. "You want something cold to drink? I've got water, beer, and ice I'm going to put in a glass of whiskey. There might be some sweet tea. Dalia seems to think I'm a hummingbird and leaves that shit in the fridge for me to drink."

"Or maybe she thinks you could use a little sweetening?" She gently put the cat down, and he trotted over to his dish and screamed his fool head off. Duffy coughed a little when I dumped half of the thinly sliced cuttlefish into his bowl. "Dear God, what the hell is that?"

"Some of the kill I got with Jonas this afternoon." She wasn't wrong. The stuff reeked, but Newt attacked it with a gusto I saw every time he came across something even remotely edible. I came back with a bottle of stout for her and a half-full glass of Jack for me. "Here you go. It's supposed to taste like chocolate. I think it tastes like a five-day-old bagel covered in carob, but when someone gives you free beer—"

"You drink it and shut your mouth." Duffy took the bottle and laughed in her smoky chuckle. "Dempsey taught you well."

She'd come bare of makeup, and in the soft afternoon light through the warehouse's high frosted windows, I could make out a spatter of barely there brown freckles across her nose and faint laugh lines at the corners of her eyes. If I looked hard enough, I might have found a stray strand of silver in her mink-brown curls, but her creamy golden skin and lush mouth were the same as that night in the brothel. Duffy caught me staring at her, and her smile brought up a hell of a lot of memories of sweaty, pleasurable times we'd shared.

"You don't look much older than the first time I saw you in Mama Cheng's place." She curled her fingernails over my chin and then brushed her thumb against the pearl-black dragon scale my body had absorbed on my last desert run. "And here I am, wearing every single one of my years and wondering how I ever was lucky enough to have someone as beautiful as the elfin boy sitting next to me."

"Odin's Birds, that's a fucking lie. Dempsey dined out for months on you taking me upstairs," I scoffed.

"Did you ever tell him I spent the whole time teaching you how to cheat at poker?" She took a sip of the stout, made a face, and then tipped the bottle back for another drink. "I mean, sure, we got *around* to doing the best of things, but I wasn't too proud to take that man's money back then."

"Fuck no." I grinned back at her. "But then, he still thinks you're really a street-licensed prostitute."

Duffy was one of the first secrets I'd kept from Dempsey and one I never regretted. Did she sleep with people for money? Yes. But it wasn't that much different from what I did for a living. Duffy's main coin was information and the influence she had on her powerful clientele. These days she spent a hell of a lot more time on the upper levels, stirring pots and taking names, but she always seemed to have a soft spot for the idiots she gathered along the way… specifically me.

"I am street licensed. Only a fool lets those things lapse. Never be too proud to do the work," she sniffed at me. "But that's not why I've come by. See, my little dragon, time's come for me to call in all of those favors you've been racking up with me. I need you to take a message to someone for me, and you have to deliver it strong enough for him to listen very carefully and do what he's told."

I peered over my glass of whiskey at her, more than a bit confused. "Sounds like you want me to break someone's legs for you."

"Might come to that." Duffy blew over the rim of her bottle and made it sing a soft, low whistle. "I need you to get that high lord of yours to do something, and baby, whatever it takes, you make sure Ryder understands I won't take no for an answer."

Three

PASSION AND eloquence rode Duffy's words as she began to speak. She started off quietly, explaining how she got connected to a man with a big heart and an even bigger wallet, only to discover that every coin he'd gathered was covered in elfin blood. Her blue eyes couldn't find a point in my face to fix on, and her gaze slid away from mine as she told me of the horrors he'd committed simply to put cash in the bank.

"In his mind, the war never ended. It'd been years since we found peace, but in Harvey's head, he was still fighting something he could never win." She crouched forward on the couch, perched nearly at the edge of the cushions, and I wondered if it was just in my mind that it looked like she was about to run. "Then one day we were at a dinner and I found out that, years before, he and his friends had gone down to the Tijuana River to hunt the Unsidhe as they fled the courts. It was a game for them. One weekend they tracked an Unsidhe woman coming through the scrub, and—"

I was right about the run. Duffy got up and on her feet and bolted for the bathroom, but she only made it as far as the kitchen. My kitchen sink had seen worse than a beautiful woman's sick in its lifetime, and it probably would see worse still. I rubbed at her back as her body spasmed and lurched as it tried to get rid of somebody else's sins. I stood there until she finished, and I stroked the hair off of her temple to let fresh air hit her face.

I turned on the water and whispered, "Why don't you wash your face? And when you're done with that, there's a packet of toothbrushes under the bathroom sink. I'll make you some tea. Okay?"

It seemed like she took forever, and I was about to worry, when the bathroom door opened and she came out, scrubbing at her mouth with one of the small towels Dalia insisted I buy for guests. Duffy was the first one to use it for what it was intended for. It spent most of its existence being pushed out of the way so I had a place to hang bath sheets.

"Sit down. I'll bring you some tea." I stepped carefully around Newt, who'd taken up pole dancing around my legs. Then I handed her the steaming mug and dropped a sleeve of chocolate chip cookies into her lap. "Cookies make everything feel better. I don't know why, but they do. Chocolate makes me really happy inside. There's something stupidly comforting about a really good cookie. Besides, these go really well with whiskey."

"I slept with that man for five years," Duffy confessed in a tiny broken voice that I hated to hear coming out of her. "How can you even look at me knowing I've shared a bed with a monster like that?"

My glass was half-empty, and I'd stupidly left the bottle in the kitchen. I took a long, burning sip, swallowed, and said, "Babe, I am literally the epitome of a monster. I shouldn't *exist*. Tanic knitted me together out of magic, blood, and bone. I sleep with the monster every time I crawl into bed, so who the fuck am *I* to judge you?"

A silver gleam passed over her eyes, and their blue depths picked up a reflection of one of the Edison bulbs that hung above us. Her smile was sad as her fingers drifted back up to my face and as she traced over the shimmering hematite oval on my neck.

"It's been years since I've seen him. Well, at parties and events we made small talk, but he acted as if we were strangers. I priced myself out of his reach, hoping he would get the hint, but I finally had to tell him I didn't have time anymore. He's powerful, someone I shouldn't get on the bad side of, but my skin crawled every time I saw him. Then about six months after I extracted myself from his sphere, he was killed in one of those hunting expeditions." Duffy took a long, shuddering breath. "His lawyers contacted me three weeks later to tell me he'd left me what was a small fortune because, as he told them, *I made him laugh.*

"So I took his money, and I used it to help any Unsidhe who came across the border to get to someplace safe. It's not going to change what he did but…." She took a long gulp of the tea and then coughed. "Dear fucking God, what is *in* this? Ten pounds of sugar?"

"All I had was the iced sweet tea Dalia made for me," I replied with a shrug. "I threw it in a pot and heated it up for you. Do you actually think I'm the kind of guy who would have tea bags?"

"God, I love you so much sometimes," she laughed and combed her fingers through the ends of my hair. "And as much as I hate dragging you into this, things have gotten dangerous. Over the past eight years, I've paid for three Unsidhe to come across the border. They all headed to the interior, to a cluster of farms in the Midwest where they're sympathetic to people running away from the Dusk Court. In about a week and a half, there's going to be a young woman—a young Unsidhe—coming across. But she won't be alone. If all goes well, she'll be bringing children with her—*three* elfin children."

The Dusk Court was known to kidnap the Sidhe, mostly for pleasure, but also to increase their numbers. An elfin birth was rare. Our long life spans and our bodies' natural resistance to foreign growths hindered conception, especially for the Unsidhe. A fluke of genetic evolution allowed the elfin races to breed with one another, but the resulting offspring would only carry the DNA of one parent. A child was either Sidhe or Unsidhe, and the rival courts often went to war over the custody of a single infant.

I was the exception—a concoction of Tanic's seed and the egg of a Sidhe mother I'd never met. I was a blend of both races, with genetic markers from each side. Ryder mistakenly believed I was of the Dawn Court when we first met. Then, after an encounter with a pack of *ainmhi dubh*, he thought I was Unsidhe. The truth came out a little while later. He questioned the color of my eyes, which are a deep purple, instead of the gold or silver of a Dusk Court elfin to go with my Unsidhe black hair.

It took him a bit to wrap his head around it, but as Ryder always did, he immediately began to think about how he could make my conception and its relative success help increase the elfin population.

"Three? She's bringing three children? *Pele*, that's…." My nieces were considered miracles, although most Sidhe thought they were as monstrous as I am. But I figured beggars couldn't be choosers. For the elfin, children were as precious as the damned dragons they worshipped. "Why do you need Ryder? Hell, I'll go down there and grab her. Why involve the Dawn Court?"

"Because there's a rumor someone is auctioning off spots on a small hunting party down at the border where the Unsidhe cross that weekend, just like that one Harvey threw before." Duffy whispered, her voice shaky with fear and anger. "No one will tell me who's pulling it together, but whoever it is has all of my contacts scared to death. I don't have anyone else to help me… to help her get across safely."

"Hell, I'll do it—"

"I know you will, love." She cut me off with a wry smile. "But don't you see? I'm going to need Ryder to take them in, because no one else will. And then he has to stop these people from doing it again."

THERE'S NOTHING like a crisp San Diego morning watching the sunrise come up over the ring of mountains to the east while I sip a cup of coffee and lounge on the rooftop of my warehouse on the shore.

Pity that wasn't how I was spending my morning.

I'd spent the night uncomfortably as my body healed from the damage dealt to me by the cuttlefish—which hopefully by then was on a very slow, smoky journey to its final destination as peppered jerky. I'd dumped the rest of it into Newt's bowl and taken yet another shower because I couldn't seem to get the mollusk's stink off of me… or maybe it was just what Duffy told me the night before that clung to my skin.

Either way, I was headed toward Balboa Park and the Southern Rise Court in my beat-up old truck and with a travel mug full of hot strong black coffee.

As the crow flew, it wasn't much more than fifteen miles from my place to Balboa. According to old-timers and a lot of vintage maps, the distance had been much shorter before the Merge, but when our worlds collided, that part of San Diego tore apart and filled in with elfin forests and parts of an underground. The human population took advantage of its new tiered infrastructure, built out even farther and down to tunnel under the massive river where a major freeway artery once stood. There were still remains of old San Diego mingled in with the modern landscape, remnants of bygone neighborhoods tucked away between clusters of stacked boxy apartments and subway tunnels.

I'd found my '69 Mustang in one of those pockets—a pristine dust-covered muscle car protected by one of the largest man-eating gators I'd ever seen. Much like the cuttlefish, the gator became meat and leather. The real prize was the car. It took me forever to extract it from its cave, but once I got it back on the road, it could do the Pendle Run in eight hours at full bore.

Or least it could until I did a run for Ryder and the Mustang was a casualty of my reacquaintance with the Unsidhe and a lengthy battle with a pack of ainmhi dubh, the black dogs of the Wild Hunt. My Grande Coupe took a massive beating, but its tough exterior and powerful engine did its job. Our nieces were born on that run, in the back seat of that car, to a human surrogate who eventually not only betrayed the girls she carried but lost her life in the process.

We got the babies back, but the price I paid was not just an extensively damaged car. Tanic now knew where I was, and he had allies among the Sidhe who would be more than happy to turn me over and possibly bring Ryder's court down.

But we've all got problems.

Balboa Park's massive Moroccan-influenced domes and plateresque buildings barely survived the Merge, but the surrounding greenscapes and most of the expansive zoo next to it were consumed by ancient forests filled with magical creatures. Much like the wild animal park to the north, once the zoo's enclosures were compromised, its exhibited animals were left to roam freely.

That's why Ryder and his band of merry elfin shared their designated properties with a roaming band of grumpy pandas.

Still, coming up over the exit ramp of the 8 Corridor, Balboa and its looming ancient forest were breathtaking in the rising sun. Ryder brought with him Sidhe architects, mages with arcane skills who could coax palaces from the ground. The elfin towers were just beginning to breach the forest canopy, their delicate spires mimicking the existing architecture.

There was a spot for me in those buildings—the nearly sentient land understood the court's citizens and spurred a slowly growing tower. The Southern Rise realm recognized me, embraced me, and marked me as one of Ryder's.

I had a different opinion, but apparently there was no arguing with dirt and stone.

The entrance to the Southern Rise Court lay off of Old Sixth Street, and the broad concrete bridge sparkled in the brightening sunlight, its mica-flecked art deco sides now clean of decades of soot. Strangely enough, the forest didn't consume all traces of human existence. It left the bridge and the old museum structures, but the handblown-glass streetlamps that lined the broad drive into the Southern Rise compound now glowed from fairy lights instead of electrical bulbs.

I pulled up into the main rotunda and brought the truck to a rattling stop. The place looked a lot different from the night we rescued Kaia and Rhianna from my brother's clutches. I'd taken down his ainmhi dubh—well, most of them—and plunged into the raging waters when the human woman who'd carried them tossed them into the river. My brother, Valin cuid Anbhás, went into the water as well, but him I left.

Ryder met me on the walk, looking lordly and very Sidhe.

He was gorgeous in a way humans found delectable, but for an elfin he was... okay. He wore his gold-streaked wheaten hair shorter now, but it still fell down to skip his shoulders. His almost-too-large-for-his-face deep green eyes were shot with opal and black, and his mouth was nearly kissable, except for his upper lip being a little thin. He was also slightly taller than I was, but that could have been the hair. He was skinnier, but he was filling out and getting more muscle mass from fight training and, oddly enough, wall building. It was a curious hobby—something he claimed helped him meditate and center his thoughts. He didn't seem much calmer, but his hands were scuffed up, and his nails were a mess.

If anything, the Sidhe lord who had descended from Elfhaine to rule over the Southern Rise Court was becoming more human.

His sarcasm, however, was all Sidhe.

"You can't park that there," he drawled in his northern-accented Singlish. "If it's come here to die, at least take it out into the back where it can look at the trees as it passes."

I slammed the door to my mostly primer-painted truck and patted its hood. "This is why people don't like you, Ryder. You look down that little princeling nose of yours at their vehicles. This baby has gotten me there and back again more times than I can count, which is a hell of a lot more than I could say about you."

His smile was devastating. It ended nearly all of my control, and like always, whenever I was near him, I was struck with a need so powerful I nearly succumbed just to get relief. But I refused to be dictated by my instincts, and Ryder understood all too well the attraction riding both of us. It was the primordial and arcane drive of our blood and souls aching to quench the indefatigable fire between us.

My body thrummed with even the thought of him, and while I couldn't speak for Ryder, his pupils went large whenever they settled on me. He smelled of tea and sweet vanilla with a dash of clove for good measure. There were times when we wanted each other so badly we waged wars with our words and wit—anything to build up a defense against the genetic drive.

In the beginning, we didn't even like each other. I wasn't even sure we were friends, but we eventually circled back to each other and found excuses and common ground.

My only consolation for my lack of control and holding on by the skin of my teeth was that I drove Ryder *insane*.

"I didn't think I would see you so early in the morning. Did you hear Cari and Alexa went on a Pendle Run last night? They should be back sometime this morning if they know what's good for them." Ryder glanced back at the towers inching up toward the sky behind him. "Tell me they won't run into the trouble that we did. I do not want to lose my cousin and your best friend today."

"It's not mating season, so they shouldn't run into any dragons. They might plow through a herd of jackalopes, but I think if they see them, they'll go around." I enjoyed his look of horror. "Come on, don't be worried. Stalkers make that run all the time. *You've* made it. It's just a long stretch of black lava with a road mostly cut through it."

"It is an eight-hour full-speed haul through one of the largest gatherings of dragons on this Morrígan-damned planet—hungry dragons who are always looking to fill their bellies," Ryder hissed back. "It's suicide. There's another way around that's much safer. I know. I took it when I came down here the first time."

"That way also takes several days," I reminded him. "A Pendle Run is a hell of a lot easier than spending nearly half a week inching through mountain passes."

"You almost died!"

"That had more to do with that asshole hunt master and his black dogs than the Run." I shrugged. "And if I had a dollar for every time I *almost* died, I'd be retired by now."

"That does not make it any better," Ryder shot back.

"Are they driving the Nova Cari got from her brother? Because if they are, they'll be more than fine."

"Did you know that *nova* means *don't go* in Spanish? Why would you drive a car that means *don't go*?" Ryder frowned, more than likely perplexed at the vast range of languages humans had. The elfin, for the most part, shared similar tongues with only regional variations, some of them so thick it was difficult to understand what they were saying but easy enough to parse out. "It is good to see you, Kai, Clan Gracen, Stalker and Defender of the Southern Rise Court."

"Yeah, don't get started on that shit," I said as I nodded my chin toward the former Museum of Man, where he'd converted the upper floor into a suite of apartments and settled in while they waited for the court to finish growing. "Why don't you pour me a cup of coffee. And you might want to slip some whiskey into yours, because believe it or not, lordling, I've got a favor to ask of you."

WE STOPPED in to look at the girls, who despite the elfin propensity to age quickly out of infanthood, were still rather chubby drooling things with about as much intelligence as a golden retriever. Their nurse claimed they were brilliant and far ahead of any other child she'd ever helped raise, but the woman also liked to eat raw brussels sprouts, so as far as I was concerned, her opinion was sketchy. The babies were cute and definitely Sidhe. I couldn't tell them apart, but Ryder assured me I'd sucked egg mucus out of Kaia's blocked nose after their birth.

I'd done a lot of disgusting things in my life, but sucking on a baby's face to clear her sinuses was possibly the worst.

Their birth mother, Shannon, should never have gotten into my car. She was about to pop when we brought her down, and the surprise appearance of two eggs slithering out of her body as she straddled the back seat made me want to set my car on fire. Despite that image being permanently burned in my brain and the memory of Kaia's slithery overcooked egg white hitting the back of my throat, I was kind of fond of the kids.

"That one bites," Ryder commented as I held Kaia in the crook of my arm. "She gets that from your side of the family."

"You wish my side of the family bit you," I shot back while handing her over to the nurse. "Okay. Call me when they're able to walk and hold a gun so I can take them out ainmhi dubh hunting."

"You've already gotten to Alexa," he grumbled at my back as we walked toward his apartment. "I'll thank you to leave our nieces out of your Stalking business."

"They're going to need a job." I pushed open his front door. "Not like there are unclaimed courts just lying about the continent waiting for some lordling to show up and piss on them."

"Your misunderstanding of Sidhe politics is staggering," he replied as he shut the door behind us. The click sounded final, and my mind raced with the elaborate possibilities of what could happen in the luxuriously appointed living space that Ryder had carved out for himself. Luckily there was also a balcony, should I need to throw myself off of it. "Sit down and I'll bring you some coffee. I'm gathering by the tumbler you left in the truck you've already had some and are aching for more."

"You would be gathering right." I plopped down onto a sofa and nearly moaned in pleasure at its soft caress on my still-aching body.

Like me, Ryder arranged a bunch of couches around a low-lying table, but unlike my furniture, his was upholstered in a fine brocade and didn't have spots of dried cat horf that he couldn't get totally cleaned off. The place was airy and full of light, its outer walls filled with broad windows that overlooked the enormous cobblestone courtyard I'd driven into.

While the outside of the building boasted more embellishments than a little girl's birthday cake, its interior was much more subdued. The spaces were open and connected by long arched hallways, and most rooms were cordoned off with drapery instead of doors, welcoming any visitor to roam about. I knew from previous visits that the halls led to a library filled with enough books to make my covetous heart lust and to a study and various other rooms.

At the end of the main hall were double doors, often left wide open. They were also inviting, but for a different reason. I avoided that hall like the plague, and Ryder, amused at my discomfort, smiled every time I scowled down its cool length.

"It's not going to be a prison, Kai," he'd told me once as he gestured toward the bridge arching from his broad patio to the tower that was sculpting itself for my residency. "It will be there when you're ready… if you are *ever* ready."

Yeah. Like the plague.

The court wanted me there. I knew that. Everyone knew that. I just didn't understand it.

He returned with coffee strong enough to grow a pelt on our chests, which would be a miracle seeing as elfin didn't have a scrap of hair on us except for our heads. He passed me one of the mugs and sat on the table in front of me so our knees touched.

"You look troubled, Kai," he murmured softly and brushed his fingers over my thigh. "This must be some favor."

The elfins' need to casually touch was difficult for me, even on my best days, but I was trying to get used to it. It was like swallowing ketchup on scrambled eggs when someone served you—you tried not to make a face and gulped it down before you tasted the sweetened tomato sauce. Still, the electricity of his warmth through my jeans calmed the agitation Duffy had left burrowing inside of me.

I couldn't look at him while I recounted the tale she'd spun for me the night before. He listened as he always did, intent on my face, his dark green eyes piercing and sharp. It was odd—I had no better word for it—to see the complete trust he had in me. It played over his features, a sincere rapt loyalty, deep enough to shake me. For all we argued and fought, he was solid. He might fail spectacularly at what I needed him to do, but I could count on him on being there.

"We will offer them sanctuary here, or at least for as long as we can," Ryder said. Now it was *his* eyes that were troubled, an expression I found I didn't care for. The disruption of his arrogant confidence didn't suit his face, and my displeasure must have shown, because his hand once again settled on my leg. "It's not that they aren't welcome here. I would take any elfin into the court, but there is a complication I hadn't planned on."

"What kind of thing can complicate this? You're the damn high lord of this court. If you wanted to induct a Pele-cursed platypus into this place, nobody could stop you," I growled at him.

That growl was answered by the rumble of a big-block muscle car pulling into the main courtyard. It was the sound of American steel fueled by a hybrid gas-and-cell engine much like the one I had in Oketsu, my Mustang.

"Right there, *ainle*, is my complication." Ryder's eyes flared with anger, setting the opalescent slivers in their depths on fire. "The reason Cari and Alexa went up north was to bring down a challenger to my court. You see, Kai, there is another lord of my blood who's come to challenge me and take what I feel is destined to be mine. And that includes *you*."

Four

"He doesn't look like much," I said from my perch on the windowsill. "Kind of scrawny. Anemic even. Surprised he survived the trip down."

Ryder snorted from the couch. "He fought in the wars. Kerrick is quite sturdy."

"Yeah? Well he looks like Cari can take him. And she's wee." I studied the interloper and tried to find any resemblance to the Sidhe lord sitting behind me. His hair was long and cascaded down his back in a sleek queue, and while I couldn't quite see the range of colors in his eyes, they flashed a silvery teal when the sunlight played over his face. "Hell, Newt can take this bastard. Why are you just letting him waltz in? And how the hell does he have a claim on this court?"

"His bloodline gives him the right, just like mine does," Ryder replied smoothly, but I could hear the tension in his voice. He was disturbed by this lord's arrival, and if there was one thing Ryder hated, it was being challenged. "He's my cousin, the blood son of my mother's blood sister. He is as close a descendent to Sebac as I am, so he has every right, possibly even more. The court will eventually decide."

"What? You mean like the castle you've got growing in your backyard?" To say I was confused was an understatement. "Explain that."

"After a period of time, if it responds to his presence more than to mine, that will say the land wants him for its people." He tried to pass it off with a nonchalant wave of his hand, but I knew better. For all of Ryder's faults—mostly his pigheaded arrogance—he had a passion for his people. He would do anything for them, including defying his domineering, controlling grandmother. "We won't know until he's been here a while. If the towers accelerate their growth or react positively to him being here, then I will step aside."

"That's bullshit." Maybe this Kerrick heard me through the closed window or something caught his attention, because he glanced up and scanned the front of the building. Even with the distance between us, I could see he was a stunning man, but something in his face left me cold inside. "I've got a couple of sharp knives, and you have a very-fast-moving, deep river about half a mile to the east. I say we take care of him before the court can even catch a whiff of his ass."

He sighed heavily, an exasperated sound I knew all too well. "Kai, you just can't keep killing things or people you don't want around."

"Funny, it's worked out for me so far." I cocked my head and studied him. "And that's literally what they pay me for. Killing things is what I do."

"But not people, not unless they move against you first."

"If you remember, I told you I'd kill you if ever you began to abuse your power like your grandmother does," I pointed out. "But I'm willing to bend that to kill for you to protect your people."

His grin was a sensual tease and filled with sweaty promises. "That is the most romantic thing you've ever said to me."

"Most people don't consider premeditated murder romantic, lordling."

"Most people aren't you, Kai." He saluted me with his mug. "We will just have to wait and see."

"Answer me something. Was he at all interested in forming a court before you came down here?" I went back to watching Ryder's cousins and Cari unload the Nova. Or at least Alexa and Cari were. Kerrick just stood there, taking in the sights. "Or did he want it because you had it?"

"He has leadership capabilities and was a very high-ranking officer in the Sidhe armies. Now that the wars are over, he's probably looking to establish a legacy." Ryder shrugged. "Like I said, his bloodline gives him as much right to be here as mine does."

"You want to know what I think?" I didn't take my eyes off of Kerrick, and my breath was beginning to mist over the window. "I think your grandmother can't stand the idea of a court being established in her backyard without her dirty little fingers all through it. You waiting? That I understand. You had to gather up people and power because you knew you were going to move against her. You tried not to, but after the crap she pulled up in Elfhaine, you know she would try to undermine you because you deviate from how she runs *her* court. He isn't down here because he cares about the elfin you've gathered up. He's down here because your grandmother sent him."

His laugh was low and slightly bitter. "And here I thought you didn't understand Sidhe politics."

"Oh, I understand them just fine," I scoffed. "I just prefer the Unsidhe way of dealing with assholes who come into my yard to piss on my house. It's why I carry all these knives."

I HATED Kerrick on sight. A lot of it had to do with my surprisingly strong loyalty to Ryder, although I could've easily chalked it up to the infant nieces we shared. Mostly I hated how my body reacted to Kerrick. It wasn't as intense as my initial response to Ryder—a driving need to slide myself under his skin and share his existence—but there was definitely something there.

And I hated myself for it. I hated being a creature of magics and instinct, driven by things outside of my control. I'd already lived so much of my life under someone else's thumb. I hated to think I was nothing more than an animalistic monster beneath a veneer of humanity.

Up close, Kerrick was more than stunning. He was the kind of breathtakingly handsome that made sane people lose their minds. Luckily I only had a passing acquaintance with sanity, so I was safe. But Cari was not, and as much as I loved her, I was about ready to throw her into a closet and lock it to keep her safe.

Her hug was tight and quick, as fierce and small as she was. The only daughter of a Mexican witch and a German Stalker, Caridad Brent inherited her mother's third eye and her father's bloodlust. I'd seen her when she was wet from being born, and then as she grew up to be a Stalker like her dad. She was probably the best friend I'd ever had, and I thought of her as a little sister. She was also the biggest pain in my ass.

Right after Ryder.

And Dempsey.

"Why are you flinching? What happened?" she muttered into my chest when I returned her embrace. "Iesu, you're like a rock. What's got you all tense? Wait, let me guess. Kerrick."

"He's just the last on the list. You and me? We've got to talk." I let her go just in time for Ryder's cousin Alexa to grab me from behind. "Okay. Ribs are cracked. How about if the two of you let me go so I can stab you for bringing that asshole down the coast? Seriously, let go, Alexa. I'm bruised to hell and gone. Jonas and I took a bounty yesterday for a monster in the understreets, and the damn thing kicked my ass."

"It's just good to see you, Kai," Alexa murmured against my neck as she brushed a soft kiss on my skin. "You smell like a cinnamon bun…." She took another sniff. "And liniment."

They'd definitely done a Run, and it was kind of amusing to see Alexa mimicking Cari's behavior. She wore her red-streaked magenta curls pulled back into a ponytail, much like Cari's messy dark queue, and both had the slightly sticky feel of being caught in a car on a long haul. Even their eyes were a bit similar—Cari's the smoky blue while Alexa's were dappled with silver and gold, and despite her short time in a human city, Alexa had somehow found a pair of jeans long enough to fit her tall, slender body. The faded blue denim was nearly a mirror of Cari's.

Alexa was a handsome woman with features too strong to be considered a Sidhe beauty, but I loved her animated face and enthusiastic smile. She was the most human of them all, a relatively young four-hundred-year-old elfin woman who'd become head of security for a new court and moonlighted as an apprentice Stalker on the side.

She was Ryder's first cousin and often joked about having my children. At least it seemed like most of the time she was joking. Sometimes it was hard to tell. I doubted I would ever have children. How I was made… how I came to be… was pretty much in line with a mule. So, for all of her teasing about wanting purple-eyed babies, I didn't think she was going to get very far.

There was also the matter of Ryder claiming I was his. Alexa didn't poach on her cousin, and no matter my protests that I didn't have a relationship with Ryder, she clearly stayed on that side of the line. Besides, there were signs of a deeper friendship forming between her and Cari, something I wasn't quite sure how to feel about. Even if it was none of my business, an elfin and human relationship would only last as long as the human's extremely short life—something I tried every day to avoid thinking about.

I'd convinced Ryder not to meet Kerrick in his personal apartments. I didn't want to see the asshole measuring the windows for drapes, and Ryder surprisingly agreed. Instead I texted Cari to bring him to the court's main hall—a long, broad gathering area filled with clusters of sitting areas and tables. It was apparently very different from Sebac's main hall in Elfhaine, much more of a casual welcoming space than the rigid church-like pews she forced her clan to sit in while she lectured from a raised dais at the far end of the room.

There were other elfin in the space besides Kerrick, Cari, and Alexa when we came down, and Ryder said hello to everyone along the way and took his sweet time getting across to where they stood. The women came to meet me while Kerrick stood silently near a group of armchairs, watching and saying nothing when one of the Sidhe slipped past him with a tea tray she set down on a table.

That was more than enough to tell me what kind of man he was.

"Hello, Ryder, Clan Sebac, Third in the House of Devon." Kerrick's voice was a melodic roll of cultured Sidhe, and each syllable hammered against my soul.

The elfin's native languages triggered a feeling of sick in me, echoing remnants of a binding spell my father had placed on me a long time ago. I'd broken it, or at least I thought it had faded, but every once in a while, some combination of words or maybe the tone of the speaker twisted my stomach into knots and reminded me of the iron I once wore under my skin.

Then I reheard in my head the words Kerrick spoke, and my rising anger chased down any vomit I might've chucked up.

"You forgot something in there. It's Ryder, Clan Sebac, Third in the House of Devon, *High Lord of the Southern Rise Court*," I corrected, and because of my promise to Ryder, I hooked my thumbs into the waistband of my jeans rather than reach for the knife tied to my thigh.

There were times I regretted any promise to Ryder, and that was one of them.

Kerrick's eyes widened, and his black lashes threw shadows against his face. If his eyes were purple instead of teal, they would have resembled mine, with folds of dark pearl opal and hematite ringed with ebony, but their Caribbean hue was a startling contrast to the darker colors within them. Up close he was even more devastatingly handsome than I'd imagined, a type of symmetrical perfection the humans adored and the Sidhe glorified. Elfin beauty was probably as much the reason the war ended as was the truce the three governments hammered out. Humans loved beautiful things, and the images of fallen elfin lying next to their own dead were difficult for many to stomach.

Cute and fuzzy animals are less likely to become extinct, because someone with a soft heart will always speak up for their continued existence, no matter how dangerous the creatures might be. I'm sure there were studies on it. I knew it from experience, having seen a very green Stalker get her face eaten off by a tiny pink fluff ball with a surprisingly well-camouflaged mouth of rotating teeth because she leaned over and picked it up before any of us could stop her.

"Oh, by the gods and all the dragons, you are exquisite. Cousin, I'd heard he was astonishingly beautiful, but he goes beyond imagining. He is such a blend of our races—the wildness of the Unsidhe, but with the grace of our own kind. That black hair with…. It's like midnight with swirls of stars," Kerrick purred as he advanced on me. He lifted one elegant hand and reached for my face. "I can see why you—"

Fuck my promise to Ryder. I drew my knife and put its tip to the end of Kerrick's nose. "Swear to fucking God, you touch me and Ryder won't have to worry about you trying to claim what he's already built up."

"He doesn't like to be touched, cousin." Ryder's smile was faint, but his eyes were dancing with laughter. "Kerrick, High Commander of Elfhaine, Clan Sebac, House of Levar, I would like you to meet Kai, Clan Gracen, Stalker and Defender of the Southern Rise Court."

"Are we going to have to do this every single time I meet somebody? My name is Kai Gracen. That's all you...." I tilted my head to look at Ryder and then shifted my gaze back toward his cousin. I ran the introduction back in my head. "Wait. Clan Sebac, House of Levar. Isn't that the same as Alexa?"

"You're right, Kai," Alexa said, her words strangled with tight control. "We are of the same clan and house. You see, Kerrick is my brother."

"YOU KNOW, as much as I love Alexa and Ryder, every time I come here I feel like I'm at a dinner party wearing a trash bag," Cari grumbled as she flopped onto a couch.

We left the Sidhe cousins to talk among themselves, Kerrick rubbing at the tip of his nose, where I wasn't ashamed to admit I was more than a little proud at the blood drop I'd left there. No matter how long I lived, I would never understand why people can't keep their hands to themselves. Complaining about it to Cari would do me no good, because she hung on me like a fox stole most of the time, but we kind of grew up together, so her I didn't mind.

It was just everybody else.

"I mean, look at them." She gestured toward the other Sidhe roaming about the long space. "Everyone's dressed like they're about to go to a movie premiere instead of pulling weeds in the garden."

She wasn't wrong, but I'd been around enough Sidhe by then to know that's just how they liked to live. Every minute was spent in a bit of hedonism despite the task ahead of them. Alexa and Ryder looked out of place in their jeans and T-shirts, donning sparrow feathers in a muster of peacocks. Whatever was going on between the three of them, it was heated, but Alexa shot me a quick smile before she turned her attention back to her brother, and as I was about to tell Cari about the run down to Mexico, Ryder winked at me.

"He's such a dick," I muttered as I filled Cari's cup with a fruit-scented tea. "Did you know what Kerrick was up to before you agreed to bring him down?"

"No," Cari replied. She worked the tie out of her ponytail, threaded her fingers through her dark hair, and sighed in relief as she massaged her scalp. "Do you think I would have let him in my car if I'd known? That one is going to be nothing but trouble. I told Alexa he'd be lucky if you didn't stab him on sight. She owes me a tenner for that prick on his nose. I owe you a beer."

"Do me one better." Thankfully one of the teapots left for us was filled with coffee, and I poured myself what was probably my sixth cup of the day. It was weaker than I liked, practically see-through, but at that point, I didn't care. "I've got a job coming up, maybe in a week and a half, maybe sooner. I want you to do the run with me. He might be shit or not at all, but I'll give you what I can."

"You don't take a job for no pay unless it's something serious." Her mood went somber, and the energy in her body stilled as she leaned in to listen. "Whatever it is, I'm in."

"There's a lot of iffy pieces in this," I began, trying to ignore the cousins as they moved away from the chairs to speak to an older Sidhe who was one of the architects of the towers. "Let me tell you what's going on, and then you can decide if you want to join up."

I was trying to reconcile the little girl I'd taught how to button her jacket and ride a bicycle, and even more recently, shoot a handgun, with a woman who was now not only a full-fledged Stalker, but also a trained *hibiki*—a witch with the ability to look into the eyes of the dead and see the last moments of their lives. We'd fought a bit lately about her coming on runs with me—not because she wasn't competent, but because, in my mind, I was still teaching her how to take her first steps while she held a death grip on my index finger.

Cari was a third-generation Stalker raised in a family of hardened hunters who gave no quarter to any of its children, regardless of gender. Her mother was a plump, congenial woman who liked to stuff me with food but could also skin and bone a goat in about ten minutes flat. They were a practical people, willing to share their life skills and knowledge with an elfin chimera, so I was very reluctant to take their daughter on a mission she might not come back from.

She listened carefully as she turned her head aside to stare at an empty spot on the floor. It was a trick I'd taught her, a focusing technique I used to drown out the rest of the world around me and concentrate on what I needed to hear. I told her what I knew about the job and how Duffy believed Ryder's power could protect the Unsidhe coming across the border. Her concentration broke when I brought up the children, and she lifted her eyebrows dramatically.

"*Three*? That's an insane amount." Cari let out a low whistle. "And she really believes someone is getting together a group of people to hunt them down? To kill them like one of the Wild Hunt's black dogs?"

"I got the feeling the killing part is just the last of it." I tamped down my anger and shoved back unasked-for memories. "Duffy doesn't know who's pulling this together, but she thinks Ryder might be able to get them to stop. The two people who helped her before have died, and the one person she'd been counting on refuses to cross this guy but won't tell her who it is… or maybe doesn't know and isn't willing to risk it. Either way I'm going to be making the run, and Ryder insists on coming with me."

"Of course he does." Cari swore under her breath, asking a variety of saints for an extension on her patience. "He's the damned high lord of this court, and he wants to go traipsing off on every single run you make?"

"No, just the ones that involve the Sidhe, their fertility, or gathering up street children like they're dandelions in a field." I'd lost sight of the trio, but the main hall was busier now, filling up with elfin coming to meet the new court jester. "He says it's what a good leader does. How can he ask his people to push themselves if he doesn't get his hands dirty? So Ryder's coming along for the ride."

"As am I," Kerrick proclaimed as he broke out of a group of people to approach us. The worst part about being the only elfin among humans was that I forgot how keen our hearing was, since I was normally the only one who could hear a dog whistle. He stopped at my chair, his arm lifted up with his hand out, but he caught himself before he touched my shoulder. "If my cousin Ryder is going with you on Southern Rise business, I will as well. After all, this *will* be my court, much like *you* will be mine."

Five

"THIS ISN'T some kid's birthday party where you get an invitation just because you're in the same class." I stood up slowly and stepped into Kerrick's space. He stood his ground, but his chin came up and his jaw tightened. "And before you get any cute ideas about who I am to you, just remember I don't belong to this court. And I'd sooner gut your grandmother than spit on her if she were on fire."

"Sebac said there was some unpleasantness she regretted." Kerrick turned and shifted his hips as though to welcome a hastily approaching Ryder into the conversation. I snorted beneath my breath. It was a subtle way for him to save face, distancing our bodies in such a way as to appear as though he weren't stepping back. "She would take it back if she could."

"Grandmother only regrets gambling on my obligations and affection for Kai," Ryder interjected. He settled his hand on my shoulder, and I schooled my face not to look at him or shift away. Sidhe politics were based on connections—I knew that much—and he was showing Kerrick he had rights that his cousin probably never would. "She knew what she was doing. Her spells were meant to cripple him, maybe kill him. If you believe her lies, then you have no place here, cousin, because Kai is a crucial component to the survival of our races. He's sacrificed so much and allowed us liberties no other Sidhe would give. Without the knowledge he's willing to share with us, we are doomed to extinction."

I just had to survive the touch, because it'd been a long time for me and I knew where there was a very large bed upstairs.

God, I hated how he could make me *feel*.

"I look forward to hearing your side of the story, Kai, Clan Gracen," Kerrick conceded as he flipped the tails of his brocaded coat back in a short courtesy bow. "My purpose for being here is not to further our grandmother's agendas, but rather to establish a strong court and anchor our place on this coast."

"A strong court—*this court*—will include all elfin who wish to join it." Ryder tightened his fingers on my shoulder. "You might think my methods are unorthodox, but as you've heard me say before, if we don't change and adapt to this new world we're living in, then we will die off. Our people must not only evolve. They must also thrive and work with the humans we now share this land with. Kai's experience with the human culture and its social constructs are invaluable, and he's proven himself by defending this court against those who would try to destroy it. And that includes our grandmother."

"Let's table your grandmother for right now, because unless she's also coming along on this ride, she shouldn't be taking a seat next to us." I shifted my weight, which brought my side up against Ryder's hip, and I immediately regretted it. I knew that even if I went on a weeklong tour of every brothel in San Diego, I wouldn't burn off the itch I had for him. I took a deep breath and said, "There are only four places a party that large could easily cross, especially with the river swollen up from the rains. The one Duffy said they'll be using is not difficult to get to, but it's a long haul."

"Well, since they're coming out inland instead of by the shore, that'll make it harder to traverse. It's a rough territory to cross normally, but right now it's devil-storm season, so we'll have to go underground for the first four miles and then come up through the aqueducts." Cari stretched out her legs and leaned back into her chair. "We're talking twenty miles of slogging through sewers and buried caverns and then another five or ten through scrub brush, probably carrying about fifty pounds of gear. Enough for ourselves and whatever we bring back."

"I know of a way we can use a vehicle, but it's as slow going as hiking. It'll still lead us underground, but it's longer. The exit point is about four miles away from where we would normally come up." I tried not to breathe a sigh of relief when Ryder dropped his hand. "I think we're going to have to go that way."

I'd done the Mexican run at least twenty times before but mostly to hunt down ainmhi dubh that were terrorizing the farms beneath the devil canyons. I'd taken a vehicle to bring back pelts when I didn't want to carry them back through the tunnels, but the way was definitely longer.

"Is that the one you did with Dad and Jonas that one time?" Cari curled her upper lip. "The other way's a lot shorter. Less time on the road."

"Yeah, we could get there sooner on foot, but we're taking a wrung-out Unsidhe woman and three kids with us on the way back. They might not be able to make it the rest of the way. It'll be easier if we can load them into a vehicle." I didn't like it either, but I also didn't enjoy the idea of dragging an already-exhausted group of children through an underground wilderness while on foot. "I'm talking something like a long Jeep—transport only. We'd have to stop to let the cells recharge, but it's better than walking. Also give us some cover when the Dusk Court in Mexico sends a Wild Hunt after them. No one's just going to let her waltz out of there with those kids, no matter what race they are."

"I'm coming with you. If Ryder goes, then I will as well," Kerrick insisted. "I can do this. If anything, my cousin was never battle-tested. He—"

"He's held his own on two runs." Kerrick's nostrils flared, but I wasn't going to let him push me back. "And you don't have a damned thing to say about who comes with me. Or did you miss the part about me not belonging to this court?"

"Kai, he's not wrong." Ryder's words were a splash of cold on my temper. "He would serve you better than—"

"Do you want to come with me or not? I've got Cari on board. If you want him to take a seat on this damned ride, then fine, but you don't go, he doesn't go." Ryder knew better, and I hated seeing him step aside for an ass hat with boundary issues. I got the "more flies with honey than vinegar" thing, but a rolled-up newspaper worked great too. "Who's on the bus isn't up for a group discussion."

Kerrick scowled at me and straightened his shoulders. I was more than willing to go toe-to-toe with the asshole, but then Ryder nudged my shoulder and pulled my attention away. Ryder cleared his throat and cut through the building tension. "If you think you can find a vehicle to fit all of us, then yes, I want to go. The first Sidhe this woman meets should be the lord who is eager to take her into his court. Don't you agree, cousin?"

"DO YOU want something to eat?" There wasn't a lot in my fridge, but having food delivered was always an option. I wasn't really a picky eater, and Cari was used to chowing down on things I threw together in a pinch. We ate enough disgusting things on runs that our stomachs were pretty much cast iron, although she did draw the line at sucking at the heads of river prawn. "I've got stuff to make ramen, and if you want to wait for the rice to cook, I can make us *loco moco*."

"Make the rice. I'm going to go use your shower." She sniffed at her shirt and stuck her tongue out at its redolent aroma. "And maybe grab something from your clean clothes basket. That was a hard run to make, and I think I'm wearing it on my skin."

By the time she was done scraping the Pendle Run off of her body, the rice cooker was in steaming mode and I'd just finished up the mushroom brown gravy. I handed Cari a small hamburger patty to feed Newt to keep him out from underfoot and shooed her to go sit on the couch. The cat led with his stomach, meowing hoarsely as he batted at her ankles and tried to get her to stop walking. She'd found more than just a shirt in my clothes. She also snagged a pair of cotton drawstring pants.

"You should've gotten something thicker." The words were barely out of my mouth when Newt hooked his claws into her calf and climbed up her leg, digging his sharp talons through the fabric and into her flesh. She let out a series of hissing screams and danced her way to the couch, holding the patty up above her head while she tried to pluck the cat off of her butt. "Just sit sideways and he'll calm down. Feed him small pieces or he'll try to shove that whole thing in his mouth and horf it all right back up."

I finished up frying the eggs and then layered them on top of the two low, wide bowls with rice, hamburger patties, and the gravy I had on the counter. Then I tucked a bottle of hot sauce under one arm and two bottles of water under the other. I headed into the living area, wound around the broad storage chest I used for a table, and avoided the cat trying to snag another helping of food.

"Here. Grab something, like the water, so I can put these down." I nodded my chin toward the tangle of rebar and bolts sitting to one side on the chest. "You might want to move that to make room."

Cari grabbed not only the iron pieces but the cat and shifted everything out of my way. "Ryder still freaked out about these? I know Alexa is, even though she tries not to show it. Hard to imagine all of this being underneath your skin."

"Those are just the prettier pieces. Sparky made that out of what they pulled out." I held still as Cari grabbed the waters and hot sauce. Then I put the bowls down and handed her one of the forks I'd clenched between my fingers. "She thought I'd want something beautiful out of it. Mostly it just reminds me of where I was and probably would still be if Dempsey hadn't won that poker hand."

She shoveled a couple of mouthfuls of food in until her face resembled a plump chipmunk, chewing furiously. Then she swallowed and said, "You didn't ask about the run. Or are you waiting for me to bring it up?"

"What can you tell me that's going to change my mind about Kerrick being an asshole?" I pinched off a piece of meat and held it out for Newt to nibble on. His teeth were sharp on my fingertip, and he growled as he ate. "I noticed Alexa made herself scarce. I'm guessing her older brother wasn't too happy she came south with Ryder. Or is she choosing her brother over her cousin?"

I'd sworn I wouldn't get involved in the Southern Rise Court. There really hadn't been a need to. The place was still in its building stage, and I was oblivious to any political strife. As much as Ryder tried to get me to accept a place in its ivory towers and filigree balconies, its extravagant architecture wasn't going to be comfortable if I was surrounded by the Sidhe.

I'd suffered too much at the hands of my own people, to the point where I couldn't even hear the language without wanting to throw up. I didn't think living among them was going to do me any good, but that didn't stop Ryder from trying. He was the ultimate optimist, and as intelligent as I knew he was, he followed a lot of traditions and superstitions, the least of which was his insane worship of dragons.

There wasn't any doubt in my mind that he would step aside for Kerrick if he thought the former high commander would be a better leader, but I wasn't convinced Kerrick would be as welcoming to a small band of Unsidhe refugees.

"Why do you think that a woman Duffy wants to bring across is on the run?" Cari said after she slowed down, leaned back, and exhaled to catch her second wind. "And what's the story on the kids?"

"Probably the same one as mine," I said, tapping at the iron curls with my fork. "My guess is they're Sidhe. They could have been stolen or bred from Sidhe prisoners. Elfin kids take a long time to mature. Hell, they could have even been with that court before the Merge."

"You were probably born before any of this happened." Cari pushed her food around with her fork and cradled her bowl between her crossed legs. "That just seems so weird to me. Dad always told me I would have to get used to you not getting any older, but it really didn't hit me until the run. Kerrick is over a thousand years older than Alexa, and she's four hundred years old. She's closer to Ryder than she is to him, so to answer your question, she's not a member of the Kerrick fan club right now. I didn't get a chance to talk to her, because he was always lurking, but I know she doesn't like the Sebac. Alexa is like Ryder. She believes the elfin are going to die off if they don't do something to increase their numbers."

"Well, that's something Ryder's really working hard on. I know some think he's crazy, and they've got these ideas about natural-selection conception, but is it worth your race dying off because you're not willing to change how you think? It's kind of like social Darwinism. If you put yourself on the path to extinction, do you have the right to stop someone else from trying to survive?"

Cari chuckled and reached for a water bottle. "Do you remember when our biggest problem was trying to decide what cartoon to watch on Saturday morning as we ate our cereal?"

I didn't have the heart to tell her that had never been my life and that the times I'd spent with her on those Saturday mornings were because I was too inexperienced and too young to go on the long-range hunts with Jonas and Dempsey. My adolescence came fast and hard once I got enough food and wasn't being tortured day in and day out. My body ached from the rapid growth, and her mother did the best she could do to help ease the anguish, though she was confounded by my elfin physiology. At that time, human society was still smarting from the wars, and prejudices ran strong, but they opened their home and family to me.

I could never truly repay them, and my biggest fear would be betraying their trust and consideration by killing their daughter—even if she was one of the best damned Stalkers I knew and her family didn't expect her to do anything less than her best on a job.

"Well, since Ryder probably won't let us kill Kerrick—don't look at me like that, you know I wouldn't do it—and apparently the only thing that has a say in this is those stupid towers coming up out of the ground over there, I'm going to stick with what I know how to do." I ran through a list of my finances for the next few months, hating that I would have to borrow from the Mustang's restoration fund if Dempsey's medical bills came in before the end of the run. "Ryder's promised to fund this, and since it's directly from him to me and not through the Post, I don't have to worry about fees. I'll give you half of—"

"I'll take a quarter," Cari corrected. "I'm not equal on this one. I don't know the route, and I'm not going to be arranging for the equipment. It'll be pure grunt work for me."

"You sure?" I bit my lip, not convinced.

"Yeah, because if we split it, then I have to ride shotgun as you keep the two Sidhe lords you're dragging with us in line. That's an argument I'd rather not referee." Cari tapped my cat's nose with her finger when he tried to investigate her dish. "So if this elfin woman is bringing kids, chances are they're not Dusk Court, right?"

"Probably not. If they were, she'd have no reason to take them. Duffy's biggest concern was getting the three kids to someplace safe, where they could grow up elfin. The other people she helped across went inland, and they were adults." I broke the yolk of my egg and let it seep into the rice. "Can't say I blame her. You wouldn't want them turning out like me."

Cari's gaze flicked to my face, and a frown wrinkled her forehead. "There's nothing wrong with how you turned out."

"For me—for what I am—maybe not, but those three kids have a family somewhere in the Dawn Court. Me? Nobody was going to take me in and teach me how to be Sidhe." I shrugged at her hissing retort. "In my head, I'm human. It's hard for me to remember I'm elfin until I look in the mirror or somebody says something. The first time somebody called me a *cat bastard*, I looked around to see who he was talking about. I've got a lot of Dempsey's prejudice against the elfin, not just my own, and some layer of blind distrust underneath it all."

"But you're trying, right? I mean, you like Alexa and Ryder."

"I still don't know if I like Ryder, but Alexa's good." I put my bowl down on the crate and grabbed my water to take a drink. "For every Ryder there are twenty Sebac and maybe a hundred Kerricks. They tire me out. I feel like I have to watch everything I say and sidestep when someone touches me every other second. It's like a minefield of slender knives sharp enough to cut you, and you don't even feel it until you bleed out. Maybe if you grow up in it, it's different. For me it feels like I'm constantly under attack, and the only time I get relief is if I have Ryder in front of me. And I'll be damned if I spend the rest of my life hiding behind his skirts."

My link chimed and rattled from its spot on the shipping crate, its band hitting on the iron bars. I recognized the number, tapped it on, and answered, "Hey, Dalia. What's up? Are you at home? I've got some more stuff to make loco moco if you're hungry. Cari's here. Thinking of putting on a movie and getting sick on *arare* popcorn."

"No, I'm down at Medical. I'm on a double shift tonight." The sounds of the ER finally reached me through the line. "And there's nothing more I would rather do than watch a movie with you guys right now, but I need you to get over here, Kai. It's Dempsey. And it's not looking really good."

Six

IN THE middle of Death Valley, there was a small pond filled with bright pink water. It was fed by a cold spring and nestled under lush white-leaved trees. The water was drinkable and swimmable—an elfin oasis plucked from another world and wedged into a corner of hot, searing sands, a welcome, lovely spot that offered a weary traveler some place to rest after a long day.

Those waters were also home to a fingernail-sized lavender octopus with rainbow suckers tipped with a toxin powerful enough to paralyze an adult prismatic dragon.

It wasn't fatal, but for however long it lasted, the octopus's victim could only watch the world go by. Automatic motor functions didn't seem to be affected by it. The paralyzed creature could still breathe and swallow, but moving was impossible.

I'd accidentally swallowed one of those octopuses when I was just into my accelerated adolescence, and those were the most horrific three days of my life.

And considering everything I'd gone through until then, that was saying a lot.

The numbness creeping through my body after Dempsey's doctor was done telling me what was wrong put that toxin to shame.

I wasn't allowed to see him at first, and no one would give me the time of day until I threatened the head nurse with dismemberment. That's when someone got Dalia in front of me and she hunted me down a doctor who looked like a heron someone had dressed up as a human and slapped a stethoscope on. He started to talk, and the nostrils on his enormous beak of a nose pinched and flared as he unstitched my world.

That's when I experienced the rainbow-suckered octopus flashbacks and choked on the bile rising up from my twisted-around belly.

"It's not supposed to be like this," I said for what must have been the twentieth time since I'd come through Medical's front doors. "He's supposed to have longer than this. The healers—"

"Mr. Gracen, you can get every single healer and doctor on this planet to work on Mr. Dempsey, but the fact of the matter remains—the human body can only go for so long." The heron sniffed imperiously. "And considering everything that man's done to himself, it's a surprise he's lasted as long as he has. I give him six months on the short side, maybe a year and a half at the most."

THOSE WORDS, the number of those days, echoed in my mind, and they continued to bounce around inside of my skull even as I lowered myself into one of the rocking chairs on the wraparound porch of the Wyatts' ranch house. Dempsey sat in the other one, his gnarly feet propped up on the lower rail, his twisted toes poking out the front of a pair of house slippers that Jonas's husband gave him to wear.

I'd only seen him two days before, when I dropped off a load of groceries so he didn't have to go into town, and in those few hours he seemed to have folded in on himself, and his once robust, powerful body seemed to have shrunk. He'd become a deflated origami version of the man who used to smack me when I shoveled food into my mouth with my fingers or when I bit a Stalker on the face after he slapped my ass. Dempsey never should be smaller than me, never weaker, but there he sat, slumped down in the chair and rocking it back and forth with a lazy pump of his knees.

He'd aged five hundred years in the past few hours, his already silvery hair a grizzled, yellowing mess around his deeply lined face. The patchy scruff on his jaw was coarse and sounded like sandpaper when he scratched at it. His beefy face was leaner now, his sunken cheeks mottled with age spots, and his broad nose was red with broken capillaries. Dempsey's hands shook as he took a half-smoked cigar out of his bathrobe's chest pocket, and I sighed, refusing to fight him over the stogie. I did clear my throat at the open bottle of beer sitting on the floor next to him, but he simply rolled his watery pale eyes at me.

"Quit looking at me like that, kid," he mumbled as he cupped one hand over the end of the cigar. Dempsey struck a long wooden match against the chair leg, brought it up to light his cigar, and pulled on it to bring the burnt stump to a bright red. Shaking the match out, he exhaled a plume of acrid smoke and then pursed his lips and nodded at a flock of chickens picking at feed on the lawn. "Tell me something. Those birds look kinda blueish to you?"

The birds in question were definitely teal, bordering on a neon blue only found on stripper-joint signs and tik-tik cabs. They looked like every other chicken I'd ever seen except for their color. Then I remembered Jonas telling me something about one of his kids experimenting with a chemistry set behind their chicken coop and swearing to Hecate that he miscalculated the ingredients when he blew off the sidewall.

The Wyatt ranch was now the proud owner of a flock of teal hens, a brilliantly hued purple rooster, and an eight-year-old enrolled in witch school.

It was a great place to be a kid, I suppose. There was lots of land and a very tall chain-link fence to keep out most of the wildlife that lurked in the tall woods surrounding the back acres. The main house was large and grew with each child—a room tacked on here and there with little regard for order—but it was the kind of place people liked to gather in. A couple of trailers behind the house doubled as an office for the farm and guest houses for people staying any length of time.

A covered walkway connected a longhouse the family used for a dining room when everyone could get together for a meal, and its walls retracted up into hidden pockets when the weather was good. There was enough lawn to hold a baseball game if you didn't mind a shoe or a large rock serving as a base, and the sandy pit next to the longhouse was big enough to mold an army of dinosaurs attacking a sand castle or play a set of volleyball.

The place wasn't glamorous—not like the palace grounds at Balboa—but there was always food in the kitchen, soup on the stove, and hot water when you needed to shower. I'd licked more than a few wounds at the Wyatts' ranch and probably would again in the future. Its welcoming air was both soothing and uncomfortable. I never knew what to do or say around people as affectionate as Jonas, his spouses, and his children, but they never pushed at me. They left me to make whatever overtures I wanted.

Okay, maybe not the kids, because like all kids, they were little assholes who had to get into anything and everything I was doing. Kaia and Rhianna wouldn't give me a moment's peace because they had to know everything about the world around them.

But the chickens would take a lot of explaining, and knowing Dempsey, he wouldn't have the patience.

"Yeah, they're blue. And don't think this gets you out of talking about that stogie you've got poking out of your pie hole." I ground my teeth and leaned forward in my chair—anything to stop the gurgle in my belly. "And what's with you staying here at Jonas's place? I've got a perfectly fine guest room, and it's right next to Medical—"

"Because you're working and doing runs." He let out another puff of smoke, and the wind carried it toward me. I always hated the skunky, harsh smell of them, but a part of me didn't mind. "They've got that trailer out behind the house and hot and cold running food. Besides, I like yelling at his kids."

"But—"

"I don't care how close you are to Medical, kid," Dempsey snapped, giving his head a slight shake. "I'm not going to go back there. Don't plan on it. You heard the quacks. I don't have much time left, and I'm not going to spend it being hooked up to machines just so they can press my lungs out for one more breath. I want to sit out here on this porch, choke to death on cigar smoke, and burn a hole in my liver with cheap rotgut gin. There's no saving me now, son. And you're just going to have to wrap your tiny little brain around that."

I wasn't ready to think of my world without him in it. Maybe it was selfish or I was being naïve, but the time seemed way too short. Like I hadn't been given long enough with the asshole who'd threatened to sell me because I was pretty but also taught me how to shoot a moving target while hanging out the passenger-side window of a Chevy truck on a rough country road.

"I'm not ready to give up the fight," I argued. My throat tightened around a mash of anger and helplessness, and my voice caught on the jagged bits of pain that punctured my words. "There's got to be something we can do. Someone we can—"

"What we're going to do is, you're going to go out on runs, and I'm going to sit here and slowly die." Dempsey shut me down. "It's what we've been doing these past few years. It's just that you haven't been paying attention. I'm tired, son. So I'll be telling you things that I probably should've told you before, but I've never been one to sugar someone up, least of all you.

"I am a mean old bastard, always have been. I spent my life being the best fucking Stalker there ever was. I took chances. I risked everything. Hell, I was even willing to risk the people who went on runs with me. Doing a job with me meant there was a good chance you weren't going to come home in anything but a body bag, and that was okay with me. A few people like Jonas and Sparky stuck by my side—not because I'm a good friend of theirs, but because they're better people than I am." He took another drag of his cigar and held in the puff until his lungs spat it back out. "And then there was you."

"I owe you everything," I muttered, working my hands around the once-cold bottle of beer I'd left unopened. "I can't pay you back for everything you've done for me. There's no fucking way I can even come close to…."

I choked. I couldn't get anything out. The teal-blue hens were blurred behind a sea of tears I couldn't shed. There was no crying in front of Dempsey. I'd learned that a long time ago. I'd been brought up hard, probably harder than a lot of people would've liked, but he was all I had. He was the reason I still lived, and I owed him for every breath I sucked in from the moment he took me on.

"Don't get sentimental, not for me. I did my best by you. You turned around when I got too old and broken to do the job, and you carried me. So any debt that you think you owe me was paid off a long time ago." Dempsey hawked a bit of spittle out and then flicked a piece of tobacco from his lip. "People might disagree with how I did my job, but nobody could argue I was the best there was. Thing is, I'm human. We break down and die. I knew with being who I am, the only legacy I would leave behind was my reputation as a Stalker. That was good enough for me until I got you.

"Some people thought I should have put a bullet in the back of your head. They told me you were brain damaged, not much better than one of those damned black dogs, but there was something about the way you fought to live. In a lot of ways, you reminded me of me." He shot me a look, his broad mouth quirked into a wrinkled grin. "I knew I had to break you of... well, maybe not break you but discipline you in a way so you understood what you were doing wasn't any good. Break's the wrong word. You had a wild, strong spirit in you. You were bleeding out your back from the iron they put inside of you and starved nearly as close to death as any cat bastard can get without actually dying, but you were ready to take a piece out of anybody who came near you. And as much as I hated the elfin—and God in heaven how I fucking hate your people—I had to respect you for how much fight you had inside of you."

"Dempsey—"

"No, you let me get this out. Because I'm stoned off my ass on what the doctors gave me, and I don't give a shit what I say at this point." He slapped at my hand when I reached for him, nearly knocking the cigar out from between his fingers. "I took you in because I knew people—other people—they would try to civilize you. That's not what you needed. I knew that you needed every single little bit of fight you had in you, because I knew eventually the people who lost you were going to come looking for you. And you needed to be ready for them.

"What I didn't expect was... I didn't expect to care about you. I never imagined I would get scared about you dying on a run with me. Until one day when some asshole at the Post asked me how come I didn't sell you on a street corner because you would make me more money than us going after a pack of ainmhi dubh." He swallowed, and his Adam's apple bobbed down his thick throat. "Took five men to pull me off of him. Took another five to pick up his teeth off the floor. And I remember screaming through the red haze around me that nobody talked about my son like that. Not that there's anything wrong with being a whore, but it's a choice people make on their own. It's not what a father does to his kid."

I couldn't see anymore. Hell, I couldn't breathe. My tongue was swollen with everything I needed to say, but nothing could get my words loose. My chest was tight, and the pounding was either my heart or my fear at realizing that Dempsey was at the end of his line, confessing to everything he'd never told me because he was that much of a bastard and he'd done his best by me.

"One thing you should know before you go out on that run with that Sidhe lord—"

"I can't go on that run." There was no possible way I would leave him behind. Someone else could do it. Somebody else could drag Ryder and the remora Sebac sent down. "You're—"

"Dying? Yeah, I fucking know that. I've known that for months. Even with everything you and everybody else have thrown at this shit that's eating through me, it's going to win. Death always wins, at least for guys like me. And well, everybody else you know... except for those bastards in Balboa." He took a long swig of his beer and contemplated his smoldering cigar. "You've got to start knowing your own kind, Kai. I'd be the first one to tell you not to trust them, because they're duplicitous bastards for the most part, but there's got to be a few of them in there that are okay. I'm hoping Ryder is, because you're gonna need allies who live longer than the likes of me. So, you're going to go on that run, and you bring those people home just like I got you.

"Of everything I've done as a Stalker—every job people thought I couldn't do—the best thing that ever came out of this life was you." He chuckled. "I was the best Stalker of my time, and you'll continue that. Because as good as I am, you're a hell of a lot better."

"I'm only what you made me," I argued. We were always combative, and even then, as Dempsey flagellated his soul to bloody strips, we were going to fight about nothing and everything. "I'd be dead if it weren't for you. I know you want me to go on that run because we don't back out of contracts—"

"No, we *don't*." His growl frightened the chickens away from the porch and sent them scattering back to the yard. "I taught you better than that."

"I just don't want to...." With everything Dempsey said and the emotions he turned up inside of me, I was having a hard time getting past the decades of gruff backhanded compliments and sarcastic rejoinders. "I don't want to go on a run and come back to find you dead. It's not like I haven't seen death before—"

"Hell, you and I have waded through some fields of death together," he snorted.

"Yeah, we have." I bit my lip, trying to find the end of my thoughts to grab on to something to say, anything that made sense of the chaos inside of me. "I don't want you to die without me, old man. I know you're going to spit and swear at me as you go, but you should know I'll always have your back. I'll always be there. And even if you don't want me fighting this, I'm going to be damned if I'm not there at the end. Because no matter what you say, I owe you fucking everything, and you taught me better than to turn my back on a friend."

"You and I are friends, boy. You're my *legacy*. I'm proud that you're a better Stalker than I am. Everything I've done won't be forgotten, because you're there, fighting anything in your path that tries to stop you or make you small." Dempsey saluted me with his nearly empty beer bottle, his eyes pale behind water-sodden lashes. "No matter how you look or what blood is in your veins, you're my son, Ciméara Dempsey Gracen. And on top of that, you're the best damned man I know."

Seven

THE FIRST thing Ryder said to me when I opened the door to let him in was "I want to drive."

To the uninitiated that sentence coming out of Ryder's mouth would probably seem like an innocuous request, but I knew better. I knew *him* better. It was the initial act of defiance, the first shot fired in what would prove to be a long, bloody rebellion. I took it as it was meant to be taken—as a clear challenge to my authority.

If I didn't nip it in the bud, we would have minor tussles that would eventually lead to outright dismissal of my orders. I couldn't have that, not on a run and not in my personal life. If I let Ryder move the line, he would continue to pick it up and shove me back until I found myself trapped in a cage I'd woven for myself simply by remaining silent.

So I immediately crushed his dreams of anarchy and domination.

"*No.*"

He made another run at it and brushed against my chest when he walked through the open door. "I need to be able to drive around the city, and with you in the passenger seat—"

A quick glance outside confirmed my suspicions. Ryder had never learned the word subtle. From what I could see, none of the Sidhe had. The accounts of their armies' progress in war zones and battlefields during the conflict that followed the Merge read more like the historical accounts of the British invasions of nearly every territory they glanced at. The elfin traveled in caravans, set up elaborate tents and temporary domiciles, even sometimes built roads in places they would stay for longer than a week. They were one tea lady short of resembling a comedy skit featuring a gnawed-off leg and condemning accusations against innocent mosquitoes.

Ryder's car was further proof of the Sidhe's inability to do anything short of extravagant. Low-slung and sporting a silver-blue chameleon paint job, the roadster he'd parked in my driveway probably cost more than all the warehouses on the cul-de-sac combined. It was powerful, fast, and totally impractical to take on the gritty terrain of San Diego's understreets.

"I can't even begin to tell you how quickly that car is going to be stripped down for parts as soon as we lose sight of it." I calculated the price of the tires—numbers so high for chunks of steel-reinforced rubber that my nose was about to bleed. "Hell, maybe they'll wait till we leave."

"It has an alarm," Ryder replied as he smoothed down the crisp T-shirt he'd worn for our trip to Duffy's place, "and a defense system as well."

"Well, maybe you'll be lucky and they'll be sarcastic thieves, and they'll leave them behind for you in the middle of the road to mock you." I came back inside and grabbed my leather jacket. "We're taking the truck. And if you're lucky, I'll let you ride shotgun instead of tossing you into the back."

I WASN'T really in a talkative mood. Last night with Dempsey had stripped me raw and peeled me down to my marrow like one of Thor's goats. But I didn't feel resurrected when I woke up in the morning. There were still broken bits and parts of my soul scattered about the place, and I hadn't picked up all the pieces when Ryder knocked on my door later that afternoon. I'd spent the day cleaning weapons and working on the Mustang, anything to keep my hands and mind busy and focusing away from the black masses that were eating Dempsey alive.

The trip into San Diego's understreets was exactly what I needed. It was like a homecoming—familiar and dank and with a whiff of rotten sewage spicing the air. We'd lived in a lot of ghettos and shanties during my early years with Dempsey. Most of our money went for equipment and a seemingly never-ending supply of whiskey, so I'd grown up hard and dirty, with a hint of mean layered on top of whatever morals Jonas and Sparky tried to instill in me.

But there was always Dempsey. He wasn't the father figure most people would have wanted. Some of them thought that the way he brought me up bordered on abuse or maybe even crossed into it. I usually told those people to fuck off. They had no idea of the countless days I'd spent marinating in pain, when with each passing week, a newer, more creative form of torture was introduced to my already-fractured body.

I never went hungry with Dempsey. He never beat me until I couldn't see or carved my kneecaps out from my legs. He would slap the back of my head or shoulder when I did something stupid and grumble a lot about how much I ate, but he was always the one to refill my plate. He handed me my first gun and gave me a living by sponsoring me into a trade that most people couldn't handle, much less thrive at.

Dempsey made me more than a survivor—he made me a man. He laid down a framework for others to help fill, but in the end, he'd taught me that you don't leave family or friends behind.

Even if all that was left of them was pieces of meat, you brought them home and raised a glass to who they were. I just… wasn't ready to raise a glass for Dempsey. But it didn't look like I was going to have much choice.

"Do you want to talk about it?" Ryder asked as we slipped into the shadowed tunnel that marked the entrance to the understreets. The lights of the covered road turned the truck's cab blue and silvered Ryder's features. I saw a bit of Alexa in his mouth, and the angle of his eyes reminded me of the twins, connecting his blood to mine. "Maybe if I can bring some healers down from San Francisco—"

"He isn't going to go to any more doctors. Dempsey's done." I cut Ryder off. "Don't think I didn't try. He's tired. And no, I don't want to talk about it."

I didn't know how other people dealt with impending loss. Sure, I'd been in situations where I knew someone was going to die in the next few minutes or even seconds. That was just how a Stalker's life was. I'd known people—some of them I even called friend—who spent their last couple of breaths telling someone to take a message home or to make sure someone else knew how sorry they were for something they'd done. I've seen death come so swiftly for its next soul that the body didn't even have a chance to react, and I've sat a long vigil, bloodied and bruised from a run gone wrong, waiting for the Grim Reaper to make his rounds.

The timeline I'd been given with Dempsey was shaky, but I'd been reassured up one way and back down the other that he'd be there when I came off of the run for Duffy. He might even be around for the next ten runs. No one knew. It all depended upon him and his willingness to do what the doctors told him.

But I didn't have a lot of hope for that.

Most urban centers in SoCal had retained their expansive boundaries after the violence of the Merge, but San Diego's downtown hadn't been very large to begin with. If anything, the split-level design of the new city created a larger metropolitan area than had been there before.

And it made the divide between the haves and the have-nots even more visible.

I never knew San Diego before the Merge, but I liked the one that hugged the SoCal coast below Pendle's dragon mating grounds. There were some rumblings about fixing the Coronado Bridge because its span was patchy and missing in places. The north part of the island was practically useless, taken over by walrus and unicorn seals, but the south end, with its aging hotels and quaint village shops, was a good source of revenue. Problem was, there were only two ways to get there—one was lengthy and the other was dangerous.

Much like getting to Duffy's place.

She'd lived in the upper district for a while, but a couple years ago, she went underground. At the time she told me she wanted to get back in touch with where she came from. I offered her money so she didn't have to live below, but she laughed and told me currency wasn't a problem. I then asked her for a loan because currency is always a problem. She laughed at me then too, knowing I wasn't serious.

But I really didn't like where she lived. The old Golden Hill district was a patchwork quilt of craftsman homes woven into a landscape filled with tattoo shops, gambling dens, and the occasional brothel. The homes were beautiful but caked with the level's incessant grime. Nothing escaped the soot, and the artificial rain programmed by the weather department did little to wash it from the air and the streets.

"You're going the long way in, then, yes?" Ryder broke my silence. We'd navigated through the tunnels until I veered the truck over to an exit ramp and came out near Broadway. "The map I programmed in had a different route."

"Yeah, probably the route that you had programmed in is the one that would've taken you right next to the Ironworks. Let's just say, even in a hermetically sealed mayonnaise jar left on a porch, you'd have sucked iron filings into your lungs, and I would've had to make a U-turn toward Balboa and hoped we made it to a healer." I called the understreets map up on the truck's flickering display. "Remind me to forward the patch I had to build. It'll warn you off areas you shouldn't go and give you the police feed so you can avoid things like shootouts and nutria stampedes."

He lifted an eyebrow, which gave him a devilish air. His face resembled some propaganda posters I'd seen in some old shops, their stark, flat-colored images twisting an elfin's features into demonic proportions. "Nutria are not something to be feared, Kai. Even I know that."

"They are rodents of unusual size, Ryder." I spared him a quick glance as I pulled the truck to the left of the lane to avoid an out-of-control chicken take-away scooter careening into my path. "They're just biding their time, and one day they'll rise up and attack us, starting the great rodent revolution."

"It is times like these that I wonder if you are serious or if they neglected to give you a sense of humor when they raised you." He widened his eyes when I pulled onto the main drag, and the tiny gasp he gave was just icing on the cake. "By the gods, how does anyone live in this?"

"Careful there, Your Lordship," I cautioned with a chuckle. "Your bourgeois roots are showing."

Still, seeing the glittering but dingy district through Ryder's eyes drove home how far apart we really were.

I was comfortable there. The shops and stalls were busy that late in the afternoon, filled with people coming home from work or those about to go on shift. A tofu-dog vendor shouted out toward the crowd, his Singlish accented heavily with the round, golden tones of his native Thai. An explosion of light from the screen above his head advertised the services of a breast enhancer down the street, the before-and-after pictures of his clients splashing their pixilated chests next to a billboard that welcomed people to attend a new church being built at the end of the block. I rolled down the truck's windows to let the scents of the street into the cab.

It was a sushi burrito of everything right and wrong with the world, delivered hot through my nose.

"What is that smell?" Ryder sniffed audibly as I eased the truck to a stop. We were caught at a light that I knew wouldn't turn green for a good minute or two—a dangerous span of time to be sitting at a dead stop during some times of the night, but for right then we were okay. "It smells like… someone wrapped a flower around vomit."

"Yeah, that's the durian truck over there." I pointed it out. The cook working the grill had a pincher over his nostrils and a mesh filter taped across his mouth. He would be able to breathe and talk through it, but for the most part, the acrid smoke coming off of the cookers couldn't penetrate the barrier. It made speech sound like you were underwater, but he probably preferred sounding like a cartoon prawn to choking on a day's worth of cooking durian. "Normally it's in something sweet, but lately people are eating it like chips—deep-fried and with curry on top."

"Do you want to stop and grab some?" I caught Ryder scraping his tongue against his teeth. It was a noble gesture, offering to sit in a cab with me as I ate durian, and I appreciated it, but it wasn't necessary.

"I would rather suck the egg mucus out of our niece's nose again than eat that, but thanks for asking."

The light turned green, and I pulled the truck forward, taking us deeper into the brightly lit streets. "But if you see a street cart serving *lau-lau*, give me a shout-out, and I'll show you what really good food tastes like."

No matter how hard San Diego's local government tried to normalize living under tons of concrete and steel, they couldn't replicate the sky or actual sunlight. They made attempts with tracks of brightening and dimming bulbs able to throw off a diffused light that closely replicates the outside, but they often fell to disrepair or were stolen. Considering the so-called ceiling was more than twenty stories high in most places, I had to give those thieves credit.

That part of the understreets didn't need sunlight. If anything, it could have used a dose of darkness, because half a block out of the exit, the air burned with a kaleidoscope of colors bright enough to burn a man's eyes out.

Everything was lit up. The sides of buildings abounded with banners and LED lights, all of them shouting for attention. Nudity was big, but it was so commonplace that no one seemed to notice. People scurried by, holding the hands of their children as they dodged through puddles left over from the morning's scheduled rain. But no one looked up. They were intent on getting to where they needed to be and out of the glorified consumerism shower they'd been forced to bathe in.

Tik-tiks dove up and down between cars, grabbing passengers from the street and then climbing up the thick cables that connected them to the overhead trolley lines. A monorail train loaded with people rumbled past us on the right as it climbed its creaking steel track and gained speed to barrel through tightly packed apartment buildings. Traffic was thick and hampered by a couple of cop cars with flashing lights that blocked in a tiny red roadster. The police were huge and towered over the sports-car owner, a twitchy, skinny guy in an ill-fitting suit. I don't know what he did, but from the looks of things, he was about four words away from wearing a pair of cuffs and eating jailhouse sandwiches for dinner.

The taller of the cops spotted us, and he narrowed his eyes as he tracked the truck. Elfin were rare in human cities and not often seen underground. I'd been the only one of my species in San Diego for a long time, but now there were more, and Ryder's face was often seen on their screens when they caught him on a charitable junket or attending some dinner with little food and a high price tag.

Two of us in a truck cruising the brothel strip was not only unprecedented, it would probably get us pulled over eventually.

"There are some times when I really wish we could make you look more human," I muttered as I turned onto a side street. "If the cops come after us, please let me do the talking."

"I have diplomatic immunity for anything that I do in the city and the state." Ryder frowned at me, and a very familiar look of confusion formed over his handsome face. "And we've done nothing wrong. We're simply driving. Just like the people next to us."

"See, that's the difference. Right there." I nodded at the couple staring at us from their SUV in the next lane over. "Those are actually people. We are elfin. Try to remember that."

"How can I forget?" he drawled. "You remind me every five minutes or so."

"There. Right there. *That*." I stabbed at the air to emphasize my point. "That's why people don't like you. Because you're sarcastic when they try to help you."

"I would make a remark about a pot and a kettle, but I don't think they've invented a color darker than black just yet." Ryder leaned forward and studied the map on the screen. The heat of his body was welcome against my arm, and his breath ghosted over the back of my hand as I shifted. "We should be there shortly if I am reading this right."

"Actually, we're there now." I turned left into a narrow alleyway between a row of tightly packed-in houses. "She's got a garage in the back we can park in."

"So we could have brought my car, and it would've been safe." Ryder shot me a hot look. "Admit it. You just don't want me driving."

"You bet your sweet ass I don't want you driving." I counted out the houses as we passed, since the lane's tall cedar-plank fences and detached garages all looked alike. "And if you haven't figured that out by now, you are dumber than you look."

"Well, at least you like my ass," he muttered under his breath.

The area was mostly houses for a block and a half—beautiful two- and three-story structures built in a time when television sets were barely a blip on the technological horizon. In many ways the area was experiencing a renaissance. New families were moving into the slightly dilapidated large homes and refurbishing them over long weekends with a lot of sweat equity and pizza parties to pay their friends for their help in retiling floors and painting ceilings.

Duffy purchased a near-mansion of a house. Its sloping roof extended out to cover its wraparound porch, and it promised to cost a fortune to replace its ancient glass windows with newer panes. I questioned her sanity when she moved in, more than slightly horrified by the falling plaster walls and whatever used to live underneath one of the bathtubs. I helped out a couple of times with her renovations, mostly because some of the quotes she got from contractors gave me heartburn, and while she'd been willing to cough up that kind of cash, it just didn't sit right by me.

But I did take the nail gun away from her the one time she tried to help us, and it took Jonas four minutes to pull out all the spikes she'd shot into my upper arm.

"It's later than I thought it was," Ryder commented as he peered out at the glowing canopy above us. "Is your clock right?"

"Yeah, the environmental system on the site is glitchy. I think someone has it set for a time zone or two ahead, because there are seasons when the sun gets up a lot earlier than the rest of the city, and it goes dark by about five o'clock in the afternoon." I grimaced when the streetlamps began to flare on. "You think somebody would be able to get at least that straight."

"I am grateful that she's willing to meet with me." His smile was warm and oddly reassuring as the sun lamps began to dim quickly toward a dusk the outside world wouldn't experience for another hour or so. "I know that she has given you all the particulars for our rendezvous, but I wanted to thank her personally for all the help she's given our kind."

"She's probably got to stop after this, but I think she's hoping you pick up the banner. Mostly she does it to make sure they end up someplace safe. The area the Unsidhe cross is dangerous, and if the land doesn't kill them, the people living on that side of the river might." I shook my head, recalling the times we'd stumbled across an encampment of old soldiers hidden in New Tijuana's twisted canyons. "A lot of folks out there are still fighting the war in their heads. They see an Unsidhe, and things go bad really fast."

We got to the tenth lot, and every alarm, siren, and klaxon attached to my senses went off. The garage's rolling door was up, and the door connecting it to the backyard was wide open. The neighborhood itself was fairly safe despite the surrounding area, and it was still the kind of place where neighbors took in each other's garbage bins and the nosy neighbor next door baked apple pies on holidays and left one on everyone's porch. I knew that last one was certainly true, because I'd been there when she dropped off the pastry and startled her when I opened the front door.

But Duffy never would have left the house wide open.

"I'm going to grab my guns from behind my seat." I parked the truck sideways on the cement pad in front of the garage and gestured toward the glove compartment. "There's a Glock in there with two clips. I'm not going to say that you need it, but I also know I won't be able to stop you from following me. Whatever you do, just don't shoot me in the back… or the front either, for that matter."

"Do you think this is really necessary?" Ryder asked even as he unlatched the compartment. "She knew you were coming. Perhaps she—"

The sound of gunfire was all I needed to get me out of the truck. I quickly grabbed my weapons and strapped them on as I ran. It was something I could do in the dark, something I've done tens of thousands of times before—going into a fight fully loaded and primed without knowing what was waiting for me on the other side of the wall.

It didn't matter. Duffy was in trouble, and all I'd brought with me to the fight was a Sidhe lordling and a handful of weapons. It was going to have to be enough.

But I couldn't help smiling when I heard Ryder fall in behind me.

Eight

TEN STEPS into the backyard and the ground was black beneath my feet. Something was driving the light away from the house, drowning it in shadows. My brain fought to make sense of the dimness, especially since I could see the light touching the rest of the world beyond the tall wooden fence. It made no sense, but there was a line of smoky darkness cutting through the yard, a clear demarcation that circled the house itself.

The lower level of the city was far from silent. Even in the depths of the deepest sections, life existed. Birds still sang and bees built hives wherever they could find a cool spot. The fluctuating environment was a struggle, but nature always adapted and filled in the crevices of an artificial environment as easily as it did an open field or a riverbank.

Despite the sound of gunfire—if it even *was* gun-fire—I stopped dead in my tracks to try to make sense of my surroundings.

It was magic. That much I knew. But at a scale I'd never seen before in a human city.

Humans had magic. It was either awakened by the Merge and the shove of the elfin world into theirs, or perhaps it had always been there, simmering beneath the surface and unacknowledged by a species driven forward by science and technology. Cari came from a long line of witches, and their power blossomed following the cataclysm of the Merge, but it took them a while to harness their magic. Still, they were nowhere near as powerful as the elfin.

Whatever engulfed Duffy's house was not human in any way, shape, or form.

The grounds were deafeningly muted, as though sealed off behind tight glass. I heard nothing from the house, and then a crash of something being toppled over. The sound rolled out from an open window upstairs but whispered away into nothing nearly as soon as I heard it. That was the one thing about living beneath the underbelly of a city—sounds echoed and bounced in the strangest of ways.

Then I heard a whisper of Unsidhe. Its velvet crackle ribboned through the air, a sibilant Möbius strip that strengthened the surrounding shadows.

"Fuck," I ground out. "Duffy!"

I mounted the back steps at a full sprint and slammed into something I couldn't see. My face stung, and my forehead throbbed where I'd struck it, but when I reached my arms out and pressed against the invisible barrier, it didn't give. A few feet down the porch got me the same results—an impenetrable obstruction I couldn't get past.

"Shielding spell." Ryder finally caught up with me. I was relieved to see he kept his weapon pointed down, his hands loose around its grip. The grayness around us enveloped him and muted the brilliance of his hair and eyes. "The trick is to ease in slowly. Like it is quicksand."

"I've got a better idea. Cover me." I put my gun back into its holster and secured it on my thigh. "I'll be back."

Taking the steps in a few short leaps, I was suddenly immensely grateful for Duffy's old-fashioned taste. She'd styled her garden in an old California fashion and left it alone after she discovered I couldn't use any of the wrought-iron lawn furniture without getting sick to my stomach with prolonged exposure.

Rich plump falls of bougainvillea cascaded down the left side of the yard from old shrubs trained to follow the line of the planks. A three-tiered fountain splashed merrily despite the shadows that drowned the yard. It was a plaster-and-concrete tea-tree-looking lawn ornament I'd brought up with me after a run through San Diego's buried underground. At some point those fountains were a dime a dozen, but they had become difficult to find. I'd gotten a lot of shit from Cari about loading it into the back of the truck with the black dog carcasses, but the smile on Duffy's face when I rolled up with it was worth every bruise and scrape.

She'd designed her entire Spanish-SoCal-influenced gardens around it and set the three-foot-high fountain into the middle of a larger pool. Then she coaxed a bunch of lilies to grow around its base, planted what looked like a thousand rosebushes, and she found the perfect piece to finish off her dream sanctuary—a vintage wrought-iron table set with six chairs, each heavy enough to kill a cow or bring one elfin chimera from zero to puke in less than half an hour.

I gritted my teeth against the inevitable, grabbed the captain's chair by its arms, and hefted it up over my head. The black paint she used to refinish the metal did little to shield me from its poisonous bite. I didn't know what they made the old tables out of, but they were a hell of a lot more dangerous than anything I'd run across. My skin burned where I touched it, and the strength in my legs wavered as my muscles rebelled from the proximity of the metal.

"Get out of the way!" I shouted at Ryder. Then I took the stairs as quickly as I could and hoped I wouldn't collapse or puke on the way. My stomach was threatening to starfish out of my mouth, but I swallowed and held it back. It wasn't hard to figure out the moment Ryder came too close to the chair, because his face flushed green, his jaw clenched, and his neck muscles bulged out against the strain.

I was the most magical elfin thing I knew of, and these chairs made me sick as a dog after a three-day binge on a garbage scow.

The shielding spell had no chance.

I was used to hefting up large objects and struggled with more than my fair share of unwieldy, monstrous bodies, but I rarely handled eighty pounds of poison. Its presence against my skin and bones weakened me and stole the strength from my muscles. My upper arms shook with my struggle to hold on, and then my back nearly folded over, unable to support the weight I was swinging about.

"Kai, what are you doing?" Ryder recoiled and staggered away when I swept the chair back. "We won't be able to—"

I was still hurting from the battle Jonas and I had fought with the cuttlefish. It was mostly bruises, but the proximity to that much iron had me feeling every bit of torn muscle and mangled flesh beneath my skin. The waves of pain sickened me nearly as much as the presence of the metal, but I wanted to get inside. I needed to find Duffy and rescue her from whoever and whatever had sealed her into those spells.

My shoulders wrenched as I twisted about, and there was too little space on the wraparound porch to get momentum, but I couldn't risk what I planned on doing from the lawn. The craftsman's porch was lined with wide posts and thick solid short walls—perfect for lounging on but impossible to throw things through.

I got in as many revolutions I could, spinning in place to build up centrifugal force. Then, just as a wave of sickness hit me, I let go of the heavy chair and prayed to Pele.

The flung wrought-iron behemoth hit the spell with a sizzling crunch, and the world broke apart.

Ryder caught me in midspin before I fell off the porch, and we were both flung away from the house by the explosion. Smoke billowed out of Duffy's house, and flaming sparks and ash formed a storm of dancing devils when the shield collapsed. I couldn't tell if the dampening enchantment disintegrated when the obfuscation broke, because the black dust that billowed through the air made it impossible to see. My eyes stung from the acrid smoke, turning everything blurry, but I could see well enough to find the house, or what remained of it.

The upper story was engulfed in flames, and the roof was collapsing in on the right, above the dining room. The lower level looked gutted, but the left side of the house was still mostly intact. Despite my palms being raw and blistered from the iron, I broke free of Ryder's hold and headed in.

He tried to keep me there, attempted to drag me back down to the ground by grabbing at my shirt and jacket. But strength surged through my thighs, and I twisted loose and easily evaded his second attempt. The porch was beginning to crackle, but the back door was unlocked, though the knob burned my already-injured hand and seared the flesh closed on the blisters I'd gotten from the iron chair. I didn't have time to deal with the pain. My sole focus was Duffy and my hope that she was alive somewhere in the inferno that had been hidden by Unsidhe magic.

The back door opened up into the kitchen, and there was little left of the counters I'd helped put in. If it was difficult to see outside, inside was a soup of flames and soot. Inhaling ash set my lungs on fire, but I pushed on and headed toward the front rooms. She would've wanted to serve Ryder in the formal setting of the rarely used parlor that she'd taken forever and a day to design.

That's where I found her, exactly as I imagined.

Except for the gaping hole that stretched down her chest and belly.

My heart felt as though it'd been punched through, and I fell to my knees, gathered her up, and looked for any sign of life in her open, sightless eyes. Her fingers were curled in, her nails painted her favorite scarlet red. I scooped her up and tried to stagger through the house, but the walls seemed to move, and I kept banging them and jostling us despite my very best effort to get us free.

"Kai!" Ryder's voice echoed through the smoke. "Where are you?"

His voice was enough to lead me at least a few feet, and then strong hands grabbed my arms and turned me around. I was in a hallway I'd been down countless times before, but confusion settled in on my thoughts and masked my sense of direction. Something insidious whispered in my brain, then again around my head, and wrapped around me as tightly as a vine strangling a tree to death.

"The obfuscation enchantment is still going. You only weakened it." Ryder hooked his arm into mine, loosening my hold on Duffy. "I'm going to try to lead us out, but if you see the door, pull us that way so I can follow."

He said nothing about me holding her, but I saw his gaze slide away from her still body.

A sliver of light became our guide, although it seemed as though it moved every time we got close. The whispering continued. It wove through my thoughts, and I couldn't seem to catch my breath. Ryder was practically holding me when we burst out of the back door, engulfed in fumes and smoke. I stumbled on the stairs, cradling Duffy to me, and I fell and hit the stone walkway that cut through the lawn.

"You're too close to the house." Ryder pulled at my arm, trying to get me to my feet. "You've taken in too much smoke. I've got to get you to fresher air, Kai."

"Not leaving her," I growled back as I scooped Duffy up once more. I was on my knees, and my legs refused to straighten, but I wasn't going to let her go. I couldn't. A harsh tickle started in my belly, worked its way up through my lungs and throat, and I began to spasm and cough uncontrollably. Still I held on.

Ryder lifted me up, wrapped his arms around my waist, and yanked me to my feet. He struggled to drag me away from the house to put distance between us and the now-raging fire. Sirens were going off above us, triggering a focused water dump on the area, but the flames were too fierce and turned the deluge into banks of rolling hot steam.

Ryder got us as far as the garage before he collapsed into a coughing fit. I joined him. My lungs seized up inside of my chest, and I spat out what came up—a sticky black mass splattered on the concrete floor of the garage. My eyes were still stinging, and my hands were cracked and singed across my abused palms, but the pain was something I was going to have to live with because Duffy lay broken on the floor next to me.

Her long brown hair was missing on one side of her skull, but so was the skin it was once attached to. Her mouth was a mimicry of a grin, and where the intense heat of the fire had peeled her lips back from her teeth, a splash of scarlet lipstick remained to match her fingernails. Her eyes were swollen and bruised, and she stared up at the ceiling.

I got to my knees, slid my arm under her shoulders, and lifted her up from the cold floor, hoping to find some sense of life in her stillness. But as much as I wanted to ignore them, the gaping wounds in her torso were too real, too permanent.

"This can't be happening," I cried out, my voice scalded into a tortured croak. "Not Duffy. Not like this."

I could still feel the endless labyrinth of words woven around the house, and the power in them haunted me. It wasn't fair. It wasn't as though I didn't know that life wasn't ever fair, but Duffy didn't deserve the end that came for her. No one should die for trying to keep others safe. And even if I hadn't known all of her secrets, she entrusted me to take care of her legacy because it grew too big for her, and now it had gotten her killed.

"There's got to be something I can do. She can't be dead." I held her lifeless body, but I'd held her countless times before, and I'd always felt the beat of her heart against my arm or my cheek when I laid my head on her chest or felt her pulse when I pressed my lips to her long, elegant throat. "I can't let you go like this. You can't leave me like this."

Something dark flared inside of me, and its sickening call seduced me and drew me in. The whispers plaguing my thoughts became clear, familiar words that I'd never spoken but somehow knew the meaning of. Death seemed so useless, so ridiculous, and something easily overcome with a bit of power I didn't possess. I needed a way to undo the damage done to her, to peel back the death wrapped through Duffy's existence and expose her fragile body to the life around her.

I so badly wanted her to breathe. I ached to feel her heart beat again, and I couldn't imagine a world where I didn't hear her laughter when I showed up on her doorstep holding a box of chocolate cupcakes I'd gotten from her favorite bakery. I wasn't going to live without a New Year's kiss from her every time the calendar turned over, and I refused to live a life without her gentle flirtations, even though we stopped sleeping together years before.

There was no way I was going to fucking live like that. I wasn't going to live without *her*. The darkness in me grew and spread through my chest until it strangled my senses and confused my thoughts. I couldn't see a way out of the sticky veil that covered my sight. But then I felt death itself in Duffy's body, and her limbs stiffened as I held her tight. Where sorrow and denial once reigned, my rage was born, kicking and screaming against the futility of fragile flesh and waning souls.

The whispering returned, but this time the words were different, focused on the rebuilding of flesh instead of fire. I had to close the hole in her chest. She wouldn't be able to survive unless her lungs could expand and her heart beat beneath her now-shattered ribs. Her flesh had to be whole, and shaping her flesh, an impossible task only moments before, seemed so simple once I listened to the threads of sound that echoed through the crackle of the raging fire.

Something in me broke open, and the pain that filled my body gushed forward and carried the darkness out.

Duffy blinked.

Something had changed. There was a spark of life in her, something I'd missed or simply hadn't seen because I was so overwrought. But she *blinked*.

Then her heart beat. It was sluggish, but it was there—a tiny hiccup of blood movement at her throat—and I looked up, unable to trust my own senses.

"Ryder, she's alive. We have to get healers," I begged him through my tears, trying to blink away the soot that clung to my lashes. "Or get her to Medical. They can save her."

I didn't understand the pity in Ryder's expression or how slowly he was moving, and I couldn't seem to shake the spell we'd gone through on the porch. But its lingering effects didn't matter, not when I could feel Duffy moving in my arms. The nausea was back, and my guts cramped as they responded to something malevolent moving through me. Duffy shifted and then blinked again, but this time I noticed the brilliant blue of her eyes was fading, slowly changing to a milky white.

I glanced back to look at Ryder, unable to make sense of what was going on, and Duffy's head turned as well. Her charred hair slithered down my arm when she tilted back, and my vision wavered as I caught a flash of my own face, a hard sculpt of Sidhe features with a wealth of black-purple hair I could only have gotten from my Dusk Court blood. I'd only ever seen myself in a mirror or reflected back in water, but before I could focus, I blinked, and the vision was gone.

"Kai, you've got to let her go." Ryder slowly approached me, nearly crawling to get to my side. He was as filthy as I was but still as perfect as he'd been the moment I first saw him. The filth and trauma of what we'd gone through hadn't dimmed his natural beauty, and despite the ash smeared over his face, his gentle smile was a comfort. "Listen to me. You don't want to do this. This isn't you. The spell is doing something, and I don't know what exactly, but it's calling to your father's power. I need you to hear me, Kai. Duffy is gone."

"You're wrong. I can feel her heart beat," I argued, but it was difficult to think with the sick moving through my belly and clouds forming in my brain. It was getting harder to think—to focus—but Ryder gripped my chin in his hand and forced me to look at him.

"Listen very carefully to her heart, Kai. Does it beat in time with yours?" Ryder kept a firm hold on me, refusing to let me go, keeping my gaze on him. "Do you not see how she moves with you?"

"The iron from the chair." I gasped as I fell into another coughing fit. I couldn't seem to catch my breath, and as my chest worked to pull in air, Duffy's rose and fell in staggered jerks.

My hands ached, much like my back had for ages when I'd been in my father's possession—when I'd *been* my father's possession. It'd been so long since I'd been used in his enchantments, since the iron in my flesh served as a focus for his foul magics. Parts of him still lingered in me—arcane traps I would never break free of—and something in the spells surrounding the house, combined with the poisonous metal flakes I'd probably driven into my skin, awakened the Unsidhe horrors lying dormant in me.

The reality of death consuming the woman I held in my arms had stolen my sanity away. I wanted nothing more than to see Duffy rise from the black pit she'd been thrown into. My father's necromancy could resurrect the shell that once carried her soul, but it would never bring back the woman and her sultry laughter. I knew that, but I still couldn't let go.

"Would you want this for her? Would you want her to live as your puppet?" Ryder's words were gentle, but they abraded my already-raw heart. "I don't think so, Kai. You would want her to have peace, not this soulless existence as your plaything."

It took everything I had inside me, but I slid Duffy's body into Ryder's arms and then broke away, leaving me with only my grief to hold.

Nine

THERE WASN'T enough whiskey in the world.

Ironically the cops we'd seen on the road were the ones who responded to the call Duffy's neighbor made when the obfuscation spell broke. The tall baldheaded one turned out to be a former Stalker who'd left the Post's service with a chip on his shoulder and a perforated intestine. He knew who I was as soon as he rolled onto the scene and got out of his car. He called out my name in a questioning tone while his hand rested on his gun holster.

He wasn't adversarial, but Ryder's diplomatic immunity went a long way in getting us handled with kid gloves, especially once the Non-Mundane Crimes unit hit the scene. The human wizards poured over the site and got in the way of the firemen responding to the call. And once they cornered Ryder and me against my truck, I knew we were in it for the long haul.

I checked out. Ryder fielded most of the questions and then stepped in to answer everything they threw at us once I caught myself staring at a boggle-eyed human dressed in purple robes embroidered with metallic gold symbols. The sigils he wore on his clothes were familiar, but I couldn't place them—at least not until I realized they were a string of the elfin alphabet I'd seen painted on the nieces' bedroom walls.

At that point I just wanted out. I hated bureaucracy and its red tape. Nothing I said or did was going to bring Duffy back, and from the looks of things, the Dusk Court was responsible for her death. There was no way in any of the hells that the SoCal government or San Diego's police department would bring down her killers. That was the worst part about the Merge— the glaring fractures in law enforcement and justice. Even if an Unsidhe lord walked out of the engulfed house and claimed responsibility, there was nothing any of us could do.

Well, I could put a bullet in his head, but that wouldn't change anything. It would make me feel better, but it wouldn't change anything.

Freed by the cops with a warning to make myself available for any future questions, I handed Ryder the keys to the truck and let him drive us back to my place. There were lingering cobwebs in my mind, and the numbness creeping through my body refused to be dislodged.

I didn't remember the ride home, but Ryder eventually got us there. A few minutes later, after I fought with the front door, I plopped myself down on the couch and wondered if I shouldn't have thrown up in the kitchen sink first. Newt came over to chew on my nose and then screamed his fool head off when Ryder walked into the warehouse and closed the door behind him.

"Does he need to be fed?" He headed to the kitchen—the one with the sink I should have used—and opened up the cabinet where I kept my booze. The bottle he pulled out would've been my first choice if I'd made it over there, and for the first time in my life, I was thankful Ryder paid attention to what I drank. "You give him a full can of food, right?"

"He's lying to you. I fed him before we left. He just likes screaming at people." I scratched at my cat's ears and folded them back from his face. He seemed to like it, just like he enjoyed getting the spot next to his tail scratched and me rubbing my thumbs between the toe pads on his back feet. A bit of drool formed on Newt's lips, and his eyes rolled back and showed their whites. His purrs were loud and uneven, a rumbling glitch that would have sent me to check the timing on my engine if he'd been a car.

I never understood the lure of the single place to live until I bought the warehouse and molded it into where I wanted to spend time. Everything there was something familiar and permanent I'd pulled through the door and set in place. Even the cat was a set fixture, a companion of sorts for the nights when I lay in my own bed instead of crashing on an air mattress in the back of my truck. Don't get me wrong. I loved to go on runs. I loved the hunt, but I loved having a home—someplace I could lick my wounds and heal.

There just wasn't any guarantee that I was going to heal from this.

Ryder brought a bowl of grapes and a package of *arare* with him, an odd accompaniment to the whiskey, but I probably didn't have a lot in the refrigerator or cabinets. I didn't think I had grapes, but Dalia must have dropped them off while I was out. He tore off the plastic wrapper around its neck, cracked open the bottle, and handed it to me.

"You can go home." I took the bottle and slid my hand down its neck until the edge of my palm rested on its square body. "Thanks for driving."

"I am going to ignore the insult you just gave me, thinking I would leave you at a time like this," Ryder murmured as he sat down on the couch next to me.

My first mouthful of whiskey was bitter and harsher than normal. The sour mash wasn't the top of the line, but it was my go-to when my life felt rocky beneath me. I liked the smokiness of its amber wash, the hint of charcoal beneath its sting. The second swig went down smoother, but my throat was raw from the fire, and the burn went all the way down to my belly.

I was overwhelmed, which seemed so very strange considering I'd been through much worse. My own father periodically skinned me, sometimes even going so far as to debone my torso, and at the moment, that kind of pain seemed preferable to what I was experiencing.

Having Ryder pressed up against me should have been a disturbing, erotic sensation, but not this time. My skin still tightened over my flesh, and there was no question my body knew he was there, but I didn't want to crawl into him. Leaning against his long, hard form was enough. I needed to feel the life coursing through him, anchoring myself to the world with his every breath and the rustle of his hair against my cheek when he reached for the bottle and took it from me.

He took a sip. Then he gasped and coughed at the strength of the sour mash. He was more of a wine-and-brandy person—elegant alcohols served up in pretty glasses—another sign of how disparate we were. I liked drinking from a bottle, the realness of it, the gritty reminder of days spent on long, unsuccessful runs where there was nothing to do in the evening but drink and talk.

When Ryder passed over the bottle, Newt mewled at him and offered up his nose for Ryder to scratch. I cradled the whiskey in my lap and sat as still as I could while the cat climbed my shoulder and butted Ryder's jaw when he was finally in reach. Ryder's soft fingers brushed my neck as he attended to the cat's needs and worked Newt into a drooling stupor.

After about the seventh or eighth swig from the bottle, the anguish burning in my heart flared as the bright prickles in my brain subsided. It was too early in the day to get drunk, but I didn't care. I'd never felt more adrift than I did at that moment. Still smarting from the past few days, I'd been blindsided first by Dempsey's unwillingness to forge on, and then to have Duffy taken… it was just too much.

My tongue loosened, and I leaned my head back and turned it so my cheek rested against the couch and I could stare at Ryder's pretty mouth.

I *really* did like his mouth.

I liked a lot of things about him, and I also hated how he affected me, but having him against me made me feel better. There were too many things spinning out of control, and even though I knew I couldn't have done anything to save Duffy, a part of me wished I'd had a solution of some sort. There were quite a few if-only scenarios going through my head. I'd spoken to her not more than five hours before we drove up to the back of her house, and from what the department captain told us, the fire was started by an incendiary device set to go off hours after it was triggered.

She was dead long before I headed over, and there was nothing I could do to change that. I could feel vengeance and hunt down her killers—I still might— but I wouldn't stop her from dying, even though I did stop myself from forcing her to live.

That was going to have to be enough. It was all the satisfaction I would get.

Now I was sitting on the couch with a cat I'd rescued from the underbelly of the city and the lordling who sometimes yanked on the leash he put around my neck. But damn me if I didn't want to spend the night pressed up against him just to feel the warmth of another body on mine.

It really didn't hurt that I liked his mouth.

"Talk to me, Kai," Ryder purred along with Newt. "Tell me about Duffy. Tell me about your friend."

"She was my first, you know?" I mumbled as I held up the surprisingly depleted bottle. I liked how the burnt-gold liquid played with the light and folded over into lighter tones, much like Ryder's hair. "Well, not my *first* first, but she showed me it didn't have to hurt. Hell, she showed me sex didn't have to be so serious, that you could have fun with it.

"But it wasn't just sex. I mean, there was a lot more to her than that. Some of the best times I had with her were when we would spend the entire night on her couch watching movies, old ones from before the Merge, and she would teach me how to cook." I snorted, recalling some of the more outlandish things we'd thrown together. "She was a horrible cook. Anything past the bare basics and we probably would've given somebody food poisoning, but Duffy showed me how much better some foods were if they were crispy around the edges—like grilled cheese sandwiches and marshmallows, and peanut butter cookies. Okay, practically every cookie, but mostly peanut butter and chocolate chip cookies. Mostly she taught me how to feel normal and how to laugh."

"I'm glad she was there for you." Ryder took the bottle from me, swallowed a long sip, and then gave it back. Newt remained perched between us, half on his shoulder, half on mine. "I would've liked to have met her. You told me once that you didn't sleep with people whose names you knew. Clearly she was an exception."

"Yeah, that was a lie because *you* get into my brain." The bottle went down a little bit more, keeping pace with the increasing numbness of my limbs and tongue. "I just didn't want to care about anyone I slept with. I mean, I was friends with Duffy, but that was different. She was different. Everyone else was physical.

"I can't even tell you when we stopped having sex, because it really wasn't important. It was more about being her friend—her being *my* friend—than anything else. I love her," I confessed with a slur I couldn't shake. "Not like Cari or Sparky, but something else, something I can't explain."

"The first woman I had sex with was an older cousin," Ryder whispered as he ran his thumb over the back of my hand. "It's common for the Sidhe to initiate sexual relations with a younger man or woman on the edge of adulthood. It's a very formal, ritualized encounter."

I snorted and muttered, "Of course the Sidhe would go out of their way to fuck up something as simple as sex."

"That's not how it is." He laughed at me. "Our races are very sensual people, and it's important to understand what brings pleasure and not only how to ask your partner to be aware of what you like but also to learn how to listen to their needs, whether those are vocal or subliminal. My cousin Chela was my initiator into the pleasures of the body, and I have an immense fondness for her memory. There is nothing like the first of so many things, moments you can only experience once, and if someone you like or love brings you that moment, you cannot help but equate their presence in your life with that pleasure—much like you equate Jonas with your first taste of chocolate. He will forever be associated with that mind-opening experience."

"Yeah, there's not much difference between sex and chocolate," I agreed. "Do you see your cousin? Chela?"

"No." His voice dropped, and his expression was somber. "She was one of the first casualties in the war. We lost her when humans attacked the Sidhe's first contingent of envoys to the governmental hub of San Francisco. They were unarmed and defenseless, bringing a message of peace that no one was willing to listen to until too many died. Her insistence that we could live harmoniously with one another is what drives me. Up until that point—up until the day she died—I sat with Sebac's philosophy that humans and the Unsidhe were little more than animals who could talk.

"I'd planned on marrying her. Or at least I wasn't immune to the idea, but her schism from set Sidhe beliefs was difficult for me to swallow." He wistfully smiled at me. "She was older than I was by a thousand years, but at the time, I believed she was thinking like a child. After they brought her body back, I finally understood that she'd expected her death—anticipated it—and was still willing to die so our people could live. That was the beginning of my break from Sebac and my awakening to the realities of this world."

I handed him the bottle. He seemed to need it, and I was at the point of not being able to feel my lips.

"I tried to cut the tips of my ears off once." I chuckled at Ryder's rueful grimace. "It made sense at the time. I was just learning how to work the job, or at least Dempsey felt like I was big enough to hold a gun and shoot it. So he took me on a contract with a couple of other Stalkers to hunt down a large pack of ainmhi dubh in Arizona.

"On the third night of this trip, one of the guys told Dempsey I would probably get shot on a job one day because people hated my kind, and there was no way I could be a Stalker because I would always side with the monsters… because I *was* a monster." I didn't remember the man's name or even his face, but his words resonated and stuck with me over the years. "I'd been skinning black dogs for several years by then, so I had my own knives. Dempsey caught me before I sawed my way through the left tip, but I still got a couple of notches there. Never healed. Which is weird because I've always healed."

"I've got a theory on that but tell the rest of your story." Ryder patted my leg. "How does Duffy fit into the story? I assume you met her later."

"Yeah, a lot later. There was a long time between that guy having to pick his teeth up out of the fire from Dempsey's punch to when she took me into her bedroom for the first time." I fingered the triangular piece missing from my ear tip. "She asked me what happened, and I told her about the time I believed I could make myself look more human because I didn't want to be elfin. And she told me it didn't matter what I did to my body. It wouldn't change the person I was inside—that no matter where I went, there I'd be. I couldn't run from what I was any more than I could run from who I was. And then she made some noises about me being pretty. But by then, I was done talking."

"Well, you are *extremely* pretty," Ryder teased. "And you are the most human of humans I've ever met. I like who you are, Kai Gracen. Today you were faced with an impossible decision, brought to you on the heels of wild magic and a bloodline you cannot control, but the choices you made were good ones. You let her go."

"I don't know what happened back there any more than I understand what happened in the mountain. I called those ainmhi dubh to me." The whiskey suddenly tasted like the ash I'd gotten in my mouth while I ran through Duffy's house. I wasn't just battling with grief and sorrow. Fear had a hold on me and was digging into recesses of my soul that I thought I could protect, but I was wrong. "I'm going to tell you something, Ryder, and if you speak about it to anyone, I'm going to deny it and then gut you."

"Anything you say to me is kept between us," he reassured me, his shoulder pressed into mine, the heat of our bodies warming my cat.

"I don't know what I'm more afraid of—my father hunting me down to reclaim me or me becoming him without noticing." The bottle was nearly empty, but there was enough for me to take another short sip. "Today I could see how to keep Duffy's body going, even though she wasn't quite there. I knew for just a minute how to fix everything to keep her alive. I promised myself I would work on restoring her soul to her, but that didn't matter, because I would still have a piece of her. The entire time those thoughts were going through my head, I was getting sicker and sicker. I was torn between restoring her and killing myself for wanting her to exist in that shell. I had to let her go because she was already gone, and I hated myself for making a decision."

"It was the right one to make," Ryder whispered. He placed a soft kiss on my temple, and I didn't pull away. On some level I needed that contact, that affection to quell the disturbances roiling through me. "I promise you this—just like I took up Chela's cause, I will assume Duffy's fight. Anyone fleeing the Dusk Court will be welcome in mine, and I will use everything within my power to ensure they make it safely across."

"Then you better reconsider me getting rid of that cousin of yours, because Kerrick isn't going to go away." I drained the bottle when Ryder shook off my offer for the rest of it. "And the last thing San Diego needs is one of Sebac's puppets leading the Southern Rise Court. If there's one thing I know for certain, the only elfin worse than my father is your grandmother, and that's not someone I want in my backyard."

Ten

"IESU, THIS thing's ugly." I walked around the vehicle Sparky and Jason had hauled down from her place up north. "What did you do? Let a rhino fuck an old Jeep?"

"Look, you know what your problem is?" Jason grumbled at me as I inspected the monstrosity he'd backed down the ramp of the flatbed hauler. "You want your cars to be like you—pretty, fast, and can take a beating. That's just not how shit works, Gracen."

"Dude, there's ugly, and then there's... *this*." I rolled my shoulder, trying to work out a kink in my arm. "Convince me that thing can outrun a dragon."

"It can take a dragon hit." Sparky spat out a bit of sunflower shell. "And it'll run for three weeks at full bore without any sunlight, so you won't have to worry about being underground for too long. Nothing's shittier than running out of juice when you've dropped down a gulch. So shut your yap, Kai."

Jason sniggered, so I punched him on the arm and went to inspect the latest of Sparky's hybrids.

I owed both of them a hell of a lot. Sparky was one of the few people Dempsey hadn't driven off with his winning, toxic personality, and she'd done me right by spending a few long, excruciating days removing all of the iron bars and geegaws from my back. She understood me from the moment she almost ran me over to right now as I nitpicked my way through one of the rugged creations she built up at Sparky's Landing, a refueling and storage depot on the edge of Pendle's boundary. I stored the Mustang there in preparation for my runs through the lava fields. Rebuilding it took time, so parking it in the warehouse meant I could work on it when I had a couple of hours.

Not being stupid, I still paid Sparky to hold my storage bay, which was a prime enclosed spot with cooled air and access to a cell-fueling port.

They were an odd pair, but at the heart of their relationship was a love for all things mechanical. Sparky was Dempsey's age, maybe even older, and like the old man, her rawboned whipcord body had seen its share of bumps and bruises. Weathered from sun exposure, her nut-brown skin was wrinkled around her sharp eyes and thin lips, and her silvery-white long pixie cut framed her narrow, hard-boned face. Dressed in slightly grimy overalls and chewing through a handful of sunflower seeds, Sparky looked nothing like anyone would expect an energy-conversion engineer to look, but at her heart, she was a motor head, and tinkering with engines was her greatest love.

Jason was her brawny, shaved-pated bruiser of an apprentice and one of the best tattoo artists I'd ever met. He'd laid down more than a bit of the ink I had on my body, rendering gorgeous dragons across my hips and thighs, but like Sparky, his true loves were a Frankenstein rough-bodied hauler, powerful engines, and the human woman who used to break my heart every time she smiled—Dalia Tanaka.

I didn't begrudge their relationship. Hell, I encouraged it. Dalia and I had flirted with the possibility of being more than close friends, but the reality of a human-elfin relationship was a painful one, and I'd gladly stepped aside to give Jason room to woo her. Dalia deserved a happiness I could never bring her. Children, Sunday picnics, and romantic evenings on important days were things a Stalker wouldn't deliver on a consistent basis, and Dalia couldn't spend her lifetime watching time eat away at her body while I remained young.

"It'd be unnatural," Sparky scolded me when I told her of my crush a few years ago. "A woman might not want a house, kids, and sunsets, but she does want someone to grow old with. Besides, you think anyone wants to sit at home for weeks on end wondering if you've left them for someone else or didn't come back because death got you on a run and there was no one to bring back the news you'd lost your damned head? Walk away from all of that, boy. Girl's too good of a person to spend her life in that kind of pain."

I liked Jason. *A lot*. He was the kind of solid guy Dalia deserved, and he adored the hell out of her. I couldn't ask for a better partner for one of my best friends, and she loved him to the point of being sickeningly sweet. It was hard sometimes not to hate them both, seeing them move on with something I'd never have—which only emphasized Sparky's point.

"Do you want it or not?" Sparky elbowed me in the ribs and chortled under her breath when I winced. "Sorry. Forgot about the hits I heard you took the other day. Shit, that reminds me, Jase. We've got to stop over at Jonas's place on the way back. He's got some smoked cuttlefish for us. Says it might stink like angry pissed-off cat, but it tastes good enough."

"Funny," I growled back at her. "Why don't you show me what this thing can do? You know what happened the last time I pushed a button you didn't tell me about."

"Shit, I drive by that crater every time I make a run up to Rainbow. Almost lost a tire to it the other day," Jason groaned. "I want to put a sign up that says 'Kai Gracen is an asshole for making this.'"

"Mark the buttons." I shrugged and took a few short strides toward the monstrosity that squatted in front of my driveway. "And always tell me when one drops ten concussion grenades."

None of us were mentioning Duffy. For me it was too soon, too raw. For Sparky and Jason, they probably had no idea what to say. We were used to losing our own on a run or even to stupidity, but she was outside of that circle. Violence and death dogged our every step, but someone like Duffy should have been safe.

Lots of *should haves* that meant nothing.

"Forget what I said before. It was a ménage à trois. The rhino and the Jeep had a threesome with an accordion." I walked around the vehicle, whistling under my breath. "Iesu, this thing is *ugly*."

I wasn't exaggerating about the accordion. It looked like Sparky welded the plated accordion folds of a medical evac mobile unit with the front and back end of mismatched tactical assault vehicles. I couldn't even come up with a name for what it was. Technically I could've left off by calling it a transport, but I'd never seen one so heavily armored or as broad. Low to the ground, it resembled a flattened wheeled centipede, about eighteen feet long and mean-looking. I was about to open the folding door to peer into the cabin when I stopped myself before I touched the latch.

"Go ahead. It's not powered up to electrify." Sparky glared at Jason. "And if it is, I'll kick that one's ass."

"Come on," Jason protested. "You've got to admit it was funny. How was I supposed to know he was standing in a water puddle?"

"You're lucky he didn't shoot you where you stood," she *tsk*ed at him.

"Still might." I left that promise hanging in the air.

The interior of the beast was utilitarian—a couple of racks of sonars and other equipment we'd need to map through the underground part of our journey. I liked that Sparky enjoyed her comfort on long runs. Her preference for plush captain's chairs was a damn sight better than Dempsey's "here's an apple crate you can sit on, kid" approach to seating in a tactical vehicle. Although his lean and mean way of doing things was more because he was cheap than for any character building on his part.

"I like the fold-down bunks. That'll come in handy when we're underground." I walked the length of the cab and ducked my head slightly so I didn't hit the

ceiling. Calling out of the open door, I braced myself
for an answer I didn't want to hear. "Any weapons on
this thing?"

"It's built for power and climbing. If you get shot
at, it'll take it. There may or may not be some heavy
artillery that can pop out the sides, but all that'll do
is run hot and jam on things. I've got the slots open
if you want them, but those kinds of things usually
fall open when you least need them to." Sparky leaned
on the frame of the open door and chewed through
more seeds. "Won't take but a minute to put them in if
you're willing to get hung up on something jutting up
off the cavern floor."

She had a good point. The cleaner the outside
of the tactical vehicle was, the easier it would be
to maneuver through tight spaces. The beast she'd
brought with her was a squat, matte-black bulldog of
a machine. A few more rounds over the vehicle and
I'd located the water filtration system she'd worked
into the back as well as the charging solar plates on its
roof, which would be handy when we popped out of
San Diego's tunnels.

"Lots of crap in the water down there." Jason
hooked his fingers into his belt and rocked back on his
heels. "No refrigeration, but there is a cooling system
for the air once you get back up on top. If you want something cold, there's space inside of the unit to shove
a few small things. Figured having potable water was
more important than making sure you had ice cubes
for your tea. There's a hot water spigot, though. We
could give you that."

"Cari does like to bathe when she's on a run, so
at the very least, she gives herself a whore's bath."

I didn't mind them myself. I liked to be clean after spending so much of my life covered in filth. "Now comes the hard part—how much?"

"That lordling of yours said he's picking up the bill for this, and since he didn't even blink at the number I quoted him, we're just gonna call it a done deal." Sparky grinned at me with a gleeful madness only found in scalping an easy mark. From the twinkle in her eye, I guessed she probably charged him twice the amount he should've paid. "I like dealing with him directly. And he doesn't try to shove green beans at me when he's dropping off groceries."

"You cannot keep cheating him," I groaned and rubbed at my face. "I've got nieces there to think about. Every penny you strip out of his hand is one less they've got."

Her jaw worked back and forth, a bulge of muscle set firm with stubbornness. "If he's willing to—"

"Sparky, they're my family." I was playing a trump card I'd never played, never ever had the chance to play. "I mean, sure they're just little babies now but...."

"Fuck you, Gracen," Sparky growled back. "I'll give the bastard half of it back. But that's fair market value. I'm not going to go any lower than that."

"Throw the guns in but don't mount them," I countered, "and we can call it a deal."

"I DO not understand your unwillingness to pay full price for anything," Ryder grumbled at me as we packed the squat centipede with supplies. I'd scrawled its new insect name along the side in dark brick-red spray paint—anything to give it a little personality—but there was no fighting its dreary, dull finish. "She told me a number, and I thought it was reasonable."

"I would like to take the time right now to remind you that, at one point in your life, you thought your grandmother was reasonable." I stopped packing rations into one of the overhead bins. "She was fleecing you, Ryder. From now on, you're not allowed to buy any vehicle ever again. I'm not even sure if you should be allowed to buy our food."

"Alexa did *that*." Cari climbed into the back of the centipede, her arms burdened with rolled-up inflatable mattresses. She'd taken one look at the centipede's interior and done a quick run over to Jonas's place to grab stuff out of his warehouse. "I like these. They come with pillows that blow up too."

"We're on a run," I reminded them, "not camping. What else did you bring down? A hot tub?"

Ryder was saved from being involved in our discussion by the arrival of Alexa's SUV. Its throaty roar was a mimicry of a larger engine, the sound driven by a power adapter installed on the drivetrain. It made her happy, so I didn't say anything, but if it were anybody else, I would've mocked them mercilessly.

I also was fairly certain she could take me in a fight and pound me into the ground, so keeping my mouth shut was the most intelligent thing I could do.

"Oh joy." I spotted her passenger and curled my lip. "She brought her brother."

"I will get Kerrick settled." Ryder closed the cabinet he'd filled with medical supplies. "And before you say anything, Kai, I will reiterate to him that you are in charge on this run and I will support you in your decisions."

"That'll be a first," I muttered at him as he brushed past me. "There's a couple of heavy crates of ammo out there. See if you can't drop one on his foot. If he stays behind, maybe we can fit in that wet bar Cari probably wants to put in the back."

He ghosted his hand across my thigh and brushed down toward my knee. If it were anyone else, I would've thought the touch was accidental, but this was Ryder. My eyes flicked up to his face, and there was concern in his gaze—worry for me and maybe for the job as well.

I opened my mouth to tell him to fuck off and to keep his hands to himself, but instead I said, "I'm good. It'll be okay."

It must've been what he needed to hear, because he gave my wrist a quick squeeze and headed outside to deal with his cousin. I turned and found Cari staring at me with a stupid grin plastered across her face.

"Why don't you help me put away supplies instead of smiling your fool head off?" I picked up the first crate I saw and shoved it at her. "We're going to be on rations all the way over, but some of them are the high-protein, high-cal-count I grabbed this morning. Leave those in the boxes and shove them in the back. We need to save those for our refugees after we pick them up. They're probably going to need that kind of fuel to get them up to fighting weight, since from what Duffy said, those kids are in pretty bad shape."

"That's one thing I don't understand about this." She took the crate I handed her and balanced it on her hip. "Children are supposed to be precious to the elfin, but the Unsidhe treat the Dawn Court kids born to them like they're animals. Well, worse than animals. I don't get it."

I continued to unpack things and find places to put what we would need along the way. It was hard sometimes to reconcile Cari's optimism with the world we lived in. Even though she possessed the power to see the last moments of the dead, the filth of our races' deviant natures never seem to sink in.

She was short and spunky, her dark hair pulled back into two ponytails on either side of her plump-cheeked face. At first glance she looked like the kind of woman who woke up on Saturday mornings and took her dog down to the beach to chase a few tennis balls before she caught a cup of coffee with her friends. There'd been a lot of discussion in the Brent household about Cari becoming a Stalker, and she'd listened quietly as arguments flew about her head.

Then she went and got licensed and hit Jonas up for an apprenticeship, which pissed her dad off so much he didn't talk to me for a few months because he thought I'd convinced her to do it. It wasn't until her mother straightened him out and Cari became his apprentice, going on runs at his side, that her father grudgingly accepted that his baby girl turned out to be a damned good Stalker.

He still looked at me funny, though.

"Anything I say is going to sound like I'm preaching at you," I said as I walked the crate over to the standing cabinets. I laid the box down on the short shelf behind the second row of chairs and contemplated what to say to her. "There's a lot of shit in being a person. You come into this world hungry and stupid.

And most of us leave that same way. I think we're
kind of like those chameleons that grab at anything
in front of us, thinking it's going to hold us up. But
it's just a piece of twig someone has pinched between
their fingers.

"We spend a lot of our time filling our bowls, and I
think since life began, there's always been people who
have worked very hard to make sure they filled their
bowls by stealing from others or convincing them to
hand over half of their food because of fear or trick-
ery." I turned and faced her. "I don't have any love
for the elfin, but that's not because I think they're less
than I am. That would be kind of hard, because I've
got the same pointed ears and teeth. There are people
out there who hate my kind because we're different,
but in reality, it's because we are a threat to their resources. I think a lot of blind hatred comes from other
people being stirred up and told that guy over there is
going to steal your pig or murder your wife so you two
can't have children. No matter what race we are, we're
driven to survive, and there are some who feed on that.
I think that's why the elfin hate each other so much.
Deep down inside, all they've got is fear."

"And the children have to suffer for it?" Her dark
eyes glittered, even in the centipede's shadowy interi-
or. "There are times I question how the gods lead us.
Why does there have to be so much pain in order for
us to expand our souls?"

"Cari, the gods don't lead us. They give us someone to swear at when we stub our toe or thank them
when there's an onion ring in our french fries. But
lead us? You'd be better off looking for someone you
respect and following their example." I chuckled and

shook my head at her. "Do I worship Pele and thank Odin? Yes. I also ask Iesu why I deal with morons, but I don't expect him to answer. It's not that the gods are deaf, it's that we're not worth listening to."

"So then why do good? Why should we go on this run to save people we have no connection to?" She gestured toward the Sidhe standing outside. "Because you're telling me that the Dusk Court only sees those children as parasites. So then why should Ryder help them? Why should we? And it's not that I don't believe we should, but what do you think we gain by doing that? Because I know why I do it. I can't sleep at night knowing someone died because I didn't give a shit. I became a Stalker to help people, but there are times when it feels like I'm banging my head against the wall."

"Yeah, we bang our heads against a lot of walls, but we also do some good. That's why we become Stalkers. It isn't just the bounty. Sure, some people are just after the cash, but you and I both know not everybody is. The pay is lousy, we could die doing it, and nobody ever comes up to you and thanks you for pulling the ass end of their cow from the dead dragon's mouth. More than likely they get pissed off because it's the wrong end of the cow, but you know they would've died if you weren't there, even if they're too scared to admit it." I had a simple truth to tell her— simplistic even—but that truth drove me to do things my gut told me not to. "I help because I *was* helped. Fucking *Dempsey* helped me, and he's possibly the shittiest human you know. But he still found it in himself to do the right thing for once in his life, so I should be able to do the same for this pack of kids and anybody else who needs me."

Eleven

DRIVING THE centipede transport through San Diego's lower level got us more than a few curious looks, and as we turned onto the main drag of the Barrio Logan district, a cop pulled me over. I knew the guy, and I tried to ignore Cari sitting in the back on the passenger side as she took selfies of herself with the cop's flashing lights going off behind her.

"Could you not flash a peace sign behind my head while I'm talking to the cop?" I muttered at Cari when the officer stepped back to his car to call off the back-up rolling in to intercept us. "It's... just *stop*."

"It's not a peace sign," she sniped back. "They're bunny ears, and I told my mom you got pulled over. She said you have to go back to driving school. Not like you went in the first place."

I couldn't argue with that, especially since I'd learned to drive in Dempsey's beat-up trucks and whatever welded-together piece of shit he'd bought off Sparky for a heavy run. The centipede was a far cry from those days—not because she got better at building vehicles but because I wasn't cheap like Dempsey and didn't intend to drive around in something that should have been left on the trash heap.

Officer Davies let me off with a slap to the shoulder and a promise from me to have a good time. Laughing at the irony of a cop telling me to enjoy a run, I fired up the transport and began the slow trundle toward the exit tunnels that led to the buried depths of the city.

The rest of the drive through the district was quiet for the most part, with a few humming tidbits of commentary from Cari—especially when we passed a churros-and-tacos stall advertising an octopus special. I told her to stuff her chortling where the sun couldn't touch it, and that only made it worse. I caught Ryder hiding a sly smile before he turned his head to look out the window and sighed.

Then, after ten minutes of stop-and-go traffic and a near altercation with a tik-tik driver, Kerrick spoke up. "We shouldn't have had to stop. We have diplomatic immunity. We are outside of human law."

"First off, only one in this car with diplomatic immunity is Ryder, and he ain't driving." His tone was haughty, or maybe that was just me. Either way, I stepped into the stream of conversation before Ryder could jump in. Pitching my voice up to be heard over a round of honking someone in front of us had started, I continued, "Second, if ever you *do* get a court and it's in the middle of a human city, you'll get along better if you're not an asshole and stop when the cops pull you over. Because, from my experience, they tend to shoot up cars that ignore them, even with diplomatic plates."

"To be fair," Ryder interjected, "the last time I had police officers shoot up my car, it was because I stopped to pick you up."

"Okay, I'll give you that one." I inclined my head to acknowledge the point. "Thing is, I don't know how they do things up in Elfhaine—'cause you know that one time I went was shitty from the get-go—but if you're going to try to get along with people, you've got to respect their society and culture."

"Like you do, changeling?" Kerrick responded, a slither of Sidhe curling around in the air behind my head. "Because I haven't noticed you affording me much respect when I'm clearly your better."

"You and I have very different ideas on what makes someone better, bucko," I shot back and glanced up into the rearview mirror to meet his hard gaze. "And I respect you fine. Well, Ryder at least. He's the one who talked me out of knifing you and tossing your body into the river."

"You've got to stop threatening to kill people, Kai." Ryder shook his head. "It's—"

"Right, because if I don't carry a couple of them out, no one's going to believe me." I cocked my head when Kerrick narrowed his eyes at me. "Don't think Ryder holds my leash."

"Trust me, chimera," he replied smoothly. "I don't think anyone has you leashed. That is *precisely* the problem."

TRAFFIC DIDN'T lighten up for another tense fifteen minutes. With a sharp word over his shoulder at his cousin and using a Sidhe slang I didn't know, Ryder prevented me from responding to Kerrick. From the look on Cari's face, it was going to be a toss-up on who stabbed Kerrick first—her or me. The silence was itchy and getting under all of our skin by the time the comm crackled open on a frequency only Stalkers used.

"Gracen. Do you copy?" The voice was a ghost from the past. Perhaps *poltergeist* was a better word. Ryder looked at me curiously, and the transmission continued. "Gracen, I know you're out there. I just heard the police scanner, and the cop who pulled you over said you were headed into the underground. I'm hoping to pay you for a quick job since you're headed that direction."

"You better answer him," Cari said with a disgusted snort. "He's just going to hound you until you do or until we can't hear him anymore."

"Who is that?" Ryder shifted in his seat and turned toward me, seemingly undisturbed by the crater-like pothole the centipede just rolled over. "And you're already on a job. Why would he think you want another one?"

"That's Mink. He is a dracologist at the University of San Diego." I reached over to answer the call and switched it over to a private line. "And he's a massive pain in the ass."

"So then he's in good company knowing you," Kerrick slid in.

"I really regret promising you that I wouldn't stab him," I muttered at Ryder. Then I turned the line to speaker and answered Mink. "I'm already on a job. I don't need—"

"I've got most of the third quadrant mapped out and ready to upload into a terrain system. I've gone all the way to four exit points down near the border, as well as to drop-offs into the river and a solid span bridge crossing over it, wide enough and stable enough to hold two tanks." Mink sliced through my argument before it even began. "It's a very small job. I just need help to get some bearded flyer eggs out of a nest so I can relocate them to a sanctuary. Won't take more than a couple of hours of your time, and depending upon where you're going, the maps could cut a day or two off of your run. I've gotten the verification but haven't loaded them in for distribution. Rights to the lines are still mine to give."

"Hold on." I muted the line and edged the centipede over to the side, leaving the trail of cars following in the wake of a slow-moving bus. I put the transport in Park and turned my chair to face Cari. She leaned forward, a contemplative look on her face. "A couple of hours, and that's a hell of a payment."

"Third quadrant would probably drop us off closer to the rendezvous point. We wouldn't have to cut across so much open land or skirt the Diablo Canyons, assuming the exits drop off to the left of those." She pulled at her lower lip, thinking. "Probably cut off two or three days. If he could prove verification…."

I switched the comm on. "Mink, give your verification code."

It wasn't hard to hear the unbridled glee in his voice as he rattled off the string of numbers. I muted the line again and quickly double-checked on the university's system. Cari crowded into the space between me and Ryder and scanned the screen as the data rolled down. It looked legit. Mink had filed enough verification points and geology readings to back up his boast of mapping out an underground quadrant. All that remained for him to do was upload the rendered maps into the system, where they would be locked down and only accessible by purchasing them through the university—something normally outside of a common Stalker's reach.

What he was offering me was pre-upload access and legacy rights to the information, all tied to my account with the university and my Stalker license through the Post.

It was a hell of a payout for just a couple hours of work.

"Something's off," Cari and I said at the same time.

"If this map is very important, I can just pay for it," Ryder interjected and then visibly started when both Cari and I shot him filthy looks. "Really? It's a map. How dear can it be?"

"One tenth of a quadrant costs more than your sports car," I informed him. "Besides, you don't pay for something if you can get it through a bit of haggling and work. I swear to Pele, I'm going to get that through your head before I die. Besides, he can't take money for it, because if he does, then he violates any payment structure he would get through the university. It has to hit the system as a virgin upload, no transactions on it. It's how their contract works. Prevents people from pulling a huge profit on something under the table, then uploading it to the university, where it's practically useless because everybody already has it."

"There's got to be a catch." Cari shook her head, then glanced back at Kerrick when he shifted in his seat. "If it's on the way, then I say yes, but I want to know what that catch is."

"You can't possibly think of derailing this enterprise simply for a map, no matter how much time it might cut off from the trip," he drawled. "I agree with Ryder. Let him upload it and we pay for it. That's my say on the matter."

Ryder gave a short burst of sardonic chuckles. "The fact that you think we have a say in any of this, cousin, is a reality you will quickly be disabused of. We go where Kai leads us. That's the condition of attending these runs. We forfeit any influence we have on our direction or what we do."

"First off, you can always speak your mind. I just might not listen to it. Thing is, it will be two to three weeks before it cycles through the university's system. No good to us then." I opened the comm, still debating my options. "You there, Mink?"

"I'm all ears, Gracen." He caught himself before his guffaw reached full throat. "Okay, that was accidental. I promise. It wasn't an elfin joke. But you've gotta admit, it was funny."

"Yeah, hilarious. Okay, two things. First, you issue legacy rights to Cari Brent too." I cut off Cari's hissing protest with a wave of my hand. "And what's the catch?"

"He does like counting," Kerrick commented to Ryder in a whisper loud enough for all of us to hear. "Intelligent as well as pretty. He's a fine asset to the court, cousin."

I ignored him. "What's the catch, Mink?"

"Small catch. About four or five feet long." He stumbled over his words and slurred them together. "There's an albino *Scolopendra maxima* at the base of the gulch where the nest's at, and well, I seem to have pissed it off."

"SO IT'S a centipede? Is that what it's called?" Kerrick frowned as he tried to make sense of our conversation. "Isn't that what we're driving? A centipede? We're going to go fight a transport vehicle?"

I understood his confusion. Hell, I was confused myself. But then this was Mink, and wherever the nutty professor went, chaos followed.

Mink had crossed my path a few years back when I found him in a ditch out by Lakeside. I'd been coming home from a successful black dog cull and was heading to Dempsey's to prep the skins for bounty when I noticed an orange bubble-style VW Bug sitting on the side of the road near the main turnoff. It was an unfamiliar car and seemed to be stuck in one of the deep trenches SoCalGov dug on the sides of country roads to deal with flooding during the heavy rains.

Come to find out, investigating the Bug was only the beginning of an increasingly annoying relationship with a dracologist named Mink who'd somehow gotten his car stuck in a ditch, tried to climb out of the window, and ended up lodged in an underground gulch. I heard his shouts for help and rappelled down into the newly opened crevice, where I could see him standing on a thin ledge with an all-consuming darkness beneath him. I resigned myself to dragging a little kid up to the surface while I tried to figure out a way to tell him I was not going to go look for the driver of the

Bug—Mink was *that* short. He resembled a twelve-year-old, and at times kind of acted like one. He gave up driving cars following the gulch incident, but his work took him to dangerous places, so he now rode an old Triumph motorcycle with bulging saddlebags filled with things I didn't want to contemplate.

We'd agreed to meet in a scrapyard not far from where Jonas and I fought the cuttlefish. The guard dog on the premises was a farce—a mean-looking Rottie mix that could have doubled as an ainmhi dubh if his spittle was acidic but who rolled over and showed belly as soon as anyone with fingers walked past him. I crouched over the canine and scratched at his exposed stomach while his owner, a short Chinese woman with gold teeth, beamed proudly at our praise of her useless junkyard dog. Then she extracted a promise from Mink that he would load his motorcycle into our transport and not leave it behind, and she went back inside and left us to our business.

Mink mumbled a promise of something under his breath, his Cantonese more closely resembling Pig Latin than anything recognizable, but she smiled at me and told us to send her dog inside once he was done attacking us with his vicious licking. I complimented her on his disciplined training and told her if I had a dog, I would want one exactly like him.

To her credit, it was a great dog—slobbery, gleeful, and sweet. Probably had poops the size of a three-year-old human child, but a great dog.

"Kai calling our transport a centipede is in reference to how it looks. It's an Earth insect with mandibles, but I did not think they grew to be that large. Perhaps at the most, the length of a man's hand?" Ryder cocked his head at the dog and tentatively scratched him behind his ears. The mutt drooled, and his eyes rolled back in pleasure. Then he scooted over to sit on Ryder's foot and leaned against his leg. "But then this is a dog like Shiro, and they look nothing alike, so perhaps I have the insects confused."

"Shiro?" Cari whispered behind me. "Wait, the white puffball that the pink-haired Sidhe has? Lea's fur ball is a dog?"

"Yeah, the dog is from one of Sparky's litters from before she spayed her females. I brought it home, thinking the girls might like it, and then Lea fell in love with it, and Kai reminded him the girls wouldn't even be able to play with the dog for a couple of years." Ryder smiled at the drooling canine that wiggled against him. "It seemed cruel to separate Shiro from Lea after they bonded, so he's now Lea's."

"I thought that was some kind of Sidhe pet. It's just white fur and a black nose." She huffed. "Seriously, it doesn't even bark."

"Could we talk less about the wild animals you have roaming around the court and more about this insect this small man cannot get past?" Kerrick interrupted.

Mink bristled. "Look, just because a guy's short doesn't mean you go and point it out to everyone. It's not like they can't *see* I'm this tall."

"Kerrick, it's rude to point out things about a human's appearance." Ryder's heavy sigh lifted up at the end. "But he is right. Why do you need our help to take care of a small insect?"

"An albino *Scolopendra maxima* is a hell of a lot bigger than your hand," I informed Ryder. "Their eggs are about the size of the dog on your foot. Biggest one I've ever seen was four feet long, but I've heard they get bigger. How big is this one, Mink?"

He shifted his feet back and forth and rolled his eyes up to look at the sky as though he were trying to remember exactly how large the creature he'd encountered was. "I'd say about four feet. I didn't see any eggs or hatchlings, so I think it's a male. But it's definitely territorial, so I can't get past it."

"And you didn't think to just shoot it?" Cari asked.

"He's not allowed to have a gun," I informed her as Mink began to unravel all of his excuses about why he didn't carry a weapon. "Convicted felons aren't allowed weapons, remember? And Mink hasn't quite gotten SoCalGov to wipe his record from the time he pillaged a stone dragon's clutch."

If I listened carefully, I could've heard Ryder and Kerrick gasping in horror, but the dog's enthusiastic panting wiped out anything so subtle.

"It was an understandable mistake," he protested loudly and pressed his hand to his chest as though acting out a Regency romance drama. "I thought they were dinosaur fossils. They look *very* similar."

"Let me see the mapping so I can decide if I'm going to take this job of yours." I held my hand out for the viewing pad he held aside. "You say it's only a couple hours in, right? Is that marked on the map? Because I'm not going to go hours off course for a bunch of bearded flyer eggs, no matter how endangered they are."

"Here, I've marked it." Mink sidled up to me, and Cari peered over his shoulder with a smug look on her face, probably because, for the first time in forever, she was taller than somebody else. He pulled up the maps, showing me the extent of the caverns he'd triangulated and verified. A glowing red dot pulsed off a tunnel that skewed from the main third-quadrant cavern. "If you see the distance markers here, you can tell it's not even two hours in. I just need help to get the eggs out. They're located next to a hot spring, so I know they're active… or at least one of them has to be. I've got thermal packs in my saddlebags, so I won't need you to bring me back. I can ride my bike out, and you can continue on your way."

"I want to see the rest of the map," Cari murmured. "I want to see the exit points."

"No way. Not with Gracen standing here." Mink shook his head. "I know how his mind works. He sees that once and it'll stick there in that crazy brain of his, and he won't need the maps. You agree to do the job, I give you both the maps."

"We're wasting time here talking about this," Ryder interjected softly. "As much as I enjoy the company of this canine, we have a rendezvous to make, and if this way gets us there sooner, I think spending two hours to cut off days is a good idea."

I studied Mink. He was an ends-justify-the-means kind of guy, and I couldn't trust him as far as I could throw him, but I could probably throw him pretty far. He *really* was that short. Mink stood as tall as he could and tried to look as innocent as he could as he widened his green eyes and clearly hoped his youthful features would work on me like they worked on the food-truck guy in front of the university who always slipped him extra cheese on his loaded nachos.

"It's a win-win, Gracen." Mink had a thread of pleading in his voice—not enough to take it to plaintive, but right on the edge. "You know these maps are worth a hell of a lot more than two hours of your time. It's all I've got to bargain with, and I really want to save these flyers. I think the *Scolopendra* got their mother, or she wasn't able to get back to her nest. I watched it for five days, and other than that damned white monster, it was just me and the glow worms down there. If I can get them to the university's sanctuary, we can—"

"Okay, just stop. *Please*." I held up my hand to shut Mink up. "We'll go get your damn eggs, but I'm only going to give you four hours of our time. If we don't get in there and back out by then, the job's done, and we still get the maps."

"Five," Mink countered, "and you take me back to the main cavern."

"Five and the cavern." I calculated the risks and hedged the time it would take us and how much time we would gain with a clear shot through the third quadrant. It was a good deal, but I couldn't let Mink have the final volley. I had a reputation to uphold. "And if you finish mapping out the rest of the quadrant, you back-load the information into our access. Agree to that and we've got a deal."

"Deal," Mink said gleefully, his hand shooting out for me to shake.

As I took it and sealed our agreement, Cari muttered into my ear, "That was way too fucking easy. There's *got* to be a catch."

Twelve

"THIS DAMNED thing is not four feet long!" I screamed at no one in particular as I wrapped my arms around Ryder's waist, rolled us behind a large boulder, and skidded across a bed of damp moss. The abused moist filaments excreted a filmy white paste, and the smear burned where it touched my bare arm.

We were five minutes into the fight and things were going badly—really badly.

The third quadrant started off as a ten-foot-wide, thirty-foot-high passageway that eventually led to the initial great chamber. It was this passageway we veered off to one of the smaller chambers, where Mink served us up as dinner to an Angolan death worm.

"I take it that is not the *Scolopendra* Mink promised us." Ryder grunted as he pulled up his knees and squeezed himself into the tight space. "And yes, I agree. That is not four feet long. This brings to question any of the measurements that man has taken, including this shortcut map."

The creature's massive mandibles snapped above us, its triangular head too broad and wide to fit into the crevice we were huddled in. Acid dripped from one of its fangs, and I raised my already smarting arm up to block it from hitting Ryder. My flesh sizzled where the liquid struck, and a welt bubbled up quickly along my wrist.

"Motherf—" I bit back my profanity, mostly to throw myself over Ryder's folded-up body. Acid poured down on us in dribbles, but my shirt caught most of it. My skin beneath the fabric wasn't very appreciative about the heat, but I'd been through worse.

"Are you all right?" Ryder mumbled. "Let me—"

"Stay down. This thing's stubborn." I grinned into Ryder's hair. "Kind of like you."

"You're one to talk." He snorted. "And I don't know why humans feel the need to rename everything. What did you call it? A worm? It has legs. Worms don't have legs. *Wyrms* have legs, and that is a—"

I stopped listening to the burble of Sidhe nearly as soon as Ryder began to rattle it off. I'd broken the hold the language had on me—or rather the spell my father laid down into my bones to compel me to obey certain words spoken in my native tongue—but it still made me nauseous. Or nauseated. I was not always really sure which applied, but I was certain that Ryder would have an answer—just not one for the problem we were currently dealing with… the Angolan death worm.

The creature's fangs were getting closer, its incessant jabs chipping away at the rock face we were huddled against. Its hard shell proved to be impossible to penetrate. My guns were useless, Cari's shotgun blast to its chest only sprayed us with shrapnel, and the few shots I'd gotten in on its head created ricochets with crazy angles. Mink, being the coward that he was, ran back inside of the transport and shut the door behind him, leaving us outside to contend with the monster. Cari yelled at him for about half a second while he struggled to reopen the main cabin and set off its alarms so the chamber rang with klaxons.

So much for a quick job, in and out.

We'd come out of the passageway into a medium-size cavern, about thirty feet up. There were enough mica flecks and luminescence to see its ceiling, but I'd left the spotlight lines running around the roof of the centipede transport, brightening the chamber. Like most of the underground spaces layered beneath Southern California's now-stable lower strata, the cave was rich with speleothems and rings of columns, and stalagmites and stalactites bristled out from every direction. These chambers hadn't existed before the Merge, but nature didn't respect or care for any restrictions, and there were as many earthen creatures throughout the tunnels as there were elfin.

The Angolan death worm might have had an earthen name, but it was purely elfin in origin—and one of the meanest damned things that had crossed over into our world.

Our world. Funny how I still thought of myself as human as I lay on top of Ryder, my heart pounding with adrenaline—and not all of it from the worm attempting to bite my head off. It was impossible not to react to him, and my instincts all drove me to protect Ryder from harm, and not the way I would with Cari.

It was stupid and not something to think about when we would be broiled in acid soon if I didn't come up with a plan. But that was my connection with the Sidhe lord who brought me nothing but trouble.

Although our current situation was clearly on Mink.

We'd entered into the chambers and seen not a single sign of any insect life other than the minute cavern bugs with their glowing orange-and-yellow bodies that flashed warnings when we rolled in. Mink opened the door before I could put the transport into Park, and I should've closed it behind him and left him there. Hindsight is always a wonderful thing.

We'd followed him out, and Cari had just reached over the seat to grab her shotgun when the death worm struck.

We heard its maracas-like skittering before we saw it, a whispery clacking rhythm that echoed through the chamber. It was difficult to tell where the noise was coming from, especially with the deep crenulated folds in the sheer sides of the chamber. The cream-colored formations were ruffled, complicated lettuce forms of solid rock and slick with slime—the perfect hiding place for a massive Angolan death worm.

Mink was pointing out the nest hidden behind a cluster of rocks twenty feet above our heads when the worm's hissing caught our attention and the ticking pops of its pointed legs as it struck across the cave floor got us all moving. Cari and I stepped out into the cavern and unloaded round upon round into the worm, but nothing stopped it. I was ordering everyone back into the vehicle when Mink slammed the door shut and its failsafe mechanisms locked everything down because he'd hit the panic button.

Accidentally. Or so I deduced by the screams of apology that came through the passenger window before it slid closed the rest of the way and sealed him inside.

We scattered. Ryder and I went to the left and Cari to the right. I assumed Kerrick followed her, because he wasn't with us. Unfortunately the worm decided it preferred elfin meat. It was hot on our asses, and it was furious. A small grouping of boulders was the only protection we had in front of us, and I dragged Ryder toward them and shoved him behind the jagged rocks. The crevice behind them was deep and narrow enough for us to be out of the worm's reach—or so I thought before the thing climbed up on top to play whack-a-mole with our heads.

Most centipedes and millipedes smelled like a bit of powder mixed in with carrion. That one seemed to have skipped the pigeon-talc scent of its beauty regime and gone straight to rolling in mountains of roadkill. Cari was shouting, most of it Mexican swear words I'd learned from her brothers years before. Then she switched to German, a lingual gift her father would only share with her, and she didn't use it often enough for me to learn it. It was wholly unfair that he was stingy with his profanity, because it sounded exactly how I felt at that moment—a guttural explosion of pure rage and emotion combined with a promise to kill Mink once we got our hands on him.

Or at least that's what I got from it.

"Do you think she is trying to get its attention?" Ryder muttered from his tangled position beneath me. "And do you think it is going to work?"

"Something must've happened, because it's moved away from the rock," I replied as I risked a peek. I couldn't see the thing's head, but its odor remained, which told me it was still nearby. I pressed my guns into Ryder's hands and grinned. "Hold these for me. Don't lose them. They're my favorite guns."

My hands weren't empty for long. Pissed off and looking for blood, I pulled the knives I had strapped to my thighs and went over the rocks.

It probably wasn't the best idea I'd ever come up with, but it was all I had.

The centipede transport was still lit up like a Christmas tree. It was burning energy we would have to compensate for later, but that was fine by me. Throwing off a pool of light bright enough to illuminate the sides of the cavern we were in, it let me get a very good look at what I was up against.

Damn, that thing was huge.

I hadn't quite grasped the scope of it when I was running for my life, but as I tumbled through the air toward it, I might've miscalculated. It was easily twice as long as the transport, about as wide, and made up of ivory armored plates, a massive praying-mantis-like head spiked with fangs, mandibles, and all sorts of biting things.

It didn't really matter at that point, because I hit the worm with enough force to drive the segment I'd landed on right into the ground.

There is nothing quite like hearing the satisfying crunch of an Angolan death worm's back legs being snapped off. Sure, the broken appendages began to splatter me with fountains of indescribably horrific-tasting fluids, but that was at least four legs I didn't have to worry about. But as its head spun around on its alarmingly flexible body, I recalled that its legs weren't much of a worry compared to its teeth.

"Kai!" Cari shouted from someplace in front of the worm. I don't know what she thought she was going to achieve. I already knew my name, and the worm probably didn't care what it was as long as it got me off its back and got pieces of my body into its mouth. "You can't—"

I was getting really tired of people telling me what I could and couldn't do, so I ignored her, plunged one knife between the worm's plates, and twisted. Then I dragged the sharp edge through the softer membrane between its armor. I had another knife strapped to my shin, and its serrated blade probably would be better, but I'd gone too far, too deep. The worm bucked and tried to throw me off, and I wedged my boot through the slice I'd made into its flesh.

It worked for the cuttlefish, so I figured the technique would also work for the worm and give me a way to wedge myself against its slick body. Its hisses flicked minute specks of acid across my face and exposed arms and left tiny blisters in their wake. They didn't last long, but the burn was a flash point of excruciating pain, much like getting a tattoo in a sensitive spot. The worm's head came by me one more time, and I took a chance I would probably regret.

I leaped for its head.

Jonas liked to drag me to rodeos when I was younger. Dempsey always tagged along. He claimed he enjoyed them, but mostly he liked the brassy-haired women who followed the circuit. Jonas liked the sport of riding out-of-control animals and would often climb on the mechanical bulls we found in dive bars on country runs. After he'd been thrown through what felt like the twentieth wall, I finally asked him why he did it.

His response was, "Because it's a hell of a lot of fun."

Clinging to the triangular head of the Angolan death worm was *not* fun, but it was the only way I was going to kill the damned thing.

I lost one of my knives in the leap, so my right hand was empty when I landed. Scrambling to grab anything to hold on to, I dug my fingers into its eye and caught at the ridged carapace that protected its sensitive orb. Death worms are built funny, at least by earthen standards. Their eyes are soft, flexible, and spongy but not easily torn. I didn't know that before I landed on that one, but I filed it away for future use, providing I survived.

"Kai, I'm going to try to get the transport open," Ryder yelled at me as he sprinted across the cave floor toward our trusty centipede, where, by the brief glance I got, Kerrick was fighting to open the door and Mink was screaming his head off inside. *Brief* glance. For all I knew, they were in a rap battle and Kerrick was winning. "I saw a flamethrower."

Not what I wanted to hear while clinging to an overgrown mutant white land lobster, but it was the least of my worries, especially when Cari opened fire at its underbelly. All that did was piss the worm off, and I was off on another round of trying to hold on while attempting to get my other knife loose.

The worm's head was slick—too slick for me to grab—and when Cari's shotgun blasts to its belly angered it, the worm reared up, nearly knocking me free. My hands were damp with sweat, and my fingers fumbled to unlatch the strap that held my knife in its sheath. Up close the worm smelled worse than an ainmhi dubh, but at that point, so did I. Ryder's shouting joined Kerrick's, and I heard the unmistakable hiss of the transport's hydraulic doors opening.

"Great," I ground out. "Now I've got to worry about a flamethrower. Let's kill you quick before they make me a marshmallow."

The worm landed, rattling my teeth and shaking every bone down my spine. My hips twisted, and my limbs screamed with the effort of holding on to its vibrating plates. I kicked out, lodged myself against an eye ridge, and dug my boot into its eye. The angle made it easier to grab my knife, and it slid from its sheath, the serrated edge catching slightly on the worn leather.

Twisting about, the worm folded in on itself and brought its head down to rub on its inner coils. A plate caught me in the back, snagging on my shoulder blade, and my already-abused T-shirt ripped, leaving my side bare. Its still-intact collar dragged across my throat, cutting off my breathing, and I began to choke. I quickly slid my knife through the taut neckline and took a gasping breath, grateful for the rush of fetid air that poured into my lungs.

Another round of gunfire and the worm heaved to the right and wound through a small bristle of limestone columns that ran near the edge of the cavern wall. Cari started after it and reloaded as she widened her stance. I couldn't see where she was aiming, especially when the worm tossed its head back and its mandibles flared outward for its next strike.

It was probably already blinded by the light pouring out of the transport, but it seemed to find us quickly enough, so maybe stabbing it in the eyes wasn't going to get the reaction I wanted. I did it anyway. I gripped the serrated knife as tightly as I could, plunged it into the creature's eye socket, and pulled my arm back to do it again as it screamed in pain.

I kept returning to the same spot, and my arm grew tired and strained from holding on while the other jabbed into the worm's eye socket. Its chitinous exoskeleton seemed to be impenetrable, and the socket wouldn't give. I couldn't get to its neural system, and the thing seemed to just keep going. Cari's shotgun blasts were a distraction at best and kept it moving around in circles as she backed away to hide behind large boulders and short outcroppings.

"Get off of the thing, Kai!" Ryder's voice broke through the creature's screaming, but what he was saying didn't make much sense, especially when the worm rose up to its full length and brought me way too close to the cave's jagged ceiling. Its undulations slammed me against a rock spire and knocked the wind out of my chest. Choking on my own tongue, I coughed my airway clear and continued to jab at its slit-open eye. "I'm going to set it on fire!"

That was probably the worst plan ever, probably stupider than the one where I jumped on the monster's body. Cari must have thought so too, because she yelled at Ryder to stop, but I caught a whiff of accelerant in the air, and I knew my day was about to go to shit.

Not like the last hour had been a walk in the park, but shit was on the horizon.

I took one last stab at the worm's head and jumped off as soon as it dropped down closer to the floor—a floor that was still a little too far away for a comfortable landing.

I rolled as quickly as I could and seemed to hit every single bump and jut the cave had grown over the last few years. My shoulder took another hit, and then I got a shot to my groin from a slender column and snapped the limestone thread off across my thigh when my momentum carried me forward. I didn't wait to come to a stop. Instead I reached out, grabbed at the edge of an outcropping, and jerked myself up into the air with enough force and clearance to give me room to unfold my legs. My ankles took a beating at the shock landing, but I recovered my balance in time to see Ryder aiming a flamethrower at the worm.

All I could think was that at least he got the flames spitting and pointed in the right direction, but then he pulled down the trigger and released a stream of blue fire.

Another thing to add to the encyclopedia entry on Angolan death worms—they are apparently extremely flammable.

Thank the gods I wasn't planning on using any of the oxygen in the cavern to breathe, because it was gone.

The wall of flames was immense, a tsunami of embers and smoking chitin. Body parts twisted, cooked, and broke off into smaller piles of smoldering soft flesh, and its large plates curled upward from the immense heat and cracked like a lobster severed apart by a large English woman armed with a sharp knife and an even sharper tongue. It died as it lived, screaming with rage and flailing about, its body knotting in on itself, its legs beating a terrible tattoo on the cavern floor.

A foul odor rose up from the twisted-meat bonfire at the far end of the cave, but the smoke drifted upward, probably pulled by an opening or two hidden somewhere in the ceiling of the cavern. I dropped to my knees and regretted it as soon as I struck the hard rock, but the air finally returned to my lungs, and my legs were too shaky to hold me up any longer. Ryder was at my side before I took my third breath. Thankfully, he'd left the flamethrower with Cari or I would've found the strength to stand up and use it on Mink.

"Are you all right?" Ryder crouched beside me, his hands hovering over my shoulder and back. His face was twisted with worry, his deep green eyes soulful with concern. "Let's get you to the transport so we can take a look at you. What were you thinking, jumping on that thing?"

"I don't know. It seemed like the thing to do. How else was I going to kill it?" I grunted as he dragged me to my feet and slung my arm around his shoulder to lend me support as I walked. "How was I supposed to know that thing would go up like an aerosol can in an open flame? And why the hell do we have a flamethrower, anyway? Sparky gives me shit about putting machine guns on hard points, but she packs a flamethrower into the trunk? What else is back there? A nuclear missile?"

"Well, it's good to see that you didn't hit your head, because you sound exactly like you did before you jumped off of that rock," Ryder grumbled, but with lightness in his voice. "Let's take a look at your wounds. For a moment there, I thought I was going to lose you. When it—"

"Don't get sentimental on me, lordling." I shook my head and tried not to limp too much over the uneven floor. "It'll take a lot more than that to kill me. I'm looking forward to being a thorn in your side for decades to come, maybe even millennia."

"I'm looking forward to every agonizing second," he replied as he dragged me toward the transport. "We have Kerrick to thank for getting the door open. He talked Mink through the unlocking procedures."

"It's not that hard. Literally two—maybe three—buttons, and all of them say Open Door." I winced when Cari ran up to us, her arms spread out for a hug. "Let's not do that just yet, kid. I need maybe a beer and a new shirt. I also wouldn't say no to kicking Mink's ass once I've gotten those two things checked off on my to-do list. Where is he anyway? Did he go up the cliff to get the eggs?"

"Mink isn't really important right now." Kerrick stepped down off the transport, his boots clicking on its short steps. His face was stone, and his eyes glittered, reflecting the dying flames behind us. "I'm more interested in finding out why your pet here wears Tanic cuid Anbhás's sigil on his back."

I felt Ryder tense against me, his body coiling tight with anger, so I gave Kerrick a slow smile and said, "Well, I guess Grandma doesn't tell you everything. So which one of us has the shorter leash?"

Thirteen

MINK WAS gone as soon as Cari retrieved the bearded flyer eggs from a crevice not more than fifteen feet from where Ryder and I huddled for safety. I was stripping down to my waist inside of the transport when Mink's motorcycle revved up and Cari ducked into the main cabin holding a canvas bag and a memstick. She gave me a quick glance and then plugged the stick into the transport's console.

Mink's map began to unspool across the screen, and she shot me a triumphant look. She hit a few buttons and crowed softly, "And we've got enough connection down here that I can tap this into our main account so we won't have to wait to get back home to upload."

I couldn't quite get all of my T-shirt off, and I had a sneaking suspicion I'd healed over some of the fabric. A quick tug confirmed it. I was stuck and was going to need someone to help me. When I ducked my head, I spotted Ryder having what looked like a heated discussion with Kerrick a few yards from the transport. Since I didn't think they were arguing over the Raiders' last draft pick, I would have to wait.

"How long?" I asked her as I gave another experimental yank. "I want to be on the road as soon as we can. We're wasting too much time sitting here. Short-cut across the third quadrant is going to be useless if we don't shave time off the trip."

"How about if I drive while Ryder patches you up?" She gave a thumbs-up out the open door and then grinned at me at the fading sound of Mink's motorcycle careening out of the main cavern. "I told that idiot Mink to wait until I gave him the all clear. He didn't waste any time."

"Well, if he jacked us over, I know where to find him," I reminded her.

"Yeah, if there's one person I wouldn't want to come looking for me, it would be you. I've seen how fast you can skin an ainmhi dubh. I wouldn't want to be on the wrong end of your knife." She patted my shoulder and then leaned out of the main cabin. "Hey, Ryder. Let's roll out before we get sick off of the fumes of that thing burning. I need you to help put Kai together while I get us going. Think you can do that?"

There wasn't a mirror anywhere in the supplies we loaded onto the centipede, but it wasn't like I was expecting a fashion show. Having that much breakable glass in a moving vehicle that would probably take a few rough shots over the next couple of weeks wasn't a good idea. Still, it would've been nice to actually see my back. I was just rigging up a double-camera system off of the imaging console when Ryder came up behind me.

"Oh, by the gods, Kai...." Ryder sucked air through his teeth in a low, soft hiss heavily laden with concern. "Sit down on the bunk over there. Let me help you."

Kerrick came in behind him. If there was any doubt about him being related to Sebac, it was wiped away by the expression on his face. He looked so much like the Spider Queen that he could have been cut off from her flesh and grown in a test tube. The Sidhe lord held himself stiffly and moved as though his joints hurt. Rage set fire to the depths of his jewel-toned eyes, and his mouth was a thin slash above his firm chin. Of the three of us, he was probably the cleanest, and he was certainly much more dressed than I was.

"Why don't you sit up here with me, Kerrick," Cari suggested as she fired up the transport and the main door locked down. The centipede rumbled, its hydraulic system lifting up to level out its ride. "You'll get a better view of the caves as we move through them."

"I thank you for your offer, but I've got a few questions for your... fellow Stalker." He settled down into the chair near the door and swiveled it about to face me and Ryder. "It seems my illustrious cousin has neglected to share vital information about the person he believes is key to the survival of the Southern Rise Court."

"The *only* person key to the survival of the court is Ryder. I feel like I've said that already. Hey, watch the hands," I grumbled at Ryder's pat on my ass to move me over toward the bunk. The transport rocked a bit and shifted us on our feet. "Fine. I'll sit down."

The transport's environmental systems were working hard to cool the air inside of the centipede. After a couple of cold blasts across of my abdomen from a nearby vent, I shouted to Cari to ease back on the temperature. She complied with a rumble of profanity, but the chill dropped quickly... or least it did from the air system. Kerrick still looked as though he were encased in a block of ice.

"This would be better done on a chair where you could straddle it while I work, but this will have to do." Ryder braced himself against the wall, clutching the medical kit he'd retrieved from one of the holds. "I also would like to do this without moving."

"We've already blown off a couple of hours dealing with Mink's eggs. I'd like to get us farther into the quadrant before we break for the night." I positioned myself on the corner of a free-floating bunk and hooked my legs on either side of the frame. There was nothing to lean forward on, and Ryder would have to bend over while he sat on the opposite bunk to work on me, but it was the best we could do.

"There's a suction stool in that bottom drawer by your right foot, Kai." Cari glanced back at me. "Ryder can sit on that, maybe?"

"I'll get that. I would like to be able to be closer while I work on you." Ryder handed me the kit. "Especially if I'm going to have to dig this fabric out. You heal too quickly, Kai. Even for an elfin, it's too fast."

"Well, next time you see Tanic, tell him. So he knows for the next time he tries to grow another kid." Ryder winced with the sting in my voice, and I sighed, knowing he hadn't meant to be an asshole. "If you want to punch him in the face instead, I'm good with that too."

Tanic probably tinkered with my healing ability early on, ensuring I could take anything he dished out. I'd survived everything he'd done to me. Sure, I'd passed out from shock and blood loss along the way, but I kept ticking, coming back from horrors I refused to let my mind scrape up to the surface. The animalistic state Dempsey found me in was at least good for suppressing the memories of my time with Tanic. The less I recalled of my father's exploratory endeavors, the healthier my life would be.

But now it looked as though Kerrick was more than happy to dredge it all back up again.

"Sebac told me you were a chimera, something she hadn't seen before, but I wasn't told of your lineage." Kerrick's voice was flat, but it held the metallic taste of outrage and long-held prejudice. Or maybe I was just hearing what I expected to hear. He cleared his throat and continued, "Explain something to me, cousin. Do you not have concerns about taking the progeny of the Wild Hunt Master into your bed? Into your court?"

I could see Kerrick reflected in the glass to my right. Cari had shut down the floods on the roof of the centipede, but she left the lights on in the cabin so we could see what we were doing. Ryder clamped the stool to the transport's floor and tested it with a jiggle. For a moment I thought he was going to ignore Kerrick, especially when he made himself comfortable on the stool and arranged the medical kit on the bed next to my left leg.

Then Ryder spoke very softly, nearly in a whisper, but I knew him well enough to hear the steel cage he'd soldered around his anger. Maybe Kerrick knew him that well too, because he stiffened as soon as Ryder began to talk.

"I do not yet have the enormous honor and pleasure of having Kai in my bed. And on the day that I do, cousin, it will not be the Wild Hunt Master's son I hold against me but the man who risks his life time and time again so our people may live." Ryder drew out a scissors and a few scalpels from the kit and held the instruments out to me. "Can you open the scalpels, please? I'm going to use scissors to cut off as much of the fabric as I can, and then I'll see if I can tease the rest out."

"I don't care if you slice the bits out of me." I snuck a look at Kerrick from under my arm. "Just… we have to burn anything with my blood on it. I don't want Chuckles over there to use any of me to call up Tiamat while none of us are looking."

Kerrick nearly shot up out of his chair, but Ryder laughed, his breath warm on my spine. "Don't be silly, Kai. Everyone knows Tiamat only responds to sacrifices involving hot dogs and gummy bears. I believe one of Jonas's little girls told me that. And seeing as she's a devoted follower of our five-headed goddess, I feel she speaks with authority on the matter."

"Really?" I laughed. Pretty hard too. I never thought I would see the day when Ryder would not only make a joke but make one about dragons and elfin religion. "Paula's only seven. You going to take religious advice from someone who still drinks pretend tea from a plastic cup while surrounded by an ocean of stuffed animals in chairs?"

"I beg for you to take this seriously, cousin," Kerrick spat out. The transport jerked to the side, and Cari let out a halfhearted apology, but Kerrick acted as though we were cruising smoothly over one of San Diego's freeways. "I now understand why Grandmother is so concerned about this court. It is one thing to take in Unsidhe, but it is quite another to embrace the bloodline of one of the most evil clans ever to emerge from the Dusk Court. Tanic cuid Anbhás is the Lord Master of the Wild Hunt. He is a monster who creates other monsters, including the one you are now—"

"Be very careful about your words, *cousin*." Ryder stopped snipping away at the fabric stuck to my back and turned to face Kerrick. I watched their faces in the glass. Its smoky opaqueness blurred their features, but it was clear enough to make out the battle they waged with fierce expressions and tight body language. "Kai is not only someone I wish to have by my side as a lover but also as a friend and companion. Yes, his blood speaks to me with a fire that I haven't felt from anyone before. He may be mostly feral and too human for your liking, but he is my friend. And I will always rise to his call, because he comes to me when I ask for help.

"He has proven to be more loyal to me in the past year that I've known him than any of my own people have been through the centuries that I lived in our courts. You call me cousin because that's our connection—a thread woven in blood only. You speak against Kai, who sits here and waits for me to cut into him because of injuries he sustained defending my life." Ryder shifted on the stool, turned his back to Kerrick, and lifted up a piece of fabric from my back, the tug on my skin sharp but brief. "Your words are filth, cousin. They're nothing but old rotten eggs from an impotent clutch. You may try to challenge me over the court, and I won't fight the land's decision should it respond to you. But hear me, if you speak or move against Kai in any way, it will be my knife you should fear, not his."

"THIS SHIRT has tiny unicorns on it. Why?" The offending shirt was comfortable, but the mockery of a line of flowing-maned horses with golden horns sprouting out of their foreheads prancing across my chest was almost too much to deal with. "Do you have any idea how much of an asshole a unicorn is? Seriously, I'd sooner face a dragon with a sore tooth and indigestion from eating a nightmare than deal with a unicorn."

"It was a present. From Cari's mother," Ryder replied. "Besides, I was not the one who placed an open container of fruit punch on your duffel bag. You needed something to wear, and that is what I had. Unless you would rather wear something of Cari's. I wouldn't mind staring at your belly while you drove, or your back either. At least that way I can make sure you don't pick the dermafilm off before your injuries are fully healed."

"Yeah, well, we've got fresh water, so I'm going to see if I can rinse out something. I don't want to use the transport's power cells to wash my clothes. We've still got a couple of days to go underground." I eyed the large pond we'd found tucked into a side cavern off the main chamber. "Bad enough we used a big chunk of juice to scan the cave. I don't want to waste our energy on stupid things. We might need it later."

When we scanned the cave and shallow pond for any type of thermal signature and determined it was free of anything that would come up and eat our faces, parking the transport seemed like a good idea. Steam vents and hot springs made scanning difficult, but where we were was chilly, especially compared to the cave of the bearded flyer nest. That place lit up like fireworks, while this pocket of darkness left off tiny twinkles of sparks in the water and darting blurs that we could see were small fish.

I just really didn't look forward to rinsing out my citrus-scented shirts in an ice-cold pond.

"I'll do that really quickly so we can lock down inside the transport." Cari had the interior lights on, a soft glow bright enough for me to see by. We pushed through the main chamber, a gray stretch of moist rock with the occasional flurry of bats and midnight butterflies that swooped in to investigate the moving lights. "I'll be fast. How about if you guys pull out some of the self-heating rations so we can eat when I come back?"

"I don't like leaving you out here by yourself," Ryder grumbled. "I know you say it's safe, but every time we stop to take a breath, something happens."

"Promise you, nothing's going to happen. Chances are we took out the biggest predator down here a few caverns back. It'll be some time before something else moves in." I hefted the tote with my soiled shirts. "Now, may I go take care of this? Because I refuse to spend the next couple of days wearing unicorns."

"You just want out of that shirt because it smells like me," Ryder responded, giving me a sly smile. "And it bothers you that you like it."

"Yeah, keep telling yourself that, Skippy." I shoved at his shoulder and pushed him toward the transport. "Just someone try to come and save me if I'm wrong and there is a nine-foot-long alligator living in that pond."

The water was damned cold, but I pushed my way through the icy grip that settled over my skin. Rinsing my shirts out required little effort, but it took a while until I couldn't smell the juice on any of them anymore. Behind me the sounds of Cari bossing about two Sidhe lords kept me entertained, and by the time I got around to wringing out my first T-shirt, my teeth were chattering. I hunkered down and was shaking my hands out to get the feeling back into my fingertips when Kerrick joined me.

"I owe you an apology, Stalker Gracen." He loomed up behind me, and his shadow fell on the water. The bioluminescent prawns living beneath the surface scattered, minuscule dandelion flecks of light rippling around the uneven floor of the pond. "We have, as they say, gotten off on the wrong foot."

"I know exactly what foot I got off on, and it wasn't the wrong one." I bravely picked up another shirt, only to find that one as sopping wet as the first. Gritting my teeth, I began to roll it up and braced for the bite of cold against my skin. "You want to take over the Southern Rise Court, and I don't want you to. Pretty simple. I don't see how we're going to get over that."

"There was a time not long ago when you did not want my cousin Ryder to take over the court." He settled down on the floor a few feet away from me. I caught the wince when his ass touched the cold stone, but he braved it out. "In fact, you didn't want him here at all. Perhaps you'll have the same change of heart with me."

"I doubt it, because *you* are your grandmother's creature." I twisted the fabric and hissed at the pour of water over my hands, but it would take several tries before I could dry it in the transport. "Which is funny because you think I'm my father's puppet and I've somehow ingratiated myself into Ryder's court so I can eventually betray him."

"And my grandmother said that your intelligence was little more than a dog's." Kerrick's laugh was as cold as the water on my skin. "She is losing her grip on our clan. There have been too many changes and too many power shifts for her to control. Some of her ideas I agree with. I will not lie to you about that, but I disagree with her methods. I came to the Southern Rise Court for the same reason Ryder did. It's a central node of power that one of us can shape into a political dynasty—one outside of her influence."

"I don't care why you came down here," I replied. "I only care about how quickly you're going to leave."

"There are people in Elfhaine who believe Ryder is insane for challenging our grandmother, but they're blind to how the world is evolving. Do we need to learn to live with the humans? I cannot say we agree on that, but I do empathize with Ryder's insistence that we increase our numbers." He shifted, probably trying to ease the cold that was eating through the seat of his pants. "I understand why he believes you're vital to his court. And he is right that we must make peace with the Unsidhe, because our races must find common ground before the humans overwhelm us.

"While you are proof that it's possible for the elfin bloods to be combined, your existence is not sustainable. Or rather your creation is not. I do not bear ill will against the Unsidhe. In fact, I don't believe we can survive if we don't mingle our courts. That is why San Diego is so vital. That is why I wanted to come on this run. I need to hear for myself how the Dusk Court below the border would react to pledging fealty to me." He shook his head at my snort of laughter. "This woman we're rescuing is bringing three children with her. *Three*. That number is incredible now, when once we could easily have had fifty to a hundred children in Elfhaine at one time. The Unsidhe are fertile and increasingly birthing Sidhe offspring from a mixed coupling. They're an answer to our biggest problem and one Ryder is not willing to entertain."

"That's where you're wrong, because I know for fact he welcomes everybody into his court, regardless of what kind of elfin they are. The Dusk Court down in Tijuana has been a vicious cesspool of murder and kidnapping for as long as they've been down there. I've been on raids to rescue human children because the Unsidhe down there collect them as pets." I worked on another shirt, suddenly not feeling the cold. "They put out bounties for kids with certain eye or hair color like someone getting the pick of a litter. Now I'm going to point out something that Duffy never questioned. Those three kids that woman is bringing up might not even *be* elfin, so if I were you, I would hold off on your plans about conscripting the Unsidhe. As another saying goes, don't go counting your chickens until they're hatched."

Kerrick studied me while I worked through the shirts. As I wrung out the last one until no more water could be squeezed out, he sighed. "It pains me to admit that you thought of something I have not considered. This little discussion of ours has drastically altered my view of you."

I held my hands up, my wrinkled fingers now light blue. "Probably because I'm changing colors as we speak. I'm about to head back. Do you have anything else to say that I should *really* listen to?"

"I understand now—truly understand—what Ryder sees in you. You have a strategic but angled way of looking at things. You come at problems in ways that none of us anticipate or even dream of. I now know why he values you so much, and not just because you're beautiful."

He smiled in a way I'd grown used to seeing Ryder smile at me. My hands weren't the only cold thing on me, because the chill that ran up my spine could've made ice cream. Kerrick stood with a graceful flow of Sidhe arrogance, but his smile never warmed.

"I look forward to the day I make you *mine*."

Fourteen

I SPENT the first hour of my watch pacing the perimeter of our camp. Avoiding Kerrick seemed the best way to keep him alive, especially since he'd stalked off away from the pond with a righteous stomp. Dinner was a hastily gulped down Italian-style hero and potato chips Cari had stuffed into the space by the cooling unit Sparky told us about. It was her surprise dinner, something she thought we would enjoy on our first night. It was good—greasy and full of cheese and a few hot peppers. Ryder ate it in layers, because he's a freak that way and likes to take things apart the first time he eats something. Kerrick sniffed at it and then chowed down as though he were suffering through the experience.

It was very difficult not to laugh when the pepper seeds hit the back of his throat. There are times when my sense of humor is on a par with Jonas's youngest child, who thought flaming bags of dog poop were the best thing in the world. Ryder passed him a bottle of water and kicked me in the foot when he went by.

Sure, I could have told Ryder that water would only make it worse, but why would I spoil my fun?

I'd spent a little energy topping off the water tanks from what was in the pond and running it through the transport's filtration system. We hadn't used much of anything, but it was always good to grab resources as we went. After everyone settled in, I dimmed the lights inside, leaving the main cabin door open but rolling down the screen to keep any bugs from flying in. I took one of the suction stools with me and attached it to the cave floor a few feet away from the door, close enough so I could lean on one of the centipede's enormous tires.

With the lights mostly off, the cavern came back to life as its glowing subterranean creatures reemerged from their shelters. The soft glow from the transport's running lights would keep most invasive underground species away, especially the kangaroo rats with their love for electrical wiring, but beyond the reach of the lights, the cave lit up like a field of stars.

There were spots in the world where being underground plunged you into a black so pitch-dark it felt as though your breath lightened it every time you exhaled. San Diego's caverns were a far cry from that kind of stygian depths. Some chambers were open to the sky, while others had natural chimney shafts punching through their ceilings, letting in air and sunlight. This cave had no opening, but the creatures living in its cracks and crevices more than made up for it as they spread out a tiny galaxy around me. Grateful for the quiet, I opened the tumbler of hot coffee I'd brought out with me and settled in for a quiet two-and-a-half-hour stretch.

A few minutes later, the screen door opened and Ryder stepped out of the transport carrying another stool. He'd changed into the unicorn shirt I'd discarded and a motorcycle jacket he'd scrounged out of my closet once. I let him. It was too small for me, and at least this way the thick leather would prevent road rash if he somehow fell out of a moving vehicle. His hair was still damp from the quick shower he'd taken earlier, but the gold in its strands was hard to mute. Their metallic sheen was brilliant, even under the cave dwellers' soft, inconsistent lights.

He locked down the legs of the stool, settled in next to me, leaned back against the solid side of the centipede, and then held his hand out for my cup. "Tell me that's coffee and you're willing to share a sip?" His mouth quirked to one side. "Unless it's whiskey, which would surprise me because you are on watch, but I would understand, considering the day you've had."

"Coffee. Sadly, no whiskey, because yeah, no one's going to die while I'm on a run because I couldn't take a few bruises or deal with your asshole cousin." I handed him my coffee and grinned when the potent brew left him with a grimace. "Careful. This late at night? I like it strong."

"That could grow hair on a Sidhe. Gods, no wonder you're foul tempered," he coughed out, but he took another tentative sip before he handed it back. "And once again, I must apologize for my… asshole cousin."

"How he acts doesn't rub off on you." I shrugged. "Because if I were going to think like that, your grandmother would have stained you something fierce."

"True, Grandmother's much worse than Kerrick." He shifted on his seat and glanced at me from under his long lashes. Then he dug into the pockets of his jacket and pulled out two long, flat rectangles with a glint of silver at their edges. "I have something for you. Here. I was going to save this for later, but I think after today, you probably need this more than you need a shot of whiskey."

I wondered sometimes if he truly understood me. Most often Ryder heard me, but his head seemed to be at a constant quizzical tilt, so I was never sure if anything I said or anything I did sank in. The fragrant foil-wrapped rectangle he held out to me proved me wrong in so many ways.

It was *chocolate*.

Not only was it chocolate, but it was the kind of chocolate I love most of all, a demi-bittersweet mixed with a silky milk and crackled through with macadamia-nut bits. There was no wrapper, just *foil*. And when I unfolded it, the bar was thick but uneven, scored every inch or so to make it easier to break apart. I snapped off an inch, put it on the tip of my tongue, and closed my eyes at the glorious sweetness spreading through my mouth.

It was *perfect*. The balance between the salty, savory nuts and the sweet bitterness of the chocolate made me purr. I took my time sucking on the tidbit I'd stuck in my mouth, aching for another taste but wanting to make the bar last. In the stillness of the cavern, I could hear Ryder opening the foil on his bar and then the snap as he broke off a large chunk.

I was stingy when I ate chocolate. Jonas used to tease me about it. Hell, he still did. Dempsey once raided one of the few Halloween stashes I'd ever had—ill-gotten booty because I could fake being human one night every year and knock on doors to get candy. It took Jonas, Cari's father, and a couple of his sons to get me off of Dempsey and take away the knife I pulled on them.

Needless to say, he never touched a piece of my chocolate ever again.

I was glad Ryder had brought his own, because I didn't want to share. It was *that* good.

"Where did you get this? And can I lock whoever made it into a bathroom so I can keep them prisoner like Rumpelstiltskin did with that girl and the spinning wheel?" I opened my eyes when Ryder laughed. "What?"

"I made it. And while I would not mind being locked in your bathroom, it would make running the court very difficult. I suppose people could shout at me from under the door, but our nieces would probably eventually need raising. I could leave that to you." He laughed again at my horrified expression. "I'm glad you like it. I wanted to do something special for you, something maybe no one else has done? Or at least no other Sidhe has done."

To say I was speechless would've been an understatement. I was gobsmacked, not because the idea of Ryder standing in a kitchen concocting chocolate seemed ludicrous, but at the idea that he would make something so specifically for me. I didn't know what to say. "Thank you" seemed trite, even though most people would think what he did was nothing because it was just chocolate.

For me, there was no such thing as *just* chocolate.

"Go raibh maith agat," I murmured, my Sidhe heavily accented by Dempsey's Irish. There were many regionally shared words between the elfin and human languages, but the Emerald Isle seemed to anchor itself in my people's native tongue. *Thank you* was one of those phrases, firmly entrenched in a Gaelic laden with peat bogs and fairy tales. "This means a lot to me."

"It was fun to make. I couldn't get it as pretty as the chef did, but I think I got the flavors right." He folded the foil back over his bar and shoved it into my jacket pocket. "You keep this one too. I just wanted to make sure it tasted okay, or I would've had to risk a fatal injury and smack it out of your hand before you could eat it."

"I like how you think that throwing it on the floor would somehow prevent me from eating chocolate," I retorted. "I'm not too proud to admit I've sucked up chocolate pudding that had fallen out of a cup and onto the kitchen floor. It's chocolate. And honestly, my favorite kind."

"I remember Cari describing your face when you had a truffle made from this kind of chocolate, so I wanted to see if I could recreate it for you." He was close enough to lean against me, and when he did, his weight against my shoulder wasn't that bad. "I wanted to say thank you for everything that you've done. Not just for the court or even for the girls. But today, when you trusted me enough to cut the fabric out of you, I realized how much of a gift your friendship is to me. Because, my dear chimera, if someone had done to me what your father did to you, I wouldn't let an elfin near me with a blade for the rest of my life."

Shit.

I'd let Ryder cut into me.

I not only let him, I unwrapped the scalpels for him.

I should have been freaking out. The panic and the fear of an elfin carving into me, even being that close to my blood and flesh with a sharp object, should have had me bristling with violence. But I'd straddled that bunk and leaned forward, hissing when the blade went deep and refusing any numbing medication because I wouldn't be able to feel if there was anything left under my skin, and we would have to slice back into me again later if we didn't get it all out.

Ryder.

He'd slithered past my defenses, charmed me by being an asshole and butting heads with me whenever I told him no. And I told him no a lot. Apparently there were also a few yeses in there as well.

I *liked* the bastard. That was a dangerous thing to do, but if someone had asked me in the morning if I trusted Ryder, I would have said it would depend upon the situation. Obviously I was lying to myself, because I'd let him bleed me and would probably let him again.

"Well, *fuck*. I didn't even think about it," I admitted softly. Then I scraped my teeth against another tidbit of the bar. "I don't even know what to think now."

At that point my sanity was fragile. Everything that I was tilted and made room for Ryder in my consciousness, every bit of me screaming to shove him away, but the stupider piece of my brain kept circling back to the chocolate and his gentle touch as he peeled back my skin to work the T-shirt fragments out without causing me pain.

"I didn't notice myself. It was just natural. You needed help, and I wanted to be there for you, to help you out of the pain. I know Cari is sometimes clumsy with delicate work, so I didn't want her to touch you. I didn't want her to hurt you, even though I know you love her." Ryder chuckled. "And it wasn't as though I was going to let Kerrick near you. I didn't think about how easy it was, how stoic and firm you felt beneath my fingertips. You *trusted* me. It came to me afterward, while we were eating dinner and you smirked when I kicked your foot for laughing at Kerrick.

"He doesn't understand how I feel about you. He sees you as an asset and a resource." Ryder gave me a rueful expression. "I will admit to thinking about you that way when I first met you. You were a piece of society's puzzle that I could fit into the court and perhaps make it easier for us to interact with the humans. Then, as I got to know you, I realized that your unique nature makes it impossible for you to interact with practically anybody. And I think, Kai, that's what I love about you the most. Because, my chimera, I find myself thinking about you with great affection despite how much you exasperate me."

"Since we're laying all of our cards out on the table," I said, saluting him with my coffee cup, "I apparently don't hate you either."

"What amazes me and intrigues me about you is how close you are to the dragon that we've come from," Ryder murmured.

"Well, Tanic did use a dragon egg in his stew when making me." I fingered the spot on my neck where the black pearl dragon had slid a scale beneath my skin. "But I thought that was mostly to bind the incompatible elfin genetics. Maybe it left its mark."

"It's more than the egg. You are what our races need. And maybe even what we once were. You're stronger in a lot of ways, and your mind is nimble. You leap to conclusions we never think about. You're a leader who leads by action and wisdom—your own kind of wisdom, but still astute and perceptive." Ryder eased my tumbler out of my hand to take a sip. "People follow you through fires and destruction because they know instinctively that you will fight for them to survive. You're not a ruler of a court, and I am sure the thought of trying to mediate arguments or stabilize an infrastructure would be one of your worst nightmares. Yet still I would turn to you for your opinion, because you see things I do not."

"I think the problem with the Sidhe—and maybe even the Unsidhe—is that you drifted too far from having to live in a world that would tear you apart if given half the chance. Sometimes the best way to know you're alive is to come close to death. You guys mute everything. You don't laugh too loud. You don't drink too much. You don't eat till you want to puke and then find room for another spoonful of ice cream." I nodded at the coffee he held in his hand. "It wasn't until you had to face an army of humans that you experienced loss and fear. See, that's all I'd ever known. So maybe that's why I look at things differently. And I can tell you one thing—I sure as hell wouldn't be able to do what you do. Just the thought of everyone coming to me to solve all their problems gives me hives."

"It's easier than you think," he countered. "For the most part, people just want you to reaffirm the decision they've already made. Or, sometimes, guide them away from a very stupid mistake. But in the end, it's always their choice. The court makes demands on all of us. My duty is to provide them with a safe home and a prosperity they would not find elsewhere. Most of the Sidhe who have followed me down to San Diego are those who don't fit well into the structure of other courts. In a lot of ways, we are misfits, just like you."

"Just make sure they learn to think for themselves along the way," I cautioned. "I think that's how corruption of power happens—when someone controls choices and feeds people dogma instead of solutions. You don't get strong by going the easy way. There's got to be challenges. You've got to know what it's like for life to kick you in the teeth every once in a while, so when it kicks you in the balls, you already know what pain feels like. That way you're not surprised."

"Probably," Ryder agreed. "But—and you might hate me for saying this—there is also a lot of your father in you."

"Now you're just being mean," I shot back.

"Hear me out."

He took another sip and then handed it back. I could taste Ryder on the edge of the tumbler when I drank my coffee, but his familiar essence did nothing to calm the frisson of alarm his words sent through me.

"When I first came here and saw you, I believed you would eventually become a working member of my court and leave your human ties behind."

"I think that was maybe the first time I told you to fuck off." I grinned to let him know I wasn't ruffled by his arrogance.

"It was in a way. You are feral, cynical, and possess the biggest heart of anyone I have ever met," he said, reaching over to squeeze my hand. "The duality of your personality and soul perplexed me until I discovered where you came from, who your father is. When I look at you now, I see your wildness and the need to be free. You truly *are* the closest to our dragon blood. You are a Stalker, not just because that's how you defend your society, but also because you were born to hunt. It's in you as strongly as anything Dempsey taught you or what Jonas gentled in your fierce nature.

"Despite everything done to you, you hunt for the greater good. You take a gift given to you and don't use it in the ways others have in the past." Ryder bumped my shoulder and smiled at me. "I could no sooner stop you from hunting than I could pull the stars from the skies. I realize that now. No, I embrace that now. That is who you are. That is who you will always be. And I will have to reconcile myself to understanding that I may one day lose you to that greater good, because you cannot and will not be changed. You speak of challenges the Sidhe must endure—no, *conquer*—and you're right. My greatest challenge is not trying to tame you but rather trying to match your passion for life. And I would like you to know that I will meet that challenge. I vow it."

"Well, you took a big step by making me chocolate," I teased as I rested my temple against the top of his head. "We're still going to fight once in a while, you know. Okay, maybe a lot more than once in a while, but I guess today proved I can trust you."

"I can't imagine living my life without fighting with you," Ryder confessed with a low chuckle. "And if all it took for us to have this kind of conversation was a bit of chocolate, I would have bought you a candy store months ago."

"Oh hell no. That kind of shit leads to glass elevators and little men singing songs as you get sucked up a vacuum tube." I laughed and settled my shoulders back against the ridges of the tire. "But if you want to make me the occasional bar with macadamia nuts and maybe chili pepper once in a while, that's totally okay by me."

Fifteen

AFTER ABOUT six hours, I decided I would let Ryder drive. Maybe he slid something into the chocolate. I wouldn't put it past him, but I doubted it. Mostly it was because my hands were tired of gripping the wheel and my shoulders ached from fighting the rough terrain. Cari was catching a couple hours of sleep on the bunk. She strapped herself down and nodded off as though she'd eaten the whole turkey and needed to digest to get room for pie later on. Kerrick was reading up on San Diego history in a long treatise written by some bombastic professor in the Elfin Studies Department. Ryder had made friends with a few of the intellectuals at the university and had been trying to get me to speak at one thing or another for the past couple of months.

I'd taken jobs every time he brought it up. Sure, Dalia was probably sick of watching Newt, but I didn't have to stand in front of a bunch of privileged kids who stared at me like I was a frog they wanted to dissect. It was good for my savings account but hell on my friendships. He didn't necessarily wheedle or nag me, but there was definitely disappointment in his eyes. He brought it up once again when we were about ten minutes away from the second large chamber, so I offered to let him drive.

All conversation about me speaking at the university was dropped, and I put the centipede in Park to switch chairs with him. *That* got Kerrick's attention.

"Are you sure that is wise?" our spare Sidhe lordling drawled from behind us. "He can't even ride a horse."

"Really?" I slid back between the two seats to let Ryder slide over. "Luckily, this isn't a horse."

"I can ride a horse just fine," Ryder replied as he settled into the driver's seat. "You put me on a pooka when I was just ten. I could have been able to ride with the Wild Hunt and not control that beast. If anything, you should be grateful I didn't tell my parents exactly how I ended up almost drowned in a reed-filled pond."

"Right up until now, I really doubted the two of you were related." I snapped the latch on the seat belt and buckled myself in. "But you guys argue like Jonas's kids do."

"Anything to keep you entertained." Ryder carefully eased the centipede into first gear, pressing down tightly on the brakes. I'd given him a quick rundown of automatic shifting but thought it would be a good idea to run him through the gears before we got into rougher terrain. "I appreciate your trust in me, letting me do this."

"The more kinds of shit you know how to drive, the more often I can take a nap in the back," I confessed. "Just go slowly and follow the tracks on the screen. It'll tell you where we need to head and if the ground is stable enough to take this kind of weight. Mink might be a pain in the ass sometimes, but he knows how to map and always tests for stability. That's why his patches cost so damned much."

The centipede was pretty easy to drive, and when we punched in the calibrated map diagrams, the drive system laid out a green line on the main screen for us to follow. Sparky had built in beam indicators around the front of the vehicle, a handy thing to have underground, especially since the dim light projected out to the end of our safe zone. It was kind of like training wheels for a new driver or a visual guide for tight passes. But all of it depended upon how accurate the map was, and this route was going to be virgin territory because no one except for Mink—that I knew of—had ever tracked a clear path through the third quadrant from San Diego to the outer regions.

"Just be sure you keep an eye on the ground in front of us. We're probably not the only ones down here, and this thing can roll over practically everything." I settled back in the chair, mourning the fact I'd left my chocolate stashed away in my duffel bag. But it was considered rude to eat in front of somebody, and I didn't want to share. "Do you see that bend? You're just going to turn slowly to the left. The back end takes a while to follow, so you'll want to straighten out quickly to bring it all back in line."

"It vibrates through you," Ryder murmured as he eased into the curve in the passageway. "I would imagine after a few hours, your muscles would ache."

"Just go slow and try to keep the bumps down to a minimum. Then you'll be okay," I reassured him.

It felt good not to drive, and more importantly, sitting in the passenger seat gave me a chance to watch Ryder's face when we entered the second large chamber. Until that point in the connecting caverns of the third quadrant, the rock ran to a dull beige or gray, often wet… with water or other things I never truly investigated. While I'd been through quite a few of the side passages in the area, hunting one thing or another for a museum or collector, I always made sure to stop and marvel at the chambers.

The small cave we'd spent the night in was a child's broken-down planetarium projector compared to what Ryder was about to experience for the first time. His gasp of wonder did not disappoint, and I leaned over to put the transport into Park before he drove us off a cliff or something. Kerrick murmured, either in awe or maybe in envy of the glorious display. It didn't matter as long as he was quiet while Ryder communed with the beauty around us.

"Can we get out?" He glanced at me and then ducked his head down to peer out of the windshield. "Do you mind? I know it takes time off of our—"

"Could you just get out already?" I swung my door open. "We made good time today, but I'd like to get through this area and over to a spot that Mink marked with usable water. I give you one hour. After that, we're back on the road."

Our boots crunched through the tiny rocks that littered the cavern floor. The second chamber was bisected with a natural road that curved through the enormous space that stretched up above us to the sky. Deep gulches dropped off on either side of the one-hundred-yard-wide mesa, and the cave ceiling was open in several areas above the flat expanse, letting in streams of watery afternoon sunlight. The rays were diffused by nearly translucent cave kelp, and their crystalline threads cast out rainbow sparks to dance across the sheer red-rock walls of the cavern.

Wind or water shaped the cave, much like the ribboned canyons in Antelope Valley. The variegated strata glistened crimson and sunset, and the diffused brightness threw its juts and weaves into sharp contrasts of shadow and light. It also exposed the most glorious collection of dragon bones embedded in the beautiful stone of the natural cathedral.

Many were a jumble of shapes that took a moment to understand, but there were a few breathtaking stretches where it was easy to follow the sculpt of a magnificent lizard with its talons out and wings spread behind it, its tail whipped about as though to balance it on its endless flight through timeless rock. There were a couple of smaller skeletons, a bit larger than the average elfin, woven around a column close to the entrance of the chamber, but it was the enormous warlord dragon with its spine curved in nearly a figure eight and its impossibly large wing expanse stretched out on either side of its embedded body that stole Ryder's words.

I knew how he felt. It often stole mine.

"Can you imagine how big that would've been when it was alive?" Ryder whispered as he crossed the flats to get closer to the dragon skeleton bathed in scintillating flecks. "If you get too near it, you can't see all of it."

I tried to see the dragons through their eyes, but I knew I would never truly understand their worship of the beasts who hunted me through Pendle Runs. I had a healthy respect for anything that could outfly a powerful engine and had teeth longer than my body. They made my life difficult, but I loved to watch them fly.

There was a brutal grace to their forms, and whether fighting or mating, a dragon's no-holds-barred way of life called to me. They ran the gamut from ugly to the heartbreakingly beautiful, but what I loved most was their honest, stark existence. Not overly sentimental—hell, most of them hardly ever sat on their eggs to hatch them—they took life and their opponents as they came to them. But my imagination couldn't wrap itself around the existence of lizards the size of the ones captured in the walls of the cavern.

It wasn't hard to see our alleged draconian ancestors in our features and structure. Or at least I could see it in Ryder and Kerrick. I was thicker-bodied than they were—taller and brutish-looking compared to their sleek elegance. It could have been the way they held themselves or maybe even the "how to float on air when you walk" lessons they probably got as kids, but both Sidhe reminded me of the prismatics that glided on the thermals above Pendle's lava fields.

"This place is sacred. No one should be here," Kerrick finally whispered. When his awe took the edge off his arrogant tone, his Singlish failed him, and

he reverted to Sidhe—a burbling, potent string of ven-
eration mixed with wonder. I didn't understand all of
it, but it sounded like a prayer, a plea for his soul to be
lifted and his troubles calmed.

Yeah, we all want that, but I'm not praying to a
wall of dragon skeletons hoping to get it.

"It's a protected area, and, well, you can't get
down to the bones. Cliffs are too sheer, and the rock's
too hard to punch into, so coming down from the top
is practically impossible." I pointed up at the ceiling
as a rush of air from the natural skylights sent the cave
kelp into a gentle sway and started a faint concerto
of harpsichord chimes through the chamber. "It's not
like you can get any heavy equipment down here, or at
least not without someone noticing. People have tried
a lot of things, and those gulches go down forever. No
one's all that interested in retrieving their bodies."

"You have, as always, a very morbid way of looking at things." Ryder spared me a quick glance. "How
much time do we have? I'd like to walk a bit."

"Maybe half an hour." I checked my link. "The
encampment spot's a bit of a hard ride down the pass,
so get what sunlight you can now. We're going to be
heading into the dark after this."

Ryder slid his hand under my jacket and rested
it against the small of my back but didn't pull his
gaze from the cavern walls. His breathing fell into the
kelps' sweet-ringing melody, and despite the fabric of
my T-shirt, I felt his pulse slow through the press of
his palm.

"Thank you for this, Kai. We'll have to come
here again some time when there is nothing tugging
us along." He sucked in his breath as a flock of birds

broke through the kelp to shoot across the cavern and exit out another opening moments later. "I will make you chocolate every month, enough so you don't have to hoard it."

"Hell, hoarding's half the fun." I chuckled. "Go take your walk, lordling. I'll be here when you get back."

WE EMERGED from the caverns a day and a half later, desperate for sunlight and fresh air. It'd been a hard push to get to the open prairies, but I was grateful for the long hours of driving and short sleep shifts. The Sidhe fell to the darkness first, or that could have just been Ryder and Kerrick rubbing against each other wrong. Cari spent a lot of time napping when she wasn't driving, and I took the longer hauls, listening to the books she'd loaded into the system.

That's when Kerrick discovered how explicit sex scenes got in romance books.

The constant dark wore us down, and the natural lamp lights could only do so much. I purposely chose smaller alcoves to park the centipede and illuminated the camping niches as much as possible to defray the agitation that was growing among us, but the ceilings and walls of the caverns pushed down on us constantly. It was oppressive, driving deep into the bowels of the earth and then slowly climbing back up toward the surface.

Ryder and I spent the first shift mostly sitting quietly, thankful for the running lights and the occasional creature that skittered just outside of the illumination range. We grew quieter with each passing hour until it seemed as though we would forget how to speak.

Then the words would rush out of us when someone broke the silence—anything to create a ripple in the tightness that sealed us in.

We'd drowned in the shadows for so long that Cari broke into song when we rolled out into the late afternoon sunlight. I didn't blame her. I would've sung too if I didn't sound like a mostly thawed-out seagull being torn in half with a rusty chainsaw.

It took me a little while to orientate myself on where we came out, so I parked the centipede and opened the doors so the fresh air could wash over us. We were miles from the canyons where we would meet this Unsidhe whose name no one seemed to know, but we had firm coordinates, and unless there were hordes of women fleeing the Dusk Court with elfin children at that exact spot, I thought we would recognize her.

"What are you doing?" Kerrick stood up in the cabin behind me but bent over slightly to study the screen on the dashboard. "Do you know where we are?"

"Theoretically, yes. I've made a lot of runs down in this area, but it's constantly changing, and I've never come out of that gulch before, so it's going to take me a while to pinpoint in my mind where we are." I shot a quick look at Cari, who was about to leap out of the centipede. "Hey! I'm going to turn up the light-sensor sweep, but it's going to be dim because of the sun. Ground here is kind of shaky. I don't want you wandering off. There's a lot of pockets of caves and tunnels beneath us, so give me a few minutes to plot out a solid course. Then we can head to a campsite I know about nearby."

"Does this campsite have hot and cold running water? Or better yet, a margarita bar?" She pursed her lips at me.

"Funny you should say that, because there is a hot spring, and it's drinkable once you let it cool off." I shrugged and wiggled my hand back and forth. "It'll have to go through the filters, but we can top off there. I want to start moving in fifteen minutes. If we get there while it's still light, maybe I can snag us some fresh meat."

"Now that's the best idea you've had *ever*." Cari grinned at me. "I don't want to go far. I just want to stretch my legs and drink in some air that doesn't smell like boy."

"I happen to like how some of the boys smell," Ryder teased her as he opened the passenger door. "Or at least one of them. I'll join you on your stretch, but I agree, not eating rations would be heavenly."

We'd come out on the rolling prairies, stretches of hillocks and small mounds covered with fragrant seeded tall grasses and pockets of cotton-candy-colored bushes. It was late enough in the season for the herds of bison and antelope to have migrated through, leaving vast swaths of cropped vegetation in their wake. On a rise a mile or so in front of us, a tower of spotted giraffes kept company with a dazzle of zebra, their long necks sticking up out of a scrub-brush stand frilled with black-and-white-striped equines. I didn't realize how far the escaped wild animals had strayed from the defunct safari park in Escondido.

"I fought a battle near here." Kerrick slid into the seat Ryder had abandoned moments before. His eyes were hooded and troubled, his handsome face a mask of hard porcelain. His attention was focused on memories instead of the landscape outside. I'd seen that look on a thousand faces, usually on veterans nursing a drink in a dive bar where they paid for cheap beer with a few coins and a part of their liver. "The spot… in Underhill… was where my father and I would capture wild horses—our kind of horses, not Earth's—and spend the season gentling them. I wonder if the outpost we used is here or if it was swallowed up in the Merge."

"Well, you and your dad can take a trip out here and check," I suggested. We'd come to a détente of sorts. Mostly we avoided talking to one another, and I tried not to stab him out of respect for Ryder's wishes. He'd toned down the imperious proclamations about half a day after we left the dragon chamber, but every once in a while, he would say something to get on my nerves, and I would have to take a deep breath. "Just be sure you get a good mapping system, because the ground is unstable in places."

"My father and I will not be doing anything together. He did not… he was not among the elfin who…." Kerrick huffed out a sharp hiss and twisted his mouth into a mocking smile. "He is not on the side of the Merge. He and one of my mothers were traveling to Auberdain—that is San Francisco here—but they are like many people who are unaccounted for. Perhaps there is a world where I am missing from their family. Just as Alexa is… and her daughter."

"I guess I never thought about those losses," I admitted, my focus shifting from the map plotting to the Sidhe lord sitting next to me. Of course families were torn apart when the worlds intersected that day. The confusion and chaos of the sudden shift of land was something I couldn't imagine. I'd seen footage, but the tremors were the only warning each side got before the world unfolded and then filled in with massive amounts of elfin landscapes and cities. It was over in a matter of minutes, but it brought a cataclysmic change no one seemed to have recovered from. "I'm sorry about your dad. No matter what, it's shitty when family is taken away from you. I didn't have family until Dempsey, and while he's definitely not the most prizewinning pig at the county fair, I'm kind of used to him being a part of my life."

"Dempsey is the human who won you, yes?" He cocked his head and bit his lower lip. "Alexa told me a bit of the story, but she didn't have a lot of details."

"There's not much detail to tell. Dempsey doesn't remember most of it, but that's not that unusual with him." The map glitched, and I tapped the screen again to work out a different route. "Dempsey was three sheets to the wind, and an Unsidhe guard put me up on the table as part of the pot. Even drunk off of his ass, Dempsey can play cards, so next thing he knew, he was stuck with me."

"That is what confused me. Where was this guard, and how did he come to have you with him?" Kerrick eyed me in a way people normally reserved for selecting lobsters out of the tank or choosing which dog to bet on in a race. "You were mostly uncivilized, and from the little I know of *what* you are, I can't imagine Tanic letting you slip out from between his fingers. Not that I know the Lord Master of the Hunt personally, but his reputation precedes him. He is as disciplined as he is cruel. Didn't you ever ask?"

"No one to ask. The guard was gone before Dempsey woke up the next morning, and I was chained to one of the metal loops welded on his truck bed to

secure the ainmhi dubh he brought down." I was nearly done with the course and craned my neck around to
see where Ryder and Cari had gone. They were only
a few feet away from the back door of the centipede,
laughing about something—probably the half-grown
zebra colts prancing along the hillside. "If you want
to stretch your legs, you better do it now. I'm almost
done here. Just stay inside of the green-light marker."

"I think I just want to stare at the hills for a while."
Kerrick reached behind me to grab the long coat he'd
left on his seat. It was elaborately embroidered and
typically Sidhe, much more formal than anyone needed to be out in the middle of the prairies, but it'd taken
Ryder a long time to change how *he* dressed, and he
still favored his fancy trousers over a pair of jeans. "I
will try not to wander too far."

"Try not to wander at all," I muttered, mostly to
myself, as he stepped out of the cab and walked toward a nearby clump of bushes. "I don't want to be
chasing any of you around the place. I still got to find
us something for dinner."

Most of my attention was on the screen... like
nearly all of it. At least it was until I heard the cracking of the ground. The air filled with plumes of red
dust, and the prairie wind caught the tiny storm flurry
and carried it away. Panicked, I looked up and saw
Ryder and Cari turn around. Then the ground shook,
and Kerrick disappeared.

Sixteen

RED DUST choked me as I sprinted toward the growing crevasse. The grit stung my eyes as I shoved Ryder aside, not wanting him to follow down the rabbit hole after his cousin. I shouted for Cari to get me a climbing rope from the centipede. Then I lay on my stomach and inched toward the still-crumbling opening and hoped he hadn't fallen into a dark pit stories below.

There was enough afternoon light for me to see Kerrick about ten feet down, his fingers bloodied and his arms caked with dirt. His pale face shone nearly as brightly as a star in the darkness as the sun caught on his sharp cheekbones and the glisten of sweat across his temple. He'd grabbed a jut of rock with his right hand while his left had a death grip on a sheaf of grasses still rooted at the lip of the crevasse. His weight was too much for the vegetation, and the grasses were slowly tearing, snapping, and pulling up from the ground.

A hot wind picked up across the rolling hill and sent the grasses into a ruffling whisper. More dirt slid over the edge, creating a light shower of rocks and debris that tumbled over Kerrick's shoulders. The fall had torn his shirt and ripped much of his right sleeve away from his arm. He was more muscular than I would've given him credit for, but Ryder said he'd been a commander in the military. That was decades ago, but his hidden strength would come in handy now because he was going to need every bit of it to hold on to the nearly smooth wall.

"Don't let go." It seemed stupid to say that, but at least Kerrick would know we were going to get him out of there. Whenever I was hanging by my finger-nails on a cliff, it made me feel a hell of a lot better knowing the people I'd been with planned on helping me out. And since Kerrick wasn't one of my favorite people, he might have had a few doubts. "Just give me a couple of minutes."

The damned asshole had gone too far away from the transport, and from what little I remembered of the screen, the ground was riddled with empty spaces and deep gulches. We were way out of the green zone, but shit happens on a run, and sometimes a person's got to learn to follow what they're told… even if that person's a Sidhe lord.

"Shit, I just got the *last* one trained," I muttered to myself. I scooted back a little when the ground began to crumble inward. Then a pocket opened up by my right hand and gave me a good idea on how wide the crenulation was beneath me. "Okay, we've got climbing gear—"

"What do you want me to do?" A long shadow fell across me—a very Ryder-shaped shadow—and I glanced up, looking at his waist. "I can help Cari—"

"No. Give me your belt first." I held my hand out for the leather strap, hoping to give Kerrick a few seconds at the very least. I couldn't see anything beyond the darkness, so I didn't know if the cave below was a simple drop that he would survive or if he would plunge to his death and we would have no way to recover his body. "Then grab the flashlight out of the compartment in front of the passenger seat. We need to see how deep this thing is. Kerrick, can you see anything down there? Can you see the floor?"

"Shifting is a problem." Kerrick grunted between his words as he struggled to stay in place. "There aren't enough holds on this rock face. I can't get my feet wedged."

"Cari! Where the fuck is that gear?" I grabbed at the belt Ryder left by my side and inched closer to the clump of grasses Kerrick dangled from. I wove the leather in and out of the stalks, slowly tightened the belt, and drew them into a solid mass. Testing the belt's integrity with a tug, I glanced back over my shoulder when Ryder returned with the flashlight held out for me to grab. "Put that down and back away. I don't want to risk your weight on this ground. Go to the left over there and grab on to the belt. Hold it as tight as you can. We need to take some of the pressure off the root system, but if you feel it snap, you let go. I do not want both of you to die down there."

"Well, cousin, at least I know for sure where his loyalties lie," Kerrick sniped bitterly from the shadows.

"You should've known that before you decided to go spelunking without any equipment," I shot back as Ryder got into place. "Save your complaining for when we get you out."

Cari jumped out of the transport, her arms filled with climbing gear and a coiled rope as well as a medical kit. She skidded to a stop at my feet, careful not to get too close to the crumbling edge. She set down the kit and began to uncoil the steel-and-nylon-thread rope. "What do you need me to do? I brought out the anchoring kit too."

"Tether one end to the transport with the mini winch while I take a look below. At the very least, clip it first. In case things go bad, I can do a loop and rappel down to grab him. He's up against the cliff face, so at least we know there's solid rock underneath, but we need to get anchored, and I want to see the bottom of that cavern." I grabbed the flashlight, flicked it on, and turned the powerful beam down into the hole, careful not to catch Kerrick's face and blind him. "Well, shit."

I didn't like what I saw—or rather, what I didn't see.

The beam was a thick, bright, powerful concentration of light. Pity it didn't penetrate the end of the cavern—not even the other side of the wall. Warning Kerrick to close his eyes, I flashed it over the cliff face, hoping to find a shelf or something thicker than what he was already hanging from, but it was nearly glass smooth in most places. He was damn lucky to have something to hold on to. I felt the grasses tug and almost panicked until I saw Ryder getting a firm grip on the belt, his heels wedged up against rocks embedded in the ground.

"Here." Cari knelt down by my feet, holding open the harness she'd attached to the rope. The other end was tethered to the transport with a mini winch anchored against its side and the climbing cable running through it, the lever locked down to hold it in place. "You sure you don't want me to go down?"

"No. Just help me get it going." I sat up, shed my jacket, and tossed it aside. Then I looped my arms into the harness and tightened the straps while Cari fed the line through the back. "In case something goes wrong with that winch, you're not going to have the strength to walk both of you up the side of the cliff. You've hooked the end of the cable to the transport, so if the winch does blow, we'll at least be caught. Let me get him secured. Then, when I give the word, you and Ryder ratchet us up. You good with that, lordling?"

"I am beginning to hear that as a term of endearment at this point," Ryder hissed as he tightened his grip on the belt. "We're going to have to hurry. This will not hold together once it comes out of the ground."

The harness was tight around my chest and cut a little into my ribs, but I didn't have time to mess with it. A headlamp was going to have to provide me with enough light, because there wasn't going to be anybody to hold the lantern for us. I just hoped the mini winch would be able to pull us both up.

"I'm going to come down, Kerrick." Peering into the chasm, I gauged where I could safely scale down the cliff and get to him if the grasses snapped. "Ryder, try to hold on as long as you can. I'm going to do a fast drop down and snag him. Once he's secure, I'll call out and you and Cari work that winch as quickly as you can without dislodging the cable. I'm going to try to walk up the wall, but I don't know if that will help."

"Kai, I should go down—" Ryder began to protest, but I was already on my belly, inching backward toward the break.

"Will you just do as I tell you? Just this once, don't argue." I glared up at him. "I gave you a job. Go do it."

I didn't wait to hear him counter me. There were a lot of reasons for me to go down—the first was that I was stronger, and the second was that I didn't trust Kerrick. His arrogance drove his every decision, endangering not only himself but now the entire team. This was my run, and I was responsible for all of their lives. I would be the one to yank him out of the gulch, just like I would be the one to tear a strip off of his ass once I got him onto solid ground.

I hated the taste of dirt, and the grit falling into my mouth when I went down over the edge tasted of Unsidhe.

There were times back before Dempsey when I would crawl around the underground block where my father imprisoned me, scraping at the corners of the walls until I got a teaspoon of dust on my hands. My fingernails were usually bloodied after the effort, torn from the constant digging, but the moisture made it easier to pack the dust into a damp ball.

Stitched together by my father's spell, my flesh could take a much greater beating than most. No matter what Tanic did to me, my body survived it. He was clinical in his sadism, patient in his work to fully understand how flesh and bone could be shaped. I'd been created for pain, and he was more than happy to deliver it, including long, countless days without sunlight or food. I had no concept of time. My life was marked off by those tiny amounts of dirt held together by my own blood.

I knew the taste of this dirt. All too well.

The headlamp gave me more light than I expected, especially when I dropped below the direct sunlight that angled into the crevasse. Dusk wasn't too far away, maybe a couple of hours, and the hills around the prairies would eat into the horizon and cast long shadows.

If the ground were more stable and I had more time, I would've loved to get lost in the sunset hues of the rock formations. But instead I was focused on the now-trembling Kerrick, a few yards below me. His hand was bloodied from gripping the sharp grasses, and a long streak of red down a good length of the stalks told me he'd had a better hold of the clump farther up but was losing his grip. His shoulders shook with the effort of keeping himself steady, his muscles locked in a fierce battle of fatigue and desperation.

I began to drop more quickly as I fed the cable out and swung closer to him, taking little hops across the scalloped orange cliff face. The mottled rock was more rippled a few feet from Kerrick's position, and if I could get him into a clutch hold on my back, I probably could get back to the spot and use the ridges to support us on our way up.

"Faster. I can't hold on much longer, chimera," Kerrick spat angrily, falling into his native tongue. "*Hurry.*"

"Almost there." I took another leap, careful not to get too close. I did another quick check of his position and crept along the cliff toward his left side. "I'm going to have to go slowly for the next few inches so I don't knock you off of the wall. I'm going to get right up against you, but let me get locked into place. I want you to grab me with your left hand on my farthest shoulder. Work your arm through the harness strap and grab my chest before you hook your leg around my hip. You got that?"

"Yes." He was panting, panic pulling a wildness through his teal-and-opal eyes. Sweat and blood matted Kerrick's hair and stuck it flat against his skull, and the scent of his suppressed terror rolled in waves off his skin. I had to give him credit for gritting his teeth and riding out his fears. His limbs were struggling with the effort of holding up his entire body weight with only a few inches of bone and skin to anchor him. "I'm losing my hold on the grass."

My attention flicked up, and I saw the edge of his palm touching the seed husks at the end of the stalks. I moved as quickly as I could and bit down the roll of bile that curled up my throat when I pressed against Kerrick. There could be very little room between us when he made the transfer, but something had changed in our chemistry over the last few days. Maybe it was my increased connection with Ryder or Kerrick's challenge for the Southern Rise Court, but the harmonic longing I'd felt for him when I first met him was gone, replaced by my familiar, ingrained revulsion at another elfin touching me.

It was good from a psychological standpoint, but pretty shitty for trying to save somebody.

"Go slowly. And whatever you do, don't wrap your arm around my throat." There wasn't anywhere for my right foot to hitch into, but my legs were long enough for my left to find purchase on one of the faint folds nearby. I cinched the cable into place, locking myself into position, and then motioned Kerrick over with a nod. "There's a canvas loop dangling on either side of the harness. Try to get at least your left calf into the one by my hip and then move over."

"I'm going to let go and try to get my arm under that strap. I can't get my hand open." His sweat was slick across his flesh when I dropped a little below him to make it easier for him to grab on. His left hand resembled a claw, his fingers frozen in their hooked position. "It's going to put all of my weight on the grasses."

"I know, but it was too risky to come down the right side. The ground there is worse." I braced myself for his weight. "Just go slowly."

I angled my hips so I was easier for him to get to. Rock climbing wasn't something I did on a day-to-day basis, but I'd done my share over the years— never on something this slick and not with as deep of a drop. Most of the time I was geared up for the sharp-glass jaggedness of glistening black lava fields, where climbing required a pair of thick gloves and one eye out for dragons who viewed dangling Stalkers as a delectable appetizer before the main course.

His weight dragged me down, and I clenched in tightly and held my position as Kerrick slid his leg through the strap. He had just gotten his knee in when the grasses snapped, and he flailed as he strained to hook his arm through the harness. The limb was loose and unresponsive, refusing to unfold out of the bent position he'd held it in while we'd scrambled to reach him. I did the only thing I could do. I turned, slamming his knee into the cliff, rolled him over to wedge him against the wall, and left my arms free to wrap around his waist.

Unfortunately, this left us swinging loose against the sheer rock.

Kerrick's breath was hot and sour with fear. He'd probably thrown up at some point, and I didn't blame him. Ryder was shouting something above us, but I couldn't make out anything through the pounding of my pulse in my ears. We'd jostled the ground at the edge of the crevasse enough to send a shower of rocks and dirt down on us, and the patter of stones striking the cliff reverberated in the cavernous silence. Moments later it all disappeared into the void below us. I heard nothing strike a floor or water. But then I heard a soft rumble.

"What is that?" Kerrick got out through his panicked breathing.

"Doesn't matter. I need you to get into the back of the harness so we can get out of here." I kicked at the wall and used my momentum to turn us back around but kept a firm grip on Kerrick's right leg. "I need you on my back. I won't be able to hold on to you and climb up at the same time."

His pants were torn, exposing his thigh, and I caught a glimpse of a scarring pattern running across his hip and down toward his knee—long delicate fronds spreading out of a larger keloid. It was old enough to have lost most of its pinkness, but it was deep enough to weaken Kerrick's leg. Bruises were already beginning to form from the strain of holding up his weight, and his torn muscles were hot wherever I touched him. The shaking was back in his limbs as the adrenaline that pumped through him during the fall now left him weak as it eased away.

He worked to get himself in place, but it was the longest three minutes of our lives.

Then I heard the rumble again, closer this time. The sky above us was still blue, but flash storms were common in the desert. I needed to get us out of the gulch if there were rains rolling toward us, or the mud and the wet rock would make it too difficult for us to get over the edge of the crevasse.

"Okay, I believe I'm in as far as I can get." Kerrick looped his left arm over my chest, but his right dangled down my side, hooked through one of the secondary straps by my waist. "I can't lift my arm above my shoulder. It's tingling."

"Probably popped it out. I think it'll be okay. We'll get you set back into place once we're above ground." I tilted my head back and shouted for Ryder and Cari to pull us up. Then I eased my knees into a bending position and got my feet against the wall. Pushing against the rock, I used the tension in the rope to angle us out and took a step when the winch jerked us upward. "Just hang on."

The ascent was painful and slow. The rope would yank up an inch and then stall for a few seconds. Thinking the winch was stuck, I tried to climb the wall, but Kerrick's dead weight on my back slowed me down. My thighs ached with the effort of climbing up the cliff, and the twenty feet I'd rappelled down in seconds now seemed like miles.

"Ryder! What's the problem?" I shouted when the cable jerked us to the right and I nearly lost my hold. "What the hell is happening?"

This time the low growling sound rolled over us, and I felt something burning and wet strike my cheek. Kerrick sucked in a quick breath and hissed when he leaned his head back. The motion pulled us farther away from the cliff, and I could see what was now waiting for us at the edge of the crevasse.

The cliff face smoked where the spit hit it, and the acidic saliva pocked and scored the rock. I couldn't see it clearly, not with the sun behind it, but its outline was fairly horrific. It seemed mostly ursine in shape, but it was rough skinned, and patches of bristly fur poked out at odd places. It sniffed at the air with a long snout, and then its glowing red eyes tracked down the cliff face and found us easily. Its stench reached us a moment later—a perfume of sewage and rotted eggs carried down with another shower of pebbles and dirt dislodged by its massive claws.

"Ainmhi dubh," Kerrick spat. "This looks like one of your brothers has come to find us."

"Remind me again why I came down here to get you?" I said through gritted teeth. The cable jerked again and lurched us up a few inches. Then the foul black dog howled with an eerie rattling screech strident enough to send a shock wave of pain through my eardrums. I wrapped my hands around the cable and warned Kerrick, "I'm going to pull us up. If you can, press against the rock wall to ease some of your weight from my back. I'll have to do this in stages. I think they put the winch on auto."

We went up another six inches, and the ainmhi dubh clawed at the edge of the break in the ground. The sounds of fighting reached me—Cari shouting for Ryder to get down and then the unmistakable boom of a shotgun. The ripple of sound startled a flock of small birds, and the tiny swarm swept overhead and blocked out the sun for a brief moment. The black dog above us didn't flinch. It dug its claws into the ground as though we were rabbits down a hole it could excavate.

My foot hit the edge of an outcropping. It was slender but enough to give me a little bit of relief, and I dug my toe into the space, hoping to push off of it and increase our ascent. I had two knives on me—not enough to kill a black dog, with its acidic spit and nearly impenetrable skin—but they were going to have to do. Kerrick couldn't outrun it, and I doubted he could fight with his shoulder popped out of joint. Another splash of spit and I could almost swear I heard the ainmhi dubh cackling at me with the high-pitched rolling growl that emanated from its toothy maw.

This time the rumble came with a shake of the ground, and just as I cursed the skies for adding a thunderstorm into our mix of bad luck, the rock wall blinked, and I found myself staring into a black-slitted golden eye as wide as I was tall.

Seventeen

I DIDN'T know what we were on. But whatever it was, it wasn't happy. Kerrick was swearing up a storm on my back, and the ainmhi dubh yelped and scrambled back from the ledge. The walls shook and rolled beneath my feet, and then the earth tore apart and cracks appeared on the cliff face on either side of us.

"Climb!" Kerrick shouted in my ear. "Get us to the surface!"

If the sheets of rock that tumbled from the cliff didn't motivate me, the animalistic groaning coming from an opening slit among the cracks got me moving. Kerrick obviously knew what it was or at least had an idea. All I had going for me was the pressing instinct that we were going to die a horrible death if I didn't get us out of that cavern.

There were niggling whispers in the back of my skull, urging me to grab hold of the black dog and use it, turn it to my will. Kerrick would be its first kill, followed by—I shook my head and refused to listen to the madness that crept through my thoughts. I could *taste* the ainmhi dubh in my blood. It was an odd awareness hovering in the back of my mind, and it was insane. I couldn't control the black dog any more than I could control the weather or the creature breaking out of the cliff. But there was something residual lingering in my essence, perhaps a genetic memory my father left behind. Tanic cuid Anbhás was the Lord Master of the Wild Hunt, the bogeyman that other monsters were afraid of. I did not have his powers. I would never be him.

The feel of Duffy's body coming to life beneath my hands flashed through my scattered thoughts and fought for dominance with the burning pain in my thighs and shoulders and my very real fear of whatever was going to chew me off of the cliff.

I was sweating, my hands nearly too slick to hold on to the rope, but I was giving it my best panicky sprint-up-a-vertical-wall that I could. Whatever was in the rock was waking slowly enough for me to get clear of its debris-shaking movement.

And then the ground fell out from underneath my feet, and Kerrick and I were catapulted into the air and flung out of the crevasse by a massive twisted coil.

I'd like to say I landed on my feet. But then I'd also like to say I woke up every morning to a cup of hot coffee and chocolate pie, but that was a lie too. We tumbled in the air, an eight-limbed beast with two fronts and a joined back. Halfway through the arc of our fall, Kerrick dropped out of the harness, his unresponsive limbs unable to hold on to the straps and loops. The loss of his weight altered my trajectory, skewing me away from the front end of the transport, and I landed a few feet beyond and rolled through the grasses and dirt.

Right into another sinkhole.

"Shit! Shit!" Skidding, I grabbed at anything I could and finally snagged a small bush while I windmilled my feet, trying to find purchase on the rocks. My joints jerked painfully when I finally came to an abrupt stop, and then my spine twinged and reminded me I'd just taken a pretty hard-core beating against hard rock.

Panting heavily, I wasted no time. It took me a good half a minute—agonizingly long seconds—to pull myself out, but when I finally did, I paused to reassure myself that my knives were still in their sheaths. Then I shed the harness and left it on the ground. The transport blocked my view of what was going on, but the monster from Kerrick's fissure reared up onto its hind legs, gave me a very good view of its stony mass, and dropped back down into a hunch.

It crouched on the ground between the transport and the enormous fracture we almost died in. Hunched over, it was hard to tell how tall it was, but I guessed that, if it stood up, it was easily fifteen feet. With bony plates I now recognized as the scallops set into the cliff face, it resembled a pangolin, with an armament of jutting horns covering its face and running down its spine.

Every inch of my body ached, and I'd pulled something along my ribs, but I was going to have to suck it up. Another of Cari's shotgun blasts got me moving. I broke into a full-out sprint through the grasses, and the stalks whipped at my bare skin and left a thousand tiny cuts behind. I rounded the front end of the transport and immediately slammed into the sticky, scaly haunch of a snarling ainmhi dubh.

I have skinned more than my fair share of the Unsidhe black dogs, and in return, more than a few of them have taken their pound of flesh from my body, both before and after my escape from my father's clutches. Most of the Wild Hunt monsters I took down for a bounty were ainmhi dubh that had gotten loose from their masters by overpowering them and then breeding, or the Unsidhe who created them died in the Merge. There are ainmhi dubh who are so ancient that they grew wings and could take flight—massive creatures that continuously grew more powerful, fed by arcane power through the tether to their creator.

They were eternal machines, hard to kill and even harder to tire out. Shaped into whatever form their master preferred, they were driven by hunger and viciousness, and while they could reproduce, the original magic that made them disintegrated through the generations as each litter became weaker and more malformed. If left unchecked, the ainmhi dubh could ravage the countryside of its people and wildlife within a year. And those were just the weak ones.

The one I'd just run into was definitely not weak. And it most definitely had a master.

Whoever made it knew what they were doing. The ainmhi dubh was a powerful-bodied creature. Its nearly hairless hide gleamed in the late afternoon light, and a blue-black sheen rippled over the darker mottled spots that clustered about its haunches and ridged back. About the size of a half-grown bear, it was formidable, and as I drew my weapons, the ainmhi dubh's muscles bulged, and it coiled back.

It launched itself at me, eyes glowing red and long fangs shimmering with its caustic spit. I didn't know if it was the one that had stood over the edge of the crevasse or if there were multiple ainmhi dubh circling the transport, but there wasn't really time to do much more than react.

Pity all I had on me was a pair of knives and a bunch of blown-out bruises.

The giant rock-encrusted creature looming just outside of my peripheral vision was a distraction. So were shotgun blasts, but I was more concerned with the ainmhi dubh. It struck me with both its front paws and drove me down into the dirt. I had a brief moment before the wind was knocked out of my chest, and I sent Pele a prayer of thanks for giving me the knowledge that the ground beneath me was solid.

I brought my arm up, jabbed my elbow into the creature's throat, and dug down as deep as I could to hit its airway. It gave me the response I wanted. The black dog began to choke and gag on its pressed-in flesh. Disoriented, it staggered to regain its balance and stepped off my torso.

It was risky, but I chanced a quick glance at the melee behind me, hoping to get a good look at what was going on before the black dog struck again. It wasn't good, but it wasn't bad.

I couldn't see Kerrick, but I also didn't know where he'd landed. Cari stood a few feet away from me, armed with one of my shotguns, her back toward the transport as she kept another ainmhi dubh at bay. In true stubborn Sidhe lord form, Ryder was armed with a long dagger and a determined grimace. I couldn't tell if the black dog was bloodied or simply wet with frothy sweat, but they definitely had it cornered.

Unfortunately, right behind it was the orange-and-red striated rock creature we'd woken up.

Ryder caught my eye, and the relief on his face was visible. I gave him what I hoped was an encouraging nod and jumped onto the ainmhi dubh I was wrestling with. Bullets could penetrate the skin, and it was my preferred way to kill a black dog, but the knives would have to do.

My leap was a good one, and I caught the ainmhi dubh as it rose up. Growling, it snapped at my leg and ripped apart my jeans, but they were already meant for the trash after the fall into the cave. Still, its spit hit my skin, and the burn from the acid traveled quickly. Blisters bubbled up in tiny pockets of seared flesh and then quickly disappeared and left behind a ghostly pain as my arcane-concocted body absorbed the damage.

Much like the ainmhi dubh, I was hard to kill, but that didn't mean it couldn't be done.

The creature twisted on itself and snapped its massive jaws at my face. I yelped and nearly lost my balance, but the edge of the transport caught me in the middle of my back, and I rolled around its bumper as the ainmhi dubh slammed into its armor-plated front end. Despite the transport's sophisticated shock system, it rocked back and forth at the impact. The ainmhi dubh's dense body absorbed the hit, but it shook its head, probably trying to shake off the reverberations through its bony skull.

The massive cave creature chose that moment to rear up as far as it could go and stretch its long front limbs up in the air. Its shadow swallowed up the sun and dimmed the light in our clearing. Throwing back its blunt head, it cracked open its short snout and screamed, blasting the prairies with its outraged cries. I didn't know what it was, but I certainly felt the effect of its immense weight when it slammed back down onto its curled-over front paws and sent a shock wave through the entire area.

The boom was larger than any blast I'd heard before. I was knocked off my feet, facedown in the dirt, and as I tried to right myself, the grasslands came alive with fleeing animals.

Creatures I'd never seen bolted from their hiding places—everything from a herd of tiny yellow deer the size of Chihuahuas to a giant sloth, its brindled fur tinged green with moss. The sloth ate the ground up with its elongated strides and kicked up dirt where it dug its claws in. A pack of laughing dogs, their enormous mouse-like ears pressed flat against their skulls, rushed past the transport from a clump of frilled stalks.

The ainmhi dubh was confused, unbalanced, and ravenous in its rage. I took advantage of that. There were no rules for trying to survive. Ryder liked to hold philosophical discussions about ethics and morals, and most of the time I agreed with him, right up to the point where I was facing down something with a lot of teeth and the idea that I was lunch.

I hit the black dog while it was disoriented, stretching my body as far as I could after I leapt at its head. It wasn't easy to take an ainmhi dubh by surprise, but I hurt too much, and the bruises under my skin were slowing me down. Something hitched in my ribs, making it hard for me to breathe, and I tasted blood back in my throat—a sure sign I'd broken something in me.

There were times when I felt Odin and Pele heard my mewling pleas for their benevolence. It was hard to ask for mercy from gods with a taste for destruction, but they were the ones who called to me and required little of my interaction. Mostly we went our separate ways. I didn't attend any church and never made any formal sacrifices other than consecrating the occasional spilled beer or shot of tequila to one of them just so it didn't go to waste.

But whether it was luck or the hand of a god steering my aim, my knife plunged straight into the ainmhi dubh's eye.

It began to buck as it tried to throw me off, but I scrambled to get onto its back. Digging my heels into the bony plates along its belly, I fought its contortions while I gripped the hilt of my knife with one hand and pounded at the pommel with my fist.

An ainmhi dubh skull was hard, but I liked living. It spun about, and its slimy pelt twisted loosely between my clenched legs. I continued to pound the knife through its socket, and then its teeth caught my knee and a fang ripped my calf open. The pain was incredible. My muscle was massively torn, and the hit of acid that cauterized the edges of my lacerated skin nearly made me lose my hold. I hung on out of sheer fear. If I dropped to the ground, it would be the end of me, and the ainmhi dubh would feast on my bones.

Another slam of my fist and I felt something give beneath the tip of the knife. Another hit and the crunch was both edifying and frightening. I knew what was coming. I'd done it before, but if I was in pain now, it was about to get much worse.

One final blow of my hand against the end of my knife and the ainmhi dubh's skull split open.

Its death throes were a storm of movement, and I forced myself to hold on as I yanked my knife toward me to leverage the bone apart. The blade caught on something, and I twisted it, more to make sure the ainmhi dubh would die than to hold on to my weapon, but one final thrust of its strong haunches and I was sent spinning from its back.

I broke something when I landed—something in my right arm. Numbness hit me immediately when I slammed into the ground, but I needed to get as far away from the ainmhi dubh as I could. Even with its brain cleaved in two, its instincts would drive it toward its prey, and I was the closest thing to it.

Or at least thought I was.

A boulder landed next to me, at least four feet from my right side. Another followed, slamming into the ainmhi dubh and pulverizing it into the ichor-soaked dirt. I blinked, wiped the blood from my face, and realized the boulders were actually the rock creature's front paws. It straddled me, and its long torso blocked out the sky as its legs tensed, its body stiffened, and it craned its neck forward.

Its bellow deafened me, momentarily shocking me into a silent world. With blood running from my ears, I got to my feet, stumbling as I moved. Fifty yards to the left and the creature would take out the transport, leaving us stranded in a no-man's-land where getting to the nearest civilization would take days of walking through inhospitable prairie lands and canyons.

"Get in," I screamed at Ryder, who was aiming at the second ainmhi dubh in the clearing. "Get into the transport and go. I'll find Kerrick."

"I'm not leaving you," he shouted back as he fired at the black dog. It took the hit to its chest, and the impact pushed it back. My hearing was spotty, and Ryder's words faded in and out. "Cari, do you see Kerrick?"

"I see him. He's behind the transport," Cari yelled back. She ratcheted out a pair of empty shells from the shotgun and reloaded before they hit the ground. "Kai, can you get into the centipede? Ryder, cover me and I'll grab Kerrick. Start moving. I'll be on your six, Gracen!"

Trust was hard, but I was with two people I trusted a lot. Ryder had gained a lot of my respect over the last month, and while I still didn't think he could hold his own in a bar fight, I had faith he would do his best. Cari was one of the best Stalkers to ever strap on a gun, but it was hard to not see her as a little girl. I was too hurt to do anything but trust that they would complete the job, and as hard as it was for me to let go, I left them to get Kerrick into the transport and battled my way into the driver's seat.

Because as much as I believed they could retrieve Kerrick, I didn't think either one of them could drive the transport out of there without killing us in the process.

I left a trail of blood across the seats, but I didn't care. I could feel my skin sealing up around my broken bones and torn flesh as the tormenting and agonizing healing process began. Firing up the transport took a couple of jabs of my finger, and I was more than grateful to see the mapped-out egress flare up on the main screen. The centipede's engine drew the rock creature's attention, and it slowly turned its head and studied the long metal vehicle.

There was no way to read its expression. Up against the cliff face, it'd been invisible, and standing against the sun, it looked like a carved statue, some-thing a mad hermit would leave behind after a lifetime of isolation. There was no intelligence in its golden eyes—not like the ainmhi dubh had—and there was no way of knowing if it would pursue us or drop back down into its canyon once it no longer felt threatened.

Considering it had an ainmhi dubh smeared through its toes, I couldn't even begin to imagine why it thought we could threaten it, but I didn't want to stick around to ask.

"Got him!" Her voice was fuzzy, but I under-stood her. Cari heaved a semiconscious Kerrick into the main cabin. His head lolled back, but his eyes, while clouded with pain, tracked my movements. Cari pushed him in as far as she could and then grabbed her discarded shotgun and laid down cover for Ryder. "He's close. Get ready!"

I gunned the vehicle as soon as I saw Ryder slide through the open doors. Without waiting for Cari to close the transport up, I put the centipede into gear and shot as much power through the cell chambers as I thought the engine could hold. The tires spun in the dirt and then grabbed at the ground and the centipede lurched forward.

"Come on, baby." I patted its dashboard and urged it to go faster. Sparky didn't build for speed as much as she did for durability, but no matter how many plates she welded onto a vehicle, there was no way anything was going to survive that creature's direct hit. "Just get us out of here."

The grasses whipped around the transport. It passed through the uneven prairie and left a wake of chaff and torn leaves. Something hard struck the centipede's rear end and skewed it to the side, and I heard something crumple on the roof, but that wasn't the time to stop. There was always the chance the creature could move at a greater speed than the transport, but I didn't have any C-4 to shove down its throat or any hope I would live long enough to detonate it.

Ryder fell into the passenger seat and was half thrown into the door when the transport hit a hidden boulder. We rolled over a short hill, and the engine picked up speed and carried us away from the cavern's inhabitant. I glanced at the side mirror as I navigated through the labyrinth of green and red lines laid out on the screen and tried to keep us on a safe route, but at the same time, I needed to know if the creature was following.

An animated column of furious rock, it ate up much of the sky as it stretched out its limbs and screamed one final time, with a hurricane of rage I could hear even through the muted ringing in my ears. Then it slowly dropped back down, and moments later, it disappeared from sight.

I didn't let my foot off of the gas.

"Are you good to drive?" Ryder asked softly. There was concern in his voice—probably not as much as on his face, but I'd already endangered us by looking at the creature. I wasn't going to fall into the pity party he was having for me on the next seat. "You should pull over—"

"Not until we're someplace far away. The campsite is less than forty-five minutes out. I can make it," I growled at him, and I tried not to hiss when a jostle sent sparks of pain down my spine. "What was that thing back there?"

"I think it was a henge guardian, probably a juvenile." He laughed when I risked giving him a look of disbelief. "They normally only wake up during solstices, and they're known to be foul tempered when they're young. They stop eating meat at a certain point and subsist only on the rocks they carve out to make their dens. That is only the third one I've ever seen and the youngest. I'm more concerned about the ainmhi dubh. They came upon us quickly and circled us."

"Someone's controlling them, but they could've just been patrolling a range. We *are* in Unsidhe territory," I reminded him. Another jerk of the transport and I couldn't hold back my grunt of pain. "Those were a master's work. Somebody powerful has their leash and probably won't be happy that they lost one. That kind of ainmhi dubh takes a long time to grow in a vat. So either the area is protected by someone powerful or there's been a Wild Hunt called on the kids we're trying to rescue."

Eighteen

It'd been two years since I'd been in the can-yons. Post-Merge SoCal stretched hundreds of miles from the coast to its eastern border. It picked up a lot of land when the Underhill crashed into it. I didn't know a lot about what the elfin world was like and how its landscape looked, but from what I'd heard, this part of the country was a bit of a jumbled mess. The low prairies were left behind about twenty minutes back, and we'd entered a wide labyrinth of wind-sculpted canyons and mesas. The campsite I'd been to before was a literal oasis in the parched, baked red rock, com-plete with a fairly decent-sized spring-fed pond and overhangs large enough to provide cool shade in the hot summer months.

I'd bowed down to the crippling pain after half an hour of driving. There didn't seem to be any en-raged ten-foot-tall stony armadillos following us, so

I let Cari bully me out of the driver's seat and switch sides with me in the cab. The ground was green on the scanner, so there wasn't any danger of us ending up in a subterranean tomb. I'd stopped coughing up blood a few minutes after we left the creature in the dust, but the area we'd been in was riddled like wormwood, and there was only so much trust I could give out on any given day.

"Pull in over there." I pointed toward a spot a few yards away from the crystal-blue pool. "It'll give us a good view of anyone coming in or out of the canyon."

"Sometimes I think your paranoia goes a bit too far, Gracen." Cari muttered a profanity but did as I told her. "Then I remember that everyone who meets you does eventually want to kill you."

"I've had those moments," Ryder interjected from behind me, "but then it always seems like someone is trying to beat me to it."

"Funny. Just remember, everything that happened in the last few hours was because of your cousin back there," I pointed out. "Let's just get camp set up, and then I can take a look at my ribs."

The vibrant walls of the moon-shaped canyon were muted with a bluish wash as dusk crept up on us. Like most of the smaller pockets, the ground was mostly made up of hard-packed sand and small gravel with a few small cacti and bushes hugging the perimeter of the broad pond. Something small splashed at the far end—a fingerling minnow being chased by something larger—but I knew from experience there was nothing more dangerous in the water than the occasional long-pincher prawn. Fresh air swept down through the opening at the other end, curled around the rise in the ground, and held a slight bite—a promise of a cooler night ahead.

Cari parked the transport and angled the cab toward the pond so we could use its spotlights to illuminate the area. She watched me as I opened the door and then gave a good scold when I moved slower than she liked.

"Check on Kerrick. Those painkillers you gave him are probably going to make him sick to his stomach in a few minutes. They always do that to me." I gave her a smug look when a groan came from one of the bunks behind the seats, along with a sound I more equated with Newt coughing up fur from his belly. Cari bolted to hover over somebody else. "There's a bucket in the compartment next to you. You'll probably have to dump the stuff out of it, but it'll give him something to throw up in."

Ryder stayed exactly where he was and swung open the main doors to the back cabin. "Do you intend to wash up in the pond? Because you're covered in blood and dirt, and I want to be able to see what I need to stitch up on you."

"You might have to rebreak my arm and reset it. Everything else's pretty much going to be taken care of." I looked longingly at the pond. A bath sounded great, and I knew where the circulation pattern was so I wouldn't dirty the water for drinking. "I can't feel my fingers. So, if you're willing to do that, come on down."

I left Cari to deal with Kerrick. He was mostly road rash and gave off a yelp when she popped his shoulder back in, but by the way he was moving his arm, it seemed fine. I was less lucky. The break was fairly clean and about halfway healed when Ryder clenched his teeth and pushed everything back into place when I showed him where to grab. Luckily, I held my stomach and didn't foul the pond, but it was close. Stripping off my clothes was an experience in patience, but I hadn't healed into any of the torn fabric on my body, so I put that into the win column.

The water was cold, or maybe I was just too hot. Either way, I sat down in it, rested on a natural stone shelf a few feet below the edge, and leaned back, grateful for the water sluicing over my bruised body. The hematoma over my ribs bordered on alarming, but it was healing rapidly, probably driven by my fear that Cari would slather her mother's witch balm over my wounds and its minty aroma would bring out every feline creature within twenty-four miles.

"Och, look at your leg," Ryder exclaimed softly. "Did that thing take a bite out of you?"

"Small one, but it's almost healed over. Hurts a bit, but it'll stretch. Meat's easier to heal than bone." Rotating my arm around, I was happy to not hear any crackling-rice sounds coming from the area I'd broken. "You did a good job with this. Slid right into place."

"I hate that you live a life where you know how your bones sound when they are broken." I got another long-suffering sigh from Ryder. "And yes, I know it's your life, but I still don't care for it. Maybe it reminds me of how dangerously you live."

"Not like we're on a walk to the donut shop here, lordling." Rubbing at my calf made it feel better and eased away some of the ache as the muscle rebuilt. "I don't know why you insist on coming along when you know damned well you could get killed. Hell, I don't know why Kerrick is here. All he had to do was sit back in Balboa and wait to see if you came back."

"Ego, mostly," Ryder replied. "And he's competitive. I did not fight in the wars, and he did, so he probably feels he would lose face if I risked my life and he did not. My part of the family is forbidden from conflict because we are a fertile clan. I was surprised they took him or that Sebac allowed it. Still, he acquitted himself well, by all accounts."

"Yeah? Then why didn't he pitch in while we were fighting off that damned worm?" I made a face as I recalled how he'd worked to get the transport unlocked, but I didn't want to give up the argument. "Hell, the asshole could have picked up a rock and thrown it. *Something.* I mean, it's not like I'm asking him to come out with a flamethrower or anything."

He chuckled, and I scrunched back down into the water and hoped the cold would numb the rest of my body.

Sitting on the pond's edge, Ryder took off his boots and socks and eased his feet into the water. I could practically hear him thinking, and I didn't blame him for staying silent. I welcomed it at the moment, but there were a lot of questions pressing down on us, things we would have to figure out before we went any farther.

"Do you really think those ainmhi dubh were part of a Wild Hunt?" he asked when I finally opened my eyes to stare up at him. "Unsidhe magic killed Duffy, and there's so much we don't know about the Dusk Court below San Diego. Everything I've heard says their clans and houses are in a constant battle—to the point where they're starving their people because resources are spent feeding armies instead of villages."

"I know that the humans have abandoned the area." I splashed water over my face and then cupped some into my mouth to ease the dryness in my throat. The water was sweet and held a hint of the ginger grown in farms along the river. "There were some cities down there, but most are ghost towns now. Mexico lost a lot of its land to the Unsidhe in the Merge, and with its people gone, there is no incentive to gain it back. Cari's mom had family down there, and they all fled north to SoCal."

The crunch of footsteps on gravel brought us both to attention, and Cari held her hands up and chuckled as she showed me the small duffel she'd carried over from the transport. She set it down by my elbow and joined Ryder in shedding her shoes to soak her feet.

She gazed out over the pond and sighed.

"I brought you some clothes, since yours look like they're about ready to fall off of your body. Kerrick threw up mostly water, so it wasn't too bad. I told him he should come out here and at least get a sponge bath, but he passed out again. Said something about how the Sidhe sleep off their wounds. Apparently it's better for them to heal that way. I told him the only Sidhe I knew was you, Kai, and you would sooner drop dead than admit you were hurt." She grinned when Ryder snorted. "So what do we do now? We know there are Unsidhe in the area, as well as those assholes on their hunting party. It's too late to call in reinforcements, and even if we did, I don't know what good they would do."

I thought about it for a moment and then replied, "I'm hoping the ainmhi dubh were a patrol, because they didn't seem focused on any one person in particular. If they were looking for elfin, they would've gone after Kerrick and Ryder specifically. Or even chewed on me a bit more." I didn't mention the hunger I'd felt from the black dog I'd fought with or the ache to control it that I'd experienced. "Duffy told me she used to get some help from the people in the area on other runs, but that all dried up. Something's changing out here, and I don't know what it is. If the Tijuana Dusk Court is running patrols this far north into SoCal, then it makes sense for farmers not to want to stretch their necks out for runaways. They have their own to worry about, especially if the Unsidhe are moving up here. I mean, the nearby area's marked as Dusk Court territory, but it's been mostly a buffer zone. One thing to mark it on a map, but it's another if they're actually starting to move in. Something's changed to drive them up."

The Dusk Court didn't have the cohesiveness to protect an area or to even make insurgent runs into SoCal territory. They were on arid land that was nearly impossible to make viable, even with everyone's cooperation. I knew the Sidhe had people who could shape plants and land, forcing nature to provide a higher yield at harvest, but I couldn't say the same for the Unsidhe. And of course, humans had to do things the old-fashioned way, with irrigation lines and backbreaking work through hard soil. Still, there were acres of fruits and vegetables about twenty miles to the east of us, and that kind of arable land would be attractive to a starving Dusk Court.

"It seems uncharitable. If someone is fleeing for their lives, why wouldn't you help them? Why wouldn't you extend them any protection?" Ryder leaned forward to rinse his hands off. "Running a patrol of ainmhi dubh requires a lot of control and support from a clan. They wouldn't just have one pack. It would have to be multiple groups to cover an area this wide."

"Yeah, it makes more sense that what we ran into was a Wild Hunt rather than a patrol." I didn't like it, but Ryder's logic made sense. "We should move toward our rendezvous point as quickly as possible. We're guessing the three kids who are coming up are Dawn Court, but suppose they're not? Maybe they're from a clan that's dropped out of favor and someone wants those kids dead?"

"Your mind is like a telenovela," Cari *tsk*ed. "Why do you always pick apart problems and make them intrigue?"

"Everything is an intrigue with the courts. I haven't even been around them that long, and I know that," I replied. "Just ask Ryder here."

"He is not wrong." Ryder inclined his head and glanced back at the transport. "I'm going to go check on Kerrick and then maybe ask him why he's here with us, because it does not seem as though his intentions line up with ours."

"Do you mean because he didn't help with the giant centipede back in the cavern and then disobeyed me when I told him not to go too far?" The cold was getting into my bones, and I reluctantly resigned myself to getting out of the water. "It's almost as though he has an agenda and he wants you to fail. He's walking around with the idea he's some high lord commander in charge of an army so he doesn't have to listen to some mutt like me. Does that sound about right, Cari?"

"Yeah, it does. But I think he had a 'come to whatever god you guys worship' moment back there." She cocked her head, ran her hand through her hair, and then winced at the speckles of dirt she found. "I don't think he expected Kai to go down after him… or anyone else, really. Alexa told me a little about what it's like to live in Elfhaine, and she said the farther you are from the center of the clan, the happier you'll be. Kerrick doesn't strike me as being too happy, so I'm going to guess he's in the thick of things."

"I would say he is. Coming down here is both a way for him to show our grandmother that he is committed to our clan and at the same time a way to carve out a space for himself." Ryder pulled his feet out of the water, shook them off, and splashed me in the face. I growled at him, and he patted my head. "I'm going to go see if he needs something. Cari will be here to make sure you don't drown while you bathe. Are we going to spend the night here? Or are we only stopping long enough to rest?"

There were arguments to be made on both sides. We were beaten and tired. I had just had my right arm reset, and it was painful to move. Cari and Ryder were quiet, obviously waiting for me to make a decision. I wanted to sleep—I couldn't argue with Kerrick's insistence that sleep was the best way to heal—but if somebody got to those kids before we did, I didn't think I could live with myself.

"I know that look on his face." Cari groaned and reached for the duffel bag. "Let's at least get clean and get some food in us before you drag us back out. A couple of hours, Kai, that's all I'm asking."

"Three. I'll give us three hours." I took the bag from her, attempting to be stoic and not wince, but I failed miserably. There was soap and a washcloth along with a clean set of clothes. The pain along my sides cheerfully informed me it would probably take me about half an hour to get squeaky clean. "We're going to want to get our guns clean and ready for this run. We don't just have the ainmhi dubh to worry about. Don't forget, there's a group of hunters out there who want to use these little kids for target practice, and that makes them bigger monsters than any black dog I've ever met."

AT ABOUT the two-hour mark of our stay, I took a lantern to scout out the road a bit. I'd cleaned out the shotguns Cari used on the black dogs, and she loaded up a bandolier of shells for me. I grumbled about losing yet another knife, but I brought plenty. We gulped down a quick meal of lukewarm spaghetti and a spongy strawberry cake, and then I made some noises about wanting to make sure the transport could get through the next passage and set off for a walk.

I needed some breathing room and to ease the ache in my leg.

I fitted one of the Glocks into the shoulder holster and strapped the other to my side. I'd replaced the knives in the sheaths on my thighs with longer blades. It felt like there was a storm brewing. Something heavy sat on the horizon, and I couldn't carry enough weapons to make myself feel prepared for it.

There were still a few good welts on my skin, and my back looked like a tabletop gamers' map of a fantasy world. I was scared I was going to piss blood for a couple of days, considering how many hits my kidneys had taken, but otherwise I seemed to be okay. My calf hurt like a son of a bitch. It ached where the flesh was quickly growing back, and Ryder had insisted on applying a derma-layer on the area—more to keep it protected from rubbing against my jeans than anything else. The wound meant not wearing boots, so I'd have to be careful about snakes and anything else willing to crawl up my pants leg.

We were too far out for me to get any service on my link, but I checked anyway, hoping something might have bounced off of the farms nearby. Mostly I was worried about Dempsey. I'd left him stewing in the poisons of his own body. He had time left in him, but he was a man who didn't like life to control him. I would have extracted a promise from him that he had to wait for me to come back before he died, but he probably would've just slapped me.

"Wouldn't have said no to some rabbit meat tonight," I grumbled to myself. The protein would've been good. There were chunks of chicken in the spaghetti, but my body craved meat, especially when it had a lot of healing to do. I'd spotted a jackalope ten minutes into my slow stroll, but I never hunted those. I liked them too much. "Jackalopes and capybara. A man's got to have limits, 'cause dog and cat are right out."

"But you think nothing of killing dragons?" Kerrick called out to me as he slogged his way across the gravel.

I couldn't risk going too far—just enough to stretch my legs and get some air without somebody else's breath on it. Luckily for me, Kerrick was considerate enough to bring me company. Sure, I was glad he didn't die, but mostly because he was Ryder's cousin and his death would have sent the lordling into a spiraling case of guilt and depression.

"I only kill a dragon if it's trying to kill me first," I responded quietly and turned to face him. "You should head back. We're going to be leaving soon."

"We have forty-five minutes. I asked Cari if I would have time to speak to you."

"And that's what she told you? That you've got forty-five minutes?"

"No." He shook his head. "She told me that you might not want to listen to me. She seems to believe you're driven by stubbornness and pride. I told her I didn't believe you had that much Sidhe in you."

The joke took me by surprise, and I chuckled. "I was raised by the most pigheaded human there is. It's kind of Dempsey's legacy—along with knowing how to cook eggs and rice over an open fire. So talk. I'll listen."

The moons were out, mostly full and dripping with light. This far away from the city, and under such a clear sky, I could see even the rare speck moons, the tiny round celestial chunks the elfin brought with them. Above me, the stars were swirls of twinkling spots scattered through the deep blue backdrop. A few fluffy white clouds hung low enough to cast shadows on the gravel floor of the canyon.

Kerrick looked good in the moonlight. He was beautiful in a masculine way that most people would sigh over—a glorious peacock among sparrows. Humans were taken by the elfin, enamored by their beauty and grace despite the way some churches and politicians raked up fear among their followers. Kerrick would've been a good poster child for reconciliation, a pretty ambassador with smooth words who could sweep thousands of deaths under the proverbial rug.

For all I know, that's exactly what he did for the Sidhe army.

By all accounts Ryder and Alexa were reasonably attractive, but not heartbreakingly gorgeous like Kerrick, but I preferred them. I liked people who looked real. Kerrick and I had both been thrown into the air and slammed into the ground, but he appeared as though he were out for a stroll in the gardens, his pristine Sidhe tunic and lightweight trousers paired with shoes made out of buttery leather.

No, I definitely preferred Ryder and Alexa.

"I wanted to say thank you for saving me." His accent grew thicker and blurred his Singlish. "If there is anything I can do for you—"

"You can leave San Diego and the Southern Rise Court to Ryder," I suggested dryly. "It's the first thing I can think of off the top of my head. Well, the second, but somehow I don't think you're willing to take out the old lady for me. *I* can't because I promised Ryder I wouldn't."

"And I promised my grandmother I would do my best to secure this court," he said with a wide smile. "Still, I owe you my life, and while our respective promises are conflicting, I am honor bound to count you as someone I should protect."

"Just listen when I tell you to do something," I cautioned. "I'm not trying to be an asshole or to control you. I just want to make sure everybody who started off with me comes back home. I get you're used to bossing people around, but it's different out here. The cutest things can kill you. And sure, most of them came from Underhill, but they're *here* now, and I've had years to deal with them."

"It is funny you think this is the human world, because I believe it's Underhill, and the humans' world pushed into us. But that is neither here nor there. Our worlds are now one, and you are right, I have little experience with the wilderness we're going through. As familiar as some of these creatures are, they're different now, more aggressive and violent." He tilted his face up and lifted his gaze to the skies. "I wonder if that's what happened to our races as well. We've lost our way. We are no longer as courteous or polite. I want to change that. Go back to how we used to be."

"See, that's where your problem is, Kerrick." I shifted my weight, ready to head toward the transport. "There's no going back. You can't unmake a reality. It's just not possible. The only thing you can do is work hard to change it. To grow. To make things better."

Whatever Kerrick was going to say—and he certainly looked like he was about to argue with me—was lost as a hail of bullets screamed down from the mesa above us. It was a short plateau, not more than ten feet, but it was enough of a height advantage that I couldn't see who was shooting at us.

"Looks like we got a hunt." The man's voice boomed through the winding gulch. "Got us a couple of cat bastards down here!"

Laughter echoed through the canyon, and someone whooped—a deep rolling voice giddy with glee. We were too far from the transport to make a clean run for it, and I heard someone reloading, the distinctive click of a clip being slid home, and it chilled my blood quicker than the cold water of the pond had done hours before.

"Go! I'll cover you," I ordered, shoving Kerrick back. I drew my Glocks, flicked off the safety switches, and returned fire.

Nineteen

THE ONLY way I was going to stop the fire-fight was to get to the top of the mesa. Bullets scored through the rock by my feet and into the wall near my head. I wasn't going to wait around to see if Kerrick reached the transport. He was on his own.

Other Stalkers have often called me mercenary. Maybe it's something Dempsey left in my manners, or maybe I'm as cold-blooded as some think, but my first loyalty will always be to the people I love. I needed to get Ryder and Cari safe, even if it meant abandoning the run. Ryder would argue and say he wasn't as important as securing the safety and well-being of an elfin seeking asylum, but he was wrong. If he fell, then Kerrick would step in, and the Southern Rise Court would suffer for it.

I didn't need to be a hibiki like Cari to see that the death of ideas and tolerance hovered nearby. Kerrick would fight to bring San Diego's court down to its knees and mold it into something straight out of his grandmother's playbook. The kids we were trying to retrieve were a sacrifice I was going to have to be willing to make, because there were a hell of a lot more elfin back in Balboa who didn't deserve Kerrick as their high lord.

Providing I could survive getting shot at.

Iesu, my leg hurt like a son of a bitch, but I was a sitting duck if I stayed in one place. The passageway led up toward the mesa flats and would eventually get to the top. Ten feet wasn't that tall, and I'd already been on one climbing trip so far on this run, but it looked like I was going to be on another. The transport fired up, and Ryder shouted something at me. I couldn't hear him, not with the rush of anger pouring through me.

I wasn't going to survive everything life threw at me only to get picked off by a pack of rich assholes with more money than morals. That wasn't how I was going out. I didn't know how I was going to die, but Dempsey had it right. Sitting on a friend's porch, drinking whiskey, and watching blue chickens peck for seed would be my choice.

There was a dip in the wall above me where the mesa dropped a bit. The gunshots continued, but they were aimed toward the rumbling transport. I could only hope Kerrick's flashy clothes drew their attention so they wouldn't know I was coming, but I wasn't going to bet on it. I couldn't climb with my Glocks, so a knife in my teeth would have to suffice. It looked stupid and flashy—a throwback to those pirate movies Dempsey liked to watch—but it gave me a weapon I didn't have to draw once I got to the top.

I was going to need every advantage, and even though I was literally taking a knife to a gunfight, a well-thrown dagger would give me enough time to draw my Glocks.

The rock face was a hell of a lot easier to scale than the sleek walls of the cavern. I sent a cascade of dirt sliding down the cliff as I dug in, but most of the holds I grabbed were good. There wasn't any clear way up to the mesa, probably wasn't one for a long stretch, so when the transport rumbled up the pass toward me, I didn't stop climbing.

I took a quick glance to see who was driving and spotted Cari at the wheel. Ryder sat next to her, a sawed-off shotgun clenched in his hands. I pressed myself up against the cliff wall and waited for the transport to pass, hoping whoever was on the mesa wouldn't be able to see me tucked into the shadows in the rock. Cari must have spotted me against the cliff, or maybe she heard me cursing her in the back of my head, because the transport's running lights clicked off for a few yards when it rolled by.

"They're heading 'round." A panicked shout sounded above me, and I shoved myself as tightly as I could into the shallow depression I'd found. "They've got guns. Thought you said it was going to be easy."

"Easy, my ass," I muttered around my knife as I watched the transport disappear around a bend. "Just wait."

There was no guarantee Cari could even get up to the mesa or if she was driving straight into an ambush, but I was going to have to trust Sparky's machinery skills to get them through. The centipede took the hit from the henge monster pretty well. It could probably handle bullets.

"I've got a shoulder launcher in the truck," a gruffer voice belted out, more than a bit of impatience ramping up his tone. "That'll take care of them."

Okay, the centipede probably couldn't take *that*—not without being cracked open. It didn't sound like they were moving away from the edge, but I couldn't wait any longer. My shoulders and arms were on fire, strained from holding me up, and my still-not-quite-healed break shot sharp pains up through my joints. Swearing softly, I reached for the next rock hold I saw on the cliff, pulled myself up as quickly as I could, and stopped only when I heard their voices draw closer.

"There's a woman with them—a human," the first man shouted, panic riding his words. "That wasn't the plan. There's not supposed to be any people with these animals."

"Look, she knew who she was falling in with." A different man spoke, and a thick, clipped accent shortened his words as he spat them out. "She's no better than they are. Probably going to be spitting out cat-bastard babies for them in a few years, if she hasn't already. That what you want? To be overrun by those things?"

"They can't mate with humans," the tight-voiced second man argued. "It's like breeding a cat and a dog. Ain't going to happen. But that doesn't mean she's not one of them. Be like those kids down underneath the city with their pointy ears and stupid faces. We're losing what it means to be human. I say she's as much of a problem as they are. 'Sides, not like anyone's going to find her out here."

Three. I could handle three. Maybe even four if there was someone else up there. Problem was, the clouds were rolling in off the far hills, and in their heavy, swollen depths, they brought a hint of rain and darkness with them as they swallowed up the moons, spread their heft over the canyons, and hugged the land. No matter what everyone spun out about the elfin seeing better in the dark, I didn't ever find it to be that much of an advantage. Dark was dark, and I wasn't happy about the sheath of black that stretched over the night sky to the east.

I snagged the lip of the plateau with my fingers, wedged my toes into a solid chunk of rock, and crunched myself up into a ball. My ribs began to complain, reminding me I was bruised to hell and gone across my torso, and when I stretched my legs, a ball of pain tore across my injured calf.

And the metal blade against my tongue didn't taste that good.

My abdomen complained a bit when I slowly lifted myself up to peer over the edge. The clouds were moving in fast, dimming the sky, but I could still make out three large shapes moving about in the scrub bushes about twenty yards from where I hung on. A small rover sat by what looked like a curved bend a little farther back. It looked too narrow for the transport to make it up the incline, but I couldn't tell for sure. The rover sported bubble tires, nearly round balls of hard rubber meant to roll a vehicle around any terrain. They made it nearly impossible to upend, so getting to the top of the mesa probably hadn't been much of a challenge for the squat metal beast. And if I had any doubts that those guys were rich, they were put to rest when I spotted those tires—each one cost a good year's wages for a competent Stalker. Four was an unimaginable fortune.

The avarice demon I had inside of me begged me to steal the rover, but that kind of thing always led to no good, so despite my intense and sudden desire for a four-seat rover with balls at its axle points, I forced myself to focus on the men.

"Get in the car!" The gruff-voiced man I'd heard scolding the other two earlier was huge and loomed over the other men. What little light there was glistened across his bald head, and a flash of silver traveled over his smooth pate as he moved. "That thing won't make it up the hill. We'll be able to meet them at the gully and corner them."

"This isn't what we signed up for." A smaller slender man broke out of the group and backed away from the rover. "We're supposed to—"

I didn't wait for him to finish. Surprise was all I had going for me, and the moment the tall bald guy rounded on his client, I went up over the edge of the mesa, slid my knife back into its sheath, and drew a Glock right before the shouting began.

As stupid as it was, I had a hard, fast rule about holding my fire unless I was being shot at. Being a Stalker meant living on the edge of lawlessness with less-than-honorable people who would sooner gut a man for his boots than give him a sip of water. I'd heard stories about Dempsey's ruthlessness over the years, but he *never ever* shot first—or at least not while I was around.

And I sure as hell wasn't going to break that creed, even if these three had already laid down a blanket of fire on me earlier.

"Drop your guns," I ordered, keeping my voice as steady as I could. "You don't have to die tonight."

The anguish of my torn muscles and bruises thickened my voice, pulling out the growl in my words, but I knew I still *sounded* human. And in the dark—as they say—all cats are gray. Betting they couldn't tell I was elfin, I wanted to make them stop and think about what they were doing.

The tall bald guy blew that straight out of the water. Bringing up a sawed-off shotgun he'd held down against his leg, he bellowed, "Shit, it's *Gracen*."

In the movies, fights were always one-on-one, or the biggest guy would hold the others back with a shout of *He's mine!* before engaging the hero in an epic fifteen-minute battle of trick shots and impossible acrobatics. That's not how any of it worked. Instead what happens is a bunch of guys I never saw come barreling out of Pele-knew-where, and everyone starts shooting at me.

And that is exactly what happened.

I don't know where the other two guys came from, but they were ready to kill me based solely on the tall bald guy's say-so. I don't know who they were expecting to hunt down near the rendezvous point, but they'd come loaded with more weapons than I would have brought along for a nightmare hunt. The guys by the rover were struggling with high-powered rifles— the kind of weapon used more to show off than to do the job. Bald Guy was a worry. His stance was solid, his grip casual on the stock of the shotgun, and I knew he would give me trouble.

His first shot opened up the game, and if I hadn't seen him dip his shoulder, he might've blown me clean through. Being out of range helped. So did jumping out of the way. And as the ground ate the blast he'd unloaded at me, I came up firing.

Unfortunately, so did the two guys who came out of the bushes.

The only thing that saved me from becoming a sieve was the transport surging its way up onto the mesa and slamming into the rover.

It was always great to see backup arrive, especially when I was outnumbered. The two guys holding the rifles hit the dirt and flung their weapons out of reach. The bald guy was much more savvy. He rolled to the side and out of the way of the rover. The men by the bushes didn't even stop to blink as they turned their guns onto the centipede and began unloading their clips into its front end.

I did not fare as well. As I brought my Glocks up to return fire, one of the rover's tires broke loose and barreled toward me. Dodging a four-foot-wide solid ball of rubber was difficult on the uneven ground of the mesa. I feinted to the right when the damn thing hit a rock. It changed its trajectory, and instead of rushing past me, it caught me straight in the ribs.

The tire picked me up, or rather, it ground me down. I ate dirt and then a bit of blood and spit out both as I fought to catch my breath and scramble to my feet. A round of gunshots exploded, some headed my way, but they went wide, probably thrown off by the tire as it rolled by me. The bouncing ball of rubber went over the lip of the mesa and crashed into the gulches below. I heard another pair of engines firing up, smaller than a car or rover, and as I began to sprint toward a boulder to give myself some cover, a pair of dirt bikes broke from the bushes, carrying the men I'd seen emerging earlier.

If the bald guy was concerned about their desertion, he didn't show it. He backed himself up against the turned-over rover, threw down the shotgun, and reached for the handgun holstered to his thigh. He let off a shot, aiming for my head, and it whistled through the dried leaves of a tall sage near my ear.

"Drop your damned weapons," I shouted again. "There's no way you're going to get out of this!"

The lights on the roof of the transport flared on, and I got a very good look at the man trying to kill me. I knew his face. I'd seen it before, but my impression was fleeting, and my attention was drawn by the revving engines of the dirt bikes as their riders pulled the two hunters behind them. They roared away, slightly off balance from the added weight and the uneven ground.

"Cari, cover me," I shouted at the centipede, not knowing if anyone inside could hear me. The driver's door swung open, offering Cari shelter as she crouched down behind it and leveled a shotgun at the retreating motorbikes. I knew she wouldn't pull the trigger, not unless I told her to or someone on the bikes opened fire.

One of the bikes teetered and hit something hard on the ground. Its riders tumbled, and the impact of their bodies striking the mesa echoed loudly through the dusty air. The bike skidded to a stop, and one of the men lurched to his feet and grabbed at its handlebars. Cari's shotgun trained down on him, prepared to let loose a blast if needed, but he climbed onto the machine and tore away, leaving his passenger behind.

"We do not want to kill you," I called out, hoping the guy on the ground would stay there. It didn't look like he was moving. "Don't make this shitty. It can go really badly for you."

"Too late for that," the bald guy yelled back at me and began to fire.

Most of the time when I'm getting shot at, it's not personal. I was either in the wrong place at the wrong time… or maybe the right place at the right time, because more often than not, if anyone's pointing a gun at me, it's because they're on the other side of the law. While a Stalker is technically a bounty hunter, we're allowed to arrest people and bring them in. This guy knew me, knew my name, knew my face. The chances were, he also knew I could drag him back to San Diego and throw him into a courtroom without much trouble.

I was wondering why he was so resistant about being taken in, considering the only thing I could really charge him for was perhaps attempted murder if the judge was particularly elfin-tolerant. I would've had better luck if they'd fired on Ryder, seeing as he was an official diplomat of the Sidhe court, but it would've been harder to make it stick. I was fair game. Caught in a no-man's-land of races and societies, I fell between the cracks of practically every legal system except for the Stalkers. We didn't like people who came after our own. We usually let the law deal with things, but I knew for a fact there were some who believed that vigilante justice was best served by the people who'd been trespassed against.

Hell, Stalkers even stood up for Dempsey when a couple of wheat farmers ambushed him because he had me riding along with him. I'd heard one of the men finally learned to walk without too much trouble, but the other would never fully use his right hand again.

That was the only thing I could think of that would make a man reluctant to throw himself on the mercy of the law—until I saw his face clearly and the remaining moonlight filtering through clouds washed everything in a sea of blue.

His button-down shirt and cargo pants were crisp despite the desert trek he'd made. Considering where he and his clients were, I guessed they'd left nearly as soon as I'd seen him last… standing in the middle of Duffy's garage, his stern face softened by what I now knew had been fake concern. He'd probably been jumping for joy inside of his tight little mask, reveling in her death as he shook my hand while her blood still clung to his skin.

That's why he was so close to the scene and probably why Duffy let him in. In that neighborhood, who wouldn't open the door for a cop, even one as nasty-looking as the asshole in front of me?

"You killed Duffy." I came out from behind the boulder where I'd taken cover. "For what? Money?"

"Whore got in the way. She already fucked up one of my last trips. Lost me a hell of a lot of easy cash." His grin sickened me. It was a bone-white slash beneath his hooked nose. "I'm not going to let you take me in. You know that, right?"

I circled around him, keeping Cari in my sight as well. The motorbikes were long gone, and the rattling growl of their engines faded in the distance. "I don't remember your name, but I know Davies. He works out of the same house you do."

"Don't try to connect with me, bastard," the cop snarled at me. "You're what's wrong with this world now, all of you. San Diego used to be a decent place to live until you showed up. And then more came with you. I didn't even mind that bitch screwed up my side business, but bringing them into our city—*my city*—that's too far. Too much."

"But you used Unsidhe magic to blow her place out," I reminded him, edging closer.

I could probably take him down if I was lucky. There was a lot of muscle beneath his massive chest, and he was used to carting around fifty pounds of gear while running in a full sprint. It would be close. Keeping him talking seemed like the best idea, but I didn't know where it would take us. I did want answers, and he seemed like a talker. Zealots were like that. If I could just keep his tongue wagging, I would find out who led him to Duffy, because the guy on the ground Cari was dragging into the transport didn't look like he was going to be talking any time soon.

"Yeah, I used your own shit against her." He laughed, a mocking deep rumble nearly lost in a roll of thunder. A drop of water hit my face. It was as cold as the pond in that canyon we stopped in. "Unsidhe detonation spells are a dime a dozen, especially right on the border near Tijuana. They're desperate for anything. They'd sell their own mothers for a month's worth of food, because those animals are starving each other out. Makes business really good. They run up here looking for someplace safe to live, and I get a couple of coyotes to feed them through the canyons.

"Then it's just a matter of finding a bunch of traditionally minded guys who want to balance the world out. All it costs me is some gas and the price of a few bullets. But you had to go and fuck that up." He lifted his gun, and I tensed and raised mine in response.

"You're crazy if you think I'm going to let one of your kind take me out. And I'll be damned if it's some half-assed cat bastard Stalker like you."

The single gunshot was lost in the storm as it broke above us. The weather systems in the canyons moved swiftly, and wild winds and pounding rains were ushered in with a clatter of lightning and booming thunder. He dropped where he stood, landed on his knees, and then rolled back to rest on his haunches, his sightless eyes pinned to the horizon. Sighing in frustration and disgusted by his stupidity, I stood in the deluge, dropped my gun down, and slowly walked toward his swaying body. I got about halfway when gravity toppled him over, and his slack face splashed in a muddy puddle forming over the dirt of the mesa. The rains would carry away his blood, the ground too hard and dry to soak up any moisture, and I was still standing there when Ryder approached.

"Why?" The Sidhe lord's befuddled expression was nearly comical, and I would've laughed if I weren't standing vigil over a dead cop. "They live such short lives. Why would he do this?"

"Same reason why moths fly into open flames," I offered as I slid my Glock back into its holster. "He was a cop, Ryder. If I took him back, he would've lost everything. There was a good chance he'd be stripped of his pension and tossed in jail, not the best place for a corrupt cop. And even if they only gave him a slap on the wrist, every single Stalker in the area would have made his life very uncomfortable. So, instead of backing away, he took a dive into the fire. Can't say I blame him."

"How can you think that?" Ryder's anger rode his voice like the thunder rolled through the storm. "Is that a choice *you* would make? Because I would not want that for you. And I demand you tell me—you promise me—you will never ever consider that as a way out. I need you with me. I need you by my side."

I stood and stared at the Sidhe lord I'd dragged on more than a couple of runs. We weren't pretty. There were cuts and bruises on our faces and arms, and the cold rain had plastered our hair and clothes down. Still, his emerald-shard eyes shone with a compassion and an optimism I never had. Ryder was something I never would be—someone who believed the world could become a better place if only he worked at it. I didn't share that optimism. Hell, I didn't think people would do the right thing even if somebody paid them. I'd been turned away by Medical too many times, so I knew that was a truth.

But there he stood, with a man's blood trickling around his feet, demanding loyalty from me.

I laughed and then winced when my arm began to ache. "Don't forget the promise I made you, lordling. I'm not going anywhere, because somebody needs to kill you if ever you become your grandmother. So expect me to be your shadow for however long this whole thing lasts. Now, if you don't mind, this rain is really cold, and we've got a few kids to take back home."

Twenty

"I COULD have done the dead-eyes thing," Cari argued under her breath and poked at me between my shoulder blades. "I have all the stuff with me. We could have learned something."

"Yeah, you would have learned what it looks like to blow your head off while staring at me." I shifted to my right, hoping to avoid another jab. My back was bruised, much like a lot of my body, and her index finger seemed to have the uncanny ability to find a particularly painful spot each time she prodded. "Not worth the risk. Doing that wipes you out, remember? Anything you might have learned isn't worth you not being able to shoot straight for a couple of hours."

"Still…." She wasn't willing to give up the argument, even though she knew I was right. "How often do I get to do it? A hibiki gets better the more she uses her powers."

As much as I'd have loved to squeeze information out of the dead cop's brain by using Cari's witch magic, I didn't think we could learn anything we couldn't learn by squeezing the guy we'd picked up off the mesa floor. And since invoking Cari's third eye meant me chewing up peyote buttons and other things—including my blood—and spitting it into her open mouth, I had to be really in the mood or desperate for information.

I also didn't want to deal with being stoned off of arcane spell ingredients while I dealt with the local sheriff, especially in the dead of night with no sleep and very little food in my stomach.

We strapped the dead cop to the roof of the transport and loaded the still-unconscious hunter onto one of the bunks and secured him with a bunch of duct tape. The medical kits we had on board were good for injuries but crap for anything beyond stitches and splints. There was a short debate about whether to drive to the nearest farm and dump the survivor on someone else or see if we could patch into someone's link and call in to the regional sheriff's station.

In the end we lucked out because someone in the area amped up their signal, and we caught the edge of it, reached out to the local cops for help, and found out the sheriff himself was making rounds only a few miles away. He was willing to meet up with us at a farmer's feed outpost—a forty-five minute detour—and I didn't want to drag a possibly dying human around with us.

The outpost was actually an old barn attached to what looked like it had been a garage before two of its four walls fell over. Still, the structure was solid enough to serve as a carport, and the sheriff's beat-up military rover with its regional seals sat beneath its slightly sagging roof, a thick layer of dust covering the vehicle's boxy lines. I angled the centipede into the drive and left room for its wide doors to swing open so we could move the injured man. Flicking on the spotlights drove the damp night back so the sheriff could see, and Cari extended the canvas overhang from the roof of the transport, giving us some protection from the incessant drizzle.

Sheriff Graham turned out to be a large barrel-chested man who wouldn't have been out of place starring in an old spaghetti western. Standing a few inches taller than me, he was as broad as a bull and moved slowly, as though he'd grown up in the proverbial china shop and had been told to always be careful. He could easily have picked Cari up by her head with one hand, but his light gray eyes beneath his bushy salt-and-pepper eyebrows were gentle. He took off his cowboy hat briefly toward her when I did a quick round of introductions.

Since we'd left our unconscious passenger on the bunk nearest the main door, it was fairly easy for Graham to peek his head in and see what kind of shape his newly acquired prisoner was in. We stood outside to give him room, but I moved in closer when Graham asked me to fetch him a scanner from the back of his rover.

I returned with the visor, and the sheriff admitted that he did double-duty as an emergency medic when he was out in the field. He spent a bit of time examining our slightly pudgy, soft-faced patient, but eventually the sheriff proclaimed him okay to travel to the nearest hospital, where he could regain consciousness while under arrest for attempted murder and other charges.

"Yeah, I should be able to move him. I've got a huge rover with a stabilizing gurney in the back. It should hold him." He took another peek at the man's eye and let the lid close back down. Graham fired up the head scanner he'd fitted onto the man's head and then shot me a curious look. "Gracen. You came through here about three years back, didn't you? Took out a nest of mega rattlers that were chewing up Johnson's flock, didn't you?"

I remembered the job. Vaguely. Mostly I recalled getting caught in a herd of nightmares by myself and having to find a replacement bumper for my truck after one of the damned things tore it off while he chased me clear back to Lakeside.

"Yeah," I mumbled, nodding. It'd been a quick bounty, a short run out to eradicate a nest of about fifteen rattlers large enough to swallow two adult sheep, one after the other, without stopping to burp. "Johnson's wife gave me a peach pie."

"Yep, that woman can bake." His eyes turned steely for a moment. "You 'bout broke my deputy's heart, if I recall. Boy moped for days after you left. Told him not to expect a call. 'Specially not from a Stalker."

Now I remembered the run. "Umm—yeah, about that…."

"Just giving you a hard time." Graham's grin lifted up his rosy cheeks. "Kid was dragging his feet afterward, but he met up with a cop from Houston at a training thing. Guy moved out here about a year back.

They're married now, but I don't think I'll mention you came rolling back through."

"Might be best," I agreed.

"Oh no, I'd love to meet one of Kai's ex… can a one-night stand be considered an ex-anything?" Cari piped up, and I shushed her with a hard dead-eyed look I'd picked up from her mother. She listened to me about as well as she did anyone else, which was to say, not at all. "Kai's hard to pin down. Just ask Ryder here."

"I'm not trying to pin him down," Ryder mumbled. "I'm trying to get him to join my court."

"Sounds like you've got more than enough problems to go around, boy, without adding Dwayne to the mix." Graham guffawed. "Now how about you tell me about that dead guy you've got tied to the top of your vehicle and what you want me to do about him?"

"Dead guy's SDPD with a side business of taking rich guys like the zombie over there on hunting trips. Problem is, some of his big game are Unsidhe running the border." I watched Graham's expression closely to see where he fell on the line of good cop or bad. His frown was immediate and fierce and wiped away any of the jovial teasing he'd given me earlier. "Killed a friend of mine back in the city to cover his tracks. This guy's one of his clients."

"He fired upon my cousin Kerrick and Stalker Gracen. Or at least we believe it was him. We recovered a pair of rifles from the mesa." Ryder slid into the conversation smoothly, asserting his place as the reigning high lord of his court. Kerrick interrupted his examination of an old chicken coop and squared his shoulders, ready to interject, but Ryder continued,

"We can turn the weapons over to you. They fired on the transport as well, but I don't know if there are any bullets lodged in its outer plating to match to the rifles."

"Picked some vid off of their rover." I slid my hands into the pockets of my jeans and rolled my shoulders back to loosen the tightness along my back. "They had it rolling as they were shooting. Or at least that's what it looked like. Ran through it quickly while heading over here, but the thing goes belly-up once their vehicle got hit."

The tape would show a lot, and some of it—like the cop deciding how he was going to go—wouldn't be there because of Cari plowing into their expensive rover, but it was all I had to offer. Well, that and the tires.

"Pulled the bubble tires off their rover and tossed them into the back of our centipede. Behind that storage wall there." I jerked my thumb toward the far end of our segmented transport. "Expensive-as-shit pieces of rubber, and if I left them out here, they would probably be cooked before someone could retrieve them. Pulled out as much of their gear as we could and chucked it back there as well."

"Officer… Sheriff, if I may interrupt," Kerrick cut in. "We appreciate your assistance in this, but we have a meeting to make. Is there anything else you need from us?"

"Not much else, really." Graham's gaze moved from cousin to cousin, and then he decided he'd rather deal with me than either of the elfin lords that karma had dumped in his lap. Ryder excused himself, hooked his arm into Kerrick's, and dragged him away from the open door. They'd gone only a couple of feet away when they fell into a heated conversation, and Cari rolled her eyes and excused herself to take a walk around the property and look at the sheep huddled inside the open barn.

"Pretty girl. If I were a few years younger…." He laughed and then shook his head. "Well, she'd probably be the death of me. So, Gracen, you're remanding the dead cop and this one over to me, right? We can process the arrest on your badge if you'd like the points at the Post."

It was generous of the sheriff, but I knew what he was avoiding. There was always going to be someone with a badge on that would be looking for trouble, and a cop-on-cop arrest always stank to high heaven, even if the dirty cop was caught with his hand in the proverbial cookie jar. Someone would also want to sweep it under the rug, but that was a political stew I didn't want to dish up. I didn't know the bastard's name, but I wasn't going to be sad about his death.

"If it'll be easier on you, I can take it," I replied. "I don't want to cause you any problems. Easier for me to take heat from a couple of the boys in SDPD."

"I ain't scared of anyone coming out to find me. Plenty of room and caves for someone to get lost in. Land out here takes care of its own." Graham did another check on his patient's reading and grunted, apparently more satisfied with what the scanners scrolled out than the last time. "You said you're intercepting a couple of Unsidhe coming across the river? Down which crossing?"

"Marker's Hang. Or at least nearby. We're going off coordinates we were given." I glanced at my link, not happy about how low of a charge it was holding. "We're a couple of hours from the spot, but they're not supposed to be crossing over until late tomorrow. I'd like to get rested up before we head down. There's been too many fingers in this, and that kind of attention makes me nervous."

"Most of the time that mess down there doesn't care if someone does a runner across the border," Graham drawled. "But then, it's also been a hell of a lot quieter in the past few months. One of my buddies does trawling across the river, and he's said some of the courts are ghost towns now. Sure they need a walkover?"

"Yeah. Promise to my friend, remember?" I stopped myself from sharing any more. As much as my gut told me to like Graham, I didn't want to show all our cards. The less he knew, the better, and if something went belly-up, I'd like to die thinking he'd been a good man who hadn't backstabbed me. "I just want to see it through, and well, there's still three of these guys floating out there somewhere. I'm thinking they went back to the city, considering we've got all their guns and gear, but I can't rule out them deciding to continue with their stupidity. Some people never learn, you know?"

"Yeah, I know that for sure." Graham was silent for a moment as he watched the cousins bicker. "Seems kind of strange those two are with you. Brent—well, she's one of yours—but those two are like tits on a fish, and you don't seem like the kind of man who'd drag along dead weight with you."

The fact he'd called me a man told me everything I needed to know about Graham. It rolled off his tongue as easily as Dempsey told a lie, and I was glad my gut hadn't done me wrong.

"Ryder's okay. The blond one. High lord. Arrogant as shit and sometimes doesn't have the sense Odin gave a turkey to come out of the rain without drowning, but he tries." I cracked a grin at the sheriff. "The other one's a pain in the ass, but at least I know where he is. They're out of their element. Even if a lot of this land is Underhill, apparently neither one of them really was for roughing it, and from what I've found out on this trip, it's crazier now than it used to be. There's things out here even *they* haven't seen in a long-ass time, so I think we're all on a level playing field."

"Yeah, things do get wild out here. No getting around that." The visor made a rapid-fire burr of noises, and then its surface flashed with a cascade of green lights. "Well, that's repaired some of the bruising on his brain. I should be good to get him on the table in my rig so you all can move along. Or if you want, leave that thing parked here and get some rest. There's a shower stall in the barn. You've got to fire up some wood under the tank so it'll be hot, but it's better than nothing. The guy you helped last time you were out owns the place. Told him I was meeting you out here, and he said you can crash out here if you want. Even grab some eggs from the chickens up in the loft if you can find any. Eggs. Or maybe chickens. Jungle fowl really. Don't think anyone's going to miss a couple if you decide you need a bit of *pollo* in your rice in the morning."

"Thanks. I think we'll take you up on that." I stood to help him move the guy from the bunk, but Graham stopped me and put his hand on my arm.

"Just do me a favor, son. Be careful. Okay? That buddy of mine says there's some big changes moving through the Unsidhe down there, and I don't want to see good folks like you get caught up in that." He nodded toward the cousins still having their heated argument in the rain. "Those people down there would as soon kill those two as look at them. Might be better off leaving them here while you go meet those people you're expecting."

I didn't know what to say. I clapped my hand on his shoulder and squeezed. "I appreciate that, Sheriff, but if you hadn't noticed, I'm one of them too."

"Well, elfin, yes, but Sidhe?" He ducked his head when he stood up, probably used to hitting it on the ceiling of most transports. "Son, with that hair of yours, no one's going to be thinking you're anything but Dusk Court. And honestly, that's got me worried too. Those empty towns? Where'd those people go? Not up here. Not through here. I'd have noticed that much activity. And no one goes south. Getting past Old Mexico City is like serving yourself up on a platter to all those dragons down there. Something is going on down there, so my bit of advice to you is, be careful and don't linger. Last thing I want is to find you nailed up onto one of those trees like I've found some of the other Unsidhe who pissed off someone bigger than them."

GRAHAM WAS right. The shower was glorious. I was the last one in the beat-up wooden stall with its "punctured bucket on a pulley" showerhead, but I stoked up the fire under the massive metal tank next to the barn and stood under the hot water long enough to turn my skin pink. Washing in the faint ambient glow of the powered-up transport was a bit difficult, and I'd spent a good ten minutes clearing out a spider's nest from the converted horse stall before Cari would use the shower, but it was still damned good.

I didn't even mind that the soap she left behind smelled like lavender and black tea.

"Do you need more light?" Ryder's voice broke through the darkness, and through the cracks between the boards of the shower, I could make out his silhouette moving past the sheep. "The moons are almost gone. We're going to get another storm soon."

"Same storm. It just doubled back to kick our asses again." I scrubbed at my hair, still feeling grit on my scalp. "Did you bring a lantern?"

"No, I can do *some* magic," he sniffed. "At least the rudimentary spells."

"Last time you cast magic around me, I threw my guts up, remember?" It was an ugly time back then, cornered in a Quonset hut with only a pair of metal doors and a protection spell to hold back a hunt master and his pack. "I'm really liking this shower. I don't want to clog it up with my puke."

"Small spell... and not on you," Ryder promised. "And if you start to feel ill, let me know and I'll stop."

The barn lit up with tiny glowing specks—dancing lights that hung about ten feet above me. They varied in color, mostly white but with fluctuating edges of blues and yellows. Several of the sheep stirred at the brightness and bellowed their displeasure, and I saw Ryder quickly jump over the stall wall and make sure the gate was closed behind him.

"Great, now you've pissed off the sheep," I teased. Still, it was nice to see what I was doing, especially since I'd been scrubbing what seemed like the same spot for five minutes only to discover I'd been trying to wash off a lingering bruise.

"And why is it whenever I find you these days you are either bathing or eating?" Ryder replied. From the sounds of things, he was finding someplace to sit or at least make himself comfortable. "Probably because you're always getting shot at and need to wash off all that blood."

"Funny. I didn't start it this time." Reminding him would do no good, but still, I had to drive home the point. The water was just starting to go lukewarm, and I debated asking Ryder to throw more wood on the fire, but now that I had light, I could see my fingers pretty much looked like *li hing mui*. Vowing to stand under the water until it ran cold, I tilted my head back and let the heat wash over me. "Cari and Kerrick already go to bed?"

"Cari did. Kerrick's reading up on what we know of the Tijuana courts. After what you relayed from the sheriff, it would be useful to know more. There's just not much there." Ryder sighed, and the lights moved closer and circled around the shower. "Is that better?"

"If you wanted to get a better look at me, you could just open the door," I pointed out. "I mean sure, the slats on this stall are wide, and the lights help, but you're probably not getting that good of a show."

"No, I'll wait until you're healed up. Right now you're all purples and yellows. I'll have a hard time telling where your dragon tattoos begin and your wounds end." The flippant rejoinder was light but held more than a bit of velvet burr.

There'd always been a tension between us, mostly animosity from me and overbearing confidence on his part, but things were getting easier—especially since he'd pulled his head out of his ass and admitted that life was better when he wasn't trying to control me.

I glanced down at the dragons on my thighs and hips and ran a hand over the newest one, an Asian red I'd gotten from Jason in memory of the one I'd pancaked on the Pendle Run I'd taken Ryder on. The water was definitely getting colder, but I was still reluctant to get out.

"When we were loading that guy onto Graham's rover, he told me some of the farmers who helped the Unsidhe get out of the territory were getting their farms hit. Some small stuff like ripped-up fields, but one guy had his barn burned down," I called out over the stall, hoping Ryder could hear me over the now-noisy sheep. "He thinks someone down there is pulling in the courts, but he doesn't have enough to go on. Just a hunch on his part. Think the Dusk Court's got its own Ryder now?"

"I would be more concerned that they have their own Sebac," he countered, and the lights flickered. "I'm losing hold on these. I'll have to do the spell again if it fails. Do you want me to?"

"Nah, water's cold, and I'll be freezing my balls off if I don't get out from under here." I turned the water valve off, worked the pulley back along its track, and righted the bucket after the last of its reserve drained out. Then I grabbed the towel I'd brought with me and quickly scrubbed the feeling back into my legs, warming my chilled skin. "I know what you're thinking."

"Oh?" The arrogance was back, and I could practically hear his eyebrow lifting. "What do you think I have going through my mind?"

"I think you're sitting there wondering if we shouldn't go down into Tijuana so you can strike a deal with whoever is the biggest sweet potato on the buffet. Graham said there's about thirty clans down there, small but separate. If someone's gathering them up into one or two courts, you'd want to talk." I nudged the stall door open with my elbow and fixed the towel around my waist. "Someone down there's good at making babies. And you want to know how."

Ryder's smile slashed wickedly across his handsome face, and he laughed. "I already know how to make babies, my chimera. But yes, I do want to know why. Let's go rescue our runaways first. And after they get settled and we find out how things look down below the border, I want to go down there. As soon as I get Kerrick out of my court."

Twenty-One

WE BROKE out of the canyons after half an hour of hard driving and emerged once again into grassy fields and lowland forests. Eerie rock formations punched up through the loamy soil, twisted ocher fingers clawing up at the sky. There were odd patches of sandy desert and cacti every now and then—a bit of old Earth refusing to give way to Underhill's domination—but eventually those pockets would fall, folded under the weight of the region's hard rainfall and the river separating the States from the Mexican territories of the Dusk Court. I knew from experience that the grasslands would fall away to more canyons steeper than the red rock gulches and mesas we left behind.

I resisted the urge to take them through the Valley of Names. Winterhaven was far out of our way, but it was something I did with Cari when she was about fourteen. Hauling black rock out to the white sands to write our names out in large letters seemed silly now, but it'd been an adventure, a safe run for her to see if she could handle days of driving and long stretches of nothing.

She must have been thinking the same thing, because she laughed softly to herself and said, "Remember when we wrote our names in the sand that one time? Drove all the way out to the boonies so I could spell Cari on a hill."

"It was more so you'd know what it was like to have your ass fall asleep after sitting in a truck for nine hours." It'd been a good trip, and she'd been determined to prove herself. Her brother Mattias started taking her on runs after that haul, and despite her mother's objections, Cari began studying for her Stalker license. "I think your mom still hasn't forgiven me."

"Are you kidding? She loves you. She blames Mattias," Cari scoffed. "You can do no wrong. You wash the dishes every time you come over and take out the trash. Pretty sure the brothers would kill you if they thought they could get away with it. You'd kick their asses."

I was about to talk some shit about her brothers when something glistened on a nearby hill. Peering through the somewhat filthy windshield, I hit the cleanser button and got the wipers to clear off the bug specks and dirt. Ryder must have seen it too, because he murmured something low in his throat, and Kerrick shifted in the seat behind me.

"Kai...." Ryder inched in between the front seats and leaned over my shoulder. "Over there. What is that?"

"Nothing that should be there. But it's close to where we're supposed to be meeting them. Can't

hurt to look," I replied and checked the ground map.
Since everything looked green except for a few yellow
patches to the east, I angled the centipede in that direction. The thing responded sluggishly, dragging its
tires through the thick grasses. Something caught on
the axle and then snapped free, and the right side spun
out before it got traction again. "Shit. Okay. Come on,
baby. Just find your groove there."

"Are you talking to the vehicle again?" Ryder
whispered into my ear. "It can't hear you."

"Don't get him started about cars." Cari cut him
off before he could continue teasing me. "The Mustang is still sitting on blocks in his garage, and every
time he works on it, he mutters your name along with
some very nasty swear words."

Kerrick's derisive snort almost drowned out Ryder's sigh. Glancing briefly at his cousin, Ryder protested, "I told him I'd pay for someone to fix—"

"No one touches Oketsu but me. I do Pendle Runs
in him. Anything goes wrong and I go belly-up, I don't
want any doubt that it was me who fucked up." The
transport grabbed at the ground again, and we jerked
forward and barreled down the hill. "Shit, this thing's
chugging. Something's still around the axle."

"Surely we can stop and look?" Kerrick's question was a good one, and Ryder murmured his assent.
"See, even Ryder agrees. It must be a good idea."

"Yeah, I'd love to, but something's off about this,"
I countered. "Think about it. You're on the run—"

"I have never been on the run," Kerrick refuted.
"My people have always pushed forward. We stabi-
lized regions. There was *no* running."

"Yeah, fine. You were Leonidas, but what we're dealing with here is one woman and a few kids." I kept my foot on the pedal and pushed the transport through its paces. "*They're* on the run. If you were them, you'd be stupid careful about stuff. There it is again. Not rhythmic like a turbine. More like—"

The ground in front of the centipede exploded a foot off of its front end. Clods of dirt and prairie grasses struck the windshield and cracked a line across the right side. I swerved to avoid the next incoming projectile, not sure what I was dodging, but whatever landed to the left of the transport created a crater I could have put six sheep in.

Cari was beginning to load up a high-powered rifle, locking down the plasma burst shells into its stock, and Ryder was doing something behind her, probably finding the Glocks I'd given him before. I didn't know what Kerrick was good for or what weapons he could use, but then a slight buzzing behind my ear told me everything I needed to know.

I didn't know the words he was using, but I recognized the pattern of chanting. He was weaving threads of power over himself, pockets of magic he could draw on to fuel a blasting spell. Outraged at his complacency when we needed him to pitch in before, I nearly turned around in my seat to tear him apart when I met Ryder's eyes.

"He's arming amulets, badges I suppose." Ryder frowned, and I could see him look toward his cousin for a better word. "They are coins with sigils. You can activate them. Like the Unsidhe spells that were used to set Duffy's house on fire."

"So, limited resources?" I kept my query short, not trusting my temper. Logic told me he was better off saving what he had for when we really needed it—much like now—but it didn't mean I had to like it, especially since Kerrick had been holding out on us or at least not telling me he'd come armed with more than just his aggravating social skills and agitating personality. "How many do you have, Kerrick? What's the range? Can I put you on top and you hit them now?"

"Close-range, but powerful. The shorter the distance of travel, the more energy it can expend upon impact." He was messing with something behind me, but I couldn't see what it was. "These are arrowheads. A bow is a traditional Sidhe weapon. This is merely an extension of that. I'm an expert with a bow."

"Of course you are," I replied, catching sight of another dark round shape as it flew toward us. "And those can't be used in a gun?"

"A gun requires an ignition point to accelerate a bullet. If you introduce that kind of energy point to this spell, it will go off, and the person with the gun will more than likely be dead." I wouldn't say his tone was snarky, but it was borderline, as though I would've learned that in baby Sidhe school like he did. "They are a more elegant weapon in a way. They do much more damage than a bullet."

"Yeah, well, a bullet usually is a letter with someone's name written on it." I grunted as I swerved the transport to the side. "What you've got there is more like a grenade. That's more like *to whom it may concern*. And in case you don't know, that's a letter anybody can open."

The transport slid. There wasn't any warning, and I had no idea what was going on, but the tires gave out from underneath us, and the next thing I knew, the centipede was hydroplaning across the grasses. There were gulches and dips I'd marked to avoid, and the damned thing found every last one of them. The ride was rough as we jumped sideways and skipped across uneven terrain. Whoever was shooting at us lobbed another missile, but it went wide and slammed into a spot we might have been in if the centipede hadn't decided to take its own detour.

I had to give Cari this—she could teach a room full of sailors how to swear.

"Can you hold it steady?" she yelled at me as she rolled down the window. The glass rattled in the frame, and I was more scared that she'd fall out or that the windshield would shatter over her than I was at fighting the transport. "I want to take a shot at them!"

"What does it look like I'm doing?" I was working every trick in the book, but the segmented glide built into the middle of the transport made controlling it difficult, and something was wrapped around the conversion axle, because the back end wouldn't respond at all.

I tried to turn into the curve and then against it—anything to affect its trajectory—but nothing seemed to work. The grasses were thick here, slick with a milky fluid, and the centipede's heavy treads plowing through the finger-width stalks should have ground us to a halt at some point, but the viscous liquid only seemed to lubricate our glide.

We struck a boulder. I saw it coming. Hell, the thing was so big it cast a shadow broad enough and heavy enough that it was cold as we passed through it. The transport struck the enormous jut of rock with its back end first, and then the accordion fold in its middle slapped the front end around and tossed us all from our seats.

The centipede rolled—something I thought was impossible, but there I was, going ass end up, caught in my seat belt as my head slammed into the roof. The dashboard hit my knees, and the world tilted sideways as the sky slid around the windshield. We went over two, maybe three times. After the first round, I ceased counting and concentrated more on trying to find a god or laws of physics that would stop us.

A gulch saved our asses. The transport flipped into a steep divot, its angled bank almost too deep for gravity to tip us over another circuit. The centipede teetered on its left-side tires, torn between toppling over onto its roof or allowing its heavy weight to rock back against the wall of the gulch.

I guess praying to physics sometimes works, because we slammed back down on the passenger's side instead of making another go at it. Even though my brain was fuzzy from being smashed up against my skull, I was very aware that we were sitting ducks, especially with the transport slanted up and its belly exposed. My gut told me Sparky would armor the hell out of the centipede's undercarriage, but I couldn't leave anything to chance. Forward seemed to be a problem, but reverse responded, and we inched slowly back until the gulch leveled out and Cari wasn't hanging from her seat belt, clutching her rifle to her chest.

"Everyone okay?" The roar of motorcycle engines reached my ears, and I reached to undo the latch at my side and free myself from my seat. "More importantly, everyone got something to shoot with? Because we're going to have company in a few minutes."

The engines grew louder. They were throaty and out of sync. Whatever our newly found friends were driving up on, they were poorly maintained. The backfires were frequent and masked the number of bikes they were riding—more than two, I figured.

I carefully got into the main cabin. The transport was still at a slight angle, but nothing we couldn't handle. Ryder struggled with the large central door and put his shoulder up against the crossbar to force the hinges to work. Kerrick scrambled about on the floor, gathering up the arrows he'd powered before we took a dive. I was careful where I stepped, because I didn't want to blow a hole out of the centipede's belly.

We'd secured most of our equipment before the ride, but a few things were loose—mostly medical bins we'd pulled out to have ready when we picked up the woman and the kids. I stepped over a blanket and grabbed the bandolier Cari made for me and the shotgun I'd put into a tension grip mounted to the bunk support of the transport. My Glocks were still in their holsters, and my belt was heavy from the spare clip I'd threaded on that morning.

"Sounds like they're about two minutes out. Ryder and Kerrick, you two stay in the transport and lay down fire from the door. The centipede's mostly bulletproof, but I don't want you two to take any chances. If Cari and I go down, pull down the door and send out a distress call to Graham." I grabbed Ryder's arm and forced him to look at me. "Pay attention to this. I'm serious. Do you understand me?"

"I don't agree—" Ryder began to spit back at me.

"I don't care." I refused to budge. "Both of you are Sidhe lords in the borderlands between SoCal-Gov and the Tijuana Dusk Court. Either one of you is taken hostage, you're not going to like what happens to you after that. They're never going to let you go home and… they'll use the other to hurt you. If you want to spend the rest of your short life watching them peel Kerrick's skin off of his flesh, then you leave that fucking door open if we fall. And I swear by Odin's ravens that if our nieces end up in your grandmother's hands because you're not there to protect and raise them, I'm going to crawl out of the dirt hole they'll put me in and make you wish they'd killed you."

"Kai, all-terrains, not bikes. Caught sight of one when it hit a rise," Cari shouted from her position at the front of the transport. She'd hunkered down, using the wheel as cover, but she poked her head out to yell at me. "And it looks like they're chasing something right toward us—smaller but big enough to bend the grass."

The grasses were too tall to clearly see through. We could hear the motors roaring through the hills, and large swaths of stalks bent down toward us only to snap back up a few seconds later. The wind turned, and the hillside became a rippling sea of beiges and greens that masked the paths of the bikes.

"I need your promise, Ryder," I insisted. "If you can't give it to me, then I'll just lock the two of you in here. I'd rather be down two guns than risk losing either of you—which is saying a hell of a lot, because I don't like him—to the Unsidhe."

"And Cari?" he argued back, trying to twist his arm out of my grip. "You're willing to sacrifice her?"

I knew she could hear us. And as hard as it was, I had to go with what I knew she would want me to do. So my answer, as difficult as it was for me to choke out, was simple. "Yes. If she falls and I don't, I throw her body into the back of the transport and get drunk with her family. Right after we burn her body on a pyre and give her weapons out to the people she wanted them to go to. She is a Stalker. We're expendable. It's the job. You don't have that luxury. If you or Kerrick aren't in that ivory tower growing up through Balboa's bones, the Southern Rise Court is dead until it gets another lord. So the only thing I want to hear from you right now is 'Yes, Kai, I will do exactly as you say if both of you die out there.'"

"If they kill you...." His eyes shimmered and turned from emerald to a smoky, stormy green. "I'll—"

"You'll work with them if they're the ones who are breeding elfin kids like rabbits," I finished for him. "Not only is the job bigger than my life—and you are the job—you prevent the elfin from going the way of the dodo. Promise me."

"I don't want to promise that." He leaned in until our faces were nearly touching, and I felt his breath across my lips. "You have become a part of my heart. Even as combative and argumentative as you are, it would break my heart if you weren't there. I don't know if I can do this without you."

"Then I guess you better do your job and cover my ass," I teased and then kissed the tip of his nose for letting go. "That has to tide you over for, like... years. Watch my six, lordling, and I watch yours."

I was out the door before he could reply. It was getting too sugary inside of the transport for me to stand, and even though I hadn't extracted a promise from him to close those doors, I knew he could see the logic behind my insistence. As stupid as it was, Ryder and Kerrick were the future of the Sidhe court that now lived in my backyard. I hadn't wanted them there—I'd even argued against helping them—but I felt like I owed it to Duffy to continue her work in some way, and if that meant making sure the refugee Unsidhe had someplace safe to go, then I guess I had to make sure the Southern Rise Court was there for them.

Cari did not look my way, but I wasn't looking at her. I had no regrets for what I'd said. It was what she'd pounded into my head over the past few years, and it was about time I grew up enough to understand that she could stand shoulder to shoulder with me. And if she did fall, I would go back to the Valley of Names to see if the rocks still spelled out our names.

And if they didn't, I would spell them out again and return every year to make sure her mark was left.

"Maybe that's what I'll do," I muttered to myself as I wedged into the accordion bend of the centipede. "I'll go out past the inland Valley, become a hermit, and write the names of the dead in the sands."

We were about twenty yards from the break in the grasses where the terrain turned into forest. The stretches of rock scattered about the landscape began to cast long shadows as the clouds peeled back from the sun. A twisted ocher-stone column, barely as wide as a young sapling, sat at the edge of the tree line as an odd natural marker of sorts, and its tip began to tremble. The motors of the ATVs were deafening, and the sound traveled through the area and drowned out practically everything else.

The grasses parted, and a filthy young elfin woman burst out from them, dragging two very young children with her. A third—a girl kissing the edge of pubescence but with eyes as ancient as the stone that loomed behind me—emerged on her heels. Barefoot and barely clothed in rags, the children were silent, resignation and fear fighting for dominance on their young faces. I couldn't tell anything about hair color or even the fineness of their features because of the layers of dirt and grime caked into their skin.

I shouted and stood to catch the woman's attention, and she veered off and ran toward the front of the transport in a desperate panicked scamper. Holding my position, I broke a little of my cover and yelled toward the centipede, "Ryder, Kerrick, tell them we're here for them!"

Cari came around to the front end. Surprised, the woman spun about and cradled the two small ones to her body, covering them with her arms. The young girl rushed Cari, her fists flying and her teeth peeled back in a fierce, animalistic snarl. I was yards away, but I could smell them. The stink of terror and unwashed skin stuck to the roof of my mouth when the wind carried their scent over to me.

"Little one," Ryder said in Sidhe as he slid out of the transport and held his gun out to the side, staying armed but as nonthreatening as possible. "Come here to me. All of you, we are here to take you home—a new home."

The Unsidhe woman unfolded herself long enough to look up at Ryder, her arms shaking but tight around the little children she'd pulled free from the grasses. Her skin shimmered golden in spots, smears of mica flecked over her pale flesh, but it was difficult to tell how old she was or even the color of her hair through all the muck on her body.

The mica flecks were a clue. I knew the clan she came from—a vicious bunch who made runs into SoCal to snatch humans to work in their houses and fields. I'd run into them before while on another run to rescue human children they'd taken. They were mysterious and secretive, much like many of the Tijuana Dusk Court, but I'd seen the bones they left behind in their extinguished campfires. They were too long and too bipedal to be anything someone would hunt in the prairies or nearby forests.

One of the tiny children she held peered out from her embrace, and its round eyes, liquid brown and pleading, were pure human. The other's golden gaze and pointed ear tips left me without a doubt it was Sidhe. The young girl behind her shared the youngest's features, her hair falling fully away from her face, and I got my first good look at the kid. Her aquiline nose and heart-shaped face were heartbreakingly gaunt, and a thin white scar sliced down her right cheek. The cut had been deep, and something had been poured into it to mark her permanently, or perhaps she'd had an infection her body couldn't heal, but the wound had also taken her eye and left it an opaque white.

"Come here." Ryder held his hand out to them. "We are here to protect you."

The trembling woman lifted her head and took a halting step forward as though she wanted to believe Ryder, but the promise of safety was an illusion she'd evidently dreamed about for too long to have faith in now. But the young girl broke out of her fighting stance and ran toward the golden lordling who offered her sanctuary just as the grasses broke open again and three four-wheeled ATVs pushed through. Their Unsidhe riders laid down a spray of fire and cut through the Unsidhe woman embracing the children she'd fought so hard to free.

Twenty-Two

THE TIRES of the ATVs tore through the flattened grasses the transport had left in its wake and
spread deep wheaten confetti bits into the fierce winds
that had begun to whip through the clearing. I anchored my knee into the ground, dug in my position,
and blasted a round into the nearest vehicle, hoping
to pull the attention off of the kids and onto me. Out
of the corner of my eye, I saw Ryder bolt toward the
fallen woman and the screaming children. Cari was on
her feet, pumping expended rounds out of her shotgun
and reloading as she walked, working herself into a
defensive position despite the gunfire coming from the
two shooters.

At some point, the Unsidhe had bartered or purchased military-grade armor, because the two men—
or at least I thought they were men—barely flinched
when a shotgun blast slammed into a shoulder or chest.

The heavy plating should've been marked with insignia, but those spots were scraped clean, leaving silvery patches on the mottled beige tactical suit. I'd seen the insectoid helmets they were wearing on shock troops that were sent into the understreets to quell riots and large disturbances, so whoever funneled equipment to their court and clans was shopping at the National Guard armory. I didn't begrudge anybody making a quick buck, but the armor was going to make it hard to kill our attackers, and I didn't think we had enough firepower.

A bit of movement to the left of me made me glance toward the main door. At first I thought it was another Unsidhe coming up over the roof of the transport to attack from the other side, but the man's fine robes clued me that it was Kerrick before I blew him off of the centipede. He'd obviously climbed out of the driver's side and scaled the transport to give himself a higher ground to shoot from. It wasn't a bad move, and I should've thought of it, but I consoled myself with the reminder that we were there to pick up a woman and kids and needed to defend the egress. I also hadn't planned on getting into a minor skirmish with shock troops.

Just goes to show I should always be prepared for any level of military engagement, even when doing a rescue run.

The younger children were pinned beneath the dead woman's body, and in her weakened state, the young girl didn't seem able to get them free. She tugged at the woman's arm and grabbed at one of the toddlers' legs, trying to yank it out from under the body, but her arms quivered, unable to hold up even the slightest amount of weight. The children's cries were becoming weaker, either drowned out by the engines, or more alarmingly, they just didn't have the energy anymore. A few yards away, Ryder was caught in the crossfire and momentarily dove behind a large rock and then sprinted out.

He skidded into a crouch near the fallen woman, but the young girl attacked him, her hands curled into claws as she raked at his face and hands with her broken nails. Above us, Kerrick shouted something in Sidhe, but I couldn't understand him. I didn't know if he was talking to Ryder or the kids, but judging by the way he drew back his bow, I imagined he was telling them to stay down. Trapped in the skirmish with the young girl, Ryder was trying to subdue her when the ATVs came back around.

Kerrick was good with his bow. He handled it with ease, and when his arrow left his weapon, it went unerringly straight. Problem was, the ATV drivers knew what they were doing. Their driving patterns were erratic. They cut across the broad clearing, and even though it made their shooting difficult, they were almost impossible to hit.

The charged arcane arrow struck the ground, and its explosive energy left a small crater where one of the ATV's tires had left the track when its driver gunned his engine into overdrive. Pebbles pelted the dead woman's body.

I moved in and put myself between Ryder and the ATVs. There was a good stretch of land to defend, and I was firmly in Kerrick's line of fire, but Ryder needed protection, especially when the girl slashed at his face again, raking the skin on his cheek open.

Blood gushed from the skittered wound, the uneven gash probably filthy from the grime on her nails. I tossed a handful of zip ties from my back pocket onto the ground next to him. I'd grabbed a few of the long stretches of lockable plastic before we'd gotten into position. I thought we might need them for the ATV drivers. I never imagined we would end up using them on one of the children we were trying to take home.

I redrew my Glock and aimed a clear shot at the head of the nearest rider. Cari's blasts were having no effect, and Kerrick's arrows were few and far between because he was stymied by our presence at the end of the clearing. Until we got the young girl and the children into the centipede, he could only let loose his charges when the ATVs were farther away.

As though to remind me that he had his hands tied, Kerrick shouted over the roar of the ATVs' sputtering motors, "I cannot help you, Stalker, if you all do not get out of the way."

I ignored him and momentarily shut out the world. Dempsey had taught me how to shoot through practically every situation, but mostly out of the passenger-side window of an ancient truck. Many of the targets I'd been given when I was younger—way before I got my license—were vicious and moving, oftentimes an ainmhi dubh or a nightmare. I just had to concentrate and compensate for the fact that I wasn't being jostled about on a cracked vinyl seat held together by strips of thick duct tape.

That was one thing I didn't miss. I could go for the rest of my life without having to pick gummy residue from the back of my legs or my clothes.

There were slight differences between the riders, and after the third pass, I noticed the little things, like a splash of green paint on the bumper of one ATV and the red marker line scribbled over a SoCalGov ID number on the upper right arm of the other's armor. Green Paint was a better driver, but Red Marker was a hell of a shot, hindered only by the erratic weave he used to avoid getting hit. The ATVs were old and had steering systems like an old Harley—one of the dream bikes I hoped to own one day. Steering an ATV with one hand and shooting with the other meant the rider's dominant hand had a gun in it, so guiding the heavy bike around was a bitch.

Weaving about was one thing, but finesse driving was out. I hoped that would be an advantage when I stood firm as they came back around, the muzzles of their guns aimed at the children.

It wasn't that I didn't hear anything. The ATVs were still loud and needed a good tune-up, but the sound was muted as I focused on my aim. I let off both shots, one after another. The weapons kicked up slightly, but the motion was so much a part of my everyday life that I didn't pay much mind. I only needed one to find its mark, yet a blink and a half later, two black holes appeared on Red Marker's ATV's gas tank, and things went to shit.

I had no idea what they were using to fuel those ATVs, but whatever it was, it was incendiary. What should have been a small explosion turned practically nuclear, and the blast threw us all back. The gas tank blew straight up into the air, its seat following close on. A billow of smoke poured out from its engulfed frame, and I lost sight of the driver. I was hoping to give Ryder enough time to get the kids into the transport, but the explosion took us all off our feet when the blast wave hit the clearing.

My roll into the rocks was a short one. Gravel bit into my back, and my elbow scraped across the dirt, but it wasn't bad. I couldn't see Cari, but I had to assume she was okay. The other ATV was caught in the chaos and tumbled past me, but its driver was nowhere to be found. A tire went bouncing by and nearly struck my head, and a burning piece of pipe struck Ryder's outstretched arm as he still tightly gripped the young girl's wrists.

The black plume lingered and hugged the ground. The wind pushed the smoke between us and then died, only to whisper a halfhearted gust across the north end of the clearing. At least knee-deep, the thick smoke masked almost everything. I had clear visibility only when the plume grew patchy and thin. The top of the transport poked up out of the acrid screen, and despite the rattle in my skull, it didn't appear as though Kerrick was still up there. Choking on the smoke I'd sucked down, I staggered to my feet to help Ryder, grateful that the wind had begun to pick up again and carry the stinging veil out of the clearing.

Or least I was before the grasses began to rustle again.

This time there were no engines. The rumbling wasn't mechanical. The growls I heard were vicious and mean, more of a predatory warning than anything else. I scrambled to find my guns, but my Glocks were lost in the flattened grasses, and I had yards of matted leaves and stalks to dig through. I found one right away, but the other wasn't going to do me any good.

The bitter smoke shifted, thinning for a bit, and revealed a pack of black dogs slowly stalking out of the grasses at the forest line, their slinking forms rippling shadows against the roiling plumes.

I didn't have any doubt that whoever created the pack was the same hunt master who'd stitched together the dog I'd killed back at the exit of the quadrant. All of their bodies were squat and muscular, and thick rolls of power moved beneath their taut black-dappled blue skin. Their heads were broad and flat, their long muzzles wide enough to hold teeth that could rip apart a man's thigh without much effort. I counted five dogs and then mentally added up the amount of ammo my gun probably had left. If the bandolier and shotgun I'd left by the transport hadn't been knocked under the vehicle in the explosion, I would probably be able to kill one before the others fell on me.

But it might buy the others time, I argued as I calculated the distance.

"Kai," Ryder hissed through the dissipating smoke. "We've got the kids."

His voice was low, but the lead dog perked up and scanned the clearing. The shifting smoke probably made it difficult for the dogs to see, and the smell of burning gas would mask our scents, but not for long. I finally spotted Cari crouched near Ryder, her arms full of two now very silent and still young elfin. I couldn't tell if they were breathing or not, and her face was a mask, devoid of emotion, despite the trail of blood that dribbled down her forehead and into her eyes.

"Move." I jerked my head toward the transport. "Lock it down and go."

"No," Cari spat back, her words sizzling like water on hot steel. "We're not leaving you behind."

It was her voice, the temper in her tone that did us in. Carrying over the clearing, the sound of her anger pricked the black dogs' keen hunting instincts, and they were on us before I could take another breath.

There had been times when I was fairly sure I was going to die. And every time, when I found myself standing in the remains of the fight, I thanked luck, the gods, and my weapons for seeing me through. This time I was pretty fricking sure I was damned near out of all of those things, so I had to give Ryder, Cari, and those kids enough time and cover to make it to the transport.

I hit the big one first. I'd like to say I surprised it, but I'm pretty sure it saw me coming. I'm also pretty sure it laughed. Armed only with a half-full Glock and a long dagger, I was going to be a very tasty meal. But it would buy them time. They didn't have a lot of distance to cover, and those were small kids. Cari and Ryder could get them inside. Kerrick was on his own, and hopefully he would be smart enough to take cover under the transport as soon as he caught a whiff of the black dogs' rancid scent.

The ainmhi dubh met me halfway. Its open maw was a hot box of foul gases and sharp teeth, and its narrow eyes were laser focused on me, its broad paws scraping back the grasses to expose the loamy soil beneath. It hit my right side, its body hard and unforgiving. I stabbed its shoulder with my knife and dug the blade down into its flesh, hoping to find anything vital. Instead the meat tore under the sharp edge, and the knife sliced out of its leg.

It whirled about, and a torrent of black blood splashed over my bare hand and singed it. Thickly muscled, its momentum was hindered by its lack of agility, its body too massive to fold in tight turns. I heard the hiss of the transport's main door closing and then the screams of the other ainmhi dubh as they pounded the metal hull of the centipede and raked at its plated exterior with their claws.

I was alone, and I was going to die alone. Thoughts and emotions rushed through me in those few seconds I had left. I wouldn't see my nieces grow up. I wouldn't know who would win the back-and-forth war of sexual tension Ryder and I had been fighting since we first met. I wouldn't know who would take care of Newt, but I was fairly certain it would be Dalia or even the Sidhe lordling, who'd spent afternoons trying to coax the cat into liking him. I would never get my Mustang back on the road.

Then I gave a short laugh, amused beyond belief at the irony of Dempsey outliving me.

The ainmhi dubh found me in the smoke and lunged, its mouth stretched open wide enough to clip my head clean off if it could only get the right angle. Two feet away from me, it launched up off the ground, spittle flying and its partially severed flesh flapping as it arched toward me.

Shoving the Glock out in front of me, I angled it as best I could and emptied my clip into its throat.

Whoever its hunt master was, they didn't have Tanic's skills. The monster was nearly a perfect killing machine, but apparently its creator didn't thicken the bone-mass plate inside of the ainmhi dubh's mouth.

My bullets tore its skull apart. Bone chips and brains blew out in a geyser of gore, expelled through a hole nearly the size of my fist. Its momentum continued forward, the creature's body not quite understanding its brain was no longer there. Then its gait faltered, and its back legs stumbled and then gave out and slammed its rear to the ground. A few more twitches of its shoulders and the ainmhi dubh was on me.

Shoving at it when it approached took it off its course, but my arms ached from the effort of turning its heavy weight. My gun was empty, and the shots were loud. They reverberated against the sides of the transport, practically calling the other black dogs to me. I reached for one of my clips, ejected the spent one from my Glock, and turned to face the rest of the pack, only to discover Ryder hadn't shut himself inside with Cari and the kids.

The damned idiot was standing at the front of the transport, armed with my discarded shotgun and my bandolier slung over his shoulder. He gave me a tense cocky grin and lifted the weapon up, ready to pull the trigger.

"Aim for their mouths," I told him as I circled into the clearing a bit to separate the black dogs' attention. We didn't have a chance in hell of surviving. But at least I wasn't alone—even if he was a fucking idiot for standing with me.

The dogs paced, their shoulders low and their ears flat against their heads. Their leader's corpse lay twitching a few feet away from me, probably confusing them, but instinct would always win out. As soon as they got themselves sorted, the rest of them would attack. We could only hope to get in a few good shots.

I almost didn't see Kerrick come up behind Ryder. When I spotted his slender form slipping out of the wispy smoke at the end of the clearing, a sense of relief overcame me. He had a weapon that could do a lot of damage if he could get his charged arrows into their throats, but he wasn't holding his bow.

Kerrick was armed with a long dagger, and he plunged it into Ryder's ribs as soon as he got close.

I didn't remember running across the clearing. I didn't remember anything from when I saw that blade slice through Ryder's side, and then the gush of hot blood that poured out of the wound sank in and I no longer saw anything but my next target.

Kerrick was beneath me a second later. I slammed into his face with my fists, the punches weighted by the steel gun in my grip. It felt good to break his skin under my knuckles, to hear the crunch of a bone break with my next strike, and when my arm finally grew tired, I held my gun to his head and stared down at his bloodied face.

My one hand shook as I pressed my Glock into his forehead, my rage turning the edges of my vision a brilliant red, and I drew one of my hunting knives, a long wicked thing I used to skin black dogs after a kill. I didn't care that my back was to the ainmhi dubh. I didn't give a shit if the black dogs ate the transport and made themselves peanut butter and elfin-children sandwiches. The only thing I desperately needed was to taste Kerrick's blood on the flat of my blade after I was done carving his bones out of his flesh.

I made the first cut. A long shallow slice over his chest where I knew his collarbone lay beneath. I would take that out first and then work my way down his ribs, maybe even stopping to see what it would feel like to have his spine in my hand before I yanked it free. *Nothing* else mattered.

Or at least it didn't until Ryder closed his hand over my shoulder.

"Kai, I'm fine. I turned, and he didn't hit anything vital. Please, stop," he whispered. I smelled his blood, the rich scent of his body pouring out between his clenched fingers where he pressed his hand across his wound. "Don't kill him. Do not. You are better than that."

"No, I'm not," I said, looking up at him. I had one knee on the ground and the other one pressed into Kerrick's chest. His hands looked broken, and the dagger he'd been holding lay in pieces by his knee. The Sidhe lord's face was a mess of broken bones and blood, his eyes turning purple, his lashes slowly swallowed up in bruised swells. "I want him dead. He stabbed you. Yes, I know it's wrong, but he's going to keep coming after you. What's to stop him from doing this again? If he dies here, I don't have to worry about him. I don't have to worry for you. I'm pissed off as fucking hell, and your cousin has proven to be as much of a monster as those black dogs. So give me one good damn reason—other than the fact that it's morally wrong—to let the son of a bitch live."

"Yes, Ryder, Clan Sebac, High Lord of the Southern Rise Court, answer him. Give him one good reason to let your enemy live," a feminine voice called out across the clearing, and we both looked up, startled at the arrival of a slender, gorgeous Unsidhe woman dressed in tight riding leathers and stroking the heads of the black dog pack writhing in submission at her feet. "I would like to hear what answer you could give Ciméara cuid Anbhás to make him stay his hand."

Twenty-Three

THE UNSIDHE woman stood a few inches shorter than me, but her presence dominated the clearing. There was no question about who the ainmhi dubh belonged to. Their subservience was awe inspiring, or it would have been if I hadn't seen Tanic with his dogs. Her face was hard—all bones and cruel mouth—and framed with a wealth of deep-ocean-blue loose curls. Silver shimmered in the waves that cascaded past her shoulders and down her back. Her hammered-gold eyes narrowed, her black lashes curving up at the corners into sweeping wings. The ebony leathers she wore left little to the imagination as they followed the curves of her hips and breasts. And the stretch of her long legs would have made a blind man weep if you didn't pay attention to the edge of cruelty lurking in her gaze.

An air cycle sat parked at the edge of the forest line, a sleek and silent machine most people only dreamed about owning. Hers was banged up and pitted along the bumpers, probably from ainmhi dubh spit. If I were into that kind of bike, I would've cried. As it was I was just happy I had a full clip in my gun and probably more than enough time to shoot her and Kerrick so we could go home.

"You know who we are, but I haven't heard of you. Or at least, haven't heard of an Unsidhe lord like you," Ryder said in that softly arrogant lordling tone I hated so much.

We were both covered with dirt and blood—his more recent than mine—but he held himself as though he were greeting guests back at Balboa. It was hard to ignore me sitting on top of his cousin, my gun pressed into Kerrick's forehead, and blood was seeping from a cut to Ryder's side, but he forged on and performed a cursory bow.

"So, if you would introduce yourself, as I don't believe we've had the pleasure of meeting before."

"It isn't often I stray this far north," she replied. "But then you have also never been this far south in the few months you have been in the region. Is there a particular reason you've wandered so far from your nest? Meeting with the Penault, perhaps? The one you've left alive is out there still. I'm sure of it. I can send my dogs to get him. Do I need to? Will he tell me a different story from the one you will tell me?"

As though called into the conversation, a moaning sound came from the grasses, and the ainmhi dubh stiffened as one, their ears perked up into sharp peaks and their haunches firmly anchored to the ground. They sniffed at the air, and their gleaming crimson eyes followed the woman's movement as she strolled toward the black dogs' pack leader.

"We came at the request of a dead friend," Ryder explained. "We came to pick up the Unsidhe woman looking for a new life. The Penault murdered her. Killed her as she was trying to protect the children she brought with her. Do you have so many elfin in your court that you can slaughter them at your leisure?"

"Children who are not hers, and they are a distraction my people do not need. As for the woman, I knew of her. It's why I followed—mostly to ensure she succeeded. One of the other houses in the area smuggled her out so she could take the children away. Someone has a very loose mouth, so it seems everyone knew of her flight north, including human hunters who kill us for sport and the Penault, who didn't want to lose their pets."

She crouched next to the black dog and bent one knee to the ground while she kept the other up—a good position in case she needed to run. I couldn't read her face. It was an impenetrable mask, but there seemed a bit of softening to the set of her firm mouth when she ran her slender fingers across the ainmhi dubh's blown-out skull.

"Oh my dearest, what has he done to you?"

"He tried to eat my face," I said. "We had a difference of opinion on the matter, and he wasn't willing to listen. If you sent them after the kids, then he deserved what he got."

"I sent my pack to deal with the Penault. That house has been a thorn in my side for years now. I wanted the Sidhe children gone, but they are considered valuable, a bit of coin to a desperate house. I felt it was time to step in. My ainmhi dubh must've seen you as the bigger threat, and that is why he attacked. That's two of my dogs that you've killed, Ciméara." Her hard gaze found me through the dissipating smoke and locked on my face. Standing slowly, she dusted off her hand and then canted her head to study me. "You like killing ainmhi dubh. I would appreciate it if you left mine alone."

"I would leave them alone if they didn't try to kill me," I replied, and then I tilted my gun up when Kerrick shifted beneath my knee. He was struggling to get free, and I was just no longer in the mood to deal with any of his bullshit. "Stay *down*, asshole. It's not like I forgot you were there."

"Lady, hear me out. We can help each other," Kerrick called out to her. "I *will* rule the Southern Rise Court. We can come to a deal, share our resources. You only have to——"

Gods, I should have stabbed him.

"I do not *have* to do anything, especially bargain with a man lying on his back with a gun pointed at his head." She took a step forward but stopped when the dogs flowed across the clearing and put themselves between her and us. Glancing at the transport, she smiled, and I followed her gaze. Cari was staring out at us through the windows of the main doors, cradling a child to her chest. "Ah, there are the children. I am somewhat surprised they got this far. The Penault is known for having good hunters. But perhaps they are not as good as you, Ciméara."

"Kai, get up off of him," Ryder said. "I have more of those ties you gave me. We can secure his wrists. And *not* kill him."

"I'd rather send him the way of the ainmhi dubh, but this is your circus, lordling." I stood up and pressed the flat of my foot into Kerrick's throat. I didn't care if he choked on my boot. He wasn't going anywhere. "What do you want, lady?"

"The question isn't what I want but rather what I will take." She inched around her ainmhi dubh and shoved them aside with her hands as though they were nothing more than a cluster of tiny Chihuahuas. She smiled in a way that set my nerves on fire, and despite the distance between us, my body whispered that it wouldn't mind a taste of her... or her tasting me. "I will make you a deal, Lord Ryder. You take the children the Penault were chasing and leave me with Tanic's son."

I aimed my gun at her face, and Ryder literally growled.

"Not anyone's pet," I said, pressing my boot down harder when Kerrick wiggled. "I don't belong to anyone but me."

"Well, it was worth a try. Mostly I wanted Chaulin to leave the Sidhe children with you, but I found out about her leaving too late to protect her. So instead, I ended up chasing the Penault in order to stop them from killing her," she drawled elegantly, giving me a graceful shrug while she stepped over the severed arm of one of the ATV drivers. Another bit of moaning crept through the air, and she flicked her fingers out and bent her wrist up slightly in a casual, dismissive gesture that sent the ainmhi dubh pack careening toward the grasses beyond the clearing. "And if you're worried, they will bring the other one back safe and sound. I have a message for him to return to his house.

I'll take back Chaulin, the woman they killed, to her family."

"I would have your name at least." Ryder took a few steps, clutching his side, but he didn't so much as wince when he walked. "You clearly know Kai but use a name he does not like. You obviously know me and believe you can manipulate me into abandoning either the children I came to rescue or Kai, someone I value above all."

"Actually, kind of hoping you put the nieces above me," I pointed out. "For one thing they're babies, and then there's the fact that I'm a Stalker and probably won't live very long."

"Kai, please try to live as long as I need you to live and perhaps even a second past that." Ryder didn't so much as glance back at me, but if I thought the woman in front of us had ice in her voice, there was a glacier in his. "I am not sure I believe your willingness to give us the children without a fight or a ransom, especially since the Tijuana Dusk Court is in shambles."

"So you'd rather I just take them from you?" She gestured to the surrounding grasses. "I have enough ainmhi dubh to make that happen if I want to."

Ryder didn't even blink. "Then I will have to ask Kai to do to you what he did to the ainmhi dubh. So choose carefully."

"And they said you were a pacifist," she purred, a smile lifting her hard face into a startling beauty. "I really *was* trying to help her, not the Penault. We are allies of sorts. The head of the Penault house and their clan usually align with mine, but lately they've taken to stealing humans *and* Sidhe. I want that to stop. We need to take care of our own."

"Allies don't bring packs of ainmhi dubh with them to start negotiations. Usually, if a Wild Hunt is in the mix, it means someone's been served up for dinner," I said as I pulled Kerrick up into a sitting position. He needed to go into the transport, out of my sight for a bit, because even though my anger had ebbed, it flared up a little bit every time he struggled. "Try pulling the other leg."

"There are too many tiny clans, and their infighting cripples our court. Our resources are stretched too thin, and we are forgetting our ways," she replied as she nudged the severed arm away with a kick of her boot toe. "I am Bannon cuid Xandras, Hunt Master and Lord of the Clan Xandras. And soon, the High Lord of the Tijuana Dusk Court."

"Ambitious," I conceded. "Good luck. That place's been a mess since before the Merge, right?"

"It's a different world now. It's time for new leadership," she replied. "While I have a reason to be here, you are on the wrong side of the caverns, Lord Ryder. If you'd meant to invade our territories, you should have brought a different army… and perhaps one that wouldn't stab you while you weren't looking. I am supposed to believe you just came down to rescue three Sidhe children?"

"It was supposed to be a simple run down to pick them up," Ryder explained.

"They're all supposed to be simple runs," I complained, jostling a grumbling Kerrick. He sat with his legs straight out, making him difficult for me to control, especially with his hands loose. "And they never are."

"The children needed sanctuary. I intend to provide it. They'll enter my court, become my people, who I've promised to protect and nurture." Ryder ignored me. "What do you want, Bannon?"

"*My* people need someone to think for them, someone to guide them," she continued, her voice growing haughty. A circuit of the clearing drew her close to me, and the desire to taste her mouth overwhelmed me. She stopped short. Her lips parted, and her eyes widened slightly, her posture not that different from the ainmhi dubh hunting through the grasses. "You are very… enticing, Ciméara. You might consider joining me."

I knew what she felt. It touched me in places only Ryder did, but with a different tingle, a different taste. If there was any doubt of my split bloodline, Bannon put that to rest. I was as much drawn to the Unsidhe lord as I was the Sidhe.

"Kai." Ryder's mouth was a thin line, tense and holding back words he couldn't speak out loud. He couldn't say I was his. I wasn't his court. I wasn't his people, but that didn't mean I wanted to dance over the border to join her. "We don't know her."

We. He wasn't speaking in the sense of a royal we. He meant me and him. We didn't know her. Didn't know who she was, didn't know what she was capable of, and there was a hint of trepidation in his voice, a wavering doubt, as though he also knew she tickled at places only he had before. There hadn't been any Unsidhe who'd made enough of a mark for Ryder to take notice, but Bannon was standing up to be counted. Right here. Right now. She was going to be a force to be reckoned with, and she would be knocking at his back door, pushing at his court, and maybe even trying to steal me out from under his nose.

It was funny how much a single *we* could hold.

I cleared my throat and jostled Kerrick's arm. He bitched back at me in Sidhe. "Sorry, lady, but I'm on a job. You can have Kerrick if you want. I'll even throw in some military rations to sweeten the deal."

"I would not take him." She laughed when the ainmhi dubh broke free of the grasses, hot on the heels of the other ATV rider. He was injured, bleeding from several places, and he held his arm tightly against his chest, but when he stumbled to the ground at her feet, the black dogs only nudged aggressively at his body and pushed him about. "And the only reason I'm taking this one is because I need him to inform everyone in his family that I am coming for them and they can either choose to join me or feed my dogs.

"You ask me what I want, Ryder? It's very simple. I want a clan and court that doesn't beg for food from humans. We're stealing Sidhe to increase our numbers, and all we get are Sidhe. Our own lines are too weak, too fragile, and that is the fault of the clans not being led by true clan heads. That has to change if we are to survive." She gave Ryder another smile, and I chuckled. "What do you find funny, Ciméara?"

"The two of you should really get together and talk dynasties," I replied, gesturing slightly with my gun in case she'd forgotten it was there. "So you're just going to let us walk out with the kids? And not get anything in return?"

"I didn't say that," Bannon disagreed. "I want you, Ryder, to stay out of my way. I will let these three go with you, but in the future, no Unsidhe will cross this border. You will promise to turn them away, to not lure them from the court. You will give me your word you will not poach my numbers. Because this region will be mine, will fall into my control."

"No. You said it yourself, these people flee because they are being starved out and abused," Ryder countered as he pulled out a couple of the zip ties I'd given him earlier. He held them toward me and gestured toward Kerrick. Then he turned to face the Unsidhe lord. "I would take in any elfin, regardless of race. If they are fleeing hunger and oppression, I will welcome them. I'm not going to send somebody off to die because you feel they need to sit at your feet."

"When I secure the entire Dusk Court, I can give all the Unsidhe a better life," Bannon said. "How about if I will give you every Sidhe I find in the houses that claim fealty to me so none of mine risks their lives crossing the border to a nirvana I will soon be able to give them? We are Unsidhe. There is too much of your kind and humans creeping into our culture. We are losing ourselves, and I cannot allow that. If all my people are doing is bringing in others, soon others will be all there are here, and we will be no more."

"You sound like you're preparing for war, not just with my race but also with the humans." Ryder stepped aside to let me hogtie Kerrick. "You say bloodlines and purity, but I hear closed-mindedness and bigotry."

"I do not want or need a war. My own people are dying. It is time to purge those houses who would sooner kill each other than put food back on our people's tables. Surely you can agree with that," she asserted. "And if you would like a gesture of goodwill, get your chimera to walk away, and my ainmhi dubh would be happy to have a Sidhe lordling as their next meal."

"No thank you. I will not sacrifice my cousin for your ambitions." Ryder sighed and glanced at me. "If your people make it to my court, Bannon, I will not return them to you, but they will have to make it into San Diego. I can promise we will not retrieve them from the border. You've already said they are starving and being taken advantage of by their houses and clans. If they want out badly enough, they're welcome, but should you provide them with a place—a safe place—for them to return to, without fear of retribution and retaliation for leaving, I will let them go. But it would have to be their choice to return."

"I will agree to that," she said, inclining her head. "But one last thing—your Stalker was right, Ryder. If you do not kill him—this cousin—he will attempt to murder you again. And if he's successful, then Kai will kill him, plunging your region into chaos, beginning a battle between the Chimera and your grandmother, the duplicitous spider. That is not a war your people would survive. So you see, it is better to feed him to my dogs."

"I like her, Ryder. She's practical." I zipped the last plastic tie around Kerrick's wrists and made sure it was tight. It wasn't in me to kill Kerrick, or at least not once my rage settled down. I hated the bastard, and I needed to get Ryder into the transport before he lost too much blood and passed out at my feet, but that wasn't a reason to kill Kerrick. "And I don't give a shit about what you say. He's getting packed back up and dumped on your grandmother's doorstep as soon as we get back."

"Hush. Killing Kerrick isn't an option, and you would never do it. Are we in agreement, Bannon?"

Ryder held his hand out to her, his fingers cupped and ready for her binding shake. "And should you ever decide to move against me, I will send my chimera to you, and he will return with not only the heads of your ainmhi dubh but with your skull for me to drink from."

As much as I didn't like everyone automatically assuming I was an extension of Ryder's court, I didn't mind him using me as a threat. Bannon had a pack of ainmhi dubh, and he needed to come to the table as some kind of fighter. Sure, he'd taken a knife to the ribs and then gotten back up as easily as pouring a cup of tea for an afternoon picnic, but the tightness around his eyes told me he was in pain. Bannon didn't seem like the kind of woman who appreciated weakness. Threats seemed to work, or at least make her pause.

Bannon hesitated—not long, but just enough for her eyes to settle on me for a split second as she debated the pros and cons of Ryder's offer. Whatever she was looking for or at, she evidently didn't like what she found, because Bannon stuck her hand out and clasped Ryder's.

"Agreed," she replied softly. "Now take your Sidhe—both the ones you came for and the one who tried to kill you—and get the hell off my lands."

Twenty-Four

"THERE. THAT should do." I tightened the last rope across Chaulin's carefully wrapped body and secured her to the back of Bannon's air glide. Having the Unsidhe lord at my back made me uncomfortable, especially since she seemed to have a hard time keeping her hands to herself. After another brush of her hand against the back of my thigh, I growled, "Swear to Pele, you do that one more time and you're going to be pulling back stubs."

"I am helping," Bannon protested softly, but I heard the mocking laughter in her words.

"I can't believe I'm saying this, but you're a complication I really don't need or want." I sighed when she stepped back, glad for the breathing room. "Besides, show Chaulin *some* respect."

"Chaulin's family will be accepted into my clan for her sacrifice in returning the Sidhe to their own people. Her body is just meat." Bannon nodded toward the open transport. "Much like that other one should be, but I understand how he thinks."

"I'd say I agreed with you right up until the part where I wanted to kill him. Ryder's right. Can't make a utopia if you kill off everyone who disagrees with you. That kind of thinking leads to people like Sebac. I forgot that. Won't happen again." I'd tucked in the flowers the children had gathered up for Chaulin's body into the folds of her clothes, but I wondered if her family would toss them away, thinking they were trash. "Can you make sure they keep the prairie flowers with her? It's all the kids have to give her."

"They will. I'll tell them." Her gaze roamed over my face, searching for something. "I wouldn't have thought you'd be sentimental. What do you care about a dead Unsidhe? You did not even know her."

"Because she died protecting those kids… kids who don't even have names," I pointed out. "Don't have to know her to respect the hell out of her."

"Kai! We're almost done here," Cari called out from the open door of the centipede. "If we're going to get to the barn before dark, we've got to move out soon!"

"Yeah, be right there." Not knowing what else to do, I patted Chaulin's wrapped shoulder and wished her soul the best. It didn't seem fair that she was going home to be buried and we were carting Kerrick back home, even though I'd rearranged his too-pretty face into something more in line with his soul. "I've got to go check on how Ryder's stitches are holding up and how well he did with securing Kerrick."

"Do you think he'd allow Kerrick to get loose?" Bannon asked.

"Probably not, but I wouldn't be surprised if Ryder hand-fed the asshole all the way home and checked every hour to see if he was comfy. If it were left up to me, he'd lose a limb or two because I cut off his circulation tying him to the chair." I shrugged and stared at the battered transport we'd fought to get righted. "We've got to refill our water supplies before those kids can get bathed. Lost too much of it in the tumble. They're my focus right now. Kerrick's just a stain we're taking with us until we can dump him."

The day was eaten up first by the resurrection of the centipede and then by harnessing Bannon's black dogs to the Unsidhe's ATV so they could drag him back to her court. She sent them on ahead, confident they'd get him there or maybe knowing they'd go half a mile and decide to eat him instead. I didn't know, and I wasn't sure if I cared. As long as I didn't see it, I was fine with either outcome. Something told me Bannon probably was too.

"You okay with your pack going on ahead?" As much as she seemed capable of taking care of herself, Bannon was also the best option to stabilize the Dusk Court. I didn't trust her, but it was just better to take what I could get.

"Are you worried about me, Ciméara?" Bannon powered up her glide and switched over to the cells she'd charged from her solar panels while we prepared Chaulin's body. "I am touched."

"Just want you to get home in one piece. There's people's asses you need to kick." I was going to wish her a good trip, but something shifted in the forest beyond—a shadow flitted against the flow of the wind. "Hold up."

Something was advancing in the sparse woods. It crept beneath the underbrush line, sunk down low to the ground. Whatever it was, its gait was jerky—a flash of ungainly movement and then a deathly stillness where it landed back in the deepening blue shadows. It was too sleek to be one of Bannon's pack circling around to take us out, but I wouldn't have put it past her. And she was tense. She held herself alert and reached for the gun she'd tucked into the console space of the air glide. If she'd been planning to double-cross us, she would have done it sooner and not waited for me to help her with the dead woman's body.

Or so I hoped.

The shadow crept closer, and I was going to have to make some pretty hard decisions. My Glocks were still on me, as were my knives. It wasn't like I was going to walk outside of the transport unarmed. There were too many things that wanted to make snacks out of anything remotely meaty, and I now had an entire tactical vehicle filled with more than enough walking buffets to feed even the most starving predator.

"Cari, close the door!" I lifted my voice, praying she wouldn't argue. If the shadow turned out to be nothing more than a wandering dog, I would take mockery. "Bannon, if I were you, I would get on that glide right now and leave."

"I'm not sure I trust you enough to give you a clear shot at my back," she argued teasingly. The shadow moved again and jerked toward another clump of bushes. "You are too far away from your vehicle to make it safely. Whatever that is, it's moving too quickly. I don't know how fast you are, but it's not something you should risk. If you don't make it, and they leave the door open for you, it could savage everyone in there. So I'll stay, and look, it's much closer now."

"Cari!" I drew my Glock as the thick bushes rustled. "Close the fucking door!"

It flowed out of the forest line—a feline abomination crafted from magic and rancid flesh. It didn't have the sleek power of Bannon's pack, but it was clearly an ainmhi dubh. And its maker was insane or desperate.

I couldn't bring myself to call it a black dog. This creature was far from the necromantic monsters my father created. I didn't know how old Tanic was, but I also never heard of anyone else being called the Lord Master of the Wild Hunt. Elfin history stretched back as far as the mountains, lost somewhere in the creation of dirt and air, but there was always Tanic cuid Anbhás. He was the stuff of legends and nightmares, the bringer of death and the creator of cruelty. I wore his face but refused to wear his name, although it followed me—my own personal ainmhi dubh.

I'd shit myself the first time I saw my reflection. There was so much of him in me, I'd fall into the terror of my memories, and it took Dempsey and Jonas a good half an hour and a bathtub full of ice to stop me from screaming. From what little I'd heard from the elfin in Ryder's court, what he'd done to me was nearly affectionate and loving. I knew that wasn't true, because the only thing Tanic cuid Anbhás loved was his Wild Hunt, and he took great pride not only in the mastery of controlling them but also in their creation.

The thing coming toward us in a full gallop was fast, a blur of rippling flesh and vomit-inducing stink, and its construction was hideous. It'd been a cat—perhaps a jaguar or maybe even a tiger—but with all of the animals loosed from the safari park and the region's native creatures, it could've been anything. There seemed to be more muscles along its body than there should have been, and its jaw opened up like a pair of mandibles when it roared, exposing a gnarly cluster of sharklike teeth lining its mouth. Its gait was awkward—its knees bending out in a flopping motion—but it sprinted across the beaten-down grasses, and the slippery broken stalks hardly slowed it down.

"Kai! I can cover you!" Cari shouted at me, but I couldn't turn to look at her. A second later I heard the door hiss and its hydraulics slowly squeak as it lurched closed. "Ryder, you—"

I didn't hear the rest of it, but good for Ryder. He finally understood when I gave an order I expected it to be followed. That was something Cari and I would have to talk about once I got out of this mess.

If I got out of this mess.

"I guess it's just you and me, then, Ciméara." Bannon chuckled.

"For the last time, my name is Kai Gracen." I planted myself and aimed at the creature's sloping head. "Try to keep up, lordling."

The boom of my gun sent a flurry of white birds scattering from the canopy of the forest. My shots plowed into the creature's head and punctured its skull, but the damned thing wouldn't drop. It felt like more than magic was fueling its rage and hunger, and I was running out of bullets.

Next to me, Bannon crouched behind the air glide to give herself some cover and rested the muzzle of her gun on the bumper of her vehicle to steady her aim. It seemed profane to be hiding behind a dead woman's body, but the dead were never around to protest.

The creature hit her. It leapt over her low-slung glide and sent it down into the ground and broke its hover. Bannon never made a sound. Instead she brought up her weapon and emptied her charge into the thing's belly. She fought to keep her head away from its chomping jaws, but I could smell the sear of her flesh when its spit dripped down onto her face, and the whimper that escaped her mouth made my decision for me.

Guns weren't going to stop that thing, but a knife probably would.

I loved daggers. I loved them almost as much as I did a finely tuned V-8 engine or the blast of blues music through the speakers in my warehouse. As much as I suffered under the kiss of iron beneath my skin, I loved the hell out of steel. I didn't really understand it, but I embraced it. I loved what it could do for me, how it could catapult me safely across miles of lava fields with dragons on my tail, or how, wrapped tightly into a string and played through amplifiers, it took my soul places I didn't think I could fly.

But mostly I loved how it parted flesh. I was often ashamed to admit that. It reminded me too much of my father, and maybe that was something else he gave me besides my face. I didn't know how much of me was simply an echo of him, and since I never saw a sign of whichever woman he'd taken to create me, I was left with only the imprint of him to fill in.

He loved carving flesh. I knew that intimately, but this was different, or so I told myself. This was mastery of the blade and using it to survive.

And I was damned good at surviving.

I took the abomination at the throat and sliced across its larynx. Most black dogs needed air to pump through their bodies. Even if they were magical creations, their existence and functions were still rooted in basic physiology. That's what separated Tanic's creations from lesser hunt masters. He didn't just animate stitched-together beasts. He understood how they worked and built them from the inside out to create nearly indestructible creatures.

Bannon's came close—very close—but I could see flaws, even though I didn't understand how, and once I saw them, they stuck out like a sore thumb. I knew why the black dog I killed earlier had succumbed to my shots. I wouldn't be able to tell her how to fix it, and I wouldn't want to, because knowing a weakness was always a benefit, but this one—*this cat*—wasn't going to fall from anything other than a well-placed blade.

The cat turned on me and let go of Bannon's arm. She was a mess, flesh hanging from her wrist and forearm, bleeding strips tangled with the remains of her shirtsleeve. Straddling her legs, I kicked back at her knee and pushed her away from the glide.

"Move," I ordered curtly as I drew my daggers. The sing of steel out of leather was to be all the warning I would give her. If Bannon didn't get out of the way, she was probably going to die. "*Now*."

I didn't have time to give her specific instructions, like *get out from underfoot* or *see if you can make it to the transport*, while I tried to kill the thing. Short and sweet would have to do. At least she got out of the way, because suddenly she wasn't beneath my legs, and the monster was on me.

Its bones didn't seem to be its weakness, so I would have to go in another way. There still was a heart and a brain, but the skull was impenetrable. I could see the divots in its sickly gray skin where my bullets went in—dimpled black craters that marked its flocked, sparse, bleached-out fur. Its canines were massive and dropped below its jaw when its mouth closed, and its claws were glittering black talons with points sharp enough to shred the grasses beneath its feet. Its disgusting odor hit me when it turned. It was so foul I could barely keep my stomach from empty- ing out the small bite of rations I'd taken to show the little boy we'd rescued that the food was okay to eat.

Growling, it opened its jaws again, its lower bone separated once more into two Y-shaped lengths, and its bright pink tongue flopped down between them. I didn't understand the purpose of its creator's design at first, until I realized the thing could clamp down on an appendage and saw it off, using the rows of teeth on all its exposed surfaces to mangle through flesh and bone.

Whatever I did, I had to make sure it couldn't get hold of me.

The bastard ainmhi dubh leapt and headed straight for me. I waited until the last moment and then ducked under and struck its chest with my shoul- der. The damned thing was heavier than I imagined, probably because its creator had thickened its bones. Flying over me, the cat tried to adjust in midair, but its back end didn't swerve like a cat's would. Whoever made it stripped away the grace of its natural design, leaving it unbalanced and unable to easily change its course. I'd been around long enough to know how a cat could fold itself in two and land on its feet, so I winced when it struck the packed-down grasses with a loud crunch.

"Bannon?" I risked calling out to her, but I couldn't see where the Unsidhe lord had gone. There was no way she could have gotten to the transport, and with the way the hydraulics were operating, I would've heard their screams over anything.

"By the glide." Her voice trembled in a painful rasp of unadulterated Unsidhe. "I'm bleeding out. I'm trying to wrap it."

Her words were ones I knew too well, and they invoked an unpleasantness from deep inside of me. I was free of Tanic's spells, the verbal commands he'd laid down on my bones and blood, but I'd shaken them off over time, as one of his disciples learned a few months back. Still, the nuances of the Unsidhe language dredged up things I couldn't deal with while I fought a monster.

And there was something so damn familiar about how it smelled.

I didn't wait for it to attack me again. As it was shaking off its failure, I aimed for its belly and struck. Its claws flashed, and I felt the sting of them on my back. One hooked into my shirt and ripped it, but it also found the scar beneath. *Something* went awry. The pain that spread through the dragon wings across my back was both incredible and agonizing. I could feel every mote of iron dust left under my flesh, every bit that was roiled into the keloids Tanic had put on me. The rush of something akin to anger surged through my body, and I felt *defiled* by its bastardized magic.

My back went wet with blood, but I didn't feel the pain anymore. I was oddly calm despite an inner rage I couldn't quite place. This ainmhi dubh was wrong in so many ways. I felt that. I knew that. And I didn't just have to kill it because I needed to survive. It had to die because it was an affront to everything ever made.

Curling around, I landed on my back and slid across the slick ground under the creature. The grasses whipped me about, and the uneven terrain threw my slide off, but it was enough momentum to carry me past the monster's belly before it could get its jaws into my flesh.

My dagger ripped through its stomach, and the hilt slammed against my palm as my glide took me under its low-hanging belly. Fluids gushed out of the wound, and I rolled to avoid them, well aware that its blood would burn. Scrambling to get out from under its thrashing body, I lost hold of my blade, which left me with only one. The grasses cut at my free hand, their sharp leaves prickly with tiny thorns, and my palms smarted from the contact.

Still, the ainmhi dubh stalked me.

The belly wound was serious, but even though it favored its left side, the creature circled around, red eyes gleaming with furious hunger. Confusion flickered in them momentarily, and then it paced about as though looking for a good angle to strike. I stood, shaking my stinging hand, and kept myself between it and the glide. Bannon was on the other side of the machine and too injured to be any use in a fight. With any luck, the blood beading on my hand would draw the creature's notice to me and away from her. I knew it could smell us in the air. We were wounded, ripe for its attack. And although I'd proven to be an inhospitable prey, I was the only one it could get to, or at least that's what I was betting on.

I was wrong.

Whatever its maker put into its back legs, it had to be part kangaroo, because the damned thing took a giant leap and sailed over me. Its wounds gushed, splayed open by the pull of its muscles, but its tiny brain only focused on one thing—the hunt. It didn't concern itself with survival. It didn't think beyond its one initiative—*to kill*.

Maybe it had been sent to kill Unsidhe, or even Bannon specifically, but whatever drove it, it ignored me.

I would've been insulted if I didn't have to kill it before it ate the only chance the Tijuana Dusk Court had to get a high lord who gave a shit about its people.

As stupid as it sounded, I grabbed its tail.

And yanked.

My dagger sliced through its flesh, but it wasn't like I was going to drop my blade in order to literally catch a tiger by its tail. The ainmhi dubh's blood stung my hands and blistered my skin, and I felt every single ounce of its weight pulling at my sockets when I wrenched my shoulders to the side and strained to throw it off course. It came down in a crash on the glide, knocking it so far off its stabilizing field the vehicle went crazy, bucking like a wild bronco.

Bannon shouted, staggered up to her feet, and with an erratic flail of her uninjured arm, blasted the creature's head with everything she had left in her weapon. The ainmhi dubh scrambled over the metal sides of the glide, its back legs raking into the machine's seat. Screaming, Bannon struck it with the stock of her emptied weapon as I yelled at her to run.

She listened about as well as Cari did.

I couldn't let go. Wedged up against the glide and with the creature's tail caught tightly in my hand, I could only reach its back end with my dagger. Blood slickened its fur, and I wouldn't be able to hold on much longer, so I spun my dagger around my knuckles to change the angle of my grip and plunged it up between the folds of its haunches.

Its meat severed off its bones in chunks and dropped to the ground as wet splats. The force of its back legs lessened, and its scrambling paws began to fling wide, missing Bannon by a mile. Its jaw caught the edge of her cheek and sliced down her face, and she reeled back, still holding her weapon up to strike.

I kept shoving my knife into its belly, not caring where it landed so long as the blade went in deep and I could feel its flesh tearing. Then one thrust got it right. The creature shuddered and coughed, and black blood splattered out of its gaping maw. I twisted my blade, wrenched it back toward me, and felt it glide through something soft.

Then the ainmhi dubh's belly opened up, and its insides burst free. Its intestines spooled out over the grasses as its body began to seize up.

I let go of its tail and scrambled over the glide to tackle Bannon before she could hit it again. Her injured arm was slack and wet, her blood soaked through the pieces of shirtsleeve she'd used to wrap up her wounds. The skin on her face was bubbled up where the acid had struck it, and her eyes were blind with rage. She fought me, nearly as viciously as she battled the ainmhi dubh, and it was all I could do to hold her down.

The things she called me—they would've made my mother weep, if I had one.

"Let me go!" She bit my ear. Literally *bit* my ear. "I will have your—"

"Bannon, think really hard before threatening me," I warned as I tried to tug free of her teeth. "And Iesu, now I know how Dempsey felt. *Stop* biting me."

The ainmhi dubh's death was violent. And worse, its magic began to unravel as it died. The stench of its rotted meat worsened, cooked by the acidic juices that surged from its organs. I pried Bannon off of me and got to my feet, aching from head to toe. The doors of the transport worked to open, its screeching hiss something I was sure would get on my nerves before we got home, especially if I couldn't figure out how to make it stop. Rubbing at my ear, I was mildly pissed off to discover my fingers came away with blood on them.

It seemed to take forever for the ainmhi dubh to die—at least long enough for Bannon to give me a gruff apology and for Ryder to give me a fierce hug, strong enough to crack my ribs. Cari remained at the open doors, which was probably wise, because I was still more than a little ticked off that she hadn't closed them when I ordered her to.

Once the ainmhi dubh was still, Bannon approached it slowly, grumbling at its crude creation. She bent over, poked at its oddly constructed jaw, and then frowned at something. She motioned with her injured arm for me to join her, and then winced and paled and dropped it back to her side. "Come look at this, Kai, and tell me if you see what I see."

Ryder strolled behind me, barely giving me room to breathe, but I didn't mind. I was tired and seriously debating letting him drive us back to the barn. Hell, if one of the kids could reach the pedals, I could be convinced to let them do it.

"What?" I tried to see what she was staring at, but it wasn't clear, not until she wiped away the blood and grass shreds from one of the monster's thick canines.

The sigils on its teeth matched the ones they'd found on the iron under my skin. There were differences. Some were subtle, while others were unknown to me, yet there was one that stood out, one so familiar that even Ryder sucked in his breath when he saw it.

"That's Tanic's symbol," Ryder whispered. "Or do I have it wrong, Kai?"

"Close, but that one above it, that makes it something else. This is one of Tanic's symbols. This ainmhi dubh belonged to Valin cuid Anbhás," I said, and I sighed as I rubbed at the ache between my eyes. "Bannon, it seems as though my brother is somewhere in your court, and if I'm not mistaken, he's just challenged you for its control."

Epilogue

"THINK KERRICK'S going to make it back to Elfhaine without any more holes in him?" I asked as I rocked my chair back on its rear legs. "Because I'd lay down money Alexa'll be happy to drill a few extra, just for shits and giggles."

"I'm not sure where that expression came from, but I can tell you, having holes put in your body does not make you giggle," Ryder grunted as he eased into the seat next to me. Hissing, he pressed his hand against his side and rubbed at where his cousin stabbed him. "I don't know how you can have this happen to you and bounce back up. Even breathing hurts."

"Whiskey helps," I replied and lifted my glass. "And what else am I going to do? Lie down on the ground and cry while someone or something is trying to kill everyone? Bleed now, weep later. That's what

Dempsey always says. Took *that* one to heart. And to the head a couple of times too."

"How is he?" Ryder carefully reached down between us and picked up the whiskey bottle I'd set there. He refilled my glass first and added a splash of the potent amber liquid to the tumbler of ice he'd brought out with him. "Does he still refuse to leave Jonas's house?"

"Yep, asshole says if he's at my place, I'd be forced to stay with him. Me staying put means I'm not out on runs, and that stops the money coming in." The whiskey did nothing to wash away the bitterness I'd been left with after an incredibly long fight with Dempsey, and I'd skulked over to Balboa, a bottle of Jack in my hand and a whole lot of anger in my belly. "I've got enough cash to float me for a couple of years if I want, especially since that jackass won't let the doctors do anything. Not good enough for him, got to be out there fighting the good fight and holding back the monsters. Damned stupid stubborn asshole."

Ryder knew me well enough to let me drink in peace for a few minutes, and I appreciated it. The silence between us wasn't as heavy as it once was, and other than the sound of kids screaming as they played somewhere in the compound, the Southern Rise was pretty quiet.

While we'd been gone, the towers had continued their steady rise, stretching outward and upward as the Sidhe architects manipulated the grounds with their sculpting powers. The land hummed with the arcane energy that flowed through it, and the ivory walls were growing more and more solid as delicate filigree gold banisters and sweeping balconies shaped themselves around the curved spires and stone mushrooms dotted with glittering lace.

Except for one.

There was one tower that refused to mold itself into the overtly beautiful Sidhe aesthetic, and I kind of liked it for fighting to remain apart from the rest. The stone mages railed and ground their teeth over it, trying to force the spire into the shape they wanted. At first it responded, but then one day it decided to say fuck it and took on a life of its own. The rooms were high and square, a defiant deviation from the gently sloping ceilings the Sidhe preferred. The doors were thick and wooden and turned golden as they formed. Their metal hasps and latches inched toward completion, all embossed with intricate knots and folds. It wasn't even close to being done, and every time I came over, something was different or the tower was sucking back a wall or closing up a window, apparently not happy about where it had gone.

What I liked most never changed, and it was becoming one of my favorite places to go when I needed to lick my wounds or talk something out with Ryder. The half-circle balcony off the main room was massive, dwarfing the grounds below and throwing most of the garden beneath it into a heavy shadow. Copper and steel knitted together into railings at the top of the balcony's short wall, its expanse riddled with an Asian weave design. Every time I saw it, the tower was different, shifting until it found its own way, but the balcony was always sturdy, and I felt as though it was eager for me to sit down, anchor my feet against its wall, and push my chair back while I stared out onto the city beyond.

I tried to ignore the fact that it was attached to Ryder's living space and that, no matter how much I denied it, the tower was trying to make me a place at the court. It was a fierce silver-flecked spire baring its metaphorical teeth at the very people who were trying to coax it into existence.

I also really liked the pearl-embedded wingless dragons the spire was shaping around the railing supports. I patted them periodically and felt foolish when I praised the tower for adding them, but I secretly hoped they stayed.

"What are we going to do about Valin?" Ryder finally spoke up. "I don't like the idea he's in the Dusk Court."

"Somehow I don't think Bannon's going to be too happy with you riding in to rescue her on that white horse you've got stored in the stables," I replied. "She seems like the kind of woman who'd sooner skewer you with her sword than let you fight her fights. 'Sides, we don't know if he's still down there. That could have been something he created and lost control of. It was a shitty black dog. Tanic would kick his ass if he saw it."

"That's someone we don't need here," he grumbled. "In fact, I'd prefer it if he and my grandmother were as far away as possible. Can you imagine the havoc they would bring if their magics were even a hundred miles from each other? I'd sooner try to mate with a dragon."

"Or they'd kill each other and we wouldn't have to worry about either one of them again." Another grunt from Ryder and I looked over at him, concerned at his discomfort. "Hey, did you let the healers get at you?"

"No, not yet. The children need their help more. It will take some time to undo the damage done to their bodies from lack of food and… well, everything else. I'll heal. Just like you do." Ryder hissed and then sipped at his glass. "Just not apparently at the same pace. While I envy your stamina, I'd like to never get stabbed again."

"Should have let me kill Kerrick, then, because that's one bastard who'll be knocking on your door *again*." The Jack was old, but it hadn't lost any of its bite. If anything, the burn in my throat was nearly as hot as a bullet passing through my flesh, but the numbness it left behind eased the aching bruises that were yellowing over parts of my torso and legs. I rocked again, careful not to tip myself over.

"Do you really regret not killing him?" Ryder asked carefully, his hooded emerald eyes fixed on some point among the city's glistening skyscrapers. Sunset was a few hours off still, but the afternoon light washed a buttery glow over the downtown upper level and gilded its nest of tall buildings and arching roadways.

I had to think about it, but eventually I sighed. "No, I don't regret letting him live, but right then I could have peeled his skin off his body and wouldn't have even blinked. Not going to apologize for that. I'd have felt the same if he stuck Cari or Alexa. You're *all*… mine. And I know that doesn't make sense, but that's just how it is. Going to promise you, though, he does it again and nothing you say is going to stop me. He comes after any of mine again and I'll end him. Simple as that."

Ryder chuckled, and I stared at him, a bit surprised at the silly smile on his face. Frowning, I sniffed at the whiskey and wondered if I'd brought something too strong for him to handle.

"Stop snuffling at your glass. You sound like an anteater." Ryder nudged my shoulder with his. "I'm just laughing at how things have changed so much since the first time we met."

"Yeah, well, you were an asshole."

"You didn't want to let me in your house."

"That's because I knew you were an asshole. Still are sometimes," I drawled. "And my cat still doesn't like you."

"Well, the feeling's a bit mutual, isn't it?" Ryder tapped his glass against mine. "I don't like the iron you have on your table."

I snorted and reminded him, "Ah, but see, it's my table. My iron too."

A peacock screamed back at the children, it was that or something was mounting an all-out assault on the compound. Either way, someone else would be taking care of it. I was done fighting off monsters for the evening. The kids were settling in and choosing names, trying out different sounds and meanings. Ryder reassured me it would take them some time and not to get used to a particular name until it hung on for more than a few days.

"I'm glad you didn't kill him, but Sebac will send someone else, someone who might break my hold on the court," Ryder responded softly. "Next time it might not be so easy to throw them back."

"Yeah. The way I see it, you're a lot like Bannon," I shot back. "You're bucking the system, and people are pissed off about it because they can't see that things are going to shit unless stuff changes. And I don't know if she's got anyone who's got her back, but you do. So, no matter what happens, lordling, I'll be here to send those assholes packing, and not just because I like the view from this damned balcony."

Maybe it was the whiskey or the afternoon sun, but there was a vulnerability in Ryder's expression, a fracture in his arrogance and self-confidence. I didn't have family. Well, I had Dempsey, and even though he'd shot me a time or two, it was by accident and we'd been on a run. As shitty as it was for Kerrick to drift down to San Diego hoping to shove his way into the court, he was still Ryder's blood.

But then so was Sebac, and she'd *invented* treachery and backstabbing.

So I did what was probably the stupidest thing I'd ever done in my life… even counting that one time I ate meat from a five-week-dead bison we found floating in a river while we chased ghost wranglers.

I leaned over and kissed Ryder on the mouth.

He tasted of whiskey and melancholy with a dash of brightness that I figured he'd soaked up from the sun, and as my lips touched his, he stiffened. Scared I'd stepped over a line, I was about to pull away and apologize when he brought his hands up and tangled them into my hair and pulled me in closer.

We'd danced around it, exchanged brief flirtatious touches, but this was the first time we truly drank deeply from each other's bodies, and my need for him flared and brimmed over the edges of my control until all I could see and feel was his presence, all gold, emerald, and warmth pushing through the darkness

I cradled in my soul. If Bannon was a complication, then Ryder was a catastrophe. I would lose myself in him, give up every bit of humanity I'd held on to, and finally surrender my tooth-and-nail fight against my elfin blood.

I needed space… room to breathe… but I also didn't want to let go—not yet, not now. But the sensations flowing through me were too much. If he'd gotten my blood surging before we touched, my nerves were now drenched in a symphony of falling stars.

All from a simple kiss.

The ground shook, and the balcony trembled under us. A whisper of rolling stone breached the mind-numbing stillness we'd pulled around us, and the sky erupted with spikes of deep shadows as the court thrust up enormous spears of ivory stone into the air, and their massive honeycombed shafts pushed back the thick soil and heavy foliage of Balboa. The forest rolled back away from the compound. Ancient trees crashed down to the hungry ground that waited to be fed. Sweeps of evergreens and oak stands fell beneath the court's ravenous need, easing down into the rich dirt to wait to be pulled into the towers by the architects of the Southern Rise. Boulders sank beneath the surface and opened up a wide expanse of soft, rolling hillocks dotted with smaller trees and exposed underbrush.

A wave of birds took flight from their disappearing roosts and landed in other trees, only to move again when those fell as well. Breathing heavily, I tried to make sense of what was going on as the shafts thickened, straightened, and settled into place around the established buildings of the court. Archways were beginning to form between the shafts—slender granite tendrils that unraveled from the structures and reached out to connect to the framework nearby. There was a flash of black-and-white fur gamboling hastily across one of the new clearings, a roly-poly bearlike creature only visible for a second before it crashed into the thicker forest a few yards away. Herds of deer and smaller animals followed the lone panda, and then there was quiet as the court finally came to a rest.

There was shouting from the main compound, and Ryder stood carefully and took in the new expanse of woven bare shafts that now framed the court behind us. His eyes were huge, and he was speechless as he turned to me, as though I somehow had an answer for what had just happened.

Shaken to my bones, I stood and looked around. Finally I whispered, "Well, *fuck*."

The Kai Gracen Series: Book One

Ever since being part of the pot in a high-stakes poker game, elfin outcast Kai Gracen figures he used up his good karma when Dempsey, a human Stalker, won the hand and took him in. Following the violent merge of Earth and Underhill, the human and elfin races are left with a messy, monster-ridden world, and Stalkers are the only cavalry willing to ride to someone's rescue when something shadowy appears.

It's a hard life but one Kai likes—filled with bounty, a few friends, and most importantly, no other elfin around to remind him of his past. And killing monsters is easy. Especially since he's one himself.

But when a sidhe lord named Ryder arrives in San Diego, Kai is conscripted to do a job for Ryder's fledgling Dawn Court. It's supposed to be a simple run up the coast during dragon-mating season to retrieve a pregnant human woman seeking sanctuary. Easy, quick, and best of all, profitable. But Kai ends up in the middle of a deadly bloodline feud he has no hope of escaping.

No one ever got rich being a Stalker. But then few of them got old, either, and it doesn't look like Kai will be the exception.

Chapter One

IT WASN'T a great day to be me.

The nick below the tip of my right ear itched, and when I scratched at it, the itch fled, traveling down my stomach and into my crotch. I willed it to go away, and after annoying me for a few seconds, it disappeared. I was cold, stinking of blood from the three elfin shadow dogs I'd already killed, and grumpy because there was still a live one out there I had to hunt down.

I smelled the last dog before I saw it. Nothing can mask the stench of an unsidhe cur. They reek like a week-old herring rolled in the juices of a bloated corpse left out in the sun. I checked the thunder gray sky for rain and sniffed for any water. Wet black dog could make a dead man vomit, and the smell would soak through the metal bed of my truck.

"Come to Kai, baby." I snuck a peek at the thing, peering around the tree I'd hidden behind. "I need some groceries."

The black dog looked like a mange-infested mastiff that'd fallen into an iguana's gene pool and was about twice the girth of the others I'd already taken down. It appeared to be male, but gender didn't matter if a dog got a lot of meat to eat, and this one looked like it ate well. Its long lizard tail doubled as a weed-whacker when it stomped through the brush, taking out huge arcs of grass with each step, and its belly dragged on the ground, a fat, happy lizard-dog bastard out for an afternoon snack.

Even though it was close to me, its forehead and short snout wove in and out of view behind boulders along the hillside's slope, keeping me from a kill shot. The coarse ebony fur on its body ran to thick, wrinkled gray flesh on its legs, long claws growing out of its reptilian paws. One of its smaller back horns was broken, probably from a mating fight, but from what I could see as it opened its maw to scent the air on its tongue, all its finger-length teeth were intact.

Good thing, because I wouldn't want to be only half-chewed when the damned thing ate me alive.

I pulled up my shotgun, cracking it open one last time to check its slugs. With the hound coming around the trees, I would have to wait for a clear shot. Dempsey liked a knife or a bow. *Stalker should hunt like a man*, he grumbled in my head. I liked having a sawed-off shotgun or a pair of Glocks I could reload.

"Fucking Dempsey and his crossbows. I'd have to shoot the damned thing five times with a bow when a damned slug can do it in one or two." When it came down to it, I'd rather be alive with gunpowder on my skin than have my picture hanging up on the Post's tribute wall to the manly Stalkers who died taking something down. "Crossbows are shit."

"God, that thing stinks." My eyes watered from the smell. Resisting the urge to check my ammo again, I waited as the wind shifted and sent a brief thanks to the slaughtered god when my nose cleared of black dog.

The dog was almost in full view, and the change in wind direction helped me more than the hound as the breeze stole my scent away. Its broad chest vibrated as it laid its head back and howled, the piercing keen of its eerie song echoing across the area as it called for the others in its pack. If I had any luck, it would soon be joining their dead bodies in the back of my truck.

The thing was going to be a bitch to drag down to the road. Bounty laws said I couldn't leave the body behind, mostly to protect wildlife from eating a black dog's acidic meat, so I'd have to drag out every pound of its dead body to the truck after I killed it. Carry out what you kill, Dempsey beat into me.

"Or find some stupid elfin kid to do it for you." I snorted.

The hound didn't have to worry about dragging me off the mountain. If it got me, it would eat me on the spot, probably spitting out the zipper of my jeans and my earring when it was done. With luck, I'd get the chance to pee myself first, because my bladder began complaining loudly, and the itch returned to my bits.

It turned, and a flicker of a red eye gleamed in the black of its face. Holding its head lower than its massive shoulders, it skulked across the ground, hitting on my scent. I couldn't hide from its nose. Damned things could track prey over anything.

The dog snagged my trail, growling as it moved its head back and forth to scent. I held my breath, letting the scent-trail draw it closer. It crept quickly over the forest floor, making a slithering sound through the leaves. If it wouldn't have given the dog the drop on me, I would have laughed. The thing was nearly as large as a tik-tik cab. The only way it could hide was if a lorry dropped down in front of it.

With its sloping body tucked down, the black dog stilled; its wide nostrils sniffed at the air. A curl of its tongue lapped around the brush of teeth, long strands of milky saliva roping down to cover a clutch of weeds. The leaves shriveled and burned when the hound's spit struck, tiny wisps of smoke rising around the black dog's head as the acid ate through the greens. The wind shifted again and caught my scent, carrying it to the dog. It turned, found me staring at it, and leaped straight for me.

Singlish is really an ugly language. It has its toes in many lingual puddles, from old Britain to Cantonese with hot dashes of wasabi Japanese, but there were times when only the ugly gutter back street Nippon would do.

This was definitely one of those times.

"*Kuso!*" I brought the shotgun down as the black dog barreled toward my hiding spot. The wind shift carried something of me on it, and the creature found me as easily as if I'd jumped out into the open and waved my arms around.

Black Dog Blues

The hound smelled the death of its pack on me, and it was pissed.

My first blast hit it between the eyes, jerking its head around. I took the recoil, easier for me than a human, but the gun bead shook, and I had to resight. For a long scary moment, I thought the shot went wide. The black dog kept coming, its earflaps laid back and its mouth opened wide enough to pop my head off with a single bite, but a trail of black gore spit up behind its head. It was hit, but not enough to bring it down.

Bringing the shotgun back around, I let loose the second round, aiming for one of its eyes. Its head jerked back again, and its cheek shattered, the eye popping into a wet mess, but the damned thing kept coming. I dropped the gun and grabbed for the Glock lying in the grass as the black dog's paws dug into the ground in front of me.

It went over me just as my hand closed on the grip. Twisting to get another shot off, I ate dirt when the black dog's weight shoved me into the ground. It hit hard, and I choked on my wind, coughing to pull enough air into my chest to inflate my lungs. Flipping over, I couldn't breathe. At nearly five hundred pounds and as fragrant as whale puke, the hound covered my legs and torso, pinning me against a bed of pine needles.

My brain told me the thing was dead, but my mind wasn't what needed convincing. The dog's mouth snapped and tore at the air near my head and shoulders as its body twitched frantically. Lines of foam polluted its pink-rimmed lips, acidic ropes of spit that burned my skin, and I placed the barrel against the creature's flat skull and pulled the trigger.

Bone chips stung my cheek, and I tasted powder before I could get my mouth closed. The blast blossomed out of the dog's head, and its skull spat out furred chunks and scaly skin. I fought to breathe as its spasms slowed, its legs stiffening out behind its body. Slowly, the glow in its eyes dimmed, turning the vivid red lights to a dull gray. It twitched once more, then went still, as dead as the rocks digging into my back.

"About time you died, damned thing." Exhaling with relief, I tried squirming out, but the dog's weight settled hard on my shins, trapping me against the forest floor.

Leaning back into a bed of dried pine needles, I stared up at the sky and sighed. "Ah, fuck me. Oh no, we're not doing this shit." Growling at the shattered head, I kicked the thing in its belly. "I am not going to lie here like some fricking bed of cabbage under sashimi. You are getting the hell off me."

It was a strain to bend forward, but I reached behind my legs to scoop out handfuls of needles from behind my knees, hoping I could give myself enough wiggle room to slide out. The ground sloped up sharply behind my shoulders, and I kept hitting my head against forest debris when I tried to get leverage. A few flailing tries and I cursed the damned thing again. The dog had me pinned, and the not-so-great day went straight to shitty when one of its enormous paws dug straight into my already strained bladder.

"Hey, mister, why'd you shoot that dog?"

It sounded like a kid, and from the silhouette I could make out when I twisted my head to the side, it looked kid-shaped. It moved into the light, and the shadowy thing turned into a dirty-faced child wearing a pair of white briefs and a thin T-shirt. Like most children under knee level, I couldn't tell if it was a girl or a boy, especially since it was wearing what looked like generations-old hand-me-downs.

"Hi. You're not out here alone, are you?" I smiled, keeping my elfin canines hidden. Sharp incisors do not a warm, welcoming smile make. I hoped the kid hadn't wandered off from some campsite. The last thing I needed was to have a lost bawler to deal with as I dragged the dog back to my truck—if I figured out a way to get out from under it. "There's a mommy or daddy around, right? Please tell me you come with someone bigger attached to you."

"Yeah, we live right there." S/he pointed behind us, up the ridge. "All of us. Mama, Daddy, and everyone."

"Is someone home right now? Maybe someone really big who can help get the big dog off me?" Someone once told me to talk to kids like I was excited to see them, told me it was easier to convince them to do things if children heard the things in a happy voice. Every kid I'd ever met had always made me a liar, but I was using as happy a voice as I had. I'd buy the kid anything it wanted, but it looked too young to bribe.

"Daddy's big!" The runty human studied me. "Bigger than you. Stronger!"

"Good," I replied. I'd be glad to lose in a size-pissing contest if it would help me get the feeling back in my feet. "Can you go get Daddy?"

"Jaime! Where did you get off to?"

Craning my neck to stare up the slope, I sent a belated thanks to Iesu and Buddha when the short cliff above me suddenly sprouted another person, taller and definitely a woman.

I kept the happy voice up, but by now it was less happy and more badly-needing-to-pee. "Who's that? Someone you know?"

"That's Mama!" The child beamed, waving its arms above its head to get the woman's attention. "Mama! It's one of those pointy-eared people! Can I keep him? He can sleep next to my turtle!"

"YOU KNOW what I miss, boy? The blood," Dempsey said around the cigar stump in his mouth. "I miss the blood the most."

Up to my elbows in said blood, I spared the human who raised me a look and offered him my knife. Isolated, Dempsey's place was a good spot to dispose of black dogs' bodies, and laying down a slab table with runnels to catch the gore into a cistern made the job even easier. "If you want to, I can leave this to you. That leg of yours is bad, but your hands still work."

"You're not too big for me to wipe my ass with." Spitting a chunk of loose tobacco off his tongue, he hitched himself up onto the bed of the truck. "And the moment you say that's because I have a big ass is the second I break that pretty face of yours with a backhand."

He'd always been a big man, with coarse features and a grizzle of beard no matter how often he shaved. A run up the coast had brought him to his knees, a swipe of a giant scorpion's tail blowing out his leg. Despite the fierce limp hobbling his walk, Dempsey hadn't changed much, even if his days of being a Stalker were done.

I'd give Dempsey this—he might have retired from the Stalker business, but he was as mean as the day he'd taken me as winnings in a card game. I didn't have any doubt that he could hand me my ass, so I kept silent, having learned from experience how quick the large man could move, even with his gimped leg. I might be stronger and quicker than most humans, but Dempsey was meaner than anything I'd ever met. Keeping my mouth shut was usually the wisest thing to do.

When he was retired out, Dempsey looked for someplace to live and found a few acres in Lakeside that were cheap. A couple of battered storage containers had been easily converted into a large home, and after a few burns from the cutting torch, I'd gotten the hang of making windows while Dempsey welded the metal rectangles into place. A few coats of paint and a deck made the place almost homey, although the gun racks in the kitchen put a serious dent into the suburban image the place struggled to put up. We'd left most of the sage and brush around the perimeter; the brambles were a natural barrier for anything large to plow through.

"Spent a lot of money and time feeding and teaching you, boy," he'd growled at me across the kitchen table, biting back a snarl as he took a shot of Jim. Too banged up to do the job, he'd had to turn over his license, and his mood roamed from mad to mad drunk. "Time to pay up for that."

Being a retired Stalker didn't come with a pension plan, and Dempsey never had been smart with his money. Most of it was spent on whiskey, poker, and women, so when the time came for him to step back from jobs, he looked to me to support him. I gave him a third of my earnings in exchange for a place to burn black dogs' bodies. Since I lived in the city, it was a cheaper way to dispose of the useless meat. The incinerator at San Diego Central Works was expensive and too often down for maintenance.

I could think of a thousand things I'd rather be doing than dragging around skinned carcasses of black dogs while looking for a place to burn them. Sitting on a fire-ant hill covered in honey came to mind.

"Took down four, then?" He stepped closer, inspecting the large alpha male I'd killed last. "Good job, that. Skulls are ruined, though. Don't know why you can't make a kill without shattering the skull. Used to be a Stalker was known by the skulls he'd collected."

"Because I'd rather be alive than have a trophy? If it makes you feel better, I waited until I could spit on it before I shot."

Bringing the dog down from the mountain hadn't made it any smaller. If anything, the thing seemed bigger, nearly impossible to get out of the bed of the truck and onto the cutting slab. The mound of black dog lying out on concrete was the last one I had to do. The others were already skinned for the bounty, and the carcasses piled up to be burned. I'd already put charcoal into the pit. After a brief discussion with Dempsey, we both agreed the dogs weren't worth wasting any precious gasoline. They'd have to burn with good old Kingston like the others before them.

"We'll get a good bounty on these." He nodded at the furs stretched on the rack, the raw skin sprinkled with salt to soak up the excess gore. The Post didn't need them tanned, but I disliked carrying decaying skins through the city, and ocean salt worked quickly on dog flesh. I appreciated him doing the salt. My skin was still tender from the acidic blood. Getting salt on the burns would be hellish. "Should get what? Five hundred for the smaller ones? Maybe more?"

"Probably more," I agreed, gripping the male's paw and slicing up around its shoulder. "The Post's offering a hundred for every hand length now. It went up last week. Lots of the dogs in the area. SoCalGov's getting flak for all the packs roaming in the farmlands. Dead people don't pay taxes."

"True. Government would want to avoid that." Dempsey walked around me, avoiding the line of blood filling the cement channels. His hand came up to scratch his nose. I flinched a little, unable to stop myself from jerking back. Growing up with Dempsey sometimes meant my lessons were given with a hard fist as much as rough words, and my body seemed to instinctively remember that, although I couldn't remember the last time he hit me.

Working my fingers under the cut skin, I separated the pelt from the black dog's body, ignoring the burn of its blood on my hands. Being elfin, I'd heal from the poison-ivy-like rash within minutes of pulling my hands from its carcass, but it still stung. Gloves were more of a bother than they were worth. Latex melted and stuck to flesh, and leather ones were too expensive to replace after every dog skinning. Even Dempsey, when he could be bothered to help with a skinning, went barehanded.

With the fur off in one piece, I began the task of taking the carcass apart. A black dog bounty paid per handspan, measured carefully by the clerks down at the Post. Bounty was paid not only for the pelt but also for the kill. Stitching together a pelt that had been cut meant waiting for the money to be released while the Post determined if the fur came from a single animal or had been cobbled together from separate pieces for a bounty. Trying to pass off strangely cut dog pelts brought in short a leg or haunch usually meant a yanked license.

A real Stalker knew all the tricks and never played them. Having a firm reputation for being reliable and honest was nearly as good as being a keen shot. Dempsey might be an asshole, but he never shorted anyone or ran off on a job. He'd left Stalking behind with his head held high, and people still spoke about runs he'd done along the coast. Other than a warm woman at night, it was all he'd wanted. Well, he also told me he wanted to die in his bed at the age of ninety-eight from being shot by a jealous husband, but a warm woman at night would be good enough.

Dempsey took over shoveling chunks of dog meat into the pit with his bare hands. He worked quickly, keeping his contact with the acid down to a minimum. Grinning unevenly, he stopped long enough to ruffle the hair at the back of my head, getting gore and guts on my neck. "You can hose yourself off outside. You stink like the dog-hugger you are, and that black mop of yours is all dusty, like you were rolling in a barn. There's some of your clothes in the back room. I'll bring 'em out for you."

I didn't argue. I'd spent the night in the truck's cab, parked under one of the tall trees, after getting to Lakeside at nearly three in the morning. The sun was barely up when Dempsey knocked on the truck window to wake me up with a cup of coffee as pitch black as the dogs I had lying in the truck bed. The tarp I'd spread over the truck's seat wasn't very comfortable to lie on, but it kept the fabric clean. I had a crick in my neck and stank from cutting open gullets filled with rotting meat. The coffee in my belly was a distant memory, and I still needed to drive back in to San Diego. A shower would go a long way in shaking me awake.

The outside shower's water was cold, leaving me with pinpricks on my skin and shivering when the wind hit my bare ass. The dog's weight left me sore, and I was covered in purple and black bruises. Moving to the side was a bit painful, and I was sure my back had suffered as much as my legs had, perhaps even more, from being rubbed against the rocky hillside. A few spots of dog blood had made it through my jeans, scorching the two hand-size Asiatic dragons tattooed on my hip and back. The blistered skin didn't look like it had lifted up any ink, but I'd have to wait a few hours to see if it healed smoothly or whether I'd have to make a trip down to the Flying Panther to fix it.

"That last damned dog was a bitch to move. Must have been an escapee from a Wild Hunt. Damned elf-in can't keep track of their own hunting packs, and we always got to go out and wipe up their messes." Dempsey gave me a once-over as he handed me a worn towel, frowning at the bruising on my thighs. "What the hell did you do? Ride the damned thing to death?"

"If I'd ridden it to death, I wouldn't have been under the damned thing when it died," I said, taking the towel and trying to use its sparse pile to soak up the water on my naked belly. The air whistled between

the outdoor spigot and the trees around it, catching on
every icy drop on my skin. He stood staring at me for
a moment too long, and I started to wonder if he'd
switched the side of the street he walked on. "What?"

"Haven't really looked at you in a few years.
Grown up a bit. You're not as skinny as you used to
be. Muscled up nice." He moved his cigar from one
side of his mouth to the other. "Finally got some meat
on that stick body of yours. Hell, I could have waited
a few years and pimped you out for money instead of
teaching you to Stalk."

"Nice of you to have a backup plan in case the
job gets too hard for me," I muttered, grabbing at the
clothes he held out for me. I looped the wet towel over
a branch then slid on my jeans, shaking out the water
from my hair as best I could.

"Not like I didn't have offers for you before. That
face of yours and those purple-blue eyes," he scoffed,
leaning on the tree. "Lots of folks thought you were
tasty, even with you being elfin, but whoring's too
much work for too little. Stalking's easier, and you
don't have to worry about someone not paying up.
Well, not as often."

I couldn't help but laugh. Part of being a Stalker meant having to take private jobs when Government Issue was lean. We'd both been burned too many
times to count after a run.

"'Sides, not like you wouldn't have stabbed anyone who pissed you off," Dempsey said. "You cut
enough people with your teeth when I first got you.
Savage little cat-bastard."

Dempsey's words didn't bother me. We'd been
down this road before. He'd been suckered into taking

a mostly wild elfin in a poker game, calling a bluff that resulted in the bluffer passing me over the table as payment. I hadn't understood a word of Singlish, and up until that point, I'd spent more time bleeding than eating. Over the years, I'd heard him wonder if it wouldn't have been more profitable just to sell me to whoever would give him a good price. But sponsoring me as a Stalker was one of his better ideas, especially on those mornings when his fondness for drink kept him in bed. I was more motivated by the hunger in my belly, where Dempsey needed only a fifth to survive on for a week.

Considering where I'd come from, Dempsey was a godsend, no matter which god sent him.

"Not that I don't want to bask in the warmth of your undying love, Dempsey, but I should head in and drop off the furs, then get some sleep. I'll have the Post drop your share into the fund," I said, pulling on a faded red T-shirt. "The account's the same, right? They can do a transfer."

"Yeah, same account," he replied. "Stay a bit. I'll bring out some food. Might as well feed you before you head back into the city. You can always eat. I've fed that damned stomach of yours long enough to know that. You probably need some more coffee in you too."

"Yeah, I could eat." I was hungry. I was always hungry, but I didn't expect Dempsey to invite me in. The woman he was with hated elfin with a passion. She refused to be in the house if I stepped into it, calling a priest to bless the place whenever I crossed the threshold. It was easier to eat on the porch with him and afterward toss my paper plate and wooden chopsticks into the fire with the burning dogs.

He gathered breakfast quickly, and we sat eating rice, cold Spam, and wet eggs as the flames burned through the dogs' bodies. I tossed my plate into the fire when I was done and lit a clove cigarette, filling my lungs with the kretek's husky sweetness to wash away the stink of burning dog.

Dempsey's plate joined mine after a few more mouthfuls. Standing next to me, he put his chewed-on cigar stump into his mouth, lit the end, then drew it back to life with a few pulls. Blowing out a stream of smoke to battle the dogs' reek, he pursed his lips and stared off into the distance.

"You could have just sent me off with some food, you know." I spotted the sun behind the gloom in the sky, surprised to discover it was only midmorning. Dempsey must have woken me up after only a few hours of sleep.

"Nah, that wouldn't be right," he growled. "You know it's not good to eat on the run, and a Stalker should always have his man's back. Be a shame if I'd spent all that time beating some sense into you and left that bit out."

RHYS FORD is an award-winning author with several long-running LGBT+ mystery, thriller, paranormal, and urban fantasy series and is a two-time LAMBDA finalist with her *Murder and Mayhem* novels. She is also a 2017 Gold and Silver Medal winner in the Florida Authors and Publishers President's Book Awards for her novels *Ink and Shadows* and *Hanging the Stars*. She is published by Dreamspinner Press and DSP Publications.

She shares the house with Harley, a gray tuxedo with a flower on her face, Badger, a disgruntled alley cat who isn't sure living inside is a step up the social ladder, as well as a ginger cairn terrorist named Gus. Rhys is also enslaved to the upkeep of a 1979 Pontiac Firebird and enjoys murdering make-believe people.

Rhys can be found at the following locations:
Blog: www.rhysford.com
Facebook: www.facebook.com/rhys.ford.author
Twitter: @Rhys_Ford

RHYS FORD

MAD LIZARD MAMBO

*"Visceral urban fantasy...set in a fascinating
world peopled by compelling characters."*
— *The Novel Approach*

The Kai Gracen Series: Book Two

Kai Gracen has no intention of being anyone's pawn. A pity Fate and SoCalGov have a different opinion on the matter.

Licensed Stalkers make their living hunting down monsters and dangerous criminals… and their lives are usually brief, brutal, and thankless. Despite being elfin and cursed with a nearly immortal lifespan, Kai didn't expect to be any different. Then Ryder, the High Lord of the Southern Rise Court, arrived in San Diego, and Kai's not-so-mundane life went from mild mayhem to full-throttle chaos.

Now an official liaison between the growing Sidhe court and the human populace, Kai is at Ryder's beck and call for anything a High Lord might need a Stalker to do. Unfortunately for Kai, this means chasing down a flimsy rumor about an ancient lost court somewhere in the Nevada desert—a court with powerful magics that might save Ryder's—and Kai's—people from becoming a bloody memory in their merged world's violent history.

The race for the elfin people's salvation opens unwelcome windows into Kai's murky past, and it could also slam the door on any future he might have with his own kind and Ryder.

www.dsppublications.com

A DEVILISH LGBTQ PARANORMAL & URBAN FANTASY ANTHOLOGY

RHYS FORD · GINN HALE · JORDAN L. HAWK

TA MOORE · C.S. POE · JORDAN CASTILLO PRICE

DEVIL
Take Me

Temptation lurks around every corner in worlds sometimes dark, sometimes lurid. Giving in is both dangerous and satisfying, though never in the ways one expects. While these enticements offer a vast range of benefits and boons, the cost is a soul and the devil expects his due. Sometimes suave and charming or calculating and cruel, these devils have schemes and desires of their own. They can be creatures to run away from… or toward.

Join the most unique and celebrated authors of LGBTQ urban fantasy and paranormal fiction for a fast-paced and unpredictable ride, from a city on the other side of reality, to a world suspended in dusk, to a twisted version of the 1960s and 70s.

Meet devils in top hats and waistcoats, a defrocked motorcycle-riding priest, and a genderfluid antihero— among many more. Full of humor, romance, horror, action, intrigue, and magic, these stories have one common element….

They're one hell of a good time.

www.dsppublications.com

INK AND
SHADOWS

RHYS FORD

Ink and Shadows: Book One

Kismet Andreas lives in fear of the shadows.

For the young tattoo artist, the shadows hold more than darkness. He is certain of his insanity because the dark holds creatures and crawling things only he can see—monsters who hunt out the weak to eat their minds and souls, leaving behind only empty husks and despair.

And if there's one thing Kismet fears more than being hunted—it's the madness left in its wake.

The shadowy Veil is Mal's home. As Pestilence, he is the youngest—and most inexperienced—of the Four Horsemen of the Apocalypse, immortal manifestations resurrected to serve—and cull—mankind. Invisible to all but the dead and insane, the Four exist between the Veil and the mortal world, bound to their nearly eternal fate. Feared by other immortals, the Horsemen live in near solitude but Mal longs to know more than Death, War and Famine.

Mal longs to be… more human. To interact with someone other than lunatics or the deceased.

When Kismet rescues Mal from a shadowy attack, Pestilence is suddenly thrust into a vicious war—where mankind is the prize, and the only one who has faith in Mal is the human the other Horsemen believe is destined to die.

www.dsppublications.com

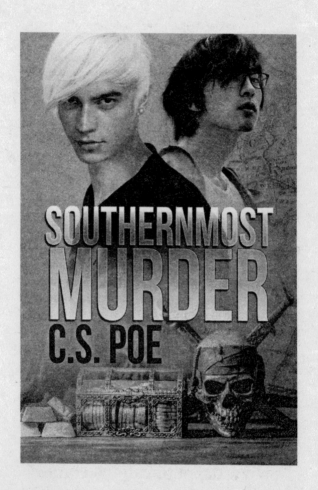

SOUTHERNMOST
MURDER

C.S. POE

Aubrey Grant lives in the tropical paradise of Old Town, Key West, has a cute cottage, a sweet moped, and a great job managing the historical property of a former sea captain. With his soon-to-be-boyfriend, hotshot FBI agent Jun Tanaka, visiting for a little R&R, not even Aubrey's narcolepsy can put a damper on their vacation plans.

But a skeleton in a closet of the Smith Family Historical Home throws a wrench into the works. Despite Aubrey and Jun's attempts to enjoy some time together, the skeleton's identity drags them into a mystery with origins over a century in the past. They uncover a tale of long-lost treasure, the pirate king it belonged to, and a modern-day murderer who will stop at nothing to find the hidden riches. If a killer on the loose isn't enough to keep Aubrey out of the mess, it seems even the restless spirit of Captain Smith is warning him away.

The unlikely partnership of a special agent and historian may be exactly what it takes to crack this mystery wide-open and finally put an old Key West tragedy to rest. But while Aubrey tracks down the X that marks the spot, one wrong move could be his last.

www.dsppublications.com